D0612285

"BEWARE OF THE SKINWALKER!"

It was the voice of death shouting this last warning to Gerrit. Then there was a cacophony of sound, shrieking as though a thousand tea kettles had boiled dry on the fire and exploded at once. Gerrit turned to look back and saw a thousand flickering eyes. And towering over all, black against the distant stars, a Shadow loomed, grinning, with his spear poised. The Prince shouted and pointed at it.

The Shadow hurled his spear and the Littleman tackled Gerrit aside. Then, prince, Littleman, and dwarf were up and racing desperately toward the distant bulk of the castle on the heights. And as they sprinted on in a race they might never win, the flickering eyes were all about them in the dark, fangs snapping at their heels, frost at their hearts. . . .

Ⓞ **SIGNET FANTASY** (0451)

WORLDS OF IMAGINATION

☐ **THE DARKLING HILLS by Lori Martin.** When the beautiful Princess Dalleena and the handsome nobleman Rendall fall in love, defying an ancient law, they invoke a searing prophecy of doom. Betrayed and exiled by their homeland, the couple must struggle to remain together through a brutal siege from a rival empire "An exciting, charming, and irresistable story."—Tom Monteleone, author of LYRICA. (152840—$3.50)

☐ **STRANDS OF STARLIGHT by Gael Baudino.** A stunning, mystical fantasy of a young woman's quest for revenge against her inquisitors, and her journey through the complex web of interrelated patterns and events that lead to inner peace. (163710—$4.50)

☐ **FANG, THE GNOME by Michael Greatrex Coney.** Here is an enthralling excursion into an age when mythical creatures roamed the lands, men fought for ideals of chivalry, and the majestic dream of Arthur and his Knights of the Round Table first cast its spell on humans and gnomes. "Rich, striking and original!"—*Kirkus Reviews.* (158474—$3.95)

☐ **THE MAGIC BOOKS by Andre Norton.** Three magical excursions into spells cast and enchantments broken, by a wizard of science fiction and fantasy: *Steel Magic,* three children's journey to an Avalon whose dark powers they alone can withstand. *Octagon Magic,* a young girl's voyage into times and places long gone, and *Fur Magic,* where a boy must master the magic of the ancient gods to survive. (152328—$3.95)

☐ **RITNYM'S DAUGHTER by Sheila Gilluly.** The third novel of Sheila Gilluly's Greenbriar trilogy—a novel of high adventure and dark intrigue. (163419—$3.75)

Prices slightly higher in Canada.

Buy them at your local bookstore or use this convenient coupon for ordering.

NEW AMERICAN LIBRARY
P.O. Box 999, Bergenfield, New Jersey 07621

Please send me the books I have checked above. I am enclosing $_____ (please add $1.00 to this order to cover postage and handling). Send check or money order—no cash or C.O.D.'s. Prices and numbers are subject to change without notice.

Name_____

Address_____

City _____ State _____ Zip Code _____

Allow 4-6 weeks for delivery.

This offer, prices and numbers are subject to change without notice.

Ritnym's Daughter

❖

Sheila Gilluly

A SIGNET BOOK

NEW AMERICAN LIBRARY

A DIVISION OF PENGUIN BOOKS USA INC.

And now, finally—and under dire threats—for my
friends, for trivial pursuits of all kinds, and tacos,
and faculty meetings, and reading manuscripts,
Salutes from—
Gilluly

NAL BOOKS ARE AVAILABLE AT QUANTITY DISCOUNTS WHEN USED
TO PROMOTE PRODUCTS OR SERVICES. FOR INFORMATION PLEASE
WRITE TO PREMIUM MARKETING DIVISION, NEW AMERICAN LIBRARY,
1633 BROADWAY, NEW YORK, NEW YORK 10019.

Copyright © 1989 by Sheila Gilluly

All rights reserved

SIGNET TRADEMARK REG. U.S. PAT. OFF. AND FOREIGN COUNTRIES
REGISTERED TRADEMARK—MARCA REGISTRADA
HECHO EN DRESDEN, TN, U.S.A.

SIGNET, SIGNET CLASSIC, MENTOR, ONYX, PLUME, MERIDIAN
and NAL BOOKS are published by New American Library, a division of
Penguin Books USA Inc., 1633 Broadway, New York, New York 10019

First Printing, December, 1989

1 2 3 4 5 6 7 8 9

PRINTED IN THE UNITED STATES OF AMERICA

The Riddle of the Hearthstone

What be the tyme?
  In the fall of the summer.
How shall ye know it?
  By the meadow's mourning.
Where is it hid?
  In the dead man's hand.
How lies he?
  Unquiet 'mongst the shadows under the scar.
What marks the path?
  The finger's long shadow,
  Thence by the gate,
  And so home.
How shall he be called?
  The Hearthstone of Tychanor.

Prologue

Muir Dach drew lightly on the reins, and the horse obediently swung off the grassy track. Next to him on the high seat of the tinker wagon, Peewit Brickleburr clutched the edges of the wooden bench and looked back to check his pony. "Careful. It's muddy. Are you sure the campsite is near here?"

The tinker spat through the gap in his jagged teeth and gave him a look for answer.

"Right," his traveling companion murmured, abashed. "Sorry, Nan Dir Nog. It's the rain, I guess."

Muir smiled at the use of his title, which meant King of Pipers, and squinted through the drips off his sodden hood. "Could have stayed put in that barn at Coombe's Echo, you know. Would have been a damn sight drier. Warmer, too," he needled maliciously.

"We'd have been hanged!" the Littleman rejoined indignantly. "You've got to stop 'freeing' horses!"

The tinker cocked an eyebrow. "Careful, there, captain. Who says I had anything to do with them horses getting loose?"

They bumped over the tussocky ground, and the smaller figure snorted and irritably mopped his bearded face.

Muir guided the horse under the autumn trees, and they made their way slowly along the dripping wooded path. He took Peewit's silence for answer. "Well, did ye see the poor beasts? Couldn't just leave them in the hands of that thug, could I?"

"I suppose not," the Littleman grudgingly conceded. "Anybody who treats animals that way . . ." From years of association with the traveling tinsmiths, he had developed some of the tinker feeling for horses. "But you might at least have let me know what had happened. Being wakened in the middle of the night by angry men with ropes is unnerving."

The tinker grunted a laugh. "Ye moved right quick, for an old feller."

The former captain of the First Watch, whose hair and beard had gone almost completely gray in the thirteen years since he'd sacrificed his career and nearly his life to save Kursh Korimson, threw Muir a gesture, and the tinker grinned happily as they passed into a small clearing in the forest. A rude hearth stood in the middle of the area, chunks of half-burned logs gleaming darkly in the rain.

While the tinker unhitched the horse and pony and rubbed them down with a bit of blanket, the Littleman set up the firescreen, a handy device for such wet fall nights as this. He took a small bundle of dry firewood from the wagon and made a blaze. By the time Muir was done, Peewit was unpacking the kettle. "There's water hereabouts, I take it?" the Littleman questioned as the man got out the feedbag for the horse and pony.

"Aye." Muir jerked his head to indicate a footpath leading through the trees. "Follow that a bit, and it'll go down a slope. The creek's at the bottom."

"Good enough." Peewit hefted the kettle and started for the opening through the trees. "Save me some of the cheese that disappeared from the tavern last night," he called over his shoulder.

"Ye mean the one the pot girl gave me," Muir parried evenly and bent to his tasks. "Will ye be wanting a taste of that loaf that wandered off from the baker's, by the way?"

The Littleman chuckled as he swung along the path. Under the trees, which were just beginning to go gold, the rain was broken a little, but the ground was spongy underfoot. Peewit absently shifted the kettle and blew on his chilled fingers. He'd be glad of a hot cup of tea.

He came to the crest of the slope and stopped in surprise, whistling low. The brook at the bottom of the ravine must have been enormously swollen with floodwaters sometime last spring, which had been one of the wettest in memory, following on the heels of a particularly snowy winter. There was a network of downed trees, scored banks, and mats of old leaves thrown up like giant mole tunnels to attest to the force of the floodwaters.

Peewit carefully made his way down the littered slope to the hurrying creek. Once he had filled the kettle, he began fighting his way back up the hill on the slippery leaves. Cold water slopped over the rim of the iron kettle, and he cursed as it soaked down one leg and into his boot. In that moment of distraction, he caught his foot in a shallow soft depression, and saved himself a serious fall only by dropping the kettle and grasping into the wet humus with both hands.

His knee gave one painful throb, and he thought for a moment he must have sprained it, but when he straightened and put his weight to it, he found it was no more than a bit of a stretch. With the damp, it would be sore tomorrow, though. Disgustedly, he bent to retrieve the kettle, resigned to scrambling back down to refill it. Reaching for the fire-blackened pot, he froze. Where his hands had turned up the earth, there was a gleam of gold.

Quickly he brushed more earth aside. The first thing he noticed was the curve of white bone. The second was the ruby that gleamed in the middle of the brooch he had exposed. Involuntarily he snatched his hand back. "Powers!"

The Littleman drew his dagger and carefully cleared more earth away from the bones. It was a rib cage. He licked his lips and paused, staring down at the remains.

"What, did you fall in?" Muir's voice startled him, and he glanced up to the lip of the ravine.

"Muir, come see this," he said quietly.

The lanky tinker came scrambling down through the loose leaves. The teasing went out of his face when he saw what the Littleman held. "Nice piece of gold work. Is there any more?"

The captain looked up at him. "This is Kursh's. It's the brooch he left for Gerrit. I know: I saw it in the bottom of his trunk."

Thick brows drawn into a line, the tinker crouched and probed at the rib bones. "Not an animal," he observed.

"No."

"Too small for an adult, though."

Peewit swallowed. "Exactly. It's a child." Their eyes met. "How did the waif come by it, do you suppose?"

The tinker thought a moment. "Knowing Gerrit Greenbriar, the young ruffian might have paid off the wee one's father with it. For the use of his daughter, say," he finished bluntly.

The Littleman mulled this. "Help me get the rest of this uncovered. There may be more to read here, though there's already enough so that I don't know how I'll break it to Kursh."

Quickly but carefully they excavated the grave. It was Muir who brushed the concealing leaf mold from the skull. Both their jaws dropped. There was gray hair still clinging to the head. It had not been a child, then.

Forgetting for the instant the Littleman beside him, the tinker blurted, "It's a Teazle!"

A moment later, Peewit sprang up, bolted a little away, and was wrenchingly sick.

The man waited till he had quieted, then told him, "It was a head wound that did it, captain. The side of his head is cracked."

Peewit wiped his mouth, tried to calm his ragged breathing, and nodded that he had heard. Behind him he could hear Muir reburying the remains. He wanted to help, but he could not force himself to do it. Never had he met any of his kin, never. And now this. He crept to a wet outcropping of stone and put his head down on his knees.

After a time, the tinker's broad hand came down on his shoulder. "Come, let's get some potcheen into you." When the captain got shakily to his feet, Muir handed him the brooch. The ruby was beaded with rain. The tinker cleared his throat. "Seems you should have this, bein' as you're the next of kin, so's to speak."

Peewit looked down at the bloodstone. "I expect I am," he said softly. A gust of breeze came over the slope and pattered them with cold droplets. The Littleman said suddenly, "Oh, Muir, I want to go Home."

The tinker dug in his ear. "Well, mebbe we'll go up to Greenbriar for the Lordling's Squiring Day, eh?" he suggested to cheer his small partner.

But that wasn't what Peewit had meant at all, and he suddenly felt very alone. He nodded a moment later and tried for Muir's sake to smile. "Yes."

Dach gestured they should climb back up to the path, and the Littleman followed him, pausing at the lip of the hollow to look back down at the fresh-turned earth. The rain dripped down the back of his neck, and he shivered. "Yes," he repeated quietly to himself. "Maybe this is the year I'll go Home. At last."

The brooch lay cold and heavy in his palm. After a moment, he clipped it inside his muddy cloak, next to his heart. It seemed somehow important to try to warm it.

BOOK ONE:

***

The Fall of the Summer

Chapter One

❧

The night threw handfuls of rain against the Rose Window high overhead. It was unusually wet weather for the middle of winter. By now Ilyria was usually neatly carpeted with a few inches of snow, but this season had been a mild one so far, alternating sleet, fog, and rain. The gardeners were not altogether displeased that the cold was not so bad, but recently talk had been of snow. Kindlefest was fast approaching, and it just didn't seem proper to be celebrating the end of one year and the rise of another without a bit of white frosting. As Queen Ariadne nodded that the servingfolk might begin clearing the dinner dishes, she was happy her roses were still showing red-speckled green stems. An errant thought crossed her mind: she could just imagine what her foster father, old Sten Cooper, must be saying about the rain that would keep the smoke low to the hearth in the snug cottage. Quite to herself, the queen smiled.

'A farthing for your thoughts,' a silver voice said in her mind.

Her smile widened, and she glanced over at the Yoriandir bard who, with the prentice harpers grouped about him on the cinnamon marble floor, was quietly strumming a nonsense little roundelay. Ariadne said, "The price of thoughts must have gone up."

Imris cocked his head. "A queen's thoughts would go for no less at fair, I think."

"Ah, you are mistaken there. Country women are too sharp to pay such a dear price for anything but a new needle, or a ribbon for the baby's hair."

The Eldest of the Yoriandir laughed. "You have the better of me, my queen. I've been to very few fairs except the ones you hold here."

"Wait till you see this one," she promised. "People are

13

coming from as far as Melethuan, I hear." She picked up her goblet and sipped the sweet white wine while her eyes searched the reaches of the hall for her son. It was the eve of the week-long celebration of the Lordling's sixteenth birthday, his attainment to Senior Squire status. At the ceremony, he would be officially declared heir to the Greenbriar throne. Because the Crystal of Healing itself chose whom of the Greenbriar line it would work with, each son had been tested with the ancient heirloom on every birthday after his fifteenth. On one of these occasions, he would be found to be king.

As she finally caught sight of him near the lower hearth, dicing with some of the younger cadets of the Watch, Ariadne allowed herself to hope it would not be this year. Gerrit, in truth, was no more ready to ascend a throne than his pet foxhound. Maybe less. The foxhound did it regularly.

There he was, gambling and laughing with the young lords, leaving his seat beside her at the high table empty, and the Nabilian ambassador stranded with no one but doddering Thurmond naBlackmore to talk to. The queen sighed to herself. Couldn't her son ever see his duty in these things? She was about to send a page to bid his attendance when he threw his head back, laughing at some no doubt bawdy jest and the friava's light from the lower hearth caught the sparkle of blue at his ear. For a moment the thick darkness of his hair, the line of the soft cheekbones hardening to manhood, and the sapphire earring reminded her so forcefully of Sal that Ariadne looked away and played with the intricate silverwork of her goblet. If the boy was spoiled, there was good reason for it, she thought.

"May I sing for you, my lady?" Imris was asking.

She forced herself away from the dark thoughts. "I'd love it," she replied quietly.

Sensitive as he was to others' thoughts, Imris had seen the direction of her look, the twirling of the goblet, and guessed what these might mean. "Have you anything in particular you would like to hear?"

The royal composure came down like a veil. "Anything you sing, my lord of Yoriand, will grace this hall."

His fir-green eyes caught her rainwater-gray ones for a moment. "How about the Song at the Edge of the Sea, then?"

Her smile was genuine. "Yes, please."

'I thought that might cheer you,' he sent.

Mindful of the listening prentices and servants, she countered, "I do like the melody on that one." The song, ostensibly about two sea gulls who met and wooed on glassy cliffs above the surging ocean, was actually the Yoriandir's tribute to the victory over the Unnamed that she and Alphonse had won at the Crystal Keep. Whether the master harper had been told by the wizard about the wooing that had happened afterward or whether he had only guessed, as was his way, Ariadne had never been able to tell. But it lightened her heart to sit now in the midst of Watchmen and potboys, waitingwomen and foreign ambassadors, and share a secret thought of the absent wizard with never a person guessing.

One of the older boys stood at the harper's shoulder and proclaimed in a clear, high voice, "Attend, lords and ladies! Hear us, gentles all! I present the Eldest of Yoriand, Master Harper Imris Gravenleaf, who will perform for your delight the Song at the Edge of the Sea." He bowed and resumed his seat on the floor.

There was a mass shushing and calls for quiet, which spread from the upper end of the hall all the way to the far corners, where the Watchmen stood against the arrases. The household servants elbowed each other for the best vantage points. Imris thanked them with a nod, smiled, and began to play. "Cloud-dreamer, wind-skimmer, Cecil the He-Gull did love the sea."

He hated it, the queen thought, amused. Gulls don't get wet and cold; we do. Of their own accord her fingers tapped out the rhythm on the fine damask tablecloth. As her mind drifted with the music, she wondered where 'Cecil' was right now. Somewhere on the run this damp night, of that much she was sure. Even after a dozen years, the Unmakers of the Meld would give the Wizard of the Three no peace.

He was Abomination to his brethren on Covencroft, having broken the strictest injunction and used the three Wardings of Earth, Wind, and Fire, which he alone of all wizards could hear. No matter that the wizard had summoned his three-stranded Warding only to beat back the power of the Unnamed, the Wild Fire. No matter that without Alphonse's help, Ariadne would not have reached the Crystal Keep. And no matter that the Queen of Ilyria loved him. He was still an outcast and a traitor to the Meld. As such, he must be stripped of his power and killed.

The problem was, no one had been able to do it, though they had tried singly and in concert. They had come very close a time or two, however. Ariadne never thought of him, but she feared the day a rider would bring her the news the wizard was dead. Despite her frightened urging or imperious orders, she could not convince him to stay by her side. He would be safe here, she argued. No, he countered steadily. It isn't the Unmakers that are the problem, you know that. Then he would kiss her hair and leave once more by the secret stair and the passage in the dungeon.

She knew what he meant. Once on a winter day they had been walking out to the garden and the pale sunshine had loosened the giant icicles that hung from the copper rain gutters on the castle battlement. So quickly that Ariadne herself hadn't even realized she had been in danger, the wizard had loosed his Fire, burning the icy spears to steam. But being startled into the action and unprepared, Alphonse had momentarily lost control of the Song that strained ever at his mind. Pearl joined the garnet of his Fire, then the gold net of the third Warding appeared, and he had thrown his power into the bog south of the castle. To this day, there was a place three miles distant where the peat cutters could get chunks of coal, if they could cut it out of the fused ground.

That was the day Alphonse had left Greenbriar more or less for good. No words of hers could convince him he would be no danger to her. So now she listened for a soft step through the tiring room of her apartment in the silent hours of the night and let all would-be suitors think her touchingly loyal to her dead husband's memory.

The harpstrings thrummed and Imris began a new verse. "Water-dipper, sun-spinner, Liselle the She-Gull did love the land."

Thank you, Eldest, Ariadne thought, I did. I do. The land and the folk on it were all that made the separation from Alphonse bearable. She was the Greenbriar and there was no help for it. She was bound to her people with her life itself. No one else could make the Elixir to heal them.

And that, my dear, is that, the queen told herself.

But she did wonder sometimes at the turn of events that had conspired to make her life so lonely. Of the people

close to her, not counting her son, only Imris could come
and go from her court as freely as he liked. Alphonse must
constantly be looking over his shoulder for Unmakers and
skulking about in the night, and Peewit and Kursh had been
lost to her.

Even under the happy lilt of the Yoriandir's song, a pain
settled in her heart when she thought on it. Peewit was
somewhere abroad in the land tonight, she knew, probably
wrapped in a wet cloak and huddled over a tinker's supper
of filched chicken or a bit of pie someone had carelessly left
by an open window. Although officially a traitor to the
Crown, the former captain was still keeping watch over the
kingdom. She was not supposed to know, of course, but she
was aware that Peewit was in touch with some of her officers from time to time and had organized the roving tinkers
into an effective spy group to keep an eye and ear on the
borders with Shimarron and the Barreners. Such loyalty
would have drawn her royal favor had it been anyone else,
but because he had dared to save a friend's life, Peewit
stood officially condemned. Though she could not say so,
the queen missed him terribly.

And Kursh. There was another sore spot. Of all the
people she knew who might possibly have brought some
discipline to Gerrit's youth, the burly dwarf was the most
likely to have made the Lordling into a decent, responsible
man first, and an heir to the throne of Ilyria second. Truly,
Tydranth had cursed both her and the dwarf when he had
driven Kursh mad, and there was no getting past what the
former First Watchman had done that day on the Sweep.
When she allowed herself to think of it, Ariadne could still
see the blood bright red against the trampled grass and the
ax lying nearby, covered with gore. There had been a crack
in one face of it, she remembered.

The worst of it was Kursh would be here soon under a
diplomatic flag as Jarlshof's ambassador for the occasion.
Nissen Olafson had broken a leg on an icy winter step. The
apologetic letter from him had arrived two days ago, too
late for her to send a refusal.

She had discussed it with her advisers. Will Quint hadn't
said so, but he had plainly been pleased. Her brother Jak,
now Lord Nevelston, had reminded her that Kursh was
Guildmaster of the Glassmakers, a title which on Jarlshof
was tantamount to royalty. If the dwarves wanted to send

him as their representative, Ilyria would have to accept him. Imris, when she had told him upon his arrival from Yoriand this morning, had gravely offered the opinion that Kursh probably wasn't any happier about it than she was.

Which was not very happy. She would gladly have had things back the way they were in the old days, but time ran backward for no one. She had spent a long, sleepless night wondering what she would possibly say to him, and whether Gerrit could master the hatred he felt for the dwarf who had maimed him.

The Eldest struck the final flourish on his harp, and she came out of her reverie with a startled awareness that she hadn't heard a note in minutes. She covered this and led the applause. "We thank you, Master Harper. Your gift of music is a delight." There was fresh applause at this public thanks, and Imris stood, bowing first to her and then to the crowd.

Over his head the queen caught sight of the Watchman on duty at the huge double doors of Rose Hall. The lieutenant's hands were flickering in the hand code of the Watch. She turned her head slightly and asked Will Quint, "What does he say, captain?"

From his post behind her on the dais, the leader of her elite force said quietly, "There's a message for you, Majesty."

"Have him bring it here." Festil, the court musician, had struck up his lute to give the Eldest a rest, and the crowd was shifting on their benches before settling to listen again.

Will's voice was puzzled. "I'm afraid that isn't possible, my lady. He says it's waiting for you in the mural corridor."

"It?" she questioned, having a sudden hunch that Alphonse might be out there to surprise her.

"The lieutenant insists you go out there to receive it. I'm sorry. I don't understand, either." With an abrupt gesture, Quint summoned the man, intending to mend the fellow's manners in short order.

Ariadne, sipping at her goblet and nodding to Festil that he could begin, knew that one did not become an officer in the Watch by being a dolt. If the man said there was a message, there was, and if he summoned her to the mural corridor, he was entirely serious. She could not just walk out of the hall without arousing comment, however, so she would evaluate things from here.

She recognized the lieutenant, but couldn't place his name.

He hesitated at the foot of the steps, and Quint irritably waved him to come onto the dais and approach the queen. "Now, Fisher, what's this all about?" the captain demanded under cover of the music.

Rory Fisher threw a salute and answered directly, "Your Majesty, it's the Greenbriar mural. You've got to come and see it."

Quint drew a loud breath to chastise him for his effrontery, but Ariadne was already rising to her feet. "All right, lieutenant. Lead on."

Heads turned to follow her passage down the aisle, and Festil lost his audience, though no one actually got up to trail her except Imris.

When the queen passed through the doors with Fisher and Quint as escort, the wide corridor was already crowded with other members of the Watch and most of the kitchen people. They fell back as she approached the left border of the painted mural. Quickly she scanned the picture. At this edge, just inside the vine-and-leaf border, the Crystal Keep stood with a sunrise sky behind it, exactly as she had found it upon her return from the Tower of the Winds. Reaching out from the center of the mural was the Greenbriar itself, the Rose that was the symbol and foundation of her sovereignty, twining into the washed blue sky as it always had. She glanced up toward the ceiling beams. Yes, the thrush was there as always. What the deuce is the matter with these people? she wondered, taking in their frightened faces.

Fisher stood pointing toward the right-hand border that joined the kitchen corridor. "Here, Your Majesty," he said quietly.

He backed up, and she stared. The hare that had always crouched under the overarching shrubbery was gone. In its place was a shattered mess, the nauseating details of a hare savaged by a fox or marten. From the painting, something bright red and liquid was trickling. Ariadne reached in shock to touch it, but Fisher's voice forestalled her: "It is blood, Your Majesty."

"It can't be," she breathed.

A fearful silence surrounded her, unbroken by the shuffling of nobles crowding out of the hall to see what was the matter. Though Ariadne felt no trance coming upon her, she experienced a dizziness for a moment, and her dinner did not want to stay where it was. All she could think was,

Not again, oh, please, Powers, not again! I haven't the strength!

Then the control she had learned took over. "Captain, I want Jamison immediately." The officer who had been Peewit and Kursh's yeoman was now in charge of the Riders, the royal couriers.

From the crowded doorway of the hall came his clear voice. "I am here, Majesty. Command me." Jamison eeled his way past people and stood waiting for her order.

She found Imris at her elbow and was not too proud to take his arm for support. "You and your men will ride at once. Find Master Alphonse and give him this message: 'The thing we have long feared has come to pass.' Then report to him what you have seen here." He was eyeing the mural.

Jamison saluted crisply. "Aye, my queen." People made way for him and he ran for the marble stairway down to the courtyard and thence to the stables, shouting for his men as he went.

Ariadne looked up at the Eldest as the rising murmur of the crowd echoed off the polished stone walls. "Tychanor's Realm, do you think?"

"Undoubtedly," he murmured.

For a moment they looked at each other. Then the queen said over her shoulder, "A council, Will. In the audience chamber, immediately."

The burly man saluted and moved away to summon cadets to assemble the other members of the council. Then he followed the queen and the Eldest as they took the stairs up to the royal apartments.

Among the crowd that stayed to stare at the trickling crimson line, Prince Gerrit stood with the dice cup still in his hand, his young lords around him. "I'll be damned," Ariadne's heir murmured to himself, rattling the dice thoughtfully.

"A most grave thing, is it not, Your Highness?" said Duncan Tregallis, whose father was the Duke of Ottergard in the Southmark.

"Um-hm. Mother's got her hands full again, I do believe." Gerrit turned away from the disturbing painting and spotted the kitchen overseer. "Hai, you—Ralf. Get this mess cleaned up, would you?" He shook the dice cup again. "Come on, lads. If the sky hasn't fallen in yet, it won't for a

while, and Dunc owes me half his allowance for the month.
I aim to take the other half away from him!" One or two of
them laughed, but they followed him into the comforting
vastness of the hall with considerable haste.

Ralf waited until the nobles were gone, then caught the
eye of his second. They had already tried to sop up the
blood before they had called the queen. "Get the mop," the
overseer sighed. As the other moved away, he called, "Better yet, get a bucket."

They were out there in the night, he knew. The wizard
sighed and stirred up the fire. The black-and-white cat doz-
ing on his bed in the corner of the abandoned beacon-
keeper's hut opened her one eye to regard him. 'There's
someone down at the shore,' she told him.

"I know, I know," he answered irritably and threw another stick on the small blaze.

'Would you like me to run down and see who it is?' she
asked, not very enthusiastically.

That brought a chuckle. "And get drenched? You won't
even cross a stream on stepping-stones if it means getting
your toes wet!"

Patience stretched and yawned hugely. 'That's different,'
she said languidly.

Alphonse grunted and stuck a bit of sodden loaf on a
stick, hoping to toast the water out of it. "No need, anyway.
It's Agosto. I can read the Warding on him from here."

The cat sat up and began to run a damp paw over her
whiskers. 'He's young for it, isn't he? Surely they can't
believe he is ready for a duel.'

Beneath his damp cloak, the wizard's shoulders moved in
a shrug, and he tugged at his bushy red beard meditatively.
"He got the Serpent last year, Nels told me when we saw
him down south." He turned the bread over the licking
flame. "Still, it does seem odd to send a first-year wizard as
an Unmaker." He grinned in the firelight, though his blue
eyes were hard. "Probably I should invite him in for tea.
The lad's no doubt half drowned with the rain."

Patience had an ear cocked at something he could not
hear. 'Possibly you should not take him so lightly.'

He glanced at her sharply, took a minute to think about
it, and then stood, setting the toast carefully on the ring of
stones that made up the rude hearth. "You're right, Mis-

tress Mousecatcher." With a word, he quenched the fire and in the total darkness stepped to the rotted leather flap that was the door. Both of them listened intently. The rain pattered off the wooden roof.

When his eyes had adjusted to the night, Alphonse lifted the flap carefully and slid around the doorframe. There was a bump and brush of fur against his legs, and he knew that the cat had crouched in the clump of last year's ragwort by the wall. She would follow him no farther; a much better hunter than he, she needed no reminder about her white fur being seen in the darkness. The wizard had the other's shielding Warding in front of him like a beacon. Without yet raising his own Warding so that he would not so easily be perceived, the Wizard of the Three struck off across the small plateau of sea lavender to meet the novice.

The boy—Alphonse persisted in thinking of him that way, though upon reflection Agosto must be nearly twenty by now—was moving slowly up the hill, waiting sometimes whole minutes before darting from one clump of scrub to another. His protective Warding was burning brightly in Alphonse's mind, but the older Wizard noted that Agosto had learned well how to call the Fire that did not show as light. Alphonse took him a shade more seriously for that.

Using the Wind's Song only, the Wizard of the Three cast a quick warding around them, but detected no other Unmakers. He had been fairly certain of it anyway; judging by the bright glitter of his Fire, Agosto was scared and brave and something of a romantic. He was also young, and had come alone. Alphonse smiled a little to himself and set one shoulder against a twisted pine to wait.

In the dripping, spattering night, Agosto circled a tree five paces away and crept across the wet rocks, staring up at the hut outlined as a darker mass against the sky. Alphonse let him get clear by another few paces, then said quietly, "Looking for someone?"

The youngster was quick, give him that. The red-haired wizard barely had time to get his Warding up before a lance of Fire—emerald, he noted with a pang—shot toward him. He did not parry with Fire of his own, he simply let the younger wizard's power slide off his shield. The canes of the beach roses by his feet burst into flame, but were quenched almost immediately by the rain.

Agosto chanted frantically a high-pitched song, and emer-

ald Fire danced across the thin ground between them. It was
supposed to have been drawn to Alphonse like oil to a wick,
but the older wizard merely drew a line with the toe of his
boot and the green flames stayed outside it.

The young wizard stared a moment, then began to sing
another Warding assault.

Alphonse impatiently snapped, "Give it up, Agosto," and
walked past the startled young man up to the hut. "There's
tea, if you can bear to shelter with the Abomination," he
called over his shoulder bitterly. "Damn fool children," he
muttered to Patience as he stepped over her into the hut
and summoned the fire to the hearth once more. Grabbing
the stick with the half-done toast on it, he hunkered down
and held it over the flame.

The flap was drawn aside. "All right," Agosto said, and
sat down on the floor with some aplomb.

Alphonse gave him a speculative look. Across the fire,
Patience's one eye glowed. "Help yourself to the kettle."
Alphonse gestured toward it. "You have a cup in your
pack?"

"No, I . . . I've been fasting, you see," the young man
said in a low voice.

Alphonse very nearly laughed aloud, and Patience sneezed.
"You'll be hungry, then." He pulled the toast off the stick
and offered it. "All we have, I'm afraid." His own cup was
set ready on a flat stone of the hearth, and he filled it and
handed it to Agosto.

Through the steam, the dark eyes flicked from Alphonse
to the cup. "What will you have?"

The Wizard of the Three got up and went to his own
pack. (Agosto flinched, but covered quickly.) From the
damp leather rucksack, Alphonse took a traveling bottle
and uncorked it. A pungent smell of licorice wafted through
the hut. "This." He tipped some of the liquor down his
throat, grateful for the warmth it lit in his empty stomach.

Agosto sniffed. "Smells like flotjin."

"It is. A friend sends me some from time to time." He
smiled behind his eyes as he thought of the letter Kursh had
enclosed with it: "Don't drink it all at once, Freckles. I
don't want to hear that you've incinerated some poor country inn."

"I like it," the younger wizard ventured.

He didn't get any. Alphonse took another swig and corked

the bottle once more. Tossing it into the pack, he stooped to rub Patience's ears. "Now," he said, eyes on a level with Agosto's, "suppose you tell me who put you up to this."

The youth swallowed some tea. "No one, actually. I . . ." He shrugged. "I just did it."

"What did Master Hrontin think of the idea?" The copper wizard, head of the Meld since old Chiswic's death, considered it his solemn obligation to rid the world of the Abomination and the danger Alphonse represented.

"I didn't tell him." Agosto smiled engagingly. "I'm supposed to be on the way to Hen's Head to pick up a scroll Master Nicodemus wants to add to the music collection."

"Then you'd better—" He broke off and stared at the door. The cat under his hand bristled and her tail lashed.

Patience hissed, 'What was that?'

Forgetting Agosto's presence, Alphonse answered, "I don't know, but it sounded like a whole village screaming."

The young wizard frowned, looking toward the door. "I didn't hear anything."

The red-haired wizard was on his feet, pulling aside the door flap and listening to the night. For some moments he remained so, while Agosto quietly finished his tea and wolfed the toast. Patience at last sat down again. 'It does not come again,' she observed.

"No, it doesn't. Just the once," the wizard murmured thoughtfully.

Agosto brushed crumbs from his cloak and scrambled to his feet. He cleared his throat. "Well, I give you thanks for the tea and food. But I'll be on my way now, if you don't mind. If Master Hrontin finds out I've left my errand for such a foolish venture, he'll curse me with warts or something." He strapped his pack on hastily.

Patience turned her one eye to Alphonse. 'He thinks you mad.'

"I'm beginning to wonder myself," the wizard answered. To Agosto he said, "It's wet out there. Why don't you share the roof, such as it is, for the night?"

"Thanks, no," the youth said firmly. "Goodbye. Guard yourself well. I . . . won't be the last, you know."

For a moment, Alphonse felt the crushing weight of his outcast status. "I know. Thanks for the warning."

The youth nodded, and after a moment's hesitation, stuck

out his hand. Alphonse shook it, and Agosto ducked through the door flap.

The Wizard of the Three watched the youth scramble and slip his way down the hill toward the small barque at the water's edge. "Agosto!" he called. When the younger wizard turned inquiringly, the Abomination said, "You're pretty good with the invisible Fire, but you want to work on your Wick Spell."

Even in the streaming dark, the boy's grin showed, and suddenly he threw a playful stream of emerald Fire that arched up toward Alphonse.

To humor him, Alphonse threw a few notes of the Fire Warding back at him. With a blast that rocked the hut, a holocaust of garnet, pearl, and gold immolated Agosto where he stood.

The blood drained from Alphonse's face. "Powers!" he gasped and launched himself down the slope toward the smoking thing. "No, Agosto, I didn't do that!" he protested insanely. He had not, had not, summoned all his Wardings, only the Fire, he was gibbering in his own mind.

But the evidence was all too clear. He bent to touch the roasted thing . . . stopped. Sinking to the ground with a despairing groan, he set his head on his knees and began to cry, and not even Patience's anxious licking at his ear could quiet him.

Fa-Salar, the Shimarrat ambassador, explained casually about the woman in town, and the guards, leering a little, opened the postern to let him out of the castle. Regardless of their amusement, he knew they would report his story. That was all right; he had paid a woman already who would swear he had been with her this night. Pulling his dark embroidered hood closer, he slipped out the door and received their ironic salutes.

The Sweep was brightly lit by the moon, and he had no trouble picking his way between the camps that already dotted the hillside, the advance guard of the thousands expected within the next few days for the celebration. His own liege, King Ka-Treer, would be here on the morrow, but there was immediate business that could not wait. He thought again of the bit of intelligence he had received and involuntarily quickened his pace toward the town. Then, cursing himself for a fool, he slowed down to an appropriate saunter and nervously listened to the very slight gurgle from the corked bottle he carried in the pocket of his robe.

The Shimarrat was nearly to the town wall when a dark shape rose from the frosted grass of the meadow and tugged at his robe. He reacted instinctively, and a jeweled dagger blossomed in his hand. He had nearly plunged it into the shapeless mass when he realized that the thing was unarmed. A slack-jawed face was turned up to him, and matted gray hair blew a little in the night breeze. A filthy hand begged a coin.

Face wrinkled with disgust at the smell of the old man, Fa-Salar struck the hand away and put the point of the dagger at the beggar's chin. "Get off, you."

But the old man did not move. The ambassador saw that the beggar was a fool, too witless to know his danger. Fa-Salar snorted, sheathed his knife, and turned on his heel. He was listening for a movement behind him and was prepared to knock the loathsome creature to the turf, but there was no sound from the beggar, and when he had gone a little way, Fa-Salar glanced back to check.

The old man was still crouched beside the boulder, one hand brushing the stone limply. Fa-Salar frowned. Crazy old fool, he thought. Then: Not too crazy to beg, though. These Ilyrians! The Shimarrat strode away, muffling himself once more in his cloak.

Behind him, Lyle Brewer, now head of Her Majesty's corps of information gatherers, brushed the gray hair of the wig out of his eyes and wondered what the Shimarrat ambassador was up to. When the shadow of the town wall had swallowed the hurrying figure, Brewer stepped into the lee of a tent, stripped off the wig to change the image, and stealthily followed.

Castlenigh, the village which had stood at the river landing below the castle for time out of mind, had in the years of Ariadne's reign burst the confines of its mud-and-wattle walls to spill out along the riverbank and grow into a city. Its warehouses were stout affairs of timber and stone, and a new roofed marketplace had been built to replace the one that had burned down when the meteor had flattened the country of Westphalia thirteen years before. Here guildsmen had established proper weights and measures, and those so inclined quickly found that giving short goods for fair money would not be tolerated. A thriving trade had grown, with merchants from all the known world meeting in the broad aisles of the Trade House to do business. By day, the roofed market was a crowded, noisy place.

By night, however—as now—the wide aisles were dark, and the wind blew freely through the broad archways, bringing in a smell of damp off the river, which rolled placidly by mere yards from the waterside entrance. Sometimes beggars tried to sleep the night in the Trade House, but there were guards posted outside by the guilds, and besides, there were not many beggars in Castlenigh. The city's prosperity was such that almost anyone who wanted work could find it.

Tonight the two guards were happily incapacitated with preholiday celebration. Fa-Salar stole a cautious peek around the corner of the inn which stood by the Trade House's southern wall and spied the two lolling on a couple of bales near the dark entrance of the market. They were idly tossing dice. The Shimarrat ambassador drew back, satisfied. He walked briskly through the innyard into the stables and out the other side through the door from which the grooms shoveled out manure into the river. A few steps along the river road brought him to the high iron gates which closed the riverside entrance of the Trade House. These were supposed to be locked, but they yielded to a slight pressure of his hand, and he slipped inside. A few well-placed silvers could accomplish wonders.

Fa-Salar walked soft-footed in his court shoes up the main aisle. As befitted a market, Trade House was dirt-floored, and the Shimarrat made little sound. When he had counted off thirteen stalls on his left, he squeezed between a stone column and a long trestle table and walked to the bales stacked three deep in the darker shadow away from the door. He sat down to wait, but then thought better of it. The person for whom he was waiting was not someone he would willingly be caught with his back to. Fa-Salar put his back to a stack of wool bales and rested his hand on his dagger hilt, flipping the edge of his cloak over so it would not be too obvious that he clutched the knife.

A low laugh came out of the darkness to his right, and Fa-Salar started. Angrily he whispered, "Why did it have to be here? The place echoes like a tomb!"

The lithe figure in close-fitting black had gotten quite near before the Shimarrat ambassador could see him. Lightly the leader of the assassins said, "How do you know? Have you ever been in a tomb?"

"That's not meant to be a threat, I hope." The ambassador's fingers tightened on his dagger.

The killer smiled: Fa-Salar could hear it in his voice as he said, "My lord ambassador, you are quite safe." He paused and must have pulled back his hood, for the ambassador caught a sudden glint of his jade ear gem. "No one's given me orders to kill you. Yet."

"I am relieved," Fa-Salar muttered, but he did not move his hand from his belt. He whispered, "I haven't much time, but I had to get this information to you: they know! The damned Ilyrians have somehow discovered there's to be an attempt on the queen's life!"

It was so quiet he could hear the river lapping at its retaining wall. Finally, the other asked, "Do they know any of the rest of it?"

"I have heard nothing."

They weighed the information. The assassin shrugged in the darkness. "It is well," he judged. "So we simply will omit that part. For the rest, we stick with the original plan. It will still work, I think."

"But they're expecting it!"

Teeth gleamed. "If they think they know what to expect, our task will actually be much easier. When our little surprises start popping, the Ilyrians will be like chickens bleeding from the ax."

Fa-Salar stroked his waxed mustache. "Yes, it is ingenious," he allowed. "To bring them down by counterfeiting an attack by their Unnamed nemesis. My lord king's plan is truly a thing of cleverness."

"And he doesn't like sheep blatting about it," the cold voice said.

The ambassador shivered in the dark. "I have the drug you ordered," he told the other, and withdrew the bottle from his robe pocket.

"Ah. Excellent. No doubt I could have broken into some apothecary shop in this wretched city, but our poisons are so much more subtle than these Ilyrians can conceive, so much more exquisite. I like to work with the best."

Fa-Salar's hand found his dagger hilt again. "The explosive is arranged?"

"Oh, yes. Everything else is done—we were just waiting for this little bottle," the assassin said with satisfaction.

The ambassador tugged his cloak up on his neck. "Yes, very well. Only remember, the nephew is not to be harmed at the outset."

"I'm a professional!" the killer hissed.

At that moment a muddled shape of rags rose up from behind the bales.

"Shaddup!" the drunk roared. "Can't a body get some bloody sleep around here?" His voice echoed under the stone roof.

Fa-Salar froze, but the assassin never hesitated, and it was doubtful the drunk ever realized what happened. The killer pushed the body behind the bales and gave the ambassador a shove. "Go!"

The diplomat wasn't quick enough, however. From the open archway at the entrance came a slightly slurred voice. "Hai, you, whoever you are—come out here!" Steps sounded on the stone threshold. "No, stay there, Will—I'll take care of it," the guard said over his shoulder as he came down the aisle.

Fa-Salar crouched behind a bale. The assassin waited.

"Come on, ye lazy bum! This ain't an inn, y'know!" the guard yelled, looking from side to side as he strode along impatiently. "Damn whoreson," he muttered. "Just when I was winning, too." He drew even with the stone column and stopped, looking toward the open river gate. "What the bloody hell?" He had turned and drawn breath to call his mate when the killer struck.

Even though the assassin's hand muffled his victim's mouth, Fa-Salar could hear the explosion of breath and the grunt as the knife slid up under the ribs, and the ambassador's stomach gave a warning lurch. He had transmitted his king's assassination orders before, but he had never seen the killer at work. When the assassin dragged his second victim past Fa-Salar to the bales, the ambassador whispered shakily, "Be sure to arrange their knives."

Fa-Salar could swear he saw the topaz eyes flare. "I know, fool! Get out, I told you!" With the hand that did not hold the bloody dagger, he pushed the diplomat toward the river door.

The ambassador did not look back. When he had skirted the crowd at the cockfight beyond the inn, he made for the

MICHAEL S. THOMAS
LEARNING RESOURCE CENTER

riverbank on the other side of the landing. Stumbling down the reedy bank under the willows, he scooped cold river water over his hands and scrubbed them, as though he himself had done the murders. When he felt steadier, he drew the hood up against the chill at the back of his neck and went up to the castle.

By the time the Shimarrat made it back to his own suite and his slave had unquestioningly set a full cup by his hand and gone to clean the dark cloak, Fa-Salar was himself once more. He drank slowly while the fire drew the river water from his shoes.

When the servant came back and bowed, the ambassador glanced up. "All done?"

"Yes, my lord. All is prepared for tomorrow. Will my lord go to bed now?"

"Yes. It's been a long day." He drained the cup and stood. "Enoki?"

"My lord?" The slave's brass earring gleamed in the firelight as he cocked his head.

"If ever you see a man with a jade ear gem and topaz eyes anywhere around me, kill him."

Lyle Brewer shrugged out of his old cloak and stood before the fire in the guard tower's watch room, warming his hands and berating himself. Unusually for him, he had lost his quarry that night, and unless he missed his guess, the ambassador had been about more than visiting a tavern wench.

Chapter Two

❧

The Master of Ledgelawn was beside himself with the preparations for his old friend's arrival. The sunshine gleamed off the polished crystal windowpanes, the brown winter lawn had been neatly raked, and the shrubbery alongside the glassblowing shed was mulched with hay. Branches

MOUNT ST. THOMAS

LEARNING RESOURCE CENTER

of holly bright with crimson berries cascaded from the window-boxes, and the air was sweet with the smell of woodsmoke.

It was all well and good when he turned the prentices out on the front lawn to inspect them in their new jerkins, barking at one to shine his boots and another to put a comb to good use, but when Kursh demanded that Trondur's wife, Lisle, find someplace else to shake her rugs, the Mistress of Ledgelawn took a hand. Wiping her hands on her apron as she peered from the kitchen window, Thyla marched down the hallway, through the living room, and out onto the lawn and firmly took his arm. Turning him so the apprentices wouldn't hear, she said, "Don't you think you might give the boys a little less of a drubbing and a little more time to do their chores? My land, Kursh, this isn't a parade ground, you know!"

The fierce eyebrows lowered. She stood her ground. After a moment, he growled over his shoulder, "All right, lads. Let's be about our business, eh? There's still the Burgher of Minstermeir's shipment to get out today, after all." They broke from ranks and walked off to their work in the crystal workshop, packing shed, or office with sidelong glances at the master and his wife. Most of them managed to hide their grins pretty well.

Kursh pulled irritably at his linen cuffs so that they showed a precise two inches under the sleeves of his scarlet velvet jacket with its gold-braided sleeves. "Where's Gretchen got to?"

Thyla patiently answered, "She's up on the hill looking for a bird's nest. She wanted to make him welcome. There's no harm in that, is there?"

"I just want everything to be right, that's all. This is Peewit's first time back, and I want to do him proper honor."

His wife's lips twitched, and she straightened the chain and flat crystal pendant hanging about his neck. "You just want to show off a little, is what you want, Guildmaster," she teased gently.

A slow flush crept up the back of his barbered neck, and the starch went out of him. "I guess I do," he admitted.

Thyla squeezed his arm affectionately. "Come in and rest yourself. Let's have some starflower."

Kursh looked slowly around the open lawn, the weathered benches set at the edge of the garden, the long views of blue sky, puffy cloud, and the city of Skejfalen that spread from their house on the hill. "All right," he said. "I guess we're ready." He tugged at his eyepatch and followed her into the house.

Kursh had arranged with Pers Half Hand to send up a rocket from the deck of his ship as soon as the *Puffin II* was moored at its anchorage in the harbor, so there would be ample time to get everybody out front to meet the coach that bore the Littleman up from the city.

The door with the insignia of the Glassblowers' Guild swung open, the small figure stepped down and had a word for the driver and a pat for the matched grays, and then Peewit was coming up the graveled walk. Kursh strode forward with a wide smile to greet him. "Hallo, captain!"

"Hello, old friend. A blessing on your household." Peewit grinned through the beard that had been part of his traveling disguise for twelve years.

As Kursh gave him a bear hug, the dwarf schooled his face not to show dismay. The Littleman looked more tired than Kursh had ever seen him, and the normally dapper Brickleburr was disheveled and unkempt. The dwarf tried to believe it was just part of his disguise. He gestured one of the apprentices to get the captain's tattered bag.

Peewit was holding him at arm's length, looking him up and down. "You're looking fit, First Watchman. Married life agrees with you."

"Most of it," Kursh agreed smoothly, drawing a chuckle from the Littleman as he escorted him up the path to where the others waited.

Thyla and Peewit embraced, and she gave him a kiss of welcome. "Goodness sake, captain, what have ye been doin' to yourself? You're as thin as a bad stew!"

"I've been fasting in anticipation of your cooking!" the Littleman told her with a wink.

"Well, good!" she exclaimed, playing along.

Then Trondur, older now and with his spectacles perched on the top of his head and bills of lading under his arm, shook his hand and presented his wife, Lisle, and oldest son, Peter. Five other children were clustered about, and he rattled off these sons' and daughters' names so quickly that Peewit knew he wouldn't be able to attach any of the names to the right faces. "A fine-looking bunch," the Littleman complimented.

"They favor their mother, thank the Powers." Trondur grinned, and Lisle laughed and colored prettily.

"Ah, there you are, mistress-come-lately," Kursh was saying as Peewit turned around. The dwarf's large hands were resting on the shoulders of a freckle-faced, raven-haired little maid of some six years, Peewit judged. Kursh's one eye shone with quiet pride. "And this is our Gretchen."

"Welcome home, Uncle Peewit." She started to fold into the old-fashioned curtsy Thyla had been practicing with her for weeks, teetered, and tripped on the hem of her embroidered dress. Before anyone could catch her, down she went—plump. Sitting there, she craned her head straight up to see her father's expression. Kursh tried to glower, but the beginnings of a smile got away from him and he tugged at his mustache to hide it.

Gretchen giggled, scrambled up, and held out the bird's nest, a symbol of homecoming. "I guess I'll never make a lady," she said matter-of-factly. She gestured Peewit to bend down, which he did with a smile, and slipped the nest into his hand. She gave him a peck on the cheek. "There. That's what I wanted to do in the first place, but Papa—"

"Would rather see a little gossip than hear her," Kursh finished pointedly.

Gretchen pursed her lips in a silent "oops" that only the Littleman could read and stepped back with an attempt to be demure. Peewit began to laugh, and Kursh motioned him to the blue-painted door. "Come in and don't stop talking, or the womenfolk in this house will natter you to death."

"Oh, shush, you," Thyla told him, steering Gretchen with her. "Don't mind him, captain. It isn't as though he listened to the half of it anyway! Just make yourself to home and there'll be tea ready in a wink, and something to go along with it."

Then they were through into the two-story main entrance and living room. When last Peewit had been at Ledgelawn, the place had gone to seed, with cobwebs in the crystal chandelier and fine carpets worn threadbare. Now the old house was alive again. As Thyla headed for the kitchen with Gretchen in tow, Kursh led the Littleman to the plush overstuffed sofa, and Peewit looked around, marveling at the changes. There was a needlepoint carpet underfoot and a gilt-framed mirror above the fireplace, which had a new blue-and-white-tiled hearth. Rich cherry planking covered the walls, gleaming with beeswax carefully rubbed in. Over all hung the aroma of lemon oil polish.

Kursh took a small package from the mantel. "I've something here for you. Thought you might be needing a new one by now."

It was a pipe, a magnificently carved meerschaum. The Littleman turned it in his hands, delighting in the scenes displayed. One showed the battlements of Greenbriar Castle with the starbursts of firerockets going off above it. Another was plainly the spire of Barak-Gambrel with a tiny kite floating above it. A third was the Greenbriar itself, twining and blooming, and the last was a honeybee, symbol of his own Hearthfolk, humming busily over a clover blossom. Peewit was about to say how much he liked the gift when the bee moved. It slowly crawled over the bloom of some flower he could not quite see, while its buzz went up in pitch until the insect suddenly jacknifed and the legs drew up in death.

"Caught you speechless, eh?" Kursh clapped him on the shoulder and passed him a lidded crystal jar of leaf.

The Littleman nearly dropped it, but caught a quick breath, and shook his head sharply while the dwarf was reaching for a decanter and two glasses from the ship's hatch that served as a table. Peewit stared at the pipe for a moment, then—not to offend Kursh—began to pack it. The heady aroma of the best leaf braced him, and by the time the dwarf turned with his drink, he was able to smile. "I'm in your debt."

"Rot. Drink up." They touched glasses, and the crystal chimed. "To friends." Both of them were poignantly aware in the moment that at one time their first salute would have been to the queen.

The black liquor sent a satisfying fire down the Littleman's throat, and he sat down with a sigh, still weak-kneed from the hallucination. "That's good."

Kursh swallowed and nodded. "Private label. The old pirate who distills it charges me a fortune, and probably sells the same lot to the dockyard taverns."

They lit up and got their pipes drawing well. Peewit made a gesture that included the room and everything in it. "Congratulations, my friend. You've done well for yourself."

The dwarf sat back in a chair covered with the softest glove leather and rested one wide-cuffed boot on the table comfortably. "A little luck, a lot of the Powers' blessing."

Peewit reminded him dryly, "There's a little talent involved, too, if I remember correctly."

"Only a little," the Guildmaster rasped, but there was pride in his voice. Being Kursh, he quickly changed the topic. Gesturing with his pipestem, he indicated Brickleburr's worn boots and clothing. "Ye look a proper tinker."

"One plays the part. Muir sends respects, by the way."

"The old ruffian! How is he?"

"As nasty as ever. He singlehandedly took on a three-man Shimarrat border patrol last fortnight and lived to tell about it."

They shared a reminiscent laugh which trailed off into silence. The smoke eddied from their pipes, and Kursh looked away. "Do you ever see any of the old fellows?"

"No," Peewit answered. "I correspond with Will and Jami, but it would never do for any of us to meet."

The dwarf nodded without looking at him. "Listen, Brickleburr—before you left last time, I never got the chance to say—"

At that moment there was a step down the hall and Thyla came in with a tray. "Get your feet off the table, Father," she said by rote, and Kursh straightened in his chair. She set the service down and grinned over the teapot at the Littleman. "I'm surprised he hasn't had you out to the shop yet."

"Just waiting for the tea, wife," Kursh gruffed, reaching past her for the covered basket of pastries. He offered it to Peewit, advising, "Try the ones with the nuts on top."

Brushed with honey and savory with cheese filling, the folded sweets smelled even better than they looked, and for the first time in weeks the Littleman felt an appetite. While Thyla poured out a cup of starflower for him, he nibbled at a corner. "Mmm."

She dimpled and handed him his tea. "Dinner will be on in a couple of hours, but this should hold you till then. I've turned back your bed, captain, if ye'd like a bit of a nap. Sea journeys are sometimes tiring."

"Thanks, no, I'm fine. The weather was good; it was smooth sailing." He sniffed the steam from his cup appreciatively.

"All right, then. I'll leave you two gents alone to pass the time. Gretchen is making something special for our dessert tonight, and I'd best be standing by to help." She straightened and looked down at him a moment. "We're awfully glad you're here," she said simply.

"I am, too," the Littleman answered.

With a nod, she headed back to the kitchen.

Kursh wolfed the last half of his pastry, licked his fingers, and tapped Brickleburr's knee. "Come. Let me show you what we do here."

Peewit hastily rose, teacup in one hand and pastry in the other, and followed the dwarf out the front door and across the lawn to the glassblowing shed. Kursh paused with his hand on the knob. "It's a bit disordered right now," he apologized. "We're in the midst of finishing a special order." He swung open the door, and the Littleman stepped past him into the sun-filled interior of the crystal factory.

If there was disorder, Peewit couldn't see it. At workbenches surrounding the central firepit, the masters blew and shaped the crystal bowls, goblets, and other pieces, while around them, the apprentices watched attentively or carefully burred and polished the completed articles. Others kept the quenching troughs filled or trundled the crystal on padded wagons out through a door at the far end. Kursh put a hand out to stop one of them, and the prentice bowed respectfully. The Guildmaster picked a goblet at random and turned with it to the light of one of the wide windows. He examined it, turning it so that the light was refracted in bright gems of color across the floor. "Master Igurrson's work, I see."

"Aye, master."

One thick finger pointed for Peewit's benefit, and Kursh explained in an aside, "He always bevels this cut a little more than the rest of us." A slight appreciative smile flickered. "It's very effective at throwing the light." As he turned the goblet again the sunlight caught the small etched trademark in the base and threw it as an enlarged shadow on the floor: a kite shape bearing across the face of it the three chevrons that had marked his rank as First Watchman. The dwarf regarded it for a moment, then met the Littleman's eye. Before Peewit could make any comment, he turned briskly to the prentice. "Very good. Get on to the packing shed with you, now, and remind Master Larson that I want the extra-thick padding this time: there's foul weather coming and this shipment's got far to go by sea."

"Aye, master." The boy inclined his head to the Littleman. " 'Day to you, sir." He trundled the barrow out the door.

Peewit followed Kursh outside. "Very efficient. I must say, I'd no idea you had so many people working for you." He drank down the last of his tea.

"Business has been good," the dwarf acknowledged. He gestured to a smaller building. "That's the office. Trondur handles that end of things for us."

Peewit looked across the lawn at a one-story shed and raised an eyebrow.

"Armory." At the Littleman's look, he explained briefly, "I tell the boys if they're going to be transporting a fortune in crystal, they'd damn well better be able to defend it."

It clicked then, the spruce jerkins, the sense of order, the intelligent eyes of the prentices that had followed them. Peewit grinned. "Senior squires."

Korimson pulled at his mustache as he surveyed the view down to Skejfalen and out to sea, and one corner of his bearded lips drew up. "I fancy my boys would match up well with anybody in livery, if they had to."

Brickleburr laughed.

Kursh led the way to a pair of benches companionably placed at the edge of the garden, and each of them fit himself into the angle of the arm and the back and swung his feet up on the plank seat. Peewit bit into the pastry. Kursh was watching him, his one eye narrowed. "Tinkering looks to be a rugged life."

The Littleman chewed slowly, swallowed, and said, "Not so bad. The potcheen helps."

The dwarf grunted. "Certain people tell me the borders are restless."

The captain finished his pastry and rubbed his fingers on his faded jacket. "Something is going on in Shimarron, but we've detected no unusual activity in the Barrens. Actually, it's been a little too quiet in the Gap."

"Has there been any coming and going 'twixt King Ka-Treer's people and those damned Wolf Cult scum?"

Peewit stared. "What made you think that?"

The Guildmaster shook his head. "Shot in the dark, you might say. But it's a natural alliance for both of them, you know, if they could stand each other's guts long enough to attack us. I mean, to attack Ilyria," he amended hastily.

"Well, actually—"

There was a shrill hail from the direction of the house, and Gretchen, pigtails flying, ran down to them, their pipes clutched aloft. "You forgot your smokes!" Triumphantly she placed the pipes in their hands and produced her father's flint and iron from the pocket of her cloak.

"Thanks, pet," Kursh rumbled. "Hush now. The captain and I are talking." Obediently she said no more, but scrambled up onto his lap. The dwarf struck a spark into his pipe and leaned to hand the flint to the Littleman. "You were saying?"

Peewit was busy for a moment with his own smoke. Then he blew a smoke ring into the light breeze. "Just before I left Muir at Waysmeet, we picked up a bit of information I don't like one bit, if it's true." He glanced at Kursh's small daughter and made a handsign in the code of the First Watch: Danger for the queen, at Greenbriar.

The former First Watchman frowned and freed one hand from holding Gretchen still to sign back: What kind of danger?

Unknown.

Both of them thought immediately to the crowd even now assembling for the Lordling's birthday celebration.

Kursh signed: Assassin?

Likely.

Gretchen twisted to look back at her father. "What are you doing?" she demanded. "If you're playing shadow puppets, you're not doing it very well. I can't see any shadows."

"That's because we're playing sun puppets," Kursh lied smoothly. To Peewit he said aloud, "Have you gotten a message to Will Quint?"

Peewit nodded, drawing on his pipe. "Muir was taking it to Greenbriar personally."

"How do you play sun puppets?" Gretchen wanted to know.

The dwarf thought a moment. "One of them"—he signed "assassin" to make clear what he was talking about—"sounds more Shimarrat than Barrener."

"Just what I thought. And, of course, Ka-Treer will be paying a state visit."

"He wouldn't be stupid enough—"

"What better cover than to do it at a time everyone would find unthinkable?"

Kursh's hand flickered in a sign peculiar to him, but the Littleman got the meaning very well.

Gretchen frowned and squirreled around on his lap. "Come on, Papa, tell me how to play!"

He put one broad paw firmly over her mouth and spoke across the top of her pigtailed head. "How about Alphonse? He'll be at court, I presume, but maybe somebody could get word to him to ward her immediately."

Peewit blew another smoke ring. "We can't find him. When last we heard anything of him, he was in Waterford. I suppose he took ship from there, but there's been no word from him all fall."

The dwarf smiled slightly. "Inishkerry." At the Littleman's surprised look, he explained, "He drops in from time to time for a game of dice and some of Thyla's cooking. Last summer he showed up one day, stayed the night, and then took himself off for that rockpile of an island. Claimed it was the only safe place for him." He took his hand from Gretchen's mouth and smoothed his daughter's hair while she blew an impatient sigh. "I gather he thought he might bring harm to us," he said quietly.

Peewit looked grave. "He's getting worse, you know. There are tales of his temper, and he talks all the time to that cat." He shook his head.

Gretchen unexpectedly piped up, "Patience talks to him!"

"Lass," Kursh said warningly.

"It's true, Papa! Master Freckles told me so himself!"

"You are a proper little nuisance, you are," the dwarf rasped.

The Littleman had a thoughtful half-smile on his face. "It is possible, Kursh. Imris could communicate with that thrush, you remember. What was her name?"

"I can't remember. Had six syllables at least." He pulled at his mustache. "Well, well," he said softly. "That explains a lot about the boy wonder, doesn't it?"

The Littleman knocked out his pipe, grinding the ash into the frozen verge of the garden soil. "Hardly a boy anymore!"

"Still plays dice like one. Ah, well. Come on up to the house. We'll have a better chance to talk after dinner, after we get this baggage to bed." He rose, swung Gretchen up, and threw her casually over his shoulder.

She squealed, "Be nice, Papa, or you won't get any dessert!"

He started for the house. "Do I want any?" he rumbled.

Gretchen winked confidentially at Peewit in a way so like Kursh's own that the captain smiled. "It's pumpkin pie."

"Hmm. Yes, well then." Her father set her on her feet

and she skipped along between them, holding a hand of each.

She looked up at Peewit and whispered, "I knew that would get him."

Years of care were stripped from the Littleman's face when he laughed.

Dinner was excellent, of course, given that Thyla had exerted herself to make the cheese, onion, and potato pie that Kursh had remembered was the Littleman's favorite. Peewit was touched by the thoughtfulness and tried to put away a fair share, though he had not had much interest in food lately. Then there was the velvet smoothness of the brandy-laced pie to follow. The whipped-cream dollops on top fairly made his mouth water just to look at them. Unfortunately, the crust was nearly as hard as rock. When Kursh put his fork to it, he had to force it through by brawn. His eye widened and he glanced quickly to Thyla, who nodded significantly to Gretchen's expectant face. Korimson forked the piece he had broken off to his mouth and made "mmm" noises. Gretchen turned a shining look to her mother, and Kursh quickly slurped some tea to soften the pie, whereupon he was able to swallow it.

Forewarned, Peewit successfully got through his portion. When the girl was in the kitchen clearing the table, the adults shared a fond and muted laugh.

Afterward, the Littleman and the dwarf repaired upstairs to the Guildmaster's study. This was a chamber that had been added like a cupola on the roof of the hillside-sheltered house. From its vantage, the view of the sunset over the harbor was breathtaking. A brassbound telescope stood on its tripod trained on the busy dockside, and Peewit had a look while Kursh walked to a cabinet built into one corner. "What will you have, captain? We've brandy, Nabilian wine, and flotjin, of course. Or tea—I see the wife has had a pot brought up for us."

"I'll have the tea, please." The Littleman sat himself in the window seat and surveyed the room. A large trestle table served as a writing desk, and the room also held a small fireplace. Carefully rendered drawings of new crystal patterns were tacked to the walls. There was a comfortable clutter of cushions, slippers, scrolls, and ledger books scattered about. Peewit got the impression Thyla had an understanding with her husband about this room. "This is your lair, I take it."

"Aye. Thyla's a worthy woman, but by Aashis's Beard, a fellow's got to have a place where he can kick his boots off in peace." Which he proceeded to do, also stripping off the velvet jacket and pitching it onto the desk.

They lit up their pipes once more and sipped tea while the busy boats came and went below them, and Kursh talked of the doings of the island in general and of the guild. "And then at the Aashnasse glassblowing competition last year, Master Jansson withdrew in favor of me, and so they elected me Guildmaster."

"Richly deserved. I wonder that it took them so long to come to it. Certainly no one else could have blown the Weatherglass from the Pipes."

The shaggy brows drew down. "I don't know about that. I think my election had a great deal more to do with the fact I'd had some military training than it did with the quality of my glass. Something's got to be done about the sea brigands. It's gotten so bad that they're taking one ship out of every five that leave this port." He brooded over the teacup cradled in his large hands.

"Have you had any success fighting them?"

"Some. And I've got an idea that seems promising if I can find a foundry big enough to do the job." He said this last almost as if to himself, then cleared his throat. "Anyway, that's one of the reasons I've got to go to Greenbriar, you see. We need Ilyria's help. A sea treaty, and so forth." He swallowed suddenly and looked away.

Peewit read his silence and said quietly, "It will go well, Kursh, you'll see."

The dwarf threw down the dregs of his tea, tugged at his eyepatch, and rasped, "Oh, aye. The queen'll be honorable, I'm sure. I'll be under an ambassador's flag, after all." Both of them were counting on this to hold at bay the sentence of death that had never been rescinded. After another moment, Korimson abruptly added, "It's just damned uncomfortable, is all. If you really want to know, I'd sooner lose my other eye than walk into that hall." He uncoiled from the window seat like a bowstring snapped and stalked to the liquor cabinet to pour himself some of the black flotjin. "And I don't think you should come with me," he threw over his shoulder.

Peewit sighed. "We've been over this, Kursh. There will be no better time for me to go back. Both of us together will be insurance for each other. Your diplomatic status will cover me, and if need be, I can make both of us invisible."

The dwarf turned with the drink in his hand. He had flushed angrily. "Come on, Peewit. You know if it hadn't been for me, you'd still be in your old station at the queen's right hand! I'll not take you back there and put you in danger again!" He gulped the flotjin.

The Littleman held his eye. "It was not you who put me in danger of my life, old friend. It was the queen. And I'll wager that in her heart of hearts, Ariadne knows I was right."

"She's made you pay a bloody dear price for being right, then! Look at you, half-starved, an outlaw!" The fist around the glass clenched until the knuckles stood whitely. And look at me, his bitten-off words said plainly, with my family around me and all my heart's desire.

Peewit read the thought as clearly as if it had been spoken. "Kursh, there is no blame to you because things have turned out well for you. By the Powers, do you think I'd grudge your happiness?" The dwarf tugged at his eyepatch. "Besides, you must understand that we all have our own fate. Yours is to be a Glassmaker. Mine is to be the Pledged of the Hearthfolk. I could not leave Ariadne's service even if I wanted to, so I had to find a way to fulfill my kin's binding to the Greenbriar."

Korimson took a swallow of his drink. "If you're thinking to make me feel better, forget it. Ye could have broken your Oath: I did." He had gone paler, but his eye was steady.

"Nonsense. You never did. Even now, you would give your life for her. Or for Gerrit."

The dwarf shook his head and said positively, "No, I wouldn't, Peewit. For Gretchen's and Thyla's sakes, I wouldn't. It isn't the same."

The Littleman sighed. "Of course not! How could it be the same? Though I have no doubt that you don't even remember it, you did kill Ka-Salin, and Gerrit . . . walks with a limp, I am told." The dwarf turned his head to hide the involuntary grimace. "But here's something to ponder: what else besides exile in the face of death would have made you come home?" Kursh's brows drew down. "And who else could the Powers have sent up Barak-Gambrel to do that job? You see? Certainly even the dreadful thing you did was worked into the pattern the Powers were weaving." Affectionate compassion was in his voice. "You make too much of it if you regard it in any other way."

Korimson set down his glass on the desk and stared at the papers there for some moments while the Littleman smoked. Finally he raised his head and smoothed his mustache. "Brickleburr, that was the biggest load of manure I've heard in an age." They regarded each other, and then the small figure in the window seat began to grin. Korimson shook his head, and an unwilling smiled tugged at his lips. "But I thank ye for it. Now if ye've done playing at Retreat Master, there's a thing here I'd like to show you." He took a key from his breeches pocket and walked to the wall opposite the fireplace. Shelves were built in there, pieces of crystal displayed along their length.

Kursh touched some lever the Littleman did not see, and the whole wall swung inward just wide enough to admit them. The dwarf gave him a glance and then led the way through to a small adjacent chamber which Peewit had not even suspected was there. Nothing was in the room but an iron safe. This the dwarf unlocked. Within were ingots of gold and silver, and resting on a velvet cushion, two Weatherglasses. Korimson took one out and handed it casually to Peewit. "Recognize this?"

The Weatherglass caught some stray gleam from the fireplace beyond the open door, and in the heart of it a pinprick of light grew suddenly into a silver fire. It was the Glass he had made on Barak-Gambrel. Peewit was struck anew at the masterful artistry of it. "Very well," he murmured. "I thought then I'd never seen anything so lovely."

" 'Tis a nice piece," the dwarf conceded. He took back the shining thing and replaced it on the cushion. "What do you think of this one?" He put the other into Peewit's hands.

The Littleman turned with it to the firelight. The Glass was cut with a wedge-and-diamond pattern around both poles, so the refracted light danced in a swarm of motes over the safe and the dwarf. In a broad band around the middle was etched a greyhound in swift pursuit of a buck which ran with its head turned back to see, sporting a magnificent rack of antlers drawn with cunning skill.

"Hold it right up to your eye," the dwarf said.

When the captain did so, he was amazed, for now he saw not just one hound and stag, but several, as there might be in a hunt, and as the firelight danced behind the Glass, the animals winked in or out of the scene as the light and shadow threw the pattern endlessly from facet to facet. "My word!"

"Interesting illusion, eh?"

"Kursh, it's spectacular!"

The dwarf pulled at his beard and said gruffly, "Not bad." Peewit put it to his eye again and made the hounds leap. Quietly the Guildmaster said, "It's Gerrit's birthday present."

The Littleman handed it back to him and matched his tone. "I'm sure he will like it."

Kursh placed it back on the cushion. "I'm not. It's small recompense for a father murdered."

There was nothing Peewit could say to that, so he merely squeezed the other's shoulder briefly and went back into the study.

After Kursh had locked the safe, he came through to find the Littleman stifling a yawn and rubbing his eyes. "The sea air catches up with you, doesn't it?"

Peewit did not want to tell him that he had not slept in nearly three days, so he merely nodded.

"Feel free to trot off to bed. There's no sense fighting to stay awake. We'll have all day tomorrow to visit, after all."

"You're sure you don't mind?"

"No." Kursh waved a hand at some of the papers. "I've some accounts that need looking after, anyway."

The Littleman stifled another yawn and nodded. "Good night, then. Oh, and Kursh—might I have the loan of a razor?" He flicked at his salt-and-pepper beard. "I'd like to get rid of this."

"Aye. Ye don't make a very good dwarf anyway, meaning no offense," he said frankly.

"I know. I haven't the nose for it."

The dwarf pitched the scarlet velvet jacket at him, and the captain ducked out the door. Kursh could hear him chuckling as he went down the stairs to the second floor.

Some time later Thyla climbed to her husband's aerie and found him standing at the bow window, staring at the distant lights of Skejfalen and the moonlight that polished the crystal dome of the guildhall. "It's late, dear," she said, going to where he stood. "Are ye coming to bed?"

He did not reply for a moment, then swallowed and whispered in a hushed and stricken voice, "Thyla, he's gotten so old."

She put her arms around his shoulders and hugged him from behind, laying her head against his broad back. "It's many a long year of care that sits on him," she agreed quietly.

His shoulder muscles bunched as he shook his head. "It's more than that," he said positively and groped for words to fit the feeling. "We've been through some tight spots together, he and I. I know him better than I do Trondur, if it comes to that. It isn't just care: he's Captain and has lived most of his life with worry. Danger, too." Kursh sighed impatiently and shook his head once more. "It isn't that. It's more like . . . like a light has gone out of him, if you know what I mean." Thyla's arms tightened around him in a reassuring embrace. "He could always make a jest, Brickleburr could. Ye'll think me daft, but there used to be a winking to his eyes. Put me in mind of some dancing brook ye'd see in the summer woods." His head sank on his chest. "When I look in his eyes now, Thyla, I only see myself looking back."

The fire crackled in the grate. She smoothed his hair and said, "He's tired, Kursh. Traipsing up country and down, in fair weather and foul, for nigh onto thirteen years—of course the lad looks worn!" She took a breath and turned him to face her. "That's why ye've got to take him home to Greenbriar, I can see that now."

His expression eased somewhat. They had argued over it.

"Ye'll take him home, and maybe the queen will acknowledge him. That's what he needs. Honor. A soft word from her."

He gently laid his large hand along her cheek. "I knew ye'd understand."

"Aye. Ye were pretty sure to go planning it without ever telling me." She was smiling slightly now, but she had not smiled, not at all, when she'd found out his decision. Thyla put her hand over his, and suddenly her expression hardened. "If she does anything to you, there will be war, you know, Guildmaster. Jarlshof will not stand for it."

"I know," he admitted.

She spoke over his murmur. "And I swear to ye, husband, I'll be on the lead ship and Ariadne Greenbriar will hear a thing or two from me, the likes of which ye wouldn't want your daughter saying!" She freed her hand to give a vigorous push at her hair where her cap would have sat if she had still been bakeress at court.

His booming laugh rose up until she shushed him with a kiss, scolding that he'd wake the girl and their guest. "Come to bed," she said.

"In a bit. I've a little more work to do here first. I don't want to leave any loose ends when I go, and Trondur's got the Lord of Hurlestone's order hopelessly mucked up."

"Ah, you!" she said with exasperation, swatting at him. But she didn't slam the door when she left, so Kursh guessed that she wasn't really angry and might yet be awake when he went downstairs. He hoped so.

Tugging at his beard to sober himself—for the next bit of business had nothing to do with Hurlestone's goblets—he set a candle in the window that faced his brother's house and sat down at his desk to wait.

Trondur must have been watching for the sign, because Kursh soon heard his light tap at the outside door. He rose and opened the bookcase wall into the safe room. When he had added this study to the old house, he had designed a secret door, patterned on the one at Greenbriar, but not so elaborate. It led up onto the hill behind the house and was not much good in the winter when everything was drifted with snow, but in the other seasons he often used it late at night to go up and watch the stars wheel slowly overhead.

His brother came in, and Kursh asked, "Is it arranged?"

Trondur Korimson polished his spectacles on his vest. "All done. Even the duplicate flag is ready."

Kursh motioned him to a seat. "Half Hand has been paid?"

Trondur hesitated. "Well, no."

"I told ye—"

"Wait a moment, will you?" The milder younger brother breathed on his glasses' lens. "Pers won't take your money, he says, and if you don't like it you can—"

"Never mind. I can imagine." Kursh was smoothing his mustache. He shook his head. "Still, he's taking a big risk, and there ought to be some reward in it for him."

Trondur rubbed his eyes and replaced his glasses. "How about a keg for payment? I don't think he'd refuse that."

"Good idea. A keg for him and his crew. Order one up, will you?"

His brother nodded and absently straightened a couple of the pillows into the window seat. "Kursh . . . are you sure you know what you're doing?"

The elder Korimson leaned on his desk. "No. I've just done the best guessing I can. We'll have to hope it's good enough." They fell silent, thinking. After a moment he asked, "How about the guild ships?"

"They are volunteers all. I'm told some of the lads came to blows for the privilege."

Kursh's eye lifted to meet his brother's troubled ones. He murmured, "I wonder how their fathers feel about it."

Trondur studied him. "Olaf Sigursson sends a message: there are a couple of strangers hanging about the tavern, not together. They've been asking about you."

The former First Watchman rasped, "Dwarves?"

His brother nodded and added, "Of course, Olaf and the others are feeding them a creel of chum. They won't hear anything of value to them, or to whoever sent them."

Kursh smiled a little. "The more tall tales they hear, the better for us." Despite his amusement, he ordered quietly, "We'll want to know where those two are at all times from now on."

"Jan Reyason is taking care of it."

Kursh relaxed. He had trained Jan himself. Not all members of the guild spent their days making glass, and Reyason had proved his worth more than once when a shipment had not reached its destination.

"Have you told Captain Brickleburr yet?" Trondur wanted to know.

Kursh picked up a crystal paperweight and held it up to the fire's light. "I thought I'd give him a chance to rest a bit first. Besides, if he's thought about this trip at all, he's probably already realized it himself." Somehow, though, remembering the flat weariness of his friend's eyes, the dwarf didn't think so. Danger had always brought a certain spark to the Littleman.

Peewit heard laughter from Kursh's study and smiled into the darkness. He leaned on the arm of the overstuffed chair in the bedroom he had been given and puffed on his old clay pipe, having put the dwarf's meerschaum carefully at the bottom of his bag. He didn't want to see it again. The hallucination had been most vivid.

Though every bone cried out for rest, he could not quite bring himself to fall into the sunshine-smelling sheets and surrender to sleep. Not yet, anyway. Perhaps if he got tired enough, he told himself, he'd be able to.

He had heard a low murmur from Gretchen's room shortly after he'd come down, and after a while had realized it was Thyla reading to her daughter. He could picture the little one's muzzy face and Thyla's serene one leaning over the book. He was glad from the bottom of his heart that the gruff First Watchman and the bakeress had found each other. Theirs were surely two names engraved on Tychanor's hearthstone, as the saying went among his people.

His head suddenly jerked up from where he had nodded in his chair. How did he know that? He had never met any of his people!

Nervously he ran a hand through his hair and knocked out his pipe. At least if he fell asleep again, he wouldn't burn the place down around their ears. He pulled Kursh's nightshirt around him, sighed, and got up to stare out the window. The shirt, six inches too long and nearly a foot too wide across the shoulders, was the cleanest thing he'd had on in an age, and he found himself wishing he could simply stay here at Ledgelawn. Kursh wanted him to, he could tell.

But that was impossible. Even now, he was extremely conscious of the stretched thread that bound him to the Greenbriar. Though he could not have told why, Peewit knew that he should be in Ilyria in case the queen needed him.

For what? he snorted to himself. She has spies aplenty and Will, Jami, and Jak to protect her. What the deuce would she need me for?

Out of the darkened, quiet house came an unbidden answer: to do something else, something they can't do.

Like what? he questioned himself morosely.

The slow beating of his heart told away a minute. To be her friend.

Sometimes you can't lie to yourself.

*   *   *

The sound came again, a groan like a wind rising.

Kursh rolled up onto one elbow and listened, trying to blink the sleep from his eye. Beside him Thyla was awake, too. "What is it?" she whispered. "D'ye suppose that dratted dog of Peter's . . ."

"It wasn't an animal." Korimson threw aside the covers and groped for his slippers. He swung off the high bed and as he passed the bureau, paused to slide open the top drawer. Something winked silver in the moonlight, and he headed for the door.

The sound swelled along the hall outside.

"Stay here," he said over his shoulder.

"Like fudge!" his wife muttered, pulling on her robe.

He opened the door quietly and went toward the stairway. A shadow came out of the darkness, and two arms clamped firmly around his middle. "Papa, I'm scared!"

Kursh let out the breath he had instinctively sucked in. "It's all right, poppet. It's just an animal. You go in with your mother and I'll chase it away." Firmly he handed her off to Thyla, who had appeared at his shoulder.

"Just you be careful of yourself," his wife cautioned, drawing Gretchen close.

"Keep Gretchen here—I've got the knife, for bloody hell's sake!" He had spoken more sharply than he intended.

Behind him he heard her "Tch!" but he ignored this and, holding the knife level and ready, crept forward.

A cold draft fluttered the nightshirt about his knees, and simultaneously the eerie moan raised the hair on the back of his neck. It seemed to be all around him, echoing slightly off the plastered walls. He dropped into a fighting crouch, though he could see no enemy, hear nothing on the stairs or from the first floor. The sound faded into silence once more. Drawing a silent breath, he ran toward the stairway.

Familiar with the house's every nook, he knew when he had reached the landing and reached for the rail. Then he heard another sound, and it froze him in his tracks. From the first room across the landing was coming the tortured rasp of breathing. "Brickleburr!"

The dwarf thudded over the landing and the few paces to the guestroom's shut door. Flinging it open, he was aware first of the terrible cold, as frigid as a midwinter night, and then of the sounds of a struggle that seemed to be coming from the corner between the window and the bed. In the confusing web of moonlight through the muntins, he made out what must be the small figure of the Littleman in his nightshirt backed up against the wall, writhing this way and that, his hands clutching something Kursh could see only as a darkness against the captain's white.

The dwarf took two swift strides and reached with his free hand for whoever, whatever, it was.

"No!" the Littleman shrieked. *"Don't touch it!"*

Abruptly his face contorted as though the thing had grabbed him by the throat. Kursh's dagger hand drove forward.

When the blade met the shadow, the dwarf was blown across the room by an icy sting that sealed his hand and arm in a vise of cold. As he lay half stunned, his eyes were suddenly dazzled by a tongue of flame that swelled in an instant to a shining light like sun striking off a mirror. A shrill scream of terror tore at the dwarf's mind, and he struggled up on his knees to try to aid his friend, though he could not make his arm work and he had to keep his eyes closed against the piercing light.

Then, suddenly, it was dark once more, and the only sound was his own panting breath. "Peewit?"

A flash of white was before him, and Brickleburr seized his numbed hand. "Dammit, Kursh, I told you not to touch it!"

"I didn't! I put a blade into it!" The First Watchman snorted. The room had warmed nearly to its normal night temperature, and blessed heat was rising up his arm. He felt as though he were toasting at a fireplace while an ice storm howled beyond the gable. But the heat was coming from . . . "By the Powers, Brickleburr, get back to bed! Ye've one hell of a fever!"

The Littleman began a laugh that ended in something that sounded in the dark like a weary sob.

Candle flame bobbed along the corridor outside the door, and Thyla's anxious voice called, "Look out! I'm coming in!" The business end of a poker slanted through the door and then her pale face beneath its night-braided hair. "What's happened? What was that awful noise? I thought ye was both dead in here!" Tears suddenly winked in her eyes, though her chin was firm.

Kursh heaved himself to his feet. "It's all right, wife," he soothed. "It's all right now. Where's Gretchen—are ye back there, pet? Aye, come and see your old dad." For a moment the three Korimsons crowded close.

The former First Watchman cleared his throat and disengaged himself, twisting around to look down at the Littleman, still sitting on the floor. Peewit had leaned his head back against the wall, and his eyes were closed. Kursh's one eye narrowed, and he snatched the candle from Thyla and held it over the captain. Brickleburr's skin was a bright, painful-looking red, as though he'd spent the day fishing on the salt water. "Peewit?"

The small figure opened his eyes and tried to smile.

Kursh crouched. "What by all the Realms was that thing, and is it going to come back?"

For a moment Brickleburr regarded him. "It was a Shadow," he said slowly, "though I have no idea how I know that. But it won't be back—I killed it. It's the third one in a fortnight." He rested his head on folded arms across his drawn-up knees.

Kursh put a hand on his shoulder. It was like touching a hearthstone. "How do ye fool?" he asked cautiously.

"Hot. Tired." The Littleman sighed.

"How about some tea, Thyla?" the dwarf directed quietly. "And cool compresses." She nodded and ushered Gretchen out with her. "Can ye make it to the bed?"

Peewit smiled. "I'm not ill. This"—he gestured to his flaming face—"seems to last only a couple of hours afterward, and then it fades." He got to his feet and, going to the window, thrust it wide to the cool night air. Suddenly he looked back at the dwarf. "It didn't get its fangs into you, did it?" Before his startled companion could answer, he was across the room, tugging at the nightshirt collar to expose the dwarf's neck. The Littleman examined it swiftly and then cast his eye over the mystified Korimson. "Ah, no blood. Good. It didn't get you, then. Sorry, I should have done that first."

Kursh shrugged his collar closed. "Why?" He followed the captain and stood by the window with him, watching Peewit's face carefully.

"Because . . ." His brow furrowed and he shook his head helplessly. "I don't know!"

"Was the light . . . you?"

The Littleman nodded but did not elaborate.

This needed some digesting, and Kursh decided not to pursue it at the moment. He folded his arms. "I knew there was something wrong. Why didn't ye tell me straight off? Ye said there have been three of them?"

Peewit leaned his head miserably against the crystal windowpanes. "I thought maybe I had shaken them off by crossing the water to come here, so I said nothing, not wanting to alarm you. I honestly thought you and your family would be safe, Kursh!"

"That's no matter now. Ye'd be welcome here if ye brought the Wild Feller himself on your trail."

The Littleman went rigid. "D-don't say that!"

Kursh started, and his broad hand came down to grip Peewit's shoulder. "By His Beard, is that it?"

Brickleburr swallowed hard and raised his head to stare over the moonlit sea. "I think so," he whispered.

Chapter Three

❧

Late at night, much later than he should have been up, Prince Gerrit Greenbriar was sitting in the window nook of the palace library, absorbed in an old book. His lips moved silently as he conned out the words. The damp weather had made his foot ache all day, and he had propped it on a stool drawn close.

At the fringe of his awareness, he knew that his body-guard, a lieutenant of the Watch named Fisher, had suddenly come to the alert at his post by the door. The prince quickly covered the manuscript he had been reading with an open book of military history. He nodded to the man-at-arms, and the other nodded back. There was a step outside, and the door swung inward.

The gray figure stopped on the threshold, peering. "Ah, good evening, Highness. May I intrude?"

Gerrit waved. "Of course, master. You've a much better claim to the room than I; you've spent more hours in it."

Fidelis smiled and received Fisher's salute, for the physician was a senior officer in the Watch. The old healer swung the door shut behind him and slowly eased himself into a chair, stretching his long legs to the fire gratefully. Though his eyes were no longer as sharp as they once had been, he nonetheless marked how the young prince shut his camouflaging book and pulled out the old manuscript once more. Fidelis smiled affectionately. "I fail to understand why you're so afraid someone will catch you."

Gerrit swung his feet to the floor and stretched. "Because a prince isn't supposed to be a scholar. It's reckoned to be odd or something. People have made it quite clear all I should care about is hunting, drinking, dicing, wenching, and the other manly sports." He grinned.

"You certainly oblige them," the doctor rejoined. "What's this I hear about the head groom's daughter?"

The boy's grin widened, but he merely shrugged.

"You know, if you'd show just a bit of this energy toward your studies, your mother would be happier," Fidelis said in his most grandfatherly tone.

Gerrit made a face. "It's boring. What do I care for declensions or" he adopted his tutor's nasal monotone— " 'the Parameters of the Plane of Dorius'?" He snorted and brushed back his dark hair.

The doctor knew he ought to say something properly didactic, but since he agreed, he wisely chose to keep silent. He and Gerrit shared a passionate interest in ancient languages, manuscripts, and artifacts, but no one outside this room knew it.

The prince stood and stretched again, then limped over to join his mentor by the fire, holding out his hands to the crackling warmth.

"Foot bothering you?" the old physician asked.

"Mm-hmm. Yours?" Fidelis had broken it badly two winters ago, hurrying to treat a scald victim down in the city in the middle of a sleetstorm.

The doctor nodded. They exchanged a smile. Gerrit sat down and made himself comfortable on the thick rug, leaning back on his hands. Both of them watched the fire dance. "I was reading—or trying to—about the Painter."

"It's grim stuff, isn't it? I remember the first time I translated it out, I kept hearing wolves howling, even in my sleep."

The prince half-smiled and murmured, "Isn't that the truth? I had nightmares all night. But actually, it was the third volume I was looking at."

Fidelis regarded the boy's profile against the firelight. "What got you interested in that particular book?"

The look he got was an exasperated arch of the eyebrows. "The mural, of course. I figured he doesn't call himself the Painter for nothing. That's the only painting around here that could possibly be that old: ergo, the fellow in the book painted our picture down there in the hallway."

"I see. And you of course want to know how he imparted magic to it."

Gerrit sat up and draped his arms around his knees. "I'm not so interested in how. I probably wouldn't understand it anyway, even if I had it writ plain before me. What I want to know is *why*?"

The physician was surprised. That was an angle he himself had never considered. Like Alphonse, with whom he corresponded, Fidelis had been wrapped up in the how. He knotted his long fingers together. "A forewarning, I suppose."

"Yes, but it's odd, isn't it, that apparently no one else in the history of the family has ever seen the thing change?" He gestured to the long rows of books on their polished oaken shelves. "For the past week, I've pored through these. Not once is it recorded that the mural has changed until some time just after Mother came back to reclaim the place. You were with her, Master Fidelis. Do you remember?"

The old man put his finger to his temple in thought. After a moment, he said, "I know that the mural still showed the Briar-and-Sword when Tristan and the others helped your mother escape from her uncle." He thought further, and finally nodded to himself. "It was right after Tristan was killed. We were missing Alphonse, and I went out to the hall to look for him. That's when I first noticed the mural had come back the way it used to be when your grandfather was king." He looked up to find the boy's eyes on him.

"You see," the Greenbriar heir said, "it all started then. But that doesn't make any sense." He leaned forward intently. "If it serves as a forewarning, why didn't the picture come back immediately when Dendron had his own insignia painted over it?" He smiled with the ironic glint that was his public personality. "You'd have thought the thing could at least have chipped in to help by throwing some fear into those damn Barreners while they drank themselves silly on Grandfather's wine."

Fidelis's eyes sharpened. "It is a warning device that works only for your family, then."

"No. It's a warning device that works only for Mother."

The doctor momentarily forgot his stiff back and sat forward. "Very reasonably argued."

"Yes," the boy answered with an arrogance that would have been distressing to the old man if Gerrit had intended it. The prince jumped up and went to lean on the mantel, staring once more into the fire. "It opens all sorts of interesting questions, you see. Foremost among them being, how did the Painter know that she would be coming along, and why was she so important to him that he should exert himself in so fabulous a manner to warn her every time the Unnamed has attacked?"

Fidelis steepled his gnarled fingers and said thoughtfully, "It may have nothing to do with your mother at all, Gerrit. Maybe the thing was triggered to change whenever the Unnamed attacked, and that has just happened to be in your mother's reign."

"All right." The youth turned to regard him. "But how did the Painter know the Wild Fellow was going to attack again at all, ever? Surely Beod's folk must have thought they'd won once and for all, especially after fighting the Skinwalker and Shadows."

"What's this?"

"You remember—it's in the torn pages. I've pieced some of them together." He jumped up and fetched the book. "Look."

The old physician gingerly laid the cracked book across his knees and peered where the boy's finger pointed. " '. . . Skinwalker, cursed creature, hath attacked agayne, taking young Darry's skin and by this means coming nigh unto my lord Berren 'fore I was ware of it and beate it back with th' medallion.' " Fidelis looked up. "Powers! It sounds like some sort of walking dead!"

Gerrit nodded. "There's a bit more—its eyes flicker, I know that—but I can't find what it is, or where it comes from. About the Shadows, Aengus was clearer. My translation of the appropriate passages is tucked in the back cover there, if you've time later, but briefly, it seems these creatures—many of them—could take different forms, beasts for the most part. Apparently they shared the flickering eyes of the Skinwalker, but they bit their victims and sucked their blood. Aengus speaks several times of 'fang marks' and poison that froze, and an infection which sounds rather like gangrene." The doctor winced, and the heir smiled wryly. "And you wonder why I can't sleep."

"I should give you a sleeping draught."

"I'd take it. I've been thinking these creatures of the Unnamed may well make a reappearance, as Beldis did."

Fidelis closed the book carefully. "I shall warn your mother, and Alphonse when he arrives."

"He may be thinking along the same lines." He held up a thin strip of paper. "You didn't by chance mark out anything in the third volume with this?"

Fidelis frowned. "I honestly don't know, my prince. It's possible. Some years have passed since I first looked into the book. It is so damaged, I eventually gave it up."

Ariadne's son shrugged. "Well, no matter. When I found it in the passage about the fresco, I figured either you or the wizard must have been looking at it."

Fidelis spread his hands. "Ask Alphonse," he repeated.

Gerrit scratched his head. "Well, that would rather let the cat out of the bag, now wouldn't it? About me, I mean. How will I ever explain to all those courtiers that their prince has actually had a thought? It's likely to cause widespread consternation," he finished drolly. At Fidelis's chuckle, he prodded, "You bring it up to him, and let me know what he says."

The doctor smiled at him fondly. "I warn you that my wizard friend is fairly good at reading people. If you expect to fool him, you'll have to be very convincing."

The prince pulled the old man to his feet when Fidelis held out a hand. "Why should Master Alphonse be any different from everyone else I've hoodwinked?"

Standing there with the strong arm around his shoulders, the physician reprimanded gently, "You are not the only extremely clever lad there is, you know."

The grin and the gray eyes were so like his mother's. "No, but all the others are studying to be Retreat Masters or wizards! As the only reasonably intelligent royal heir around, I'm in clear possession of the field! Have you seen my cousin Ka-Bril lately?" He hooted. "What a pip!"

Fidelis grasped his arm, suddenly serious. "Be careful around him, and around your uncle the king. No disrespect to you, my prince, but I do not trust your Shimarrat relations."

Heat had come into the young face, but Gerrit spoke steadily enough. "You forget yourself, Master. This is my father's brother we speak of. I am half Shimarrat."

The physician said quietly, "Come, Highness. I know you've read all the history you can get your hands on in here." He waved at the surrounding books. "You know that there were four sons of Ka-Nishon. Your father, may the Powers bless his memory, was the only decent one among them. How did the other two besides Ka-Treer die?"

Gerrit thought briefly. "One in a hunting accident—"

"A very convenient one, I am sure you will agree," Fidelis interrupted quietly.

"—and the other in a joust in one of their silly tournaments."

"His lance was rumored to have been cracked very neatly, did you know that?" Just to be sure, Fidelis drove home the point. "And how did your grandfather, King Ka-Nishon, die?"

Gerrit replied, "A bellyache." His eyes were aware. "Poison, most likely."

The doctor nodded. "Just so. Ka-Treer's way to the throne has been a rather straight one, wouldn't you agree?"

"Shall we count the dwarf Korimson among his weapons, then?" At Fidelis's stunned look, the prince said coolly, "As you say, there were four sons."

The old doctor shook his head slowly. "That wasn't the way of it, Gerrit."

Ariadne's son gestured to Fisher to open the door. "Funny," he murmured. "I asked Uncle about the rumors of how Grandfather died." He met Fidelis's eyes. "That's exactly what he said, too. Good night, master. Take a draught for your foot, now—you need your sleep."

Nothing he could say would help now, Fidelis realized. He bowed and walked slowly to the door, meeting Fisher's respectful gaze. "Good night," the old man said over his shoulder. "You might try a winter stone and some willowbark tea." Quietly, he left the library.

Behind him, the Greenbriar heir sighed and limped over to the window seat, bending to retrieve the books. "Come on, lieutenant. Let's call it a night."

"Very good, my lord," Fisher agreed. "Shall I fetch you some willowbark from the apothecary?"

Gerrit straightened, replaced the books on the nearest shelf, and then, clenching his fists, was able to walk without a noticeable limp to where the man-at-arms waited impassively. The prince told him, "Yes, please. I suppose I'd better be able to walk on the damned thing tomorrow when the guests start arriving. Bloody birthday," he grumbled. "Bloody bore."

He looked back for an instant at the Book of the Painter, then fixed his face in its habitual expression of hail-good-fellow heartiness and followed his bodyguard out into the antechamber of the royal apartments.

On the same night, as far to the northeast as the kingdom extended, something slipped in under the eaves with a contrary puff of wind that made the peat smoke from the hearth back up and fill the small room. On the bench by the fire the man muttered an oath and threw down the harness he had been mending. "Damn wind. Isn't bad enough it rains for days on end, now it has to blow inside oot."

"Hush!" his wife warned. "Ye'll wake the children." She shifted the baby to her other breast and smiled a little. "Ye say the same thing every rainy spell."

He scratched his chin. "I suppose I do at that." Resting his large hands on his knees, he leaned to see the little face swathed in its bit of blanket. "Sucks like a bull, that one," he said proudly. "He'll make a braw man."

"Aye, he has the Teazle glow on him for sure," his wife agreed. Everyone knew the Littlefolk blessed some children with extra health, extra life.

The thing that had come in with the wind curled around the rooftree, a Shadow unnoticed, a chill unfelt.

The peat turves broke apart in a shower of glowing coals. There was a bright momentary flare, and then it began to smolder. "Now look at that," the husband said, irritable once more. "The damp's got into everythin', even the turf. I swear the whole stack was cured up real good before I brought it in."

"Well," said his wife, putting the baby to her shoulder to burp it, "things will dry oot soon enough once the weather settles to cold."

"Better be soon, or spring's likely to be late. I don't see how we'll be able to pay oor tithe if the crops don't go in on time." He shook his head and stared into the fire. "I'll wager they ben't havin' this trouble away down south. Niver rains as much there as here. Them flatlanders just don't understand upcountry, else they'd niver put the same tithe on us as on them. They was sayin' down to the inn that the master hisself be worried what he'll do when the royal collectors show up."

His wife patted the infant's back. "Now ye know the queen'll be fair, Jack, and her raised by folk just like oorselves."

Moodily he picked at the harness thread. "Aye. If she don't forget it."

She stood with the sleeping baby and reached to swing the kettle away from the fire. "Now, when has she iver?"

The Shadow bared its fangs, and there was a sudden fierce gust that rattled the latch.

The man glanced to be sure the door stayed closed. At the fire, his wife said reflectively, "D'ye remember when we was courtin', and went down with my folks that midsummer to the Crownin' Day festival? The queen was so pretty in that dress."

He smiled at the memory. "No prettier than you was in yours. 'Twas yellow, I mind."

She looked at him in mock surprise. "John Fielding! This be the man who can't remember where he left his boots of a morning, but he can remember one dress a dozen years ago!"

His smile widened. "What I chiefly remember is how deuced slow 'twas to get all them laces untied when you and me went into the woods at the top of the hill that night."

Her low laugh brought him to his feet, but there was the baby to be put to bed first. She kissed the air in his direction. "I'll be right back."

Later, after the banked fire had burned down to ash, they slept twined together under the old sheepskin rug in the curtained alcove. A few feet away the cradle swayed almost imperceptibly in the drafts along the beaten earth floor, the infant milkily asleep with its tiny fist curled against its mouth.

In the darkness, a darker blot coalesced into a form, manlike if men had sharp teeth and eyes like a far-off flicker of heat lightning. Soundlessly, the Shadow flowed toward the cradle, pausing only briefly when the man drew a great snore and turned on his side. One dark hand closed on the edge of the cradle and the other swung down from its back a lumpy sack. For an instant the flickering eyes turned toward the bed, then quickly it reached into the cradle with both hands. There was a sound that might have been a small twig breaking, barely heard over the wind in the thatch. The Shadow bent to the cradle, and when it rose again, blood gleamed on its lips.

It pulled the little limp body from the blanket, in one motion stuffing the dead baby into the sack and drawing out something of roughly the same size. It tucked the blanket in and swung the sack to its shoulder. For a moment it looked into the cradle, then reached down once more and rearranged a detail. When it straightened, its shoulders seemed to be shaking with laughter.

Silently it flowed back across the floor and melded with the darkness again. There was a scuffling up the wall, as though a rat ran up a timber, then a rustle in the thatch and a draft that blew the ash from the turf and fanned an ember to brief flame. Then it was gone.

The woman murmured in her sleep, and in the loft one of the children burrowed deeper into the straw and wet his nightshirt.

In the dripping dawn, her shriek of horror woke them instantly. Children tumbled down the loft ladder one after the other, the younger ones already whimpering at the frightening cries coming from their mother and the equally disturbing hoarse gasping of their father. Both of them seemed rooted beside the cradle.

The oldest boy warned his siblings back with a look, then crept closer to see. At first he could not figure why somebody would have stuck an old shriveled-up pumpkin in the baby's cradle, and then all at once he realized that the wizened thing was a face, mottled brown and red, and that there was more of it under the lumpy blanket. A gnarled claw that might have been a hand was jammed to its horribly gaping mouth. And it was breathing.

The boy made it out the door under the sluicing eaves before his stomach came up.

There was a quick step behind him and someone stooped to hold his forehead; he kept his eyes closed, too sick to be ashamed his dad should see him like this.

After a minute, he spat, blew out the disgusting stuff from his nose, and sat back on his heels. An unfamiliar voice said above him, "Better?"

Startled, the boy turned quickly. A tall man in the queen's

uniform was leaning to pull him to his feet. A quiet horse stood ground-reined at the edge of the yard. He let the soldier help him up, nodding wordlessly.

Jamison relaxed. "Good. That's a rough way to begin—"

From inside the cottage, the woman broke into fresh cries. The Rider sprang for the door.

Inside the dim, peat-smelling house, a man was trying to support his fainting wife with one hand while with the other he pushed a couple of children roughly away from the cradle that rocked by the alcove. The queen's man stopped just over the threshold. "Give you good morning," Jamison began to say.

Anger flared in the husband's face. Unable to see Jamison as more than a dark shape in the doorway and assuming he was a ruffian, the man bellowed hoarsely, "Get away, ye rutting pig! Can't ye see we've troubles enough without ye?"

Jamison put his hand up, palm out. "Peace, sir, peace. I mean no harm. I was passing by outside, smelled your fire, and thought I might be able to buy some bread. Then I heard your wife's cry." He took a step, saying quietly, "Is it the baby?"

The man's face contorted, and he looked away. His wife mercifully lapsed into unconsciousness. The children hunkered on the beaten-earth floor, too scared to move.

Grimly Jamison crossed the room. Expecting to find an infant dead of fever, he leaned over the cradle.

Behind him the man's voice said roughly, "I don't know what it be, but that ain't oor bairn."

"By Earthpillar!" Before he could stop himself, Jamison drew back. Stomach churning with sick compassion, he put a finger lightly to the thin throat. It was dying, by the Powers' mercy.

The husband fanned his wife's face. "It's a changeling, that's what it is. Some wicked thing has took oor baby and left this in little Kenny's place." Anger and horror were in his face.

Jamison schooled his face. Belief in changelings was probably as old as the country folk themselves, a bulwark against the reality of stillborn and deformed children. "No doubt," he murmured.

The thing in the cradle struggled for breath that would not come and suddenly went quiet. The queen's Rider looked away. He said, "I will bury the child before I leave, if you like."

The man lurched to his feet. "Where's oor Kenny, that's what I want to know!" He gave the cradle a shove, and it rocked wildly, nearly tipping over. "Where's my son?" he cried in despair.

Something that gleamed dully in the dim light rolled to Jamison's polished boot. He stooped. "What's this?" He picked up a small gold box.

The man's face had sharpened. "That ben't oors. It's a Teazle box." He started for the door in bare feet. "Teazles ha' been here. By the Powers, if this be their idea of a joke, they'll soon learn Jack Fielding's no man to be trifled with! I'll track 'em till I find 'em!"

Jamison watched him stomp out. The Rider said quietly to the boy he had held, "Can you get me a mattock, lad, or a hoe? Anything to dig with." The boy scrambled up and ran out. To the oldest girl, Jamison said, "Will you stay with your mother? Put a cold cloth to her head and she'll soon be better." She let go of the hem of the nightdress she had wrung into a rope and went to the kettle on the hearth. The soldier bent to the cradle and lifted out the body, wrapping it carefully in the blanket so that the younger children would not see too much.

He crossed the muddy dooryard, hens scattering noisily at his approach, and passed the shed where the single milk cow stood at the end of her rope, placidly chewing her cud and watching with soft brown eyes as he followed the path through the neat garden plot. "Just there, under the trees, might be a good place," Jamison murmured. The boy came from the shed with a mattock and shovel.

Though it was clear the lad wanted to hang about, the Rider sent him back to his family. He quickly dug a small grave and covered over the blanket-shrouded form, smoothing a mound over the place to keep the rain off. When it was done, Jamison regarded the raw place for a moment, then cleaned the mud from his hands on the wet leaves.

The boy came running toward him. "Come quick!" he panted. "It's Dad!"

Jamison followed him along the edge of the garden and into the woods where chips and piles of brush showed the small farmstead would soon be expanded. Coming around the corner of a wood stack, they found Jack Fielding poised with a pitchfork raised high over his head and all his muscles corded to stab at something in the scrub. His face was streaming with tears and purple with rage. "Take oor boy, will ye?"

The fork began its downward swing. The boy ran forward, shouting, "No, Dad—wait!"

Jamison hurled himself at Fielding's back. The tackle carried them both into the woods, the pitchfork miraculously shoving harmlessly into the deep loam beneath the sodden trees. The farmer rose to his knees, drew back, and hit the soldier solidly in the jaw. Jamison reared and knocked Fielding out very efficiently.

He was wiping blood from his split lip when he saw, half hidden by the shrubs, a small hand grasping a root.

Jamison bent the bush aside with the toe of his boot. Tangled in a bedraggled green cloak the shade of moss, a small blond figure with a blistered face lay dead.

"A Teazle!" the Rider breathed, forgetting in that moment the other more learned names and grasping the one that everyone knew from childhood.

The boy crept near. "I seen Dad was goin' to stab her."

"I'm sorry I had to hit him," Alphonse told him. He rose with the Hearthwoman's corpse in his arms and looked over to the boy holding his father's head while Fielding raised his head and tried to focus. "Get him into the house, lad, and then a cup of tea will help."

"Aye, sir. How's the Teazle lady?"

"She is dead," the Rider answered. "I shall take her elsewhere to bury her."

The boy stroked his father's hair back. "Well, I'm still glad Dad din't kill her. 'Twouldn't have been right," he said softly. "Ye shouldn't niver harm a Teazle. Them's the Fair Folk."

Jamison smiled slowly. "You are a good boy, young Master Fielding."

He left the boy blushing and the man cursing, and headed for the beaten track that eventually turned into a road to the sea.

The dwarf had broached the subject only after dinner, when they were standing quietly smoking at the edge of the lawn. He had intended to tell Peewit earlier, but the Littleman had slept late this morning (Thyla made everyone creep around as silently as mice, and Kursh had grumbled to her, but secretly approved), and then he had seemed so much better that Korimson had not wanted to see the gray cloud of worry settle over him any sooner than it had to.

With one thing and another, the day had passed pleasantly enough, though it started on a wrong note when Peewit had come downstairs freshly shaved, and Gretchen had made the natural mistake of assuming that in accordance with dwarvish custom, he had suffered a death in his family and shaved as a token of mourning. Her eyes welled and she asked the question, and for a moment the captain had looked stunned. But then they got things sorted out, and they had taken the girl with them up on the hill behind the house to fly kites under the chin of Barak-Gambrel. Only when Gretchen had darted away to chase a sea gull and Kursh and Peewit payed out twine or took it in, guiding their kites, did the dwarf resume their conversation of the night before. "So the light was you?"

The captain nodded.

"Something you picked up from Alphonse, is it?"

Brickleburr might have smiled, but he didn't. "No. I . . . it's a Hearthfolk thing, I think. It . . . just happens."

"Oh." The kites ducked in the sea breeze. "Odd that it's never happened before."

Peewit's brow wrinkled. "Yes," he said so low that the dwarf only saw his lips move.

"Ye needn't be embarrassed about it, old sod. It isn't as if ye've grown another head or something."

"It scares me, Kursh."

After that, neither had said anything more about it, and Gretchen had run breathlessly to pull them toward an old plover's nest she had found in the tall grass.

Now as he puffed his pipe in the dusk, Kursh was thinking about it as he surveyed the shipping in the channel. "Tide's on the turn. We'll need to be aboard by the time it turns again."

Brickleburr nodded and sent a wavering smoke ring into the twilight. He waved his pipestem at the piers. "Which one is the ambassador's ship?"

Kursh pointed. "The big one with the blue hull. The *Jarlshof Star,* she's called."

"She looks first-class. We ought to make spanking time in her."

Korimson tapped his pipestem against his teeth. "We won't be going on that one," he said quietly. "We're sailing aboard the *Puffin* with Half Hand."

Brickleburr frowned. "Wh—?" Just as quickly, he saw it. "The blue ship is a decoy."

"Aye." The dwarf folded his arms on his chest.

"Sea brigands?"

"Them, too." He glanced at the captain. "It's the Shimarrats that really bother me, though." He paused. "It's the first time I've been off the island since . . . I came back here to live, and I know Ka-Treer won't let it rest, even if the queen is willing to." Peewit's pipe was smoking away unnoticed. "The Shimarrat swore he'd get me," the dwarf reminded him, "and I'm betting he'll make a try at it on the open sea, somewhere between the headland down there and Waterford Light."

The captain nodded slowly. "It's just the Shimarrat thing to do."

Kursh stroked his mustache. "Which is why quite a few ships will sail tonight from this harbor." He suddenly grinned fiercely. "If he tries anything, we'll catch the whoreson dead to rights."

Peewit raised an eyebrow. "I think you're aching for the chance, First Watchman."

"Damn right. Half Hand has told me about that silver sovereign and the look on Ka-Treer's face when Pers handed him that fish." He chuckled and shook his head. "Powers, I wish I'd been there!"

Brickleburr glanced at him sharply, but then realized that in any way that counted, Kursh had *not* been there.

The dwarf's amusement subsided and he knocked out his pipe on a rock near at hand. "Well, I've a few last-minute things to pack."

"Me, too. Oh, and Kursh, about the clothes—they're very fine and I thank you for the thought—"

"Aye. I thought if you were going to be part of the Jarlshof ambassador's retinue, ye might as well look the part."

"But I'd rather wear my own, if you don't mind," Peewit finished firmly. At the dwarf's lowered brows, he explained quietly, "No false pretenses, old friend. I'll go back as myself, or not at all."

Korimson said nothing, merely giving a quick nod and leading the way back to the lighted house.

They parted at the foot of the stairs when Thyla came bustling out of the kitchen and beckoned the captain with a wave and a surreptitious wink. Kursh pretended not to see and went on up to his study. If he knew Thyla, he guessed that she would be pressing a pouch of starflower into the Littleman's hands, with instructions on how to brew it, and an injunction to be sure her husband drank some every day. There hadn't been a day in the thirteen years of their marriage that she had ignored the ritual cup. Though both Kursh and his wife harbored a secret fear that the tea might be the only thing keeping the Wild Fire from touching Kursh's mind again, they pretended it was no more than a little wifely custom she had adopted. He grumbled sometimes about the too-sweet, flowery taste. She served him a ginger cookie with it to provide some snap and shut his mouth.

The teapot was waiting for him on his desk. He smiled briefly and poured himself out a cup. Breaking off a corner of the paper-thin cookie, he munched while he stirred up the fire. It wasn't until the logs caught that he noticed Gretchen watching him from the window seat. "What are ye doing sitting up here in the dark?" he asked, taking his tea to sit beside her.

"Mama said you'd stop and see me before I went to bed, but I didn't want you to forget." She was already in her nightgown.

He put an arm around her and she leaned into his side. "Not bloody likely," he reassured her.

They watched the fire. Gretchen asked, "You don't want to go, do you?"

She already had her mother's disturbing habit of knowing what he was thinking. "No, not much," he answered truthfully.

The girl looked up at him. "Then why are you?"

She had never been told about the murder he had done, and now he groped for an easy lie. No, he told himself. It might be the last time I ever see her. I don't want her to remember me as a liar. He licked his lips. "Once, a long time ago, Gret, I did something bad. I was . . . sick at the time, and I can barely even remember it, but a lot of other people do. Now I have to see if I can somehow make it up to them."

"What did you do?"

His resolution wavered, and he felt sweat start at his hairline. "I killed a man."

"Oh." She took it calmly, and Kursh wondered if she understood. After a moment she asked, "Was he a bad man?" He thought she might understand after all.

The sweat trickled down the band of his eyepatch. "No, he wasn't. That's why it was so . . . why I had to leave there."

"That's when Uncle Peewit came home with you, before I was a baby."

He smiled desperately at the turn of phrase. They watched the fire some more.

Gretchen sighed. "Mama doesn't want you to go, and I don't, either."

Kursh brushed a wisp of hair off her forehead. "Ye know how it is when you've had a nightmare, and you tell yourself if you only have the courage to open your eyes, ye'll see your own room around ye, and the monsters will be gone?" She looked up at him, eyes solemn. "That's how this is."

"Sometimes the monsters get you," she said unexpectedly in a small voice.

He suddenly realized part of the reason she was up here with him was the terrors of last night. He squeezed her head gently. "No," he said positively. "That only happens in tales, lass. Besides, Uncle Peewit is magical, you know, and he's put a blessing on the house here, so we're all set."

Her look lightened a little, though she still thought it important to tell him, "I'm sleeping in Mama's bed while you're away."

"That's good. Mama needs the company." She nodded, and he leaned to kiss the top of her head. "Speaking of which, isn't it about time?"

"I guess so." She slipped off the window seat and turned to face him, holding out a small cloth bag which had been beside her. "I packed these for you in case you get hungry."

The rest of the cookies she had baked a few days ago. He smiled.

"Good night, Papa. Come home quick." She hugged him tight.

"Be a good girl," he said gruffly.

Gretchen frowned. "I always am." Then she was gone, scuffing out the door in her embroidered slippers.

He finally got the damned eyepatch settled and stalked over to get Gerrit's Weatherglass from the safe. When he returned with it to the desk, he saw the flicker of a candle from Trondur's window. Time to go.

He had stowed the dagger in its spring-action sheath in a locked box on his desk thirteen years ago, but he oiled it religiously and amused himself now and again by practicing with it. Korimson strapped it to his forearm and suddenly it seemed that he had never taken it off at all. Unconsciously his hand went to his hip, where his ax . . .

Though he had not meant to slam the door on the way out, he did.

Chapter Four

Clad in two of the warm oiled skin jackets the fishermen wore, they stood at the rail coiling rope, probably badly, but it didn't matter anyway, except as disguise. The captain and the First Watchman were keeping an eye on the torchlit scene at the end of the main pier, where the *Jarlshof Star* was being noisily loaded. There was a swarm of action as the fake retinue stood about on the dock, stamping the cold out of their feet and wondering loudly who among them would be seasick. Crates of what appeared to be crystal—certainly they had the Guildmaster's own private stamp on the sides—were trundled up the gangway, and bales of Jarlshof wool were hoisted aboard by cranes, two men working the winch. The ambassadorial flag snapped at the top of the mainmast, the single silver star against its field of ocean blue.

"Looks a pretty sight, doesn't she?" Kursh murmured.

Peewit cast a look over his shoulder out past the headland light. "I wonder who is watching through his spyglass out there."

The dwarf grunted as he heaved a coil of line up to the roof of the small cabin. "Hope the bloody bastard gets an eyeful."

Pers Half Hand jumped down from the tiller half-deck. "We're ready, gentlemen, and there's rain in the Glass, so I say let's get gone." They nodded agreement. "Right. Cast us off, then, would you?" He turned for the tiller and then recollected. Gesturing to the bow and anchor lines, he winked. "That means take those and throw them back onto the dock." Korimson cursed him, and Half Hand went laughing to his station. "Oars out!" he shouted, and the fishing crew snapped to motion.

They made way slowly through the crowded slips. Just as they came abreast of the blue ship, Peewit grasped Kursh's arm. On the pier, a burly figure, indistinctly seen in the torchlight, strode down the dock. He had white hair and gray beard, and when he turned his head to say something to the smaller figure by his side, an eyepatch.

"Very convincing," Peewit said. "Who is it?"

"Fellow named Jan Reyason." He smiled faintly, thinking how much padding it had taken to make that cloak fall just so.

"Guildsman?"

Kursh glanced up at his tone. "Yes." He added, "And a volunteer. They all are."

The Littleman nodded gravely, eyes on the "ambassador" and the "retinue" which followed him up the gangway onto the ship. Then the *Puffin* swung past the blue stern and rocked out into the main channel. The tide in the bay caught them, and the fishermen eased off the oars. Half Hand quietly ordered the sails lofted, and they sped away from Skejfalen, red and green lanterns swinging from bow and stern.

Kursh straightened at the rail and dug out his pipe. "Well, might as well relax a bit. The ambassador's ship isn't to weigh anchor for another turn of the glass yet, and even then, there will be no attack till dawn at any rate. My guess is that he'll come out of the east at sunrise. That's the way they usually do. Even if this is no ordinary pirate, they'll want to make it look like one."

"How is the *Jarlshof Star* armed?"

"The usual complement of crossbowmen. Grappling hooks, that sort of thing. Also, one thing he may not be expecting." He sounded very pleased with himself.

"Really? What?"

"A catapult."

The Littleman stared incredulously. "You're joking! At sea?" The more he thought about it, the cleverer the idea was. The things had been around for Powers knew how long, but only for knocking holes in fortified walls. "Does it work?"

Korimson lifted one shoulder. "We'll see. The hardest part was lashing the bugger down so it wouldn't roll right through the rail in heavy weather."

Peewit grinned. "Even if we don't hit anything, it will certainly give the attacker something to think about when catapult stones start raining down around his ship!"

"That's what I thought." He puffed his pipe contentedly.

"You're really getting insufferably cheeky in your old age, you know."

One fierce eyebrow lowered. "Must have picked it up from someone I know."

The Littleman laughed and watched the Skejfalen headland light fall by to port.

Two hours before dawn, when the sky did not yet show even a hint of growing lighter, Half Hand ordered the running lights extinguished, and they sailed on, silent and dark, with the pole star off their stern. "Sharp watch, lads," the captain of the *Puffin* called in a low voice. "It's not likely he'll have his lamps lit, either."

An hour later they could see the lights of the *Jarlshof Star* coming along behind them, the bigger ambassador's ship making better time with her yards of canvas to the *Puffin*'s small sails. Kursh had planned for her to be closing like this: it was essential they be near enough to see, but not so near as to attract the enemy ship. The sea and sky could be distinguished from one another now, iron below and pewter above. To slow them down and provide cover, Half Hand ordered most of the sails furled and the nets out over the side. All but motionless in the heavy swell, they waited.

The sky reddened to a muddy purple; there was foul weather coming, Kursh and Half Hand agreed, quietly smoking by the tiller. All eyes were fixed on the east. The *Jarlshof Star* was a flying wedge off their stern, crowding canvas to catch the morning rise of wind. Peewit shrugged deeper into his jacket.

The sun came up red and smoking in the sea haze. And against its half disc the rigging of the attacking ship was stamped like a spider's web.

Jan Reyason gave it longer than Kursh would have liked before he sent up the fire rocket that was the traditional warning, one ship to another, of a collision course. In this case, it was also the signal for the Jarlshof coast guard boats following at a distance to tack for the ambassador's ship and close with her at all possible speed.

The other ship made no response. Half Hand had his spyglass trained on its raked black hull. "No markings, of course," he grimly reported. The *Jarlshof Star* fired off another rocket.

The two bigger ships were closing rapidly. The blue ship had run up her diplomatic flag to join the official ambassador's flag at the masthead. By all possible means, she had identified herself as a protected ship. The attacker came on.

Half Hand glanced at Korimson. "If we were really a fishing boat, we'd be getting the hell out of here."

The Guildmaster kept his eye trained on the two ships. "He's too close to worry about us now. He'll be planning to mop us up afterward."

The master of the *Puffin* signaled sharply for his crew to cut away the nets. They would need the maneuverability, and it would look like the action of a panic-stricken little boat. He had allowed Kursh to pay for the nets.

All of the fishermen crowded to the rail to watch.

The two captains must have had nerves of steel, because each held his course until the last possible moment. When they veered, the black ship and the blue one were less than fifty yards apart. A hail of crossbow bolts darkened the space between like some hideous swarm of bees. This was a preliminary tactic on the pirate's side, a means to test how strong was the blue ship's defense. They sped away from each other, fighting the swells and the wind to come about for another pass. "Get ready, Jan," Kursh murmured into the collar of his coat.

"Sailing stations," Half Hand ordered his men. They jumped for the rigging. On his word, all sails would be set. Again, they waited and watched.

The blue ship and the black closed. This time, the pirate captain raced alongside the *Jarlshof Star*, lining up for another shot. Kursh gripped the rail. "Now, by his Beard, *now!*"

On his last word, Jan Reyason released the catapult. They saw the stone, a great river boulder as round as a pigeon's egg, go hurtling through the pirate ship's rigging, bringing down sails. The dwarven fishermen cheered wildly, fists in the air.

But even as they did, they could see the pirate crew slashing at the fouled lines to clear them, and then the attacker answered. A barrage of crossbolts pounded the *Jarlshof Star*. What Kursh for all his planning had not foreseen was that each had tied to it a flask of oil stoppered with a twist of flaming rag. Within a minute the *Star* was poxed with fires.

Korimson had leaped upon the rail, spyglass to his eye. The others watching saw only a dark shape that swung suddenly down from the crane the pirates had maneuvered over the dwarvish ship, but through the telescope, he could see the tarred barrel and the fuse. "Powder!" he bellowed as though Reyason could have heard him. For an instant, the boats raced side by side, and at the foot of the crane, Kursh saw the pirate captain's mocking salute. The enemy's hand chopped down, and in one instant the barrel was cut free and the pirate tacked hard away.

There was a flat thud against their eardrums, and then the *Jarlshof Star* momentarily disappeared in a gout of fire, black smoke, and wood splinters. Kursh was knocked backward off the rail, and the fishermen threw up their arms and ducked.

"Sails!" Half Hand yelled, and, jamming the tiller hard around, he made for the rolling black cloud.

Peewit got to Kursh just as the Guildmaster was hauling himself to his feet, but the dwarf shook off his steadying hand and glared at the pirate ship racing away into the sea haze. "Whoreson cess-eating scum," he ground between clenched teeth. When the Littleman led him back to the rail, the smoke was thinning and they could see, though they desperately wished they could not.

The *Jarlshof Star* had broken her back, and the halves were already no more than whale backs wallowing in the oil-slicked sea. Half Hand had the tiller jammed under his arm. "Rudi, get out the extra sheets," he ordered his first mate, and the other nodded wordlessly and went below. They would need the spare sails for shrouds. If there were any bodies to recover.

Chunks of timber began to bump against their sides, and Half Hand stepped down some sail to slow a little. The acrid smell of powder parched their throats and made their eyes sting. An arm floated by. Nobody looked at it.

There was a splash and wracking coughing suddenly, somewhere off the port bow. Half Hand nudged his tiller a notch and took down more sail. A spar loomed in the waves, still miraculously upright, and they could see a dark form clinging desperately.

They recovered him quickly, fishermen leaning dangerously over the rail to pull him aboard. He was a mass of powder burn, and one of his legs dangled crookedly. There was blood trickling from one ear, but he was conscious enough to grin.

The *Puffin* made way slowly, trolling for survivors while Korimson cursed the rescue ships' slow arrival. Five more living they found, six altogether out of a complement of seventy-two. And the fifth was Jan Reyason.

Kursh recognized him when they saw the scarlet velvet jacket tangled in the flotsam of deck planking and canvas that had rolled to trap the air and keep him afloat. Korimson gave a hoarse shout and his face eased a little, but when they cut Jan free of the ropes and tried to lift him, he sagged like a broken door hinge. Half Hand quickly chopped a gesture to his men and they eased him back down. The dwarven captain looked at Kursh.

The Guildmaster shrugged himself out of his coat and slung it to the deck. Then he climbed up on the rail and dove into the cold sea. Peewit had put a hand out to stop him, but realized the uselessness and said nothing. They watched him surface, shaking the water out of his eye, and grasp the timber across which Reyason lay. With his other hand he reached to touch the burned face.

Jan opened his eyes. Together he and the ambassador rose and fell in the waves. Reyason licked his lips. "Did you . . . see the catapult?"

Kursh smiled. "He must have pissed himself."

A loose smile spread across the charred features. "Aye." He sighed a breath. "They were Shimarrat, Kursh. The bastard tipped his cap to me . . . and said, 'Roste!' " It was the Shimarrat drinking toast.

Korimson turned his head and spat the salt from his mouth. "They'll pay, Jan, I swear it to ye."

There was a milky glaze covering the eyes that stared up into the leaden morning sky. "My family is yours." By custom and tradition the words made a widow and her children the responsibility of a ship captain.

"I'll hold them as my own," Korimson said thickly.

"The boy's birthday is . . . at Aashnasse. He wants . . . a puppy, white . . . with spots," Reyason said faintly. His head lolled and Kursh kept it carefully out of the water, though there was no longer any need.

He stayed with the body in the wreckage until the first rescue ship arrived and began to winch the canvas and timbers up from the sea. Then he swam slowly the few strokes to the *Puffin*, and Peewit and the others pulled him roughly over the rail. Half Hand had a tankard of flotjin ready, and the Guildmaster drank it in one long pull. "Make for the *Crystal Kite*," he directed quietly and jerked a thumb at the flagship of his own private fleet, at sea anchor a half mile northeast.

No one said anything until they were bouncing in the troughs beneath the fast cargo ship's keel. When the ladder came snaking down the side, the Littleman and the Guildmaster were ready. Kursh and Half Hand exchanged a handclasp. Korimson said, "Ye've done Jarlshof service this day. The keg we agreed on will be waiting for you and your men."

A humorless smile touched the fisherman's mouth. "We'll wait for you before we drink it."

Kursh grunted, stepped up on the rail, and began to climb. With some private misgivings, the Littleman looked at the rising and falling ship's side and awkwardly followed.

They stepped through the break in the aft rail one after the other, and Peewit was momentarily surprised when Kursh received the officer's salute. "Welcome aboard, Guildmaster. Your luggage is already in your cabin, sir, as you ordered. And Captain Brickleburr, you'll have the first mate's cabin."

Korimson surveyed one last time the thin haze of smoke and small fleet of rescue ships. "Run up the flags, Jorgen. Break out a keg of flotjin and send it to my cabin. And then any man but you or Captain Brickleburr who steps through that door will lose his head. Do I make myself clear?"

"Aye, aye, sir." The officer's face was impassive.

As the officer led them forward to the companionway, ropes whistled through their tackle and two flags rose to snap at the masthead. On top was the duplicate ambassador's flag. Beneath was the flag of the Guildmaster: set on a field of rich burgandy, the gleaming white dome of the guildhall was sewn with chips of crystal to make it glitter in the sun. Kursh looked up at them once, then his gaze fell to the east. "Come back and try again, whoreson," he muttered. Ducking through the hatch, he ordered, "All speed for Castlenigh."

"Aye, sir." The officer raised his hand in a signal, and a moment later the sheets bellied from the halyards and the deck canted under them.

The Guildmaster did not come out of his cabin that night, and Peewit wisely left him alone with it.

Alphonse must be somewhere far at the reaches of the kingdom, the queen thought, or surely he would have been here by now. The Riders had ridden back in, singly or in pairs, over the past couple of days, but none had seen the wizard. Jamison was still out, however, and as her brother Jak had pointed out, that was a good indication. She glanced once more at the early sun just beginning to strike the long spire of the Guardian and turned from the window arch to look at the Greenbriar mural pensively. "Plastering didn't do much good, did it?"

Imris shook his head. They regarded the slow seep of red that showed through the fresh plaster that had been painted unobtrusive green just yesterday. "It wasn't very likely, anyway, if you will forgive my saying so."

She gave him an affectionate glance for answer, and together they walked to the wall itself. "Poor bunny," the queen murmured.

The Yoriandir bard said after a moment, "What we need, of course, is someone to read this riddle for us. Someone like a wizard, or . . ." He looked at her directly. "A Littleman."

Ariadne toyed with the Crystal of Healing on its golden chain about her neck. "I don't know where he is, Imris," she reminded the bard gently.

"And if others did, would he be welcome?"

She looked away. "If others did, would he come?"

The Eldest gestured to the mural. "If he knew of this, I do not think anything could keep him away. Even a death sentence unrevoked."

"I can't just . . ." she began, nettled. At the look in his fir-green eyes, she fell suddenly silent. "It is not so simple a thing as you suppose, my lord of Yoriand."

"Nothing is," he rejoined mildly, "my lady of Ilyria." He bowed slightly. "Now, if you will excuse me"—there may have been a glint of merriment in his eyes—"I must send a note to an old friend."

She sighed and waved acceptance. He was nearly to the marble stairway leading up to the guestrooms before she found the courage to call, "Imris?"

He turned, one foot on the stair.

"Tell him . . ." The tangle would not come straight, so she merely said, "Tell him to be careful on the way."

The Eldest fingered the carving on the balustrade as lightly as if it had been harp strings. Slowly he said, "Peewit has never been rash in anything he has done, my queen," and then he was gone up the curve of the stairs, and she was grateful there was no one to see the flaming of her cheeks.

When William Quint told her about the tip he had received, she was very glad she had decided upon a coat of mail as one of her gifts to Gerrit. "Your informant is reliable?" she questioned. He had asked for a private meeting in her garden.

The huge man's eyes slid a little. "Has been in the past, my lady."

Peewit, she thought. "Is there anything to suggest when the attempt will take place, or a description of the assassin? Or even how many of them there might be?" she added as the thought struck her.

He was shaking his head. "Nay, my lady, not a whisper. But the information was fairly definite about your being the target, not the Lordling."

"Still, the information may be wrong. You have, of course, already set extra guard on my son."

"Aye. Six of our best. But . . ." He hesitated. "We've done it quietly, so as not to frighten the lad."

So Gerrit did not know. It was tactfully left to the queen's discretion whether she would tell him. Ariadne sighed and looked away toward the slate terrace. It is the boy's birthday, her mother's heart said. Let him enjoy it! But if he is not on his guard and something does happen, he might not have another one, the queen answered. There was a long silence in her mind then, the two voices delicately balanced. "Have him sent to me here, captain."

He bowed and was turning toward his yeoman, who waited at the door into the castle, when she stayed him. "Will?

One thing more first. Is there by any chance a spare mail vest about? A sleeveless one, short and not too bulky?''

He was bewildered. "I'm sure, my lady. What size?"

"Boy-sized. A good boy-sized." This was embarrassing. Her chin came up. "It's for me."

"Oh. *Oh*."

Honest Will, she thought. He never could hide anything, and he was plainly horrified. "It would be a sensible precaution, don't you think?" she said gently.

The captain of her Watch shut his mouth with an almost audible snap. "Right. Yes. Very good, my lady. Only—"

"Yes?" she prodded.

He was red right to the roots of his hair. "Well, you know, they're . . . they're not exactly made for . . ." He drew a breath and blurted, "For a woman's form."

The queen bit her lip and pretended there was something on her sleeve. When she could, she agreed gravely, "I suppose not. Still, do your best to dig me up an old one, would you? I'd feel just that little bit better if I had something that might turn a knife."

"Aye, my lady." He was regarding her with something between dismay and respect that wanted to be awe. "They're *heavy*, you know."

"Well, I'll build up some muscles, then, won't I?" she countered cheerfully.

"Aye, my lady." He gestured toward the yeoman. "I'll just go have a word with young Mason there, by your leave."

"Fine." Behind his retreating back, she finally allowed herself to smile.

She saw him dismiss the young soldier to fetch the prince, and then, when he turned toward her once more, she held up a hand. He bowed and took up the yeoman's position by the door. She needed a few minutes alone to think. Walking slowly down the slate path toward the far terrace, she stopped to fix the corner of a burlap windscreen around an azalea, then straightened and went on. "Shall I tell him, or not?" she murmured to the bare lilac branches.

"Something wrong?"

She turned to find Gerrit behind her. He gave her a magnificent court bow for the benefit of the archers on the battlement. Ariadne smiled at the extravagance. "You've been watching Festil, I see."

"He's so wonderfully serious about it, too. I can't quite get the little toss of the head and wiggle of the—"

"All right," she said firmly, smothering a chuckle. "Master Festil has been with us a long time and doesn't merit being aped before the whole court. Now, does he?"

"I suppose not." But he took her mild tone as leeway to grin. She put out her hand and he offered his arm. They strolled back toward the birch. "Thank you for telling old Crummie I might have the day off, by the way. It's a treat."

The queen was brushed by cold, for she had not told his tutor any such thing. "You're welcome," she said. She would have Will investigate as soon as Gerrit left the garden. Casually, she looked about for the bodyguards. Yes, she thought, satisfied as she counted two beyond the boxwood, one ostensibly reporting to Will at the door, two on the battlements who were not archers, and one fellow who had marched out with one of her gardeners to check the lock on the little door on the surrounding wall out to the Sweep.

Gerrit watched her sidelong and pretended not to notice the tally. He had already marked them. To make conversation, he said, "I've got my part all memorized for the ceremony."

"Do you?"

"Mm-hmm. Been studying it all week." He let her think what she would. He'd actually scanned it once this morning. It was fairly standard as rituals went. He'd had Fisher check him on it while he was having his bath this morning.

"That's fine," she said, forcing it just a little, and Gerrit suddenly wondered what it must be like to have an idiot for a son. Ariadne looked away for a moment. When she looked at him again, he knew there was some damn good reason she'd called him here. "Well, as a little reward for all your hard work," she teased, "I think I shall let you have one of your presents early."

"Really? Where is it?"

"You'll find it in your rooms."

He gave her a sly grin. "So that's why you had to get me out here!"

Her decision was made at that moment as she saw his shining eyes and childlike anticipation. The queen said, "No, not exactly."

Alerted by her tone, Gerrit straightened on the stone bench. "You sound pretty serious about this present."

Ariadne tried not to dull the pleasure for him. "Not all that serious." She smiled. "It's a mail shirt made especially for you."

He jumped up. "Double sixes!"

"I thought you might be pleased."

"It's just what I've been hoping for!" He really had been. "Can I go try it on?"

"Yes." When he seemed about to tear away in excitement, she put a hand on his arm. "Gerrit, I want you to wear it at all times until this festival is over."

He put this together with the extra guards and came up with four. Old Fidelis had not been talking off the top of his head, then. The Greenbriar heir decided it might be time to run up the flag, just a little, to see which way the wind blew. He sat back down, asking softly, "Why?" and wondering whether finally she would allow him to grow up.

Ariadne smoothed her gown on her knee. "Well, I'm sure there's nothing to it, but Captain Quint wants to protect us a little better. There are going to be so many people out on the Sweep. Master Will gets nervous about things like this." There, she thought. That should be enough warning to get him thinking.

Gerrit pushed his hair back out of his eyes. Not quite yet, he was thinking. We get to be Baby Gerrit awhile longer. "All right," he agreed aloud. "It'll look super with my new surcoat." He looked up just as she did. "But how are we going to keep *you* safe?"

"There will be extra Watchmen. I'm hoping Master Alphonse will be here by then, too."

"Ah, yes. All right," he said again and rose. Glancing up to the battlements, he quickly did his Festil-bow and kissed her laughing reproach. Bloody serious if we need the wizard to Ward her, he was thinking.

As she watched him walk away—barely limping today, she noted—the queen thought how odd it was there should be some things you could share with the captain of your Watch that you wouldn't tell your own son.

Meara, the queen's waitingwoman, turned at the sound of the door to the antechamber, and there was a look of scandal on her face. The queen nodded to Will Quint and closed the door on the milling courtiers, Watchmen, and ladies outside. "Ah, they found one, I see," Ariadne said as she crossed the room.

"He said it was for you, my lady!" the woman said in an outraged tone.

"It is, goose." The queen laughed. She stood hands on hips regarding the short mail vest. "Looks the right size. Captain Quint has a better eye than I gave him credit for." Meara shot her a shocked glance and belatedly jumped to help her mistress out of her light wool gown. "Now, let's see . . ." She stood in her lace-trimmed shift uncertainly.

Meara folded the wool gown over her arm. "You're not really thinking to wear that, are you?" It was some measure of their relationship that she could raise an eyebrow.

"I am." The queen raised her gaze from the iron shirt to say quietly, "There's an assassin about. Will got a tip from P—from an informant there's to be an attempt sometime during the celebration."

If Meara had been comically shocked before, she was seriously so now. Her lips drew together in a straight line. "I see." The women regarded the protective mail once more. With a sudden air of decision, Meara threw the wool gown across the bed and picked the thing up. "Well, let's see, then. The laces go in back, I know."

"Yes. I remember Sal always hated it because he could never get himself out of it." She smiled a little. "But I was thinking, if I put it on so the laces were in front, I could perhaps make it fit over the bust."

"All right." Meara held it up, not without difficulty, and Ariadne stuck her arms though the armholes. The waiting woman let it fall onto her shoulders.

"Powers! It *is* heavy!"

"Aye, my lady. Be like carrying a toddler around pig-a-back all day." She stepped around, and, one working from the bottom and the other from the top, they laced the vest.

With no side-to-side give at all, the mail shirt laced well enough at neck and middle, but in spite of the fact she had pulled the ties as tightly as possible, the queen could not make it close over her bosom. The lacing crisscrossed a two-inch gap. Ariadne looked down, regarding it for a moment, then looked up at Meara. " 'Twould be a pretty poor assassin who couldn't hit *that* mark," the queen muttered.

The waitingwoman began to giggle. The queen did, too,

and before it was over, they were both sitting on the needle-point carpet laughing like idiots, Meara with the hem of her apron stuffed in her mouth and the tears rolling down her cheeks.

After a time, Ariadne sighed, "Oh, Powers," and struggled to her feet. "Well, *that* won't do, clearly." She pulled at the laces and sniffed the laughter away. Meara scratched under her cap and got up to help. This time, they put the thing on the right way and the waitingwoman began to tie the laces.

Ariadne endured as best she could, but could not help cautioning, "Not too tightly! I'll be flattened for life!"

Meara laughed, but finished the job. "There. How does that feel, my lady?"

The queen turned and gave her a look.

"You can still take it off, you know," the waitingwoman reminded her.

Ariadne shook her head. "Let's find something to put on over it." So they went into the tiring room and began considering different dresses.

"I misdoubt your old one will fit over this, my lady," Meara said, touching the sleeve of the turquoise gown she always wore for tradition's sake at the Ritual of the Rose.

"I won't have to wear the vest by then," the queen reminded her. "Alphonse will be here and he can Ward me."

"Ah, that's so, of course. I was forgetting. Well, then, since we're needing something for you to wear only for the next couple of days at most, how about the rose wool—you've always liked that one—and, um, the cream velvet for receiving the ambassadors?"

"Good."

In a few moments the queen stood before the full-length mirror, regarding her image critically. The rose gown was one of her winter favorites, because it was soft, warm, and unfitted. The front pulled across to fasten cunningly with a pin made like a leaf at the left shoulder, then angled back to her waist secured by tiny hidden buttons, there to be gathered by a handspan-wide girdle of the finest leaf-color lacework. The skirt draped to her dark green slippers. "Not bad." She turned sideways. "If you didn't know, I don't think you could guess."

"Nary a person will be the wiser," Meara agreed.

The queen straightened and sighed. "I'll need a good long soak in a warm bath tonight, though. This is already bothering my back."

There was a knock at the chamber door, and Meara went to open it. "It's Captain Quint, madam," she reported.

"Show him in. Yes, captain, what is it?"

He could not quite hide his quick glance at the bed. "The sentries have sighted King Ka-Treer's ship, my queen. Another quarter hour and he'll be here."

"Very well. The suite is ready for his retinue?"

"Aye, my lady. All's in order."

She looked at him directly. "Gerrit has received his present, I presume."

"He has, my lady. Proud as a peacock," the big man said affectionately. He nodded at the question in her eyes. "He wears it well, too, I may say. Looks older, somehow."

She straightened the clasp of the long green cloak she had added to her costume. "When a boy adopts the accouterments of war, he usually does," she said quietly. She rustled away from the mirror. "All right, Will. Let's go down." Etiquette demanded that as a kinsman and a fellow sovereign, Ka-Treer was owed the courtesy of being met on the Sweep before her gates. Privately, she'd just as soon have waited for him in Rose Hall with a complement of archers in the viewing gallery.

They proceeded through the antechamber, liveried pages hastening to form up and lead her way, and the Watchmen on duty at the double doors flung them open, saluting. Gerrit had already been summoned to greet his cousin Ka-Bril and was waiting for her with the detachment of the Watch which would be the escort.

It was uncanny, the queen thought as her son stepped forward and made the precise military bow, but he did look older and taller. His emerald surcoat emblazoned with the Briar and his own silver label of cadency broadened his shoulders, his unruly dark curls were, for once, neatly brushed back, and his hand rested naturally on the hilt of his dagger, where soon his own sword would hang.

He met her look with his own direct and proud one, only the barest of smiles on his lips.

The queen understood that he did not want her to gush. "My lord Greenbriar," she said and nodded. He returned the nod respectfully. "Allow me to say the uniform looks most well on you."

His earlobes turned scarlet, but he answered, "Thank you, madam," and offered his arm to escort her. When they were well down the hall, she gave his wrist a squeeze and saw his smile broaden slightly.

They paced down the long marble stairway and past the mural. There was a servingman stationed there with a damp cloth. Then they were out in the courtyard before the entrance, and mounted Watchmen made an aisle for her. She received their salutes graciously, thinking that Quint certainly wasn't taking any chances. Under the wide arch of Queen's Gate, she held up a hand to the captain, and Will barked an order. They waited for Ka-Treer to anchor at Castlenigh before the decorative outer gate would be opened. She could see the hordes of people lining the road up from the city. There were some preliminary ragged cheers as she was sighted, but these died to an expectant hum as people realized it was too early yet.

From around the bend just upriver, the Shimarrat king's ship barreled into view, still under full sail, even though the river current was running strongly with her and she was entering the crowded waters of Castlenigh. Ka-Treer, it appeared, was going to make his usual entrance. The queen, the prince, and the captain watched through the wrought-iron roses. Bloody show-off, Will Quint thought. If he runs down any of the merchantmen, I'll slap him with an indemnity he won't soon forget, the queen swore. Wouldn't it be funny if he piled it up on the rocks, Gerrit chuckled inwardly.

At the last possible moment, all the sails dropped like a moth landing, and the Shimarrat vessel glided in a smooth surge to the space at the end of the pier that had been reserved for her.

"That's as good an example of seamanship as you'll see anywhere," Ariadne remarked to her son.

Under the new surcoat and mail he shrugged. "They're known for it. When you're a sea kingdom, you'd better know how to sail."

She smiled. He did not sound quite so taken with his Shimarrat relations as he was wont to do. Perhaps it was the Briar he wore on his chest now.

Speaking of which, she thought, shifting uncomfortably. The pennon streaming from the mainmast was dipped, the Lion of Shimarron running half down the halyards. She heard the creak of winches overhead through the thick stone and knew that her own standard above Queen's Gate had been dipped in return to acknowledge the salute. "All right, captain," she said. Quint snapped an order, and the wrought-iron gates swung open. Pausing only a moment (the assassin could already be amongst the crowd, she thought), she and Gerrit stepped outside. The cheer went up in earnest, a good-natured rolling roar of approval for the Greenbriar Queen and her son.

Ariadne smiled and waved to them, though it broke the strict etiquette of the occasion. Gerrit was unmoving beside her, watching the ramps flung down fore and aft of the Shimarrat vessel and the swarm of grooms that off-loaded the horses, already saddled and bridled. Quint signaled the first two of the cavalry lining the road, and they drew their swords and came to parade attention. The action rippled away down the line until it reached the landward end of the pier. The watching group saw Ka-Treer, a flash of royal-blue cloak, swing into the saddle, and the smaller figure of his son beside him. Gerrit murmured, "Ka-Bril's grown some."

Ariadne glanced at him. "You have, too."

A genuine smile broke through the cool exterior.

The Shimarrat entourage came galloping up the road, robes flowing and the Lion of Shimarron streaming in the hands of the standard-bearer. They rode their horses the same way they piloted their ships, Gerrit thought as Ka-Treer, with his son a half length behind, pulled his horse back on its haunches in a plowing stop just outside the point where the queen's men would have presumed an attack. For a moment the Shimarrat king smiled at the Ilyrian cohort around the queen, his ruby ear gem glinting in the sun and his waxed mustache gleaming. Then he jumped from the gold-trimmed saddle and walked forward. "Greetings, lady of Ilyria. You are, as always, a pleasure to behold." He bent over her hand. The words were correct, but there was a too-frank quality to his look that made Will Quint's breath tighten in his chest.

Slime, the queen thought. "We give you welcome, my lord of Shimarron," she replied coolly and turned her wrist to break his lingering grip on her hand. "We are pleased you could take time from your pressing affairs to join us for our celebration."

"I would not have missed so important an occasion as when the Greenbriar Lordling comes of age." You might have thought it was toilet training he was discussing. He did not even meet the boy's eye, fixing his gaze on Ariadne instead. "Happy birthday, Gerrit."

Ariadne's son, perhaps for the first time—though it may have been knocking at the gates of his mind for some while—recognized that look for what it was. "I have not quite attained my majority yet, Uncle, but I thank you anyway." He suddenly stuck his hand out to his cousin between Ka-Treer and his mother. "Hullo, Ka-Bril, how are you?" He had quite deliberately omitted any courtesy of rank. "You've put on some weight, haven't you?"

The eyes of the Shimarrat retinue flicked to him, and behind him he could hear a very slight intake of breath from somewhere in the ranks of the First Watch. His mother's hand was steady on his arm.

King Ka-Treer suddenly smiled, and beside him the pudgy Ka-Bril echoed it vacantly. "Yes, I've had to have a whole new set of hunting leathers made!"

The Shimarrat king smiled a dagger at the queen. "Our boys are growing up."

"Young men do," she said.

Gerrit felt the understated praise like whiskey.

Ka-Treer gestured to the mail and surcoat Gerrit wore. "You've had a new wardrobe, too, I see, nephew."

"Yes, sir, though strictly speaking I have not the right to it yet." Technically, he should not have his first coat until his Senior Squire ceremony. "But I hope to earn it soon enough."

"I cannot think otherwise," the Shimarrat said smoothly. It could have been taken as a compliment, but it probably meant that Gerrit was getting the advancement purely because no one would have dared deny a prince. "And to honor the achievement, I hope you will allow your son to accept a small gift, lady."

For some reason it took all Ariadne's accumulated discipline not to stiffen. "Of course," she said lightly. "The Lordling much looks forward to visits from his favorite kinsman." She met the smoking look with a serene smile: Ka-Treer was Gerrit's only kinsman except for Ka-Bril.

The Shimarrat king snapped his fingers to one of his men, and Ariadne gave Gerrit's arm a fractionally tighter squeeze. From Ka-Treer's mounted escort a man led forward a gray stallion with a flaxen mane and tail and one white forefoot. The animal pranced lightly, a proud arch to its neck, and trappings of silver like a mirror shining. "For you," Ka-Treer said. He may have given some signal to the man who led it, because the stallion suddenly reared, lashing at the air with silver-shod hooves. "He is quite a spirited animal, as you see. Fitting, I thought, for a man's first warhorse."

Will Quint's hands fisted at his sides. The horse was a killer if he'd ever seen one.

Gerrit met his uncle's eyes and saw no hint of the portrait of his father that hung in his room. From childhood, he had known that if he was to be king someday, he would have to learn to fight from horseback, because fighting afoot in the conventional way was difficult for him. In this, he had been lucky to have inherited his father's instinctive horsemanship. Looking at the gray now, he knew this stallion was more horse than he was rider.

Ka-Treer had trapped him and his mother: he could make some laughing confession of fright and remain a boy, or he could get astride the beast.

The young Greenbriar heir smiled and forestalled whatever his mother was going to say. "I owe you, my lord king," he said into Ka-Treer's eye. Patting his mother's hand, he got free and walked to the man holding the reins. The fellow dismounted from his own horse to hold the stallion's head. It trampled, and Gerrit gathered the reins and swung lightly up. The Shimarrat retainer hurriedly let go the bit, and by that Gerrit knew instantly what he was in for.

The stallion stood up on its hind legs, screaming, then came down in a bone-jarring, stiff-legged buck. As the hindquarters rose under him, the prince lay back almost perpendicular to the ground, by his weight forcing the gray to put its feet down to balance itself. The stallion threw its head up, striking back to catch the rider, but Gerrit threw himself forward and to the side, clinging with his knees. His eye and the glaring brown one were inches apart. "Now, you bastard, let's see what you can do," the Lordling breathed, and hauling back on the reins while the horse jibbed and jumped sideways, he forced the white-maned head around, kicked the flank hard enough to get the gray's attention, and lit the horse in a wind-rushing gallop down the road toward the river.

A couple of cavalrymen, thinking the horse was running away with him, spurred to intercept, but he threw his hand up in a Watch code and they turned to let him through. He kept the hand up as long as he dared, and the Watchmen cleared the road of bystanders. The gray settled into a smooth, ground-eating gallop, Gerrit bending low on its neck and praying it didn't slip on the cobbles.

The half mile down to the pier took far less time than he had thought it would. There was a wagon across the landward end. "Oh, sh—!" the prince yelled, but the gray never even broke stride as it launched itself right over the astonished driver and landed smoothly on the other side. Down the pier they flashed toward the Shimarrat ship. The gray was expecting to be hauled back in a stop: Gerrit could feel it through the bit. "Uh-uh," he said, and pulling the animal's head over, he spurred it right off the side of the pier into the cold river.

They broke surface with the mail-coated prince still firmly astride his horse. The stallion tried to head for the bank, but Gerrit hauled its head over and made it swim yards farther than it wanted to. By the time he reined for the river banking, Gerrit was in control. They walked out of the water, and the gray got its haunches under it to heave up the slippery embankment. Passing the wagon and the astounded dockworkers, the prince called, "Excuse me, good sirs. We needed a bath." One of them hooted, and there were the beginnings of grins. He turned for the road, and at a sedate canter he rode back up to the castle.

Ariadne drew a breath, the first one that had done her any good in minutes. She had seen his hand signal to the Watch, but the terror still turned her stomach sour and made her hands shake. The mail vest weighted as heavily as all Earth-Above, and she could hear beside her Will Quint's breath whistling in his nostrils.

The cheering for Gerrit started down near the river, and by the time he came trotting up the road toward the group at the gate, hats were tossing in the air and little boys were clapping. Some of the folk saw little beyond a high-spirited boy riding hell-for-leather the way nobles did, but a few of them knew—and all of the Watch knew—what Gerrit had done and why he had done it.

The prince rode close enough to Ka-Treer to make one Shimarrat man-at-arms involuntarily reach for his dagger and reined to a halt. The gray blew quietly and shook its wet mane. Gerrit leaned slightly over the silver pommel. "He's a splendid chap, but his manners wanted mending." He grinned, extending a hand suddenly so that Ka-Treer was forced to shake it. "Thanks, Uncle."

Will Quint, openly smiling, signaled a man forward. Gerrit flung him the reins and jumped to the ground, his wet surcoat pattering them with a fine spray of river water. "Say," he said as if struck with a sudden thought. "Would you like to try him out, Ka-Bril?"

Just a shade too quickly, King Ka-Treer said, "My son owns this one's sire."

Maybe, Gerrit thought, but I'll wager six months' allowance he hasn't ever ridden him. "How lucky!" He bowed to kiss Ariadne's hand. "What did you think, Mother? Isn't he wonderful?" His gray eyes teased her well-hidden fear.

There is that moment when a mother knows her little boy is forever lost to her. "Absolutely marvelous." The smile she gave him made him duck to wring the hem of his surcoat.

"I think I need to get inside and dry off before I rust," he joked, straightening.

This drew a laugh from the men of the Watch. Ariadne joined them and held out her hand to Ka-Bril. "Yes, come, my lords. Refreshment awaits us in the hall. Be welcome."

As the Shimarrats were escorted inside the gates, Ka-Treer touched his waxed mustache and thought he really was going to enjoy hearing this little whelp was dead.

Chapter Five

❧

From the balcony of her solar the next afternoon the queen watched the big ship just showing over the city rooftops and by the flags knew who it would be. Meara, standing silently beside her, briefly patted her arm and went back inside to finish laying out her mistress's raiment for that evening's reception. Ariadne sighed, shrugging farther into her cloak, and wondered again what she would say to him.

Out on the Sweep, two figures standing by a brightly painted tinker's wagon looked down to the river landing. The Yoriandir put down his harp, and the Nan Dir Nog, the king of pipers, stowed his pipes. "Let's go down to meet them," Muir Dach said.

"Nay, not yet," Imris said thoughtfully. At the other's squinting glance, he explained, "Let us wait until they disembark tonight. That way, he cannot send us away."

There was no need to ask which he the bard was referring to, and the tinker understood about pride, too. He nodded, spat through the gap in his teeth, and picked up the potcheen jug to wet his lips.

From the deck of the *Crystal Kite*, Korimson gazed up at the proud battlements etched against the azure sky, and at the Briar rippling from the highest turret. His hand gripped the polished rail and his chest felt suddenly tight. Don't, fool, he told himself sternly and pulled his eye away.

He turned abruptly, surprising a look on Brickleburr's face before the other could become aware, a look of loss no less keen for being old. The dwarf quickly swung to the rail once more.

After a moment Peewit said, "Ka-Treer is arrived, I see." He gestured down the waterfront to the far pier. Korimson spat into the water. A faint smile came to the Littleman's face, and he changed the subject. Levering himself off the rail, he asked, "Well, we're here. Shall we go up?"

For a split second as the dwarf's eye widened, Peewit thought he saw a flash of something very near terror, and then Kursh shoved his hands deep in the pockets of his sailor's jacket and replied stonily, "Come and go as you please. Don't wait for me. The reception for the ambassadors is tonight. I'm the Jarlshof ambassador." He met the smaller figure's eye. "I'll go tonight and not before."

"All right. I think I'll just go below awhile and try for a nap," Brickleburr said offhandedly. He wandered away toward the aft companionway.

Of course you will, the dwarf thought as he watched him go. He beckoned the captain of the *Kite.* "Look lively, Jorgen. There are eyes all about."

"Aye, Guildmaster. We've seen." He gave the barest of nods in the direction of the Shimarrat ship.

Korimson grunted. "And be sure the crew knows that anyone going ashore who makes the slightest trouble—the slightest, Jorgen—will have me to answer to personally."

"That's generally understood without the saying, sir."

"Say it anyway, just for good measure. Those bastards over there are likely to try to start something with our lot. If any dwarf strikes, it's got to be self-defense." His lips drew into a grim line. "Preferably with witnesses. Make that an order: no one goes anywhere alone."

"Aye, sir. Shore leaves are going to be curtailed anyway. I've already given orders that we'll stand four-hour watches continuously from now till we weigh anchor for home. All watches to be armed to repel boarders," he added significantly.

"Good. Should have thought of that myself." Kursh frowned. You're slipping, he told himself, and ye can't afford that, Korimson, ye can't afford that at all.

Jorgen was regarding him respectfully. "You have just a few other things on your mind, sir, I believe." He saluted and left the ambassador to his private thoughts.

Kursh threw a last look up the castle before he went to his cabin. "Only one," he muttered. What will I say to her?

In the late afternoon, about an hour before sunset, Peewit tapped on the door of the cabin across from his own. "Time, Kursh," he called quietly.

The latch rattled and Korimson opened the door. For this first official function, he was attired as befit the representative of the rich merchant island. His short velvet jacket, gusseted in the back to allow for his broad shoulders, was exactly the ocean blue of his ambassador's flag, and his breeches, carefully pressed by Thyla to a crisp crease, were light gray and of the finest Jarlshof wool. His boots gleamed, and he had evidently spent some time with his barber, for he was impeccably trimmed. The heavy gold chain that marked his ambassadorial rank lay easily on his shoulders, and from it hung the flat crystal pendant that betokened him a Glassmaker. The Guildmaster's signet ring was on his right hand and a plain gold band on his left. If you did not know him very well, that might have been all you saw.

Peewit eyed the slight thickness of the dwarf's right forearm under its linen and velvet and the way that cuff was wider, looser than the other. "All set?" the Littleman questioned. "Have you got Gerrit's gift?"

"Bloody hell!" Korimson whirled and collected the padded gold silk bag from the desk. "Thanks!" They stood facing each other in the companionway. "Right. Let's be about it, then."

"Let's." Quite deliberately, Peewit raised his fist to his chest in the salute of the First Watch.

Kursh returned it, and they went in step toward the hatch.

When they emerged on deck, they found Captain Jorgen had ordered the merchant sailors on deck in precise ranks, unmoving as though for review. "Damn," the Guildmaster muttered, but he and Brickleburr marched down past them to the gangway, where Jorgen himself awaited them with a salute. The Jarlshof entourage of glass and wool merchants, secretaries, and equerries stood in a quiet, tense group nearby. Kursh scanned their faces. "All right, sirs. We know what we are here for. The guild expects us to return home with fair treaties and more orders than a dog's got fleas." There were some nervous chuckles. "I know I do not have to tell you to conduct yourselves honorably. We of Jarlshof have never done anything less." Except once, he thought. He hesitated. "If for any reason I cannot carry out this embassy"—he saw the flickers in their eyes—"Jules Larsson will be acting ambassador until the guild can elect another." The portly Larsson nodded, one hand gripping a

line tightly. Korimson turned to Jorgen. "Captain, you will
see to a safe passage home for everyone."

"Aye, sir. We shall be ready for you, come what may."

"Very good." He looked once more up to the castle, then
at the crowd of thousands packed on the Sweep. His shoulders squared, and he led the way down to the pier.

As for all the ambassadors and their retinues, the stables
of Greenbriar had provided horses and grooms, and these
waited at the road that ran along the wharfs. The head
groom was civil, indicating the black gelding that was for the
ambassador and the red roan for the former captain. "Half
a moment!" a rough voice called. "I've got his right here."
Muir rode up, leading a tawny pony with black mane and tail.

"Muir!" Peewit exclaimed delightedly. "You brought
Sandy!" The faithful Snort had breathed his last in a sunny
meadow high in the hills some years before, and the tinker
had "acquired" this pony for him. Brickleburr had thought
it better not to know exactly how, or from whom. They had
always skirted that town afterward.

The King of Pipers leaned from the back of the big bay he
rode to haul Brickleburr into the saddle. "Well, I couldn't
leave him tied to a tree somewhere, now could I? Much as
I'd like to. Fat thing's eaten me out of nearly a sovereign's
worth of grain since we got here!" He stuck a hand out to
Kursh. "Hullo, ambassador. You'll not remember me, I
reckon, but I know you well enough. Welcome to the river
country."

Despite the fellow's snarl-toothed grin and grimy clothes,
Korimson immediately liked something he saw in Muir's
eye. However, he also felt a pang at the camaraderie that
obviously existed between his old friend and the tinker: this
was the companion who had shared danger with Brickleburr
for thirteen years now. "I understand I owe ye much, Master Tinker."

Muir turned his head and spat, narrowly missing a man
rolling a barrel along the quay. The fellow gave him a
murderous look, but dared not say anything to a tinker.
"Don't know who told you that. Wasn't me." His tone put
an end to any talk of debt owed.

Peewit craned, looking about. "Is Imris here?"

"Oh, aye. Waiting up yonder a ways." The retine was
now mounted up around them. "Well, I'll be leaving now."

He meant it wasn't right for an ambassador to be seen in

company with a tinker. Korimson immediately said gruffly, "You're welcome to ride with us, Dach."

"Ah, no, Master Dwarf. I have to get back to me wagon. Some people will steal you blind, if you give them half a chance." It was exactly what the tinkers were notorious for. The stumps of his teeth showed in a jagged grin.

Peewit nudged his pony to a trot. "We'll find you later!" he called back over his shoulder.

"Aye. When you get sick of the finest wines, there's potcheen for you!"

Brickleburr laughed, and Korimson thought, Fellow after my own heart. The Jarlshof contingent moved along the waterfront and struck the road up to the castle.

There was a hail in a fair, carrying voice, and Imris, riding with neither saddle nor bridle in the Yoriandir way, guided the horse he had borrowed from Muir out into the road ahead to meet them. The silver torque that marked his rank as Eldest shone as he raised a hand and smiled. When Peewit and Kursh came up to him he leaned to grasp the dwarf's hand. "Well met, friends! I am glad to see you!"

There was a rare, open smile on Kursh's face. "Hello, Imris. Ye never change."

"The same cannot be said for all of us!" He surveyed Korimson's fine regalia, and there was a twinkle in his fir eyes. "I can scarce believe it!"

"It's all on the outside," Peewit assured him.

The bristling eyebrows lowered, and the dwarf threw him a look.

"There. You see?" Brickleburr teased.

All the while, they were moving slowly up the road, and not one of them was unaware of the open-mouthed stares, the angry glances, the sudden hush that spread over the crowd at the edge of the road as they passed. Unobtrusively, the Yoriandir slowed his horse a little so that he could cross behind the dwarf and ride on his other side, as Peewit was doing to his right. Kursh's eye flicked to him, but he said nothing.

"—cheeky whoreson," one man said at the edge of the crowd, not bothering to lower his voice, and his companion hawked and spat just in front of the ambassador's horse.

Korimson ignored it and rode on.

"Murderer!" came a sudden cry from the crowd.

The dwarf found the man and gave him a level stare with nothing of fury in it, but the fellow shut his mouth nevertheless.

Somehow there was a tallish beggarman suddenly in front of them. "Welcome back, Guildmaster," he said quietly. His hand flickered in the code of the Watch: Friend.

It took a moment, but Korimson finally recognized him as Lyle Brewer. "Thank you," he acknowledged aloud and signed back, Guard the captain.

Peewit's lips parted in surprise. "I'm all right," he protested, but Brewer acknowledged the request with a nod. From then on he kept pace with their horses, weaving in and out at the verge of the crowd, hat out and wheedling coins from the bystanders.

They rounded the last bend, and there was a cohort of cavalry waiting for them, Jak Cooper, Lord Nevelston, at their head in full uniform, beaming. As they came up, he snapped off a salute that was ostensibly for Imris, a senior officer in the Watch, but his eyes were on the dwarf and the Littleman. "Welcome to Greenbriar, gentlemen. I am your official escort. If you will follow me, ambassador?" The cavalrymen smoothly divided into two ranks and fell back to line the last climb to Queen's Gate.

Kursh rode up next to him. "This is your idea?" he rasped under cover of the horses' hooves on the cobbles.

"They are my own troops," Jak answered blandly. "Nobody said I couldn't."

"It's bloody stupid, Cooper. Ye're putting yourself in the way of a lot of trouble for nothing."

Lord Nevelston's eyes met his directly. "I wouldn't say it was for nothing," he murmured. He turned his head to Peewit. "We got your report, sir. Preparations have been made." He would not refer to the rumor of an assassin where so many people could hear.

"Ah, good. That's a relief." Brickleburr drew a breath. "And how are things between Her Majesty and King Ka-Treer?"

"Chilly," Cooper replied with satisfaction. The gate was swung open for them, and they rode under bows of the sentries. It was by the greatest effort of will that neither the Littleman nor the dwarf looked up to the arrow slits.

They drew up before the marble stairs that led into the main keep, and footmen sprang to take their horses. Doctor Theodric, who had been trained by Fidelis and taken over routine administration of the hospital when the older physician retired, hurried down the steps. "Greetings from Master Fidelis, gentlemen. He intended to be here to meet you himself, but there's been an emergency which required his attention, so he says he will see you later this evening."

"Is it Her Majesty or the prince?" Peewit asked before Kursh could.

The doctor shook his head. "Oh, no. Nothing like that. It's the Lordling's tutor, Master Crumbhollow." He lowered his voice confidentially. "An attack of stone, I'm afraid. But we're dosing him with saxifrage, so he should pass it soon enough. Well, I'd best get back to the ward. Good day to you. Nice to see you again." He nodded in friendly fashion and lumbered off with his oxlike tread.

Lord Nevelston handed his gauntlets to his yeoman and waved the visitors up the stairs. Kursh hesitated, then began to climb, and Peewit followed.

At each landing, the ornate staircase was guarded by Watchmen who snapped to attention for Jak Cooper and the Eldest. Though none was so poorly disciplined as to speak, there were a couple of frank stares and one dark look, and at the top landing where Will Quint's son Thom headed the detachment, a respectful nod.

The fresco hall was crowded with milling courtiers, ambassadors and their retinues, and liveried servants carrying trays of wineglasses and small pastries. Busy conversations in all manner of accented Ilyrian echoed off the painting and the sculpted stone lintels. Over the heads of the crowd, they caught sight of Rhys-Davies, Lord Waterford and chamberlain to the queen, standing at the broad doorway, leaning courteously to hear something the Nabilian ambassador was saying. "Each ambassador is to be announced and received individually by Her Majesty and the Lordling," Jak told them. Kursh paled.

"I will go tell him that you are here," Imris said.

"Wait." The dwarf licked his lips and looked down at the marble floor. He twisted the Guildmaster's ring. When he said no more, Imris and Peewit exchanged a glance. Korimson turned abruptly to the wall and seemed to be studying the painting of the Crystal Keep.

The Littleman turned with him, hands clasped behind him, and waited.

"I can't do this, Peewit! I can't!" Kursh muttered desperately.

Brickleburr gave it a moment, then said carefully, "And I didn't think I could strap myself in and let you push us off the mountain in that damned kite, but I did. You got us through that, my friend. You can get through this, too."

Korimson's head came up and he looked the Littleman full in the face. Peewit raised an eyebrow and cocked his head. Kursh took a breath from the bottom of his boots. "Right," he said, and gave a pull to his eyepatch. "Should have brought the bloody thing: could have flown from here to the ship." There was a wry glint to his eye that Peewit answered with a smile.

The dwarf squared his shoulders and turned to face Nevelston and the Yoriandir. "All right, Imris. Trot along if you will and tell Rhys-Davies the Jarlshof ambassador's here."

"That is news he has waited to hear," the Eldest said with a smile.

"And then make yourself scarce. You, too, Cooper. The captain and I need no wet nurses hanging about." Though his words seemed brisk, they knew he intended no offense.

"They've seated us together at the banquet," Lord Nevelston said, "so you'll have to put up with us then, old boy." Rhys-Davies made the seating arrangements at a function like this, and Jak, of course, had talked to Rhys-Davies. Kursh understood that whatever else happened, he and the Littleman would at least be flanked at dinner by friends.

"Get away with ye," he growled, and Jak gave him a laughing salute and stepped back into the throng. They saw Imris speak to the elderly chamberlain and Rhys-Davies's gravely pleased expression. One white glove lifted to beckon them forward. "Here goes nothing," the dwarf said in a low voice. "Are ye ready, captain?" There was no answer, and he flashed a look around.

"Go on," the Littleman's voice said out of the air. "I'll be close enough to help if it's called for. Otherwise, don't let on about me. I'd like to make my own peace later. Your moment is now."

Kursh nodded, drew a breath, and walked up to the door.

"Good to see you again, sir." Rhys-Davies's melodious diction could make a fellow feel like a prince, the dwarf thought as he followed the black-suited chamberlain up the wide aisle through the crowd, which was even thicker in here than in the corridor outside. Then, as he paced, he was aware of the growing silence.

Bloody, bloody hell, he swore at them in his mind. Stop staring! Haven't ye ever seen a murderer before?

His ears were raging hot, his feet were like ice, and the bone where his knees should have been had turned to jelly. Stiffly, he concentrated on putting one foot in front of the other; it felt exactly like crossing a battlefield to take yourself to the field dressing station to have a wound tended.

Rhys-Davies halted and proclaimed, "Your Majesty, Your Highness, may I present Guildmaster Kursh Korimson, the Jarlshof ambassador." And then the old man stepped aside, and there was nothing between Kursh and Ariadne but twenty paces, thirteen years, and one corpse.

Ariadne had seen him come in; she had been looking for him all afternoon, and Will Quint had bent a few minutes ago to say that the Jarlshof party was on its way up the Sweep. The well-remembered figure strode along behind Rhys-Davies, looking neither left nor right. She had never seen him out of uniform, and that was something of a shock, but it was so incidental to the turmoil in her heart that it flew out of her mind. . . . The ax bright red, the grass splattered with gore, her baby—the awful seared stump. *What will you say to him, Ariadne?* she shrieked to herself. Her ears rang so that she did not even note the tomblike silence of her hall.

Rhys-Davies's voice echoed: ". . . the Jarlshof ambassador." He stepped away.

Staring, she saw Kursh's hand clench into a fist for a moment, and then he took the prescribed five paces and went to one knee, head bowed. "Greetings, Qu—Queen of Ilyria," he began haltingly. "My . . ."

My duty to Your Majesty, she finished the stock formula she had heard repeated over and over again this day, and then I must say something to him, she thought with panic.

Kursh cleared his throat and tried again, one hand gripping his bent knee fiercely. "My duty t . . ." His head ducked another few inches and she could see the thinning hairs carefully coaxed over the balding spot. For some reason, she felt the iron fist in the pit of her stomach begin to unclench. He sucked a breath, and his head came up, eye tightly shut. "My duty to Your Majesty." Having gotten it out he opened his one eye, and it was brimming in the squares of light laid down by the Rose Window.

They might have been the only ones in the hall.

A small voice in the secret closet of her heart said, Be honest with yourself, Robin. You've heaped him with your own guilt because you knew that day, aye, even before, that you were in love with Alphonse.

True, she answered herself slowly. True. I did.

Her vision blurred suddenly, and at her heart's urging her hands went out to him. "Kursh, you old lummox, get up."

He went white and his lips parted. Then a wave of color washed through his face, and he lurched up to take her hands. Four frozen lumps clasped each other. "I'm sorry—" he began, and "I know. It's all right," she cut him off. "It's all right. Now." Her smile widened like a spring morning. "Powers, we've waited too long for this!" she told him in a whisper.

"Aye, well, the pair of us are so thick ye could pound nails with us," he allowed, a ghost of a smile buried in his beard.

She grinned and raised him up. But there was still one last thing. Ariadne beckoned forward the silent and unmoving boy who had stood behind her throne. "Ambassador, may I present my son, Prince Gerrit Greenbriar."

No need, the dwarf thought. I knew him once.

He steeled himself and looked into the smoldering gray eyes. No, there was no trace of the little one he had carried on his shoulders and piped to. The dwarf bowed. "Your Highness. Jarlshof sends felicitations for your birthday."

Gerrit's voice was cool, but correct. "Thank you, ambassador."

Korimson drew out the gold silk bag. "If I may be allowed to present a gift, a small token in honor of the occasion?"

The Lordling did not acknowledge the request, but Ariadne leaned back in her throne and nodded, pleased. A murmur ran around the hall, and people tried to crane for a view without seeming to do so. Kursh unwrapped and held up the Weatherglass, and the facets threw reflections of the Rose Window in a river of color down the aisle. There were gasps and exclamations of awe. The dwarf held the price of a king's ransom in his hand.

Kursh bowed and held the crystal sphere out to Gerrit. "With our best wishes," he said quietly.

The Greenbriar Lordling took a step forward, leaned slightly from the step, and took the gift. His face was stone as he studied first the dwarf and then the shining thing in his hand.

"It is a Weatherglass, Your Highness," the ambassador explained.

"I know what it is," Ariadne's son said curtly. "Is it Jarlshof's gift, or yours?"

The queen reddened. She looked to her son and seemed about to speak to him when Kursh answered steadily, "The guild sends it in token of the long friendship between Ilyria and Jarlshof." His voice dropped somewhat. "I crafted it myself, Lordling."

"I see. In that case . . ." He drew his arm back and hurled the Weatherglass to the cinnamon marble floor, where it crashed in a thousand fiery fragments. Into the stunned silence the prince grated, "I do not want it." He leaped off the platform and strode for the side door, crunching glass under his boots and one hand lifting to jerk a sign at the bodyguards who had jumped to follow him. They hesitated and looked to the queen.

"Gerrit!" Ariadne, her deepest misgivings confirmed, stared after him. Her gaze fell to Kursh, who stood still, regarding the shards around his feet. "My apologies, ambassador."

The dwarf's eye came up. "Unnecessary, Your Majesty." He added from the dregs of bitterness, "I understand." His shoulders squared. "And now I'll go back down to my boat. I have no wish to press my welcome. By your leave?"

Trembling and trying not to show it, Ariadne gripped the carved armrests. "Sleep aboard your own vessel if you wish, ambassador, though rooms are made ready for you. But surely you will stay to dine with us and share the evening's entertainment." She swept a look around the hall, knowing that whatever she did now would establish how Kursh would be regarded in the future. The queen looked down at the former First Watchman and summoned a smile for him alone. "We have no wish to be without your company, I do assure you."

Subtly, the tension went out of him, but still he glanced toward the doorway where Gerrit had gone. "But the Lordling, my queen?"

She took a moment to choose her words carefully. "What

is between you and my son is for the future, my lord ambassador. For now, let us deal together as well as we may. We of Ilyria welcome the continuance of the close ties that exist between ourselves and our staunch allies of Jarlshof. Relative to that, we shall ask a portion of your time for a private conference sometime during your visit."

Kursh bowed. "My time is entirely at your disposal, my queen."

She extended her hand, and he kissed it. Quietly so that the court could not hear, she murmured, "The Glass was beautiful, Kursh."

"I think he would have liked it." He pulled at the eyepatch, straightened, and followed Rhys-Davies away.

Gerrit slammed through the garden gate and made a rude gesture of dismissal to the archers on the battlement. They took themselves away, one to each turret, and he was left alone with the crisp breeze to cool his burning cheeks and the bare branches of the birch for company.

His hands were shaking and his stomach felt as if he might be coming down with something. How *dare* that whoreson old bastard try to buy him off with a piece of his sodding crystal!

Angrily the prince grabbed a stone out of the border of a flower bed and whipped it far down toward the sundial on the slate terrace.

A quiet voice said behind him, "Careful. You've broken enough for today, don't you think?"

Gerrit whirled. There stood a small figure with curly gray hair, who was lightly buffing an apple filched from the refreshment table on a patched cloak. Though Peewit could not have known, he was at that instant a figure of greater terror for Ariadne's son than a raving, ax-wielding dwarf would have been.

The prince's mouth fell open, and then he suddenly felt for the stone bench against his knee and sat down hard. While Peewit snapped back into his stillness spell to protect himself in case the archers had seen, the Greenbriar heir bent forward with his head between his knees and gave up to the familiar nightmare. . . .

It had begun innocently enough on a summer's night almost six months ago. There had been hunting and hawking for three days past to tire them all out a bit. Then they had played a delicious prank on the prince's bodyguard, Lieutenant Rory Fisher, and left that young man behind their pounding hoofbeats to explain his state of undress and the girl's giggling to her apoplectic uncle. No doubt he would catch up with them soon, and no doubt when he did there would be sulfur in the air, but till then they were all off the leash. They paid a pittance for two tuns of blackest stout in the village and carried the barrels off despite the landlord's cries of outrage. Now the moon was at the full, the woods warm, and the restraints of court etiquette a day's ride away. It was the last day of this hunting outing, and Gerrit and his friends were determined to make the most of it.

They had drained one of the kegs and were at work on the second when Duncan Tregallis, second son of the Duke of Ottergard and Gerrit's closest companion, stretched his booted feet out comfortably in front of him and looked over the leaping blaze at him. "We should have a song, you know. Can't have a decent party 'thout a song. Pity the Eldest's not here. We could use a harper."

Gerrit burped into his gauntlet and grimaced at the sour taste. "Master Imris isn't due in from Yoriand to see Mother for weeks yet, and anyway, he wouldn't like to play for a bunch of drunken pisspots like us." He grinned crookedly.

The son and heir of Hilliard neBlackmore raised his head from where he had pillowed it on a fallen tree trunk. "Old fart doesn't know anything worth listening to, anyway," he snorted.

There was a sudden hush around the crackling logs. Slowly the Greenbriar prince levered himself onto one elbow and fed a stick to the fire. He fixed neBlackmore with a stare. "The Eldest of the Yoriandirkin has forgotten more than you'll learn in a lifetime, Humfrey," he said quietly. His face twisted and he spat. "By the Powers, you're enough to give ergot a good name, neBlackmore."

neBlackmore pulled himself to a sitting position, his mouth setting in the hard line that meant he was getting ready for a fight: they'd all seen it often enough in Senior Squire's class to read him like a book.

Tregallis threw his head back and laughed, a lusty guffaw that rolled through the woods, and at the release of tension the others laughed, too. Humfrey grudgingly joined in, because he really had no choice. Gerrit gave it no more than an amused smile and a raised eyebrow, so as not to rub it in too much. You couldn't really trust a man if you'd ground his nose in the midden heap. He picked up his wooden mug and gulped some beer. "Besides, you know, that song of his—'Marian the Fair'—isn't exactly tame."

"Which is why he never sings it before your mother the queen," contributed short and round Toby Naismith, next lord of Lower Tilton. "I've only ever heard it from my father's soldiers."

Tregallis sat up and waved the rest to do the same. "Sing!"

So the woods rang with as many verses of the old marching song as they could patch together from their collective memories, sloshing stout over the rims of their mugs and yelling the refrain. The nightingales were silenced awhile.

When the song petered out finally, the Lordling surveyed his troop. "Powers, there isn't one of us who could carry a note in a bucket. No more singing! The peasants roundabouts will think we're at murder and butchery out here!" They laughed or blew rude noises at him and sucked down more beer.

"A tale, that's what we need." Toby sat up and looked about expectantly.

"Fine. Tell one," Humfrey yawned, pillowing his head once more.

"I can't," the chunky Naismith refused disgustedly. "You know I'm no good at it." He poked Tregallis in the ribs, and incited the rest of the boys with significant nods and much eyebrow waggling. "But we know who is!"

There was a chorus of "Tregallis!" and "Yea, Dunc!" until Tregallis groaned and threw up his hands in mock surrender. "All right, all right, by the Realms!" He sighed and flicked a pine needle off his sleeve. "What do you want to hear?"

"A horror story," neBlackmore demanded with relish.

"No, Toby'll foul himself," another youth jibed. "Better make it a romance," he advised, hands clasped at his heart in imitation of Festil, the court singer.

Tregallis looked across the fire. "My prince? What would you hear?"

Gerrit swilled some beer around in his mouth reflectively, then swallowed. "Something with honor in it." One shoulder lifted in shrug. "I leave it to your choice."

"All right," Tregallis said thoughtfully, scraping mud off one insole against the heel of his other boot. While the rest settled to hear him, he wet his throat. They looked to him and he glanced around. "I'll tell you the story of Rose and Tychanor, then." He drew his long legs up and sat cross-legged staring into the flames. "Long ago—aye, and longer than that—there lived Rose, fairest of all women, born of the Hearthfolk, who were the first to walk Morning's Meadows. She was the beloved of Tychanor, Lord of the Warm Fire, and such was the feeling between them that it filled the Meadows with joy overflowing."

"I'll bet," neBlackmore snorted.

"But the Unnamed, who had not yet fallen as low as he would, marked the glow that shone in his brother's eye and the maiden's blush. And for that he was comely himself and proud of it—and the elder of the two Brothers—he began to woo Rose with fair words and gifts of hunter's skill. But Rose's heart was tucked in Tychanor's jerkin, and though she treated the Unnamed with all courtesy, never did her eye turn to follow him out of sight, and the Wild Fire knew it.

"Now at that time the twin Lords of Fire were very alike in form and countenance, and only the golden cloak Tychanor wore, woven of sunbeams, distinguished them one from the other. Once on a morning, Tychanor put it aside while he helped a mare bring twin foals into the world's light. The Unnamed saw his chance.

"Casting the bright cloak about his shoulders, the Wild Fire went seeking Rose. In the dell by the Mother of Waters he found her and began to say soft words to her, and being deceived by the golden cloak. Rose listened. But of a sudden, she drew away, staring wildly. 'Your eyes!' she gasped. 'You are not my lord!' So saying she sprang up from his embrace. The Unnamed was wroth and sprang after her.

"Through the trees Rose fled, back through the hollow in the hills, past the Mother of Waters. And ever his footsteps were right behind her, though she dared not look back. Of that race, none can know the terror, but the Dark now was the same Dark then, and you would not want it behind you and you all alone."

Nervous glances went to the night woods beyond the perimeter of firelight.

"Rose raised up her voice and cried, 'Tychanor!'

"In Morning's Meadow, the Warm Fire heard the voice of his beloved and reached for his cloak of Power, but it was not there. And, 'Tychanor!' she shrieked again, desperate now, for she could feel Fire behind her, a scorch of the hair, a singe of wool.

"Out of the wood she raced toward the sun, and behind her came a huge black form draped in a cloak of gold. Tychanor ground his teeth and sprang forward to save her, crying, 'Hold, Brother!'

"But for Rose, caught between the Fires, it was too late. If she stopped, she would be consumed by the Unnamed's Fire. If she ran on the last few steps, Tychanor would attack his Brother and in that moment of fury become even like him. She chose for life. Rose let go her self, and her Light rose up pure and cool between the Brothers.

" 'No!' Tychanor cried. 'Oh, my love, do not go, for I cannot go with you!'

"The Unnamed just stared and turned away, letting the golden cloak slip to the ground. 'There. There's your power, little Brother. Go with your mortal leman,' he said bitterly, hoping in this way to lure Tychanor into a fight.

"But the Warm saw the trick for what it was and pitied the hurt behind the words. And the Unnamed could not stand such love and he went darkly away to brood.

"Standing afar in her springtime glade, Ritnym of the Earth shook her head. As Rose poured her life back into the Light, the Lady of Earth raised her hand, and there at Tychanor's feet sprouted Rose's spirit in a flower, nodding to her lord, the Sun. And that was some easing for Tychanor, though he wept to see her whom he had loved so changed. 'But I cannot follow you,' he murmured, touching with one finger the soft petals.

" 'Be of good cheer,' his sister Ritnym told him. 'Ever shall she come back to you in springtime, and at the end of our days, maybe you two will have joy of one another again.'

"So Tychanor keeps his love for Rose bright and looks ever for her coming to him across the Meadows of Morning."

The young lord of Otterard raised his head. "The end."

There was a round of applause, which Tregallis lurched to his feet to accept with a bow, nearly toppling into the fire. Gerrit threw out a restraining hand, "Whoa, steady!"

Toby Naismith shook his head. "I don't see how you memorize all that old stuff."

Duncan shrugged and eased himself back to a sitting position. "Runs in the family. My mother's people are great tale-tellers."

One of the other boys winked. "Must have some Teazle blood in him," he suggested lewdly and ducked Tregallis's cuff.

Toby Naismith frowned. "The Littlemen don't mate with others," he said innocently.

"No," Humfrey neBlackmore snickered. "The Little*men* don't, idiot."

Gerrit picked up his mug once more, idly wagging a finger at them. "Careful," he warned. "Auntie may hear you."

neBlackmore rolled his eyes. "Oo, now, that scares me."

"It should," the prince countered lightly. "If you're a bad boy, you'll get no cradle-bunny come Kindlefest." He grinned at their chorus of hoots and made a rude gesture. All of them had long outgrown the nursery tales of the old Hearthwoman who went about unseen bringing marvelous, sometimes magical stuffed toys to good children at the Celebration of the Sun.

neBlackmore picked his teeth. "I don't think there are any Teazles anymore. Maybe there never were."

Duncan objected, "There was Captain Brickleburr."

"Who says he was a Teazle? I'd wager he was just a freak—a midget, maybe, or a dwarf of some kind."

Toby threw a stick into the fire. "I wonder where the old captain went."

"Drop it," the prince snapped. "I'll hear no talk of him."

Knowing why, they all shut up abruptly, and there was only the crackle of the fire for a few moments until Tregallis had tipped the rest of his beer down his throat and gone to the keg set up on a rock to pull himself another. Turning with the dripping mug in his hand, he said, "I'll tell you what I'd like—I'd like to catch a Teazle sometime and get one of their golden boxes."

Some of the boys guffawed, and one sat up to ask, "Powers, Tregallis, you don't believe that rot, do you? Seriously?"

Duncan wiped foam from the light down that would become a beard. "The country people have been telling stories about Teazles and their magic boxes for generations. I just figure where there's smoke, there's fire, as the saying goes." He looked around at them. "And if the stories are true, and you could get hold of one of the Folk and his gold, you'd be some damn rich, now wouldn't you?" There were some interested looks. He waved expansively. "Hell, I could probably pay off his lordship over there however much it is that I owe him now."

"Two months' allowance," Gerrit reminded him complacently.

Duncan swore under his breath, only half joking; Gerrit's luck at dice was phenomenal. "Anyway, I've always had a mind to try it sometime. Just for a lark, you know. And recently I got one of our crofters to teach me an old song that's supposed to be foolproof for attracting Teazles."

Naismith looked up through the branches. "It's a full moon tonight," he said hopefully. That was one of the ingredients necessary for catching a Teazle, according to old stories.

"And we are twelve," Duncan said significantly. That was another.

"And it's summer, in a lonely place," another contributed.

In an instant the wild idea caught fire. "Let's do it! Come on, Gerrit, what do you say?"

He stifled a yawn with the back of his hand. "Oh, hell, why not? Anything for a laugh tomorrow when we get back to duty and studies." He stretched. "All right, Captain Duncan, you're the leader of this expedition. What's to do?"

"Fireflies," the other answered promptly. "Got to have fireflies."

"I've got a bottle to put them in!" Toby volunteered, digging through his pack.

"All right," Tregallis acknowledged. "That's the first order of business, then: everyone go out and catch as many fireflies as he can for the lure. Meanwhile, Gerrit and I will be drawing the figure on the ground here to hold the little bugger when we catch him." Because the Littlemen could become invisible, folklore dictated that the only way to confine one was within the matrix of a rayed sun.

Amid much laughter, the young lords scattered out of the campsite to chase the flickering lights through the undergrowth.

Gerrit still sat against his log. "This is the most asinine idea you've ever proposed, Tregallis."

"I know," Duncan chuckled, stooping to take a pointed stick from the supply near the fire. "But they went for it, didn't they? What a joke!" He looked up, grinning. "Even neBlackmore's out there, running into trees in the dark, looking for damn fireflies!"

They both began to laugh, and the harder they tried not to let hoots escape them, the worse it got. There was a sudden halloo from Toby returning, and the prince quickly scrambled to help Duncan draw the figure in the mulch of the forest floor, wiping his eyes on the shoulder of his doublet.

The troop came back noisily, stumbling into the clearing with the beer making its effect felt. "Here you go!" Naismith proclaimed, triumphantly holding the bottle aloft. "Must be a hundred of them!"

Tregallis cleared his throat and got his face in order. "Well done! Now, if you'll all take your places, gentlemen—one at each point we've marked with an X." He pointed, and they jostled to their positions, elbowing each other in the ribs.

Duncan and Gerrit were the last two to take their places. "All set?" Tregallis asked. The others nodded, a couple of them weaving slightly. There were smiles all around. "Very well, but remember: no one's to move from his post or we'll lose the Littleman."

neBlackmore muttered, "Just as if it were going to work."

"No mumbling there, Sir Humfrey," Tregallis told him crisply. "Here we go." He began to whistle.

Minutes later he was massaging his cheeks where the muscles were tiring when the beer keg toppled from the rock where they had set it and crashed apart, spewing what remained of the malt liquor over Toby Naismith and one of the other lads. Naismith drew a breath that was little short of a terrified shriek and threw himself across the circle. As the rest of the squires were still trying to figure out what had happened, a giggle came out of the dark. "Don't be whistling for help if you're not prepared for it when it comes!"

Tregallis froze.

"Son of a whore! It worked!" neBlackmore whooped and leaped the fire to run into the forest toward the voice. His shout galvanized the drunken band, and they jumped after him, yelling hunting calls.

Duncan winked at the prince. "Aren't you coming?"

Gerrit waved him off. "Go on! I'm no good in a foot chase, dammit! Go get him!"

Tregallis raced away. Gerrit listened after his troop. Across the fire by the shattered keg a small curly-haired figure flickered into view. "For shame, Gerrit Greenbriar. You have better Blood than this," the Hearthman said quietly.

The prince started and his hand dropped to his dagger by reflex, but he mastered himself and did not draw it, merely staring open-mouthed for a moment. Then his chin came up and he made a slight bow. " 'Tis naught but a prank, Master Teazle. We meant no harm."

The small figure nodded. "And I mean none to you boys. But you've used an emergency Summoning song you'd no business knowing, and you've taken me from an urgent errand for this foolishness. I'm afraid I'll have to see that the Matriarch hears about it. Now, good night to you and do be more considerate—"

Gerrit was framing a question about this Matriarch when there was a blur through the firelight, followed by a sickening thud. The Hearthman crumpled to the forest floor.

"Ha!" came the triumphant bellow. "Got him!" Humfrey neBlackmore came through the brush, sling in hand. "That ought to hold the little bastard until we can bind him."

Gerrit stared, his stomach turning, and then he jumped toward the small figure. Gingerly he reached to draw back the cloak that had fallen to cover the Littleman's head, but immediately he pulled the cloak back over the dreadful wound. Powers, I could put my fist in that hollow! he thought, suddenly sober.

When he rounded on neBlackmore, most of the rest of the band had come back and were staring down at the body. Gerrit's eyes blazed. "You poxy whoreson! Can't you ever think of something besides killing?" He threw a punch that split neBlackmore's lip. The squire angrily countered with a jab to the ribs that whoofed the air out, and then they were fighting in earnest until the other boys pulled them apart and sat on neBlackmore to keep him down.

Gerrit shook off the restraining arms, and because he was the prince, they had to let him go. Slowly he controlled himself, breathing hard and flicking blood off his chin. He could feel his cheekbone already swelling, and there was a cut that had barely missed his eye. Coldly he stared down at neBlackmore. "You damned murderer."

By now the other youth had quit struggling, beginning to realize what his attack on the Lordling could cost him. Sullenly he said, "You were as keen on the idea of catching a

Teazle as the rest of us, I noticed. It's not like I *meant* to kill him, by the Powers." Suddenly he roared, "Get off me, all of you!" Uncertainly, they looked to Gerrit. After a moment he nodded shortly, and they let neBlackmore to his feet.

The Greenbriar prince stared neBlackmore down. When the other dropped his eyes and glanced at the small body, Gerrit slowly nodded. "You're right. It was my fault."

Duncan Tregallis said at his elbow, "No, my prince. It was mine."

"It was all of us together," Toby said positively. "Any one of us might have tripped over him and hurt him." His eyes drifted to the body. "I didn't know they were so little," he murmured.

Tregallis scuffed at the fire in the silence that followed. "What are we going to do?"

The prince answered, "Take him home to Greenbriar for burial. He deserves that, at least."

There were wary looks. "But then we'll have to tell what happened," Toby ventured.

"Yes."

They looked from one to another, neBlackmore spat blood, and his eyes narrowed. "And how are you going to explain why Lieutenant Fisher wasn't here?"

At once, each of them saw the problem. If Fisher was found derelict in his duty, no matter that they had played a trick on him, he would be stripped of his rank and severely punished. By owning to their crime, they would bring Fisher down with them.

For several moments, Gerrit considered, maintaining a stone face while they waited tensely. "Right," he said finally. "I won't sacrifice Rory for you." He put a finger in neBlackmore's chest. "But from this night forward, I own you."

Tregallis put a hand on his arm, afraid that the fight would break out again. "You do anyway, my prince. You own all of us. We're your men."

"Shut up, Dunc. This has nothing to do with you, so stay out of it."

Tregallis bowed and moved back.

The prince told neBlackmore, "No more bullying the younger boys, the pages. From now on you're as nice as pie, Humfrey. Folk will marvel at the change, I bet. And just to be sure, I'll put you on your Oath. Come now—let's hear it."

neBlackmore was plainly seething, but he had apparently decided that he'd already done himself enough harm that night, for he snapped a salute of the First Watch and intoned, "Heart, mind, and spirit his. Hand, eye, and body his. My blood for the Blood, now and forever." Even though none of them was yet accepted into the Watch, they all hoped to be, and one day that Oath would bind them to Gerrit as their liege. Humfrey neBlackmore was just taking his pledge a little early.

When the other boy had finished, Gerrit nodded. "All right." He swept a look around the band of them. "That's the last any of us speaks of this. Ever." Solemnly they saluted. Gerrit's look went to the Littleman. "Let's get him decently buried out in the woods, and then I want to get out of here. We'll mount up and ride slowly toward home, and Lieutenant Fisher should catch us up within a couple of hours. He'll see the evidence of a fight between Humfrey and myself, and that should be enough to explain why we broke camp. Keep your mouths shut, and we'll come out of it well enough. To work."

In short order, some of them had dug as deep a grave as possible with their daggers, and, wrapping the Hearthman in his cloak, they laid him to rest. Tregallis tried to say something appropriate that none of them could afterward remember for staring at the small bundle. When Duncan would have scooped some earth over the body, Gerrit stayed him with a gesture and knelt on one knee. "Fare thee well, sir," he said softly. "Powers bless you." From the shoulder of his cloak he unpinned a brooch set with a ruby, a gift from his mother some years before. This he laid on the Littleman's chest. "It's all I have with me for honoring you." Then, carefully, he took a double handful of the moist earth and spilled it slowly over the body. The other boys helped and soon it was done. They fluffed some leaves over the spot.

It was just as they finished and were turning back up the hill that Duncan tripped over the small knapsack. "My lord!" he called tightly. "What will we do with this?"

Gerrit nearly groaned. He bent over to pick up the small canvas bag. "Bloody hell. I never even thought to look for one." Even as he spoke, idle curiosity made him unstrap it. In the torch's wavering light, they could all see the golden box, lying right on top. The prince's eyes went to his best friend's. "Looks as if the old tales are true," he said quietly.

Duncan looked sick. "Powers, I never really thought—" The other squires were wide-eyed and silent. "We should have buried it with him."

"No doubt," Gerrit agreed. "But there's no time to do the thing properly now. We'll have to take it with us before Fisher finds us all standing here, gawking." He put the small pack under his cloak. "Not a word," he warned them. "Especially not to Humfrey." The bruised squire had gone with an oath to keep watch on the road. There were sober nods from the rest of the boys.

By the time they returned to the campsite, Toby had directed the packing up, and the horses were saddled and ready. Tregallis held the prince's horse, and Gerrit swung into the saddle. "All right, gentlemen. To Greenbriar." He wheeled his mount and led them back to the moonlit road.

The nightmare had taken no more than a moment, as memories do, and Gerrit became aware of the cold stone bench under him. He raised his head.

A warm unseen hand touched his arm. "Brace up, lad. I'll leave for now, if you like."

Ariadne's son bit the inside of his lip and straightened, cursing himself for a fool because he knew now who it must be. He said quietly, "No need. You can come out now, Captain Brickleburr. It isn't as though I were going to kill you or anything, after all."

Chapter Six

❧

"You're taking a real chance coming here," Gerrit said, straightening his surcoat abruptly and turning up the collar of his cloak.

Peewit let his eyes roam the queen's garden, a smile of remembrance on his weary face. "Ah, good," he murmured.

"That little pear sapling lived. There was an ice storm that winter, and I wondered about it." The espaliered tree, a beautifully pruned tracery against the southern wall, showed wine-colored fruiting spurs. The Littleman turned to face the prince and studied the tense young face with the same attention he had given the pear tree. After a moment he said, "He'd worked hard on that Glass, Lordling, and had come far—very far—to lay it in your hand."

Gerrit sat as stiff as new leather. "I did not ask him to."

"You'll receive many gifts in your life you haven't asked for," the captain countered.

The gray eyes were on a level with his standing. "A new foot and father would do."

The Littleman bowed wordlessly, then measured the young man. "Both would be nice to have, but I seriously doubt from what I hear you really need either."

Gerrit flushed and his chin came up. "Why, what do you hear?"

Peewit gestured at the bench. "May I?"

People didn't sit in His Highness's presence, the Littleman divined instantly, but after a moment Gerrit made room for him. "Thank you, my prince. I have been a little troubled lately, and it is good to rest." He sniffed deeply of the woodsmoke tang drifting over the boxwood hedge from all the cooking fires on the Sweep and dangled his crossed feet comfortably from the stone bench. "Well, I've made a business the past few years of looking into some things that needed looking into, and I hear many things from many quarters. Now, on the one hand there are accounts of bawdy houses and drinking contests, of property taken from country folk at the point of a dagger, of casual hunts where the game is left to rot. All these pieces add up to the very picture of a wild young rapscallion who, if you will pardon my free speech, is exactly the sort of fellow we threw out of this castle just about nineteen years ago."

The prince's jaw was tight. "And if I choose to enjoy life, what is that to you, Mister Brickleburr?"

Not Master Brickleburr, Peewit noted, just Mister: the title one might give a servant. He had stung the youth. Good. He rocked back to lace his hands around one up-drawn knee. "It doesn't matter a wormy apple," he lied cheerfully. "But I'm intrigued by puzzles, and what I don't understand is the other stories."

Gerrit might be good at dice, as Peewit had heard, but he had much to learn of chess, for he blurted, "What other stories?" before he remembered he was pretending not to care.

The Littleman took his time about answering, lifting his face to the sun and watching a flock of birds winging southward high against the clouds. "There is the matter of that Barrener boy your lady mother took into the cadets. I understand young neBlackmore gave him harsh words and more until it got to such a point that even the men-at-arms were talking about it. One day, I hear, neBlackmore emptied the sand out of the quintain and loaded it with scrap lead, and when the Barrener made his practice run at it, the thing swung around and cracked him in the head so hard Fidelis couldn't bring him to for a day and a half. The next day, neBlackmore was found draped over a water trough in the stables, his nose broken and his eye a glorious dark sunset." The Littleman followed the overhead race of some rooks. "Given that neBlackmore's father is a rich and powerful lord who is married to a woman your mother regards as her sister, I think it unlikely that a mere earl's or duke's son would have given the little sneak a drubbing, however richly deserved. Don't you think it unlikely, my lord?"

Ariadne's son bent to fiddle with his boot. "Earls' and dukes' sons have been known to make the occasional error in judgment."

"Not without neBlackmore squealing on them." That brought a quick glance, and Peewit smiled to himself. "Then, of course, there is the little-told tale of the farmer whose poor old plowhorse took fright one day at the troop of hell-for-leather hunters that swept past. It tried to leap the pasture wall and broke its leg." There was a definite wince. "The farmer has a fine plowhorse now, strong, fattened on the finest oats. As the fellow tells it in the local tavern, the new horse was tethered in his byre one morning when, in desperation, he went out to strap himself into the harness and drag the plow into the field." Peewit's eyebrows went up and his voice took on the comically puzzled tones of the farmer. "And he has *no idea* where it came from or how it got there." The old leaves skittered underfoot, chased around the bench by a catspaw of breeze.

"Sounds like Teazles' work."

Peewit chuckled. "A tall one, maybe." Their eyes met;

Gerrit looked quickly away, but not before a smile made it to his lips and was stifled, like a child scolded for gawking at a stranger. "Last, but certainly not least, there was the little girl who went through the ice while she was out skating with her brothers last winter down at Coll's Corner. A young noble, heavily cloaked and hooded against the cold, rode by with his hawk on his fist and a Watchman in attendance, heard the children's panicked screams, and went in after her. His man pulled them both out, the two took the little one home with the brothers trailing after, and then left so hastily that the overwrought parents were never able to say their thanks." The prince's ears were red and he shoved his hands under him and looked off toward the postern into the castle without responding. The Littleman said gently, "They asked me, if I ever saw you again, to convey their gratitude. The life of a child is precious beyond price."

Gerrit swallowed. "So, what do you make of this puzzle?"

"What do *you* make of it?" The startled gray eyes met his own. "That is rather the question, isn't it?"

The prince looked away again. "That people may be other than they seem," he suggested quietly.

"Yes. Like Kursh, for instance."

The young jaw firmed. "If you think you've trapped me into admitting that point, think again. He's a murderer."

Peewit shifted, opened the pouch at his belt, and held up a brooch set with a ruby. "So are you," he said quietly.

You'd have thought it was a snake striking. Gerrit sprang up and was four paces toward the postern before the Littleman could say, "You're not the running type, Gerrit Greenbriar. You have better Blood than that."

Ariadne's son jerked to a halt, back rigid. He whirled. His lips worked and then he croaked, "That's what he said! How did you know that? How?"

Peewit held his eye and slid off the bench to quietly approach. He stood looking up at the tall youth. "I have no idea what you're talking about." He fingered the brooch. "I found this two months ago. Mu—a friend and I chanced to be camping in a small clearing off the road. I went down to the little stream to fill the water bucket. There were signs that the creek had flooded last spring in all that rain we had. At any rate . . ." He fought the memory. "There were bones, small but not a child's, and this. I know this brooch, Gerrit. I knew to whom it had been given. What I don't know is why it should possibly be in a Hearthman's grave unless it was a guilt offering."

The deserted garden was quiet. Gerrit kept silent, thinking hard.

The former captain sighed. "I've never met any of my kin," he said softly. "Still, I am the nearest to him in blood of anyone present, so I believe I have the right to demand a kinsman's death boon."

The boy with the Briar embroidered on his surcoat stared down at him, and Peewit knew he was not seeing him, but another gray-haired Littleman. Gerrit wet his lips. "If I told you I did not kill him, would you believe me?"

His hands were knotted at his sides, and a pulse was jumping in his neck. Slowly Brickleburr nodded. "I might, but I would still hold you responsible to me."

"I could accept that, sir." He straightened. "It is, you see, a matter of another's honor."

"What honor can there be in a crime that never comes out, my prince? If it's honor you're concerned with, I will give you a model: one who has lived branded with a moment's madness for thirteen years and has never refused that burden, even though he was clearly touched by the Unnamed at the time, and even though you never had to fight the Wild Fire and we did!" He knew his eyes were blazing and his face was hot. "If you don't believe me, ask the wizard someday what Kursh Korimson did on Barak-Gambrel."

In the face of his anger, Gerrit said nothing for a moment. Then he asked, "You mentioned a kinsman's death boon. What would you ask of me? I'll grant it if I may."

Peewit demanded, "Forgiveness."

"For the dwarf?"

"Yes."

Gerrit looked away. "I can't pledge something I can't give." He looked down at the small figure. "Would a chance to reclaim his former place in my mother's affections do?"

The Littleman smiled slightly. "I think so. Kursh is pretty good at beating the odds."

"The water was *bloody* cold," the dwarf agreed to Jak Cooper's speculation, the memory of the flotsam under the dark dawn sending a shiver down the back of his neck.

Imris said thoughtfully, "Roste?"

"Aye. The damn swine." Kursh drank off his goblet of Nabilian wine. A servingman appeared at his elbow to take the empty, and the Jarlshof ambassador lifted another from the tray. This one he merely sipped, however, making an effort to relax and look around casually. The queen had finished receiving them all and now had retired to dress for dinner while her guests made small talk and wondered how they could eat a banquet on top of the appetizers.

Lord Nevelston took a swallow of his own drink, waiting until two other guests had walked past before murmuring, "We've had shipping attacked, too. I've suspected the ear-gem fellows for a long time, but never have been able to prove it."

"Well, I've got all the proof I need."

The Eldest reminded him quietly, "It cannot be here, Kursh: both you and Ka-Treer are under the queen's royal protection."

"I know, I know," the dwarf rasped impatiently. "I'll not foul the nest, never fear." He straightened the eyepatch. "Unless His Royal Bastard Majesty tries to start anything for me or my men while we're here."

"Have a care not to—" Jak began to say, grasping Kursh's arm. His eyes widened in surprise, and he quickly tried to cover his dismay. "You're armed!"

"I am." The dwarf sipped.

"Kursh, it's treason to come into audience with the queen bearing a hidden weapon!"

The ambassador stroked his beard and looked around. "I know," he admitted, "but I wasn't sure of my reception, and now I'm stuck with the damned thing. Hope the Watch isn't quite as sharp as it used to be, present company excepted, of course."

Imris found his voice. "But Ka-Treer knows you always carried a dagger. Many people know it." The three of them fell silent, then reluctantly the Yoriandir pointed out, "It would make the perfect pretext, Kursh. And because of the . . . trouble . . . people would believe instantly the awful implication he would surely make of it. You must get rid of it!"

The dwarf gave him an exasperated look. "Do tell. Why don't ye give them all a mind shout and tell them to look away while I toss it into the punchbowl!"

"Powers!" Jak suddenly swore. "Here he comes!" He moved to intercept the Shimarrat party.

Immediately the Eldest threw his arm across his old friend's shoulders, azure cloak swirling with the movement, and walked with him toward the food table. To all appearances they were happily renewing memories.

From behind them a voice suddenly said above the clamor of the reception, "Ho, there, Watchman! There's work for you, I think." People nearby turned to see who had spoken so loudly, and what he had said.

Neither Kursh nor Imris took any note, deliberating now over a choice of pastries. A hush began to spread until Korimson's voice could be heard saying cheerfully, ". . . still makes the best blueberry muffins you ever tasted in your life."

"Does she?" the Eldest was laughing.

"Ambassador." The voice cracked like an ice-rimed sail.

Kursh turned in feigned surprise. Ka-Treer, a blaze of blue robe and gold circlet, stood not five paces away, with his retinue grouped about him. A Watchman in full dress uniform stood with them, obviously puzzled. The dwarf looked up at them. "King." It was not at all the correct form of address.

The Shimarrat darkened, but there was a satisfied smile carved on his lips. He came directly to it: "You are, of course, well aware of court etiquette, ambassador."

"I'm aware of *this* court's etiquette." It was a subtle point not lost on the listeners, who were by now closing in like terriers on a rat cage: Ka-Treer was throwing his weight around where he had no business doing so.

"Ah, I am glad to hear that Jarlshof is so well represented," the king drawled. He rearranged a fold of his cloak over one arm. "I thought you might have forgotten, being so long gone."

"I very rarely forget things, Lord of Shimarrat." The one eyes was steady, and if looks could have killed, the Shimarrat would have had a splinter of ice through his heart on the spot.

Ka-Treer flashed a tight smile. "Neither do we, ambassador, neither do we."

Maybe it was his imagination, but Jak Cooper could swear he felt the air crackling. His hand flickered in a code to the archers' gallery.

"Well, aren't we the good scholars, though?" Kursh said complacently and sipped his wine while the laugh rippled away through the crowd.

Ka-Treer's smile stretched. "Are you still as skilled with a throwing dagger as you used to be, I wonder? It is not an idle question: I thought perhaps you would be gracious enough to teach my son a few of the finer points." His explanation was lost in the rising murmur. He had succeeded in planting the question in several people's minds.

Korimson shrugged and let it ride.

The Watchman had got it now. His eyes flicked to Lord Nevelston and the Eldest; then he inclined his head courteously and said to Kursh, "A moment of your time, ambassador. If you would be good enough to go out into the hall with me?"

"Thank you, no, laddie. The food table's here, and I'm partial to my vittles. Is there a problem?"

Another Watchman had made his way to the silently listening group, for it was obvious there must be some trouble brewing. Others of the guards were converging. The hush spread.

The Watchman's hand rested on his sword hilt. "Well, sir, there seems to be some question over whether or not you have borne arms into this hall." His tone was polite, but firm.

The dwarf set his pastry and drink down on the table. "Search me, then," he said evenly, raising his arms slightly away from his sides, being careful to give no sudden move which might be misinterpreted, with unfortunate result.

The soldier had the grace to redden slightly: the breach of courtesy to a recognized ambassador was unheard-of. "I regret the disturbance of your person."

"You have your duty. Her Majesty would be ill served if you slighted it." Kursh was looking beyond the man at Ka-Treer, who appeared much less satisfied. The guard stepped to Kursh and ran his hands down the dwarf's sides, searching the padded velvet jacket.

One of the Shimarrat retainers as if on cue said, "Strapped to his right forearm, fellow. That's where he always carried it."

Korimson fixed him with a steely look. "I don't recollect being introduced."

Ka-Treer, knowing already that his gamble was lost from the assurance of the dwarf's manner, stroked his waxed mustache. "Ah, but your fame precedes you, ambassador."

Kursh nailed him with a stare. "Then you'll know the knife isn't just for decoration."

Meanwhile, the Watchman had found the outline of the spring-sheath under the velvet-and-linen sleeve. He stepped back, and now both soldiers had their swords in grasp and their feet planted for a fighting stance. "I must ask you to come out of here with us."

Korimson shook his head. "I wish no trouble, but I've done nothing wrong, and I want that proved here, now."

"Very well, sir. Then remove your jacket and cast up your sleeve."

Imris's fair face showed unwonted anger. "This is unconscionable!" he said suddenly. It was strictly for effect, but none of the watchers knew this, and he did it well, having profited somewhat by association with Muir Dach.

"No, it's all right," Kursh told him calmly, also for effect. "I'm willing." He undid the silver buttons and shrugged out of his ocean-blue coat. Imris reached, and the dwarf seemed about to lay it across the Yoriandir's arm when he hesitated and smiled rather sheepishly. "No, can't quite ask a king to hold my jacket, now can I?" There was a nervous titter through the crowd. The Guildmaster swept his eyes across Ka-Treer and leaned past the Watchman to fling the heavy garment at the sallow-faced Shimarrat who had spoken against him. "You'll do it, though, won't ye? Much obliged. Do keep the sleeve off the floor: my wife's the very deuce to live with when she's got her temper up." The Shimarrat lord hurriedly passed it to a servant while Kursh rolled up his sleeve. The empty leather scabbard was strapped to his forearm. A murmur went through the crowd.

The Watchmen relaxed. One saluted, saying, "Thank you for your cooperation, ambassador. My apologies."

Korimson beckoned the Shimarrat servant and turned his back, forcing the man to help him into the jacket. He settled the velvet on his broad shoulders, buttoned the coat, and turned once more, arranging his collar. "Quite all right, sergeant." He waved expansively. "No trouble at all."

Reaching for the wineglass, Kursh met Ka-Treer's eye and was certain that the Shimarrat had figured where the dagger had gone, but the foreign king could not demand that the Eldest of the Yoriandirkin be so summarily searched. Kursh locked stares with him a moment, then lifted his glass in an ironic salute, pinky finger pricked. "Roste," he said.

*   *   *

The banquet had ended at a civilized hour, and the guests had been free to come and go as they pleased. Most of the ambassadors and their retinues had retired to the apartments delegated to them, to make ready for the Squiring ceremony that would be held the next day. Kursh had indicated he would feel better if he shared the night's watch with his men aboard the *Crystal Kite*, and by mutual consent Imris, Peewit, and Muir Dach had joined him there for a nightcap and talk of old times. Finally, Peewit got up from the edge of the ship's bunk and stretched.

"Are you for bed?" Korimson asked.

"In a while. I'm going up on deck for a sniff of air first."

But the old camaraderie had been too close for the casual lie, and the dwarf studied him. "You're going up to the castle, aren't you?" He rose, reaching for a heavy cloak, and Muir shouldered himself off the bulkhead. Imris cast up his hood.

The Littleman held up a hand. "Wait, all of you. Yes, I'm going up there to see the queen." He cut off their protests. "Nobody but her Majesty will see me, I assure you. It's best that way."

Kursh hesitated. "Are ye sure?"

"Quite." He winked. "Besides, you don't want to leave Muir alone around all this crystal."

"Dammit! Why'd you have to tell him that?" the tinker swore, miffed.

The Littleman laughed and left them arguing about it. Imris stuck his head out the cabin door to call quietly, "Be careful, captain."

"Always am."

"And Peewit, remember that Ariadne cannot always say everything that is in her heart."

The Hearthman turned in the dark companionway to look back at him. "Can any of us?" he asked softly. Then he gestured at the cabin. "Watch Kursh. Ka-Treer's a bad one to make a fool of."

"Well do I know it. I have my bow, as you have seen."

"It's a hard weapon to use in the confines of a ship," the captain pointed out.

A smile appeared on the green face. 'Which is why I shall be stationed up in the rigging before another turn of the glass."

Peewit answered his smile, waved, and headed up toward

the deck hatch. Suddenly he turned. "Oh, by the way, remind Kursh to have a cup of starflower tea before he goes to bed."

That was part of the dwarf's life the Eldest knew nothing of, and he frowned. "Starflower?" he repeated uncertainly.

"Right. Just tell him 'Thyla says.' " He went off whistling, leaving a mystified Yoriandir to convey the message to Kursh.

Even by craning on tiptoe, he could not come near to putting an eye to the peephole that had been placed in the secret door at human height, but Peewit put his ear against the wood and listened. He could hear no conversation, no one moving about. If the queen was in her suite, she might be alone. At any rate, it seemed unlikely Will Quint was in attendance, for surely the man's booming voice would have carried, and it was Will that Peewit was most concerned about. The big man would not attack him, but Peewit would place the new captain in such a position that he would have to choose between friendship and duty. Brickleburr had faced that razor's edge himself; he wouldn't force it on Quint.

The former Captain of the Watch stepped back from the door and in the darkness straightened his doublet and smoothed his hair as best he might. Then he reached for the latch and let himself into the queen's tiring room, pushing aside the rustling silken gowns. He had already decided on the way up from Kursh's ship not to try stealth once he was in the apartment itself, so now he made no effort to hide the sound of his footsteps as he walked across to the connecting door and the firelit inner chamber.

The queen was alone, sitting with her back to him in one of the two tapestried chairs drawn close to the fire. On the table at her elbow two goblets stood ready with wine. She cocked her head slightly, catching the sound of his step, and he had drawn breath to salute her when Ariadne said with a teasing note, "It got so late I didn't think you were coming for Squiring Day. You might at least have sent up a fire rocket or something, Master Wi—" She broke off as Peewit stepped around in front of her and went to one knee on the hearthrug.

"Your Majesty." He kept his head bowed.

"Peewit!" She had started, and it took a moment to catch her breath. "You used the hidden stair!" the queen said inanely, trying to cope with the fact that he was here at all.

"I did, my queen. I hope you'll forgive the intrusion. I haven't Kursh's kind of courage." He raised his head, but stayed otherwise motionless.

Ariadne steadied. "You haven't the ambassador's protection, either," she said practically. She held out her hand to him, a huge smile easing her expression in the fire's dancing light as delight replaced surprise. "I knew you'd be here!" When he clasped her hand in both of his and rose, she at once threw her arms around him and gave the astonished Littleman an enthusiastic hug. "By the Powers, Master Teazle, I've missed you!"

"You have?" he asked into the sleeve of her gown.

She held him off to arm's length. "Peewit, I—" The royal composure asserted itself. "What you did was wrong, Captain Brickleburr."

He shook his head. "Not my taking Kursh away from here. My not returning to face proper punishment after I had once got him safely to Jarlshof, yes. Yes, I admit that. But you and I both know what you'd have been forced to do if I had come back, my lady, and as the Pledged of my people I could not risk that."

Ariadne waved him to the other chair. "But you are willing to risk it now?"

He sat on the edge of the chair and studied the worn tips of his boots. "I'm tired of running," he said simply.

It was the queen's turn to look at her slippers. When she could speak past the lump in her throat, she said, "I cannot reinstate you in your old place, you know."

"Oh, I didn't intend anything of the sort!" he said hastily. "Will Quint has thoroughly proved himself as Captain of the Watch, and such a thing would not set well with certain people whose opinions must be given consideration."

Their eyes met. The queen said levelly, "I don't give a tinker's damn what Ka-Treer thinks, and if you think I do, you don't know me as well as you were wont to do." He gave her a grin, and Ariadne reluctantly added, "But he wouldn't be the only one."

He crossed the tips of his boots. "I spoke with the Lordling this afternoon," he reported quietly. "I believe we've come to the beginnings of an understanding about . . . things."

Ariadne was momentarily nonplussed. "You did?"

Peewit dug in his ear and shrugged. "Well, you were

busy, my lady, and the hall was too crowded to make going about invisible very comfortable, so . . ."

She smiled, bemused. "So you helped yourself to some peace and quiet in my garden."

If she preferred to think it had been that way, that he had not seen her son's outburst in the hall, the Littleman would let it pass. "I like what you've done with the pear tree."

The queen gave him an affectionate look. "I'll see there's a pear tart made up for you. Not that the bakeress now can hold a candle to Mistress Njordson—that is, to Mrs. Korimson . . ." She stumbled to a halt.

"Thyla," Peewit filled the gap comfortably.

Ariadne stared into the fire. "Is he happy?" she asked suddenly, and the Littleman knew her thought had gone to Kursh.

"I think he will be now." When she looked at him, Peewit told her about Ledgelawn and the Guildmaster's wife and daughter, and about Barak-Gambrel and the Weatherglass the dwarf had blown on that sacred mountain. The queen tucked her slippered feet up under her and leaned chin on hand on the arm of the tapestried chair. "But the trip down the mountain!" The Littleman shook his head at the memory. "We found a kite waiting outside when we came down from the roof, and Kursh insisted that it would bear us safely down to the city. Well, I was scared to death, of course—we were way above the clouds up there—but there really was no choice, and you know Kursh when he gets going on something, so we buckled ourselves into the thing, and—"

"I saw you!" When his eyes widened, she tapped her finger on her temple in frowning thought. "I was climbing the stairs at the Crystal Keep," she remembered, "and it seemed to me that I saw things happening elsewhere. There was Gerrit, and the *Minnow* down in the estuary, and then I saw some place lit all with candles, and something rushed past me in the darkness—I thought it was a huge bird— and—" She pointed and said triumphantly, "You were both wearing green cross-gartered breeches, weren't you?"

The Littleman nodded, mouth open.

"Ha!" The queen slapped the arm of the chair. The fire crackled merrily. "I must have been thinking of you both more than I knew," she admitted.

"Well, at any rate, we got the job done," Peewit finished.

"And undoubtedly it was Kursh's power which broke the Unnamed's storm, not my own." She nodded to herself. "I see."

"It was the Lord Aashis's Power working through you both, I think," the Littleman suggested.

"Aye, Master Teazle, but the one would have been useless without the other."

"Quite so, Your Majesty."

She thought it over, and her chin came up. "It seems there is much to redress."

"No, but there are friendships to be renewed." He smiled, and after a moment she answered it. Sliding off the chair, he said, "And now I've taken too much of your time, so I'll bid you good night, by your leave." The former captain snapped her a salute, and she nodded acceptance of it. "I'll be with Kursh's entourage if you need me, my lady."

"Was it from you that Will got the tip about an assassin?"

He nodded, adding, "I hope it amounts to naught."

"So do I, obviously, but I wanted to thank you for your vigilance, and for all those years of silent service. I know about you and the tinkers."

Peewit ran a hand through his hair, a frown showing between his eyebrows. "Who told you?"

"We have our sources, Master Littleman!"

He shrugged at her teasing, bowed, and made his way out by the way he had come. His quick eyes had not missed the goblets, and he reasoned Meara had not made herself scarce just so the queen and the wizard could parley.

"By the Light!" Peewit murmured as he felt his way down the hidden stair. "Who'd have thought? Well, that's Kursh and Thyla taken care of, and Her Majesty and Alphonse. Now, if I could do something in that line for Imris." A giggle momentarily escaped him, and he scolded himself for making noise in the secret passageway. But while he clamped a hand over his mouth, the thought came unbidden: And yourself, Master Hearthman? When is it time for you to find your peace?

For a moment as he felt for the latch of the door at the bottom of the stair, longing swept over him, and he was paralyzed with Homesickness.

His lips tightened, and he told himself firmly, It isn't finished yet.

In the darkness of the stairwell he could almost hear his own voice whisper, How do you know?

The unspoken question echoed in his mind until he went still and abruptly pushed through the door into the glaring torchlight of the kitchen corridor.

Gerrit had asked Lieutenant Fisher to grant him solitude for this most important eve, and the Watchman had saluted and taken up his position guarding the door outside. For some time the prince had read from the third Book of the Painter—he had secretly removed it from the library expressly for this nighttime reading—and then he had glanced over the ritual once more to be sure he had it straight. He had drunk a little watered wine and tossed the dice idly from hand to hand. He had stared out the window into the thick fog rolling in the solitary light of the guard-tower lantern. The truth of it was, he had a bad case of the fidgets.

It was the ceremony tomorrow, and the waiting for the public spectacle, and the sudden reappearance of the Littleman. For a moment out there in the garden, when the small gray-haired figure had hailed him like an apparition from beneath the birch, Gerrit had thought himself suddenly quite mad.

He should have told the old fellow what had happened that summer's night, but there were some things one could not say, ever—even if it left the wrong impression. As he had told the Teazle, he didn't give his word if he didn't intend to keep it. That's why he had been so careful to phrase it as he had: "Forgiveness." "For the dwarf?" "Yes." "I can't pledge something I can't give."

The conversation still echoing in his mind, the prince walked slowly to stand looking up, as he had so many nights, at the portrait of his father which hung above the fireplace in the outer chamber of his suite. He traced again the subtle lineaments that proclaimed him this unknown man's son; moved his head slightly to watch the deep blue eyes move with him; searched that formal smile for a sign of recognition. Sometimes it was there.

Some nights, but not this one. Tonight the expression of his father's portrait was faintly quizzical, as though he hadn't quite caught something the painter had said to him.

Father and son they regarded each other.

Gerrit's fist came to his chest in a salute and he quietly told the dead man, "Tomorrow, sir. I swore it to you once, and I'll do it." There was no change in the painted eyes.

The Greenbriar prince blew out the lamps and went to bed.

Chapter Seven

❧

On the morning of her son's Squiring Day, Ariadne rose early and took her teacup out onto the balcony of her solar. The sun had just climbed up over the dark rampart of the Barrens across the river to the east, and the air was cold. Willowsrill steamed, the fog lying close to the water, so that only the masts of the ships and some rigging could be seen through it. Nearer at hand the woodsmoke from the cooking fires on the Sweep threaded into the brilliant azure sky, and where early risers like herself had trod through the heavily frosted turf, she could track the dark footprints. In that clear light, she could even see the droplets of heavy dew pendant from the portcullis chain above her gates.

The queen blew on her tea, bathing her face in the warm steam, and sipped. She wished her thoughts were so clear. Here it was the morning of Gerrit's coming-of-age ceremony, and she hadn't yet been able to decide one all-important detail: who should be her heir's Senior Officer? Who among her Watch should be entrusted to supervise Gerrit's year of yeoman service?

She heard a step behind her, and Meara emerged from the suite, cap askew. "My lady! You should have roused me! I don't know why I slept so late, I wasn't even very tired . . ."

Ariadne smiled. "Hush. 'Tis no great matter. You needed your rest."

The cap was straight by now, and the waitingwoman pulled her robe about her. "You've even had to get your own tea!"

"Well, it isn't as though I don't remember how," the queen said, amused. "There isn't much to swinging a kettle over a fire!"

Meara accepted her mistress's view of it and spent a moment enjoying the view. "I do love winter best. Puts me in mind of . . . oh, I don't know—hot cider and kiss-me-over-the-punchbowl," she said, naming the young couples' holiday game. The two women shared a quiet chuckle.

"Was that how you met your late husband?"

"Aye." Meara cocked her head at the memory. "He was a good player, my Darin." She waggled her eyebrows. "Very good." At her mistress's smile, she added with a nod, "Kindlefest is the best time of year for sweethearts, a good time to start a family." At once, her cheeks turned scarlet. "Not that we did!" she added quickly.

"No, of course not," Ariadne agreed.

"Not that year, leastwise." Meara grinned slyly, and the queen laughed. In a moment, the waitingwoman cleared her throat. "Now, you know you shouldn't be out here with only that bit of robe betwixt you and the chill, my lady. If it'll please you to come inside, I'll pour your bath."

"In a bit. Meara, I've got to decide about the Lordling."

The woman nodded. "I knew there was something kept you from sleeping."

"I don't know who his Officer should be."

"Aye. That's a puzzle, my lady. There's many a man will fancy himself slighted today, I'm thinking, but only one of them can have the honor. How about the Eldest? Nobody could quarrel with the choice of a king for my young lord's officer."

Ariadne looked into the leaves swirling in the bottom of her teacup. "If Gerrit would profit by the Eldest's gentle ways, I'd assign him in a minute." She raised her eyes. "But I think it will take a sterner hand than Imris's."

Tactfully the waitingwoman made no reply to that, merely suggesting, "Your brother, Lord Nevelston, then? There's family ties there."

"Only in my eyes," the queen said. "Gerrit has never regarded Jaki as his uncle, and I could not force affection where he was not inclined to give it." She sighed and murmured, "I'm afraid my son's grown into a bit of a snob, Meara." A smile flickered. "It would do him a world of good to have to muck out a barn every now and again, as Jak and I did."

"He's spirited is all, my lady. A little headstrong, the way boys are," Meara said stoutly, more for Ariadne's benefit than from any conviction that this was true.

The queen lifted her head to stare down at the foggy

river. "But that's the point: by sundown tonight, he won't be a boy any longer." She sighed. "He'll be a yeoman in the First Watch, a man with rights and responsibilities."

Meara reached to touch her mistress's arm lightly. "Come, my lady. I've ordered up porridge for your breakfast. Good stick-to-the-ribs food for this day's work."

Ariadne smiled. "You always feed me porridge on the grandest of days. Do you keep me humble, Mistress Mother Hen?"

Meara pooh-poohed this idea with a wave of her hand. "It's just I know it makes you feel homey, somehow."

The queen nodded. "It does," she admitted and lifted her chin. "So I should feel at home and let all this royalty business, all this worrying about protocol, go hang, eh? I take your meaning very well."

"It is *your* castle," Meara answered. She shrugged. "Seems to me you should be able to do what your heart tells you is right, without worrying how it will sit with everyone."

"Sounds remarkably sensible to me," the Queen of Ilyria agreed. She let Meara lead the way inside.

The trouble was, she reflected as she spooned up her porridge, her heart wasn't saying much.

He knelt before her in the audience chamber, subject to sovereign, even though he was her son. Ariadne sat a little stiffly, perhaps because of the mail vest she wore beneath her ivory-and-gold gown, and heard through the drone of the Retreat Masters' chant the rising squall of a newborn. She had never heard so sweet a sound before, or since. And now here he was, wrapped in stern iron mail and pomp, and she could not credit that sixteen years had flown so fast. Another sixteen, she mused, and he'd be . . . where she was, probably. For a moment she wondered what her grandson might look like when it came his time.

The slow roll of the chant came to an end, the Powers' blessings invoked, and the audience chamber was quiet save for a couple of coughs. The mother gave way to the queen, and Ariadne held out her hands to take his between them. Putting aside the impulse that wanted to cry, "Wait! He's just a baby!" the queen said, "Now have ye plighted thy earnest vow to me, and now I receive it with honor. For we are the Blood of Beod, and the line of Greenbriar, and the

light to our people. So have I been, and so shall ye be when
the lot shall come to ye."

"I shall," he answered with the ritual phrase, his voice
steady and reaching the far edges of the hall.

"In token whereof, receivest thou this blade from my
hand." She rose, and he stood before her, two steps lower,
hands clasped in front of him and blazing with excitement.
Ariadne beckoned Will Quint forward from his post behind
her, and across the man's broad forearms lay Gerrit's new
sword, scabbarded in a magnificent enamelwork sheath with
the motif of the Briar winding around it toward the exposed
hilt. There was an approving murmur through the crowd.

Ariadne took the sheathed sword, and before they could
think how unnatural it looked for a woman to be holding
such a weapon, she quickly drew it and held it up. The light
pouring through the arched windows glinted off its supple
silver length and the golden guard, cunningly etched to form
a rose's thorned canes.

From where he stood with the other ambassadors in the
front rank, Kursh could see very well that there was no ruby
pommel stone. The dwarf bent his head and rubbed at his
eyepatch.

Ariadne let the place get quiet, then looked down at her
son. "Powers grant that you may have no need of this, my
lord Greenbriar, but if you do, bear it honorably."

His face had clouded for an instant at her invocation of
peace, but now it cleared. "Madam, I will."

She nodded and placed the hilt in his strong young hand.
He swallowed, regarded the sword that would be his until
death, and then brought it smartly to his forehead in a
military salute. The hall dissolved in cheers, and he turned
proudly to face them. Ariadne came down off the highest
step and gave him a one-armed hug while together they
waved to the crowd. Over the roar he said with a kind of
fierce exaltation, "It's going to be a good fighter, I can tell
by the feel!"

She wanted to say she hoped it was mostly for ornament,
but she didn't think that's what his father would have said,
and she stood in both places for him, so she answered only,
"It will suit the hand that wields it, I think."

His eyes glittered and he nodded, brandishing the sword
for all to see.

When the cheers and applause had finally ended, the

queen made a little disclaiming gesture. "Thank you. I thought I did it very well, too, for all I've never held a sword before." She grinned, and there was laughter, the mood at once turning from solemn pomp to festive gaiety. She had released Gerrit, and while he sheathed his sword and attached the hangers to the new belt that went with the outfit, Ariadne said, "And now I know the new yeoman's friends are itching to congratulate him, so I invite you all to refresh yourselves with sundry food or drink, and I think in a few moments our feast will be ready in the hall. Do join us to share in this proud day, and there you shall hear the announcement of yeoman Greenbriar's Senior Officer." There was fresh applause. She gestured, and the trumpeters sounded the fanfare which officially concluded the ceremony.

"Who is it?" Gerrit asked, even as Duncan Tregallis and Toby Naismith ran forward to parade him around the audience chamber on their shoulders.

She smiled. "Ah, that would be telling," she teased, and he made a face as they lifted him.

But the truth was, her heart wasn't saying much yet, the damned dumb thing!

Kursh took a glass from a servingman's tray, tasted the wine, and winced. Bloody stuff might as well be vinegar. He had a longing for the clean fire of flotjin to wash it away.

Jak Cooper, Lord Nevelston, was looking toward the gaggle of squires clustered around the hero of the day. "He's grown into a tall boy," he said as if to himself, then recollected. "Man, I mean," he amended.

"Truly, he takes after his father," Imris agreed, cradling his harp case against his chest; Ariadne had asked him to sing for the assembled guests after dinner.

Peewit, who after his interview with the queen was numbered among those guests, stood next to the Yoriandir. He was attired in a decent spruce-green suit, courtesy of the Guildmaster's stores. On the Littleman's return from visiting the queen, Kursh had argued, rightly, that he couldn't show up at a function like this dressed like a tinker. The new clothes and clean shave ought to have made him feel like a new person, but the truth was he felt as tired as if he'd been building earthworks against an enemy attack. His stomach wasn't just right, either. Must be coming down with something, he told himself, waving away the pickled-pig's-

foot canapé Kursh offered. To take his mind off it, he said,
"It's a nice-looking blade the queen gave him."

"Very nice," the dwarf agreed while the others nodded.
But it had no ruby in the pommel. Well, what did you
expect? he asked himself. She must have ordered the sword
from the armorers months ago, and she'd not forgiven ye
then. Korimson glanced over at the queen, who was still
standing near her throne with Rhys-Davies and her foster
sister, June neBlackmore. There was a look of supreme
fondness on Ariadne's face as she watched Gerrit set back
on his feet with good-natured slaps on the back. The dwarf
sighed. Maybe she still hasn't forgiven you, for all she'd like
to. Ka-Treer blocked his view then, giving Gerrit a kinsman's embrace of congratulations, and Kursh drank off the
wine, turning to catch the Yoriandir's account of a leaf
blight that had hit some of his trees the past spring.

Across the audience chamber, the prince caught Ka-Treer's
low words and nodded shortly. "It needed no reminder,
Uncle," he said coldly and brushed past the king. He circu-
lated among the guests for a few moments, checking the
disposition of the Watchmen, not that he was expecting
trouble from that direction. His hands were cold again, and
his heart had begun to pound. He swallowed dryly and fixed
in his mind the portrait hanging in his rooms. Now, he
thought, now I become my father's son.

The thought stiffened his back, and he took one of his
new gauntlets from his belt as he strode toward the corner
where the filthy dwarf skulked. Toby asked Gerrit a question, but he ignored the pudgy face. Lord Nevelston saw
him and stepped forward with a smile, hand already outstretched and beginning to say something, but Gerrit cut
across it: "Korimson!"

The voice had a brittle knife edge, and some deep instinct
told Kursh what would happen, even as people's voices died
around him, and there was frozen silence. Resignedly, he
turned.

Gerrit slapped the leather gauntlet to the marble floor.
"Pick it up," the young voice grated.

A Watchman nearby made no pretense of ceremony: he
yelled, "Your Majesty!" and raised an urgent fist, code for
"To me, at once!" Then he plowed his way through the
crowd and stepped between the Lordling and the ambassador.

"Steady, Kursh," Imris murmured, while Jak joined the Watchman.

By now there was a cordon of Watchmen pushing the crowd back in a circle, at the center of which stood the dwarf and his friends. Ariadne was hurrying toward them, Will Quint brusquely throwing people aside out of her way.

Gerrit shouted clearly, "I claim the Blood Honor Duel!" and stood, hand to sword hilt, staring past the Watchman at the dwarf. "Pick it up, sirrah!" It was the form of address one might use to a servant of low class, or to a slave.

Korimson's mustache bristled, and his good eye narrowed, but he held himself in close check. Beside him, the Littleman murmured, "Do you want to get out of here?" He meant invisibly.

Kursh shook his head once, eye fixed on the black-haired youth.

The queen stepped into the circle, took a quick survey of the situation, and snapped, "What is the meaning of this, sirs?"

"It is man's work, Mother," her son told her calmly. "I have called out yon coward, that is all."

Ariadne was livid. "By what right do you presume to make light with the peace and free conduct of my hall?"

The gray eyes were unwavering. "It is a right any man may claim under the laws of chivalry. You have just bestowed those rights upon me, madam. I choose to use them now. I repeat: I claim a Blood Honor Duel."

The queen clenched her fists and spat, "This is ridiculous!"

Peewit's stomach was churning in earnest now. "It is no great honor that pledges its word one day and takes it back the next," he said clearly.

Gerrit looked down at him. "I bear you no grudge, Master Brickleburr. In your position, I might have done the same all those years ago. It was a bold act, though a wrong one. Step aside."

Brickleburr was rigid with fury. "You may bear me no grudge, but I certainly have one against you," he reminded the young heir.

As Gerrit lifted one shoulder in a shrug, Ariadne grasped her son's arm and ordered firmly, "You will not do this."

"Once sworn, the Blood Honor Duel cannot be taken back," the prince countered. He resumed his staring at the dwarf.

"That is true, your Majesty," Captain Will Quint rumbled worriedly.

King Ka-Treer stood behind Gerrit, Shimarrat retainers in attendance. "Of course it is true. And His Highness is well within his right to invoke it. There has, after all, been ample provocation." Not a person in the crowd could fail to think of the butchery Kursh had done to the boy's father.

Ariadne controlled herself only by mentally hanging the Shimarrat bastard's head on a pike. When she spoke, her voice was an icy, deceptive drawl. "Well, while I do not know the rules of courtesy which apply in your hall, my lord of Shimarron—or indeed, if there be any such—I do know that here in Ilyria we conduct our affairs in a civilized fashion." Ka-Treer stroked his damned waxed mustache and gave her a slight bow, a mockery of manners. The queen's chin came up. "And one cornerstone of that civility is that any guest at my court shall have absolute safety of his person. I have pledged safe conduct to all ambassadors. If you offer insult to one, you offer it to me. Let that be clearly understood." She swept a look around, landing on Gerrit. "By all."

The prince said, "The duel itself need not be fought now, madam. I will accept any time the villain names, and any place. The peace of this hall need not be broken." His jaw clenched. "But I will have my vengeance. Now or later, it is no matter to me. I tell you, dwarf, you are a marked man."

Up to this point, Kursh had remained silent. He and Gerrit stared at each other, and then the dwarf nodded to himself. "Your Majesty? May I have leave to speak?" Before she could swing her head to him with a negative reply, the ambassador from Jarlshof said quietly but clearly, "I once knew a fair amount about honor and the rules of combat, and what his young lordship says is true: a Blood Oath cannot be taken back; it demands blood payment. And as I have quite enough enemies aiming daggers at my back" —his eye was cold on Ka-Treer—"I'd rather not add another to the list. So—" He bent, and before anyone could stop him, picked up the gauntlet. "I accept this challenge."

Jak swung to face him, and Imris could not check his exclamation of dismay. "Kursh, no!"

Across the circle, Ka-Treer smiled. Ariadne's lips parted and she passed a hand over her eyes. Gerrit himself swallowed, but otherwise betrayed no emotion.

Peewit was immensely tired, but he raised his voice to be heard above the stunned reaction of the crowd. "I will be the ambassador's second."

People hushed. "And who will be the Lordling's?" Ka-Treer asked almost jovially.

No one spoke, and Gerrit began to realize just how serious a breach he had made with his mother. Heavily, Will Quint said into the silence, "I will do it, as I am Her Majesty's champion." But from his expression, it was obvious he had no taste for the obligation.

The elderly Rhys-Davies, gravely formal in his black chamberlain's robe, proclaimed, "If matters have come to such a pass—and it seems they have—then let this be done with all laws of custom." He turned to the queen and bent his head. "May I offer my service as Rules Master, Your Majesty?" There would no fairer judge of the duel.

All eyes were on the queen, who had gone white. Her lips compressed in a bloodless line as she stared at her son, who met her gaze calmly, without insolence. The silence stretched while her eyes went to Kursh . . . *the trampled grass, the ax caked with gore* . . .

Ariadne said hollowly, "I cannot stop it, but I feel I will rue this day for the rest of my life. Proceed, my lord Waterford."

Rhys-Davies bowed stiffly and turned to the combatants. "A challenge to a Blood Honor Duel has been made," he intoned formally, "against one Kursh Korimson, Guildmaster and ambassador, by one Gerrit Greenbriar, yeoman of the Watch." Quite deliberately, he gave the boy no other title, a technicality not lost upon the people watching: until his yeoman year was up, Gerrit was an ordinary soldier. The old man turned to Kursh. "Do you accept the challenge?" he asked ritually.

"I do," Korimson answered steadily.

"Then it is yours to name the time and place at which battle shall be joined between you."

The dwarf was rock-solid, arms crossed on his barrel chest. "The time shall be now. The place: the practice ground." There was a gasp and murmur at that: he was forfeiting his ambassadorial protection. He raised an eyebrow. "Well, I am sorry to ruin this proud day, but it seems to me pretty ruined as it is, and anyway, I've got a business to get back to—I don't want to leave this hanging fire for months."

Rhys-Davies nodded. "It is your prerogative, ambassador. No explanation is owed."

"It wasn't an explanation, my lord Waterford," Kursh rejoined. "It was by way of an apology to Her Majesty."

"Noted," the chamberlain said. He turned courteously to Gerrit. "And now, yeoman, the choice of weapons is yours."

Outwardly the dwarf gave nothing away, but he was thinking, If he names lances in the joust, I'm done for.

But the gift was too new for the boy to think much strategy, and he clapped a hand to the beautiful hilt. "Swords."

Jak Nevelston called clearly to his yeoman, "Wright, fetch my sword for the ambassador."

But Kursh held up one broad hand. "No need. I won't use it anyway."

Forgetting that he was supposed to be on the other side, Quint said, "There are short swords in the armory: we'll have one of those brought."

"No," the dwarf said again. "I won't use it."

Rhys-Davies frowned. "But the choice of weapons has been made, ambassador: you are required by the Rules to fight with a sword."

Korimson shook his head slowly. "No, my lord. I am required to be armed with one: but nowhere in the Rules does it say that I must use it."

There was an immediate outburst of controversy, but the Rules Master raised his hand for quiet. "I believe you are correct, sir."

A smile appeared briefly on Kursh's face. "Trust me."

Gerrit said hotly, "He can't get out of it that way! The duel has got to be fought!"

"Oh, I intend to fight you, laddie," the dwarf told him. "Make no mistake about that. And here's my weapon." Quite deliberately he made his way toward the central hearth past a few people who moved hurriedly out of his path. He deliberated a moment, picked out a fire-blackened poker from the rack, and turned to hold it up.

Purple with rage, Gerrit hissed, "I'll kill you for this!"

Unconcernedly, the dwarf slowly walked back. "Well, that is the general idea, now, isn't it? You've chosen to swear a Blood duel, so you have to draw blood, don't you? But I'm under no such obligation. So I won't." Casually he laid the poker over his shoulder. "I intend to teach you a

Lesson, though." Briefly his eye went to his old training
partner, Kelvin Miller, the Second Watchman. Together
they had made yeomen out of many a Senior Squires class,
and the Lesson, as they had come to call it, was always the
culminating exercise. Miller, gouty now and leaning on a
cane, gave him a broad smile.

"You already have, dwarf," Gerrit stated coldly, back in
control. "You have taught me how to be no man's son."

There was a death knell in his tone.

Despite himself, Kursh felt a cold touch down his back.
"I'm afraid it's worse than that," he said soberly, quietly.
"I'm afraid I've taught ye to be no woman's son, either."
He had put his finger exactly on the consequence of Gerrit's
challenge to the queen's sovereignty in her own hall, and
there was deep compassion in his gravel voice. From Peewit
or Imris, it might have been expected, but Kursh was not
known for such things, and his words poured cold water on
the swelling eagerness in the crowd for a fight as nothing
else could have done. He tugged at his eyepatch and sighed.
"All right. Let's get on with it."

Rhys-Davies bowed. "To the practice ground, then. Du-
elists fifty paces apart, please." The distance between them
was designed to make certain the fight did not start before it
could be supervised. He waved Gerrit toward the door.
"Will you witness, Your Majesty?"

Ariadne glanced at her son, who had turned without a
word, and then her look went to Kursh and stayed there for
a long moment. "Aye, my lord." She took the chamberlain's arm and allowed him to conduct her toward the door.

Peewit fell into step beside Kursh. "This is the bloody
stupidest thing you've ever done."

"Seems I've heard that phrase a time or two before. I
must cap each stupidity with another." Korimson handed
his weapon to Imris and began to unbutton his jacket.

"A poker!" The Littleman threw up his hands.

"Oh, come on, Peewit—the boy's only sixteen; how much
experience d'ye think he has with a sword in a real fight?"

"How much do you have with a poker, by the Powers?"
At the dwarf's grunt, the former captain said seriously,
"Kursh, the fact is, he *is* sixteen." He grasped the brawny
arm and halted him. The press of people divided around
them and flowed on toward the stairway down. "You're
not, old friend."

A shadow appeared in the deep-set eye. "Brickleburr, there's no way out. Shall I wait and face him when he's a man full-grown, then?"

There was no answer for that. Wearily, the captain shook his head and they fell into step once more. The dwarf lifted off his Glassmaker's flat crystal pendant on the Guildmaster's chain of rank. "Hold on to this for me, would you?"

Absently, Peewit took it. "Guard your left side."

It was Kursh's blind side. The dwarf gave him a brief glance of understanding. "Aye."

The river of people carried them slowly down the stairs and out onto the chilly practice ground.

The boy did not deign even to circle. He had gone to guard stance, of course, when Rhys-Davies released the queen's handkerchief to flutter to the hard-packed earth, but that was all. Steadily he watched the short practice sword the dwarf had been forced to arm himself with. Kursh held it loosely in his left hand, as one might hold a billet for the fire, and wondered who the boy's weapons master had been all these years. Gerrit was well trained, no doubt of it. He was holding back, not rushing to the attack, cool as marble, and that gave Kursh pause. He had hoped the lad's challenge had been a hot-headed, spur-of-the-moment expression of his newfound official maturity, but it was evident now that Gerrit had been planning this Blood Duel for a long time. That was not a good sign. He wasn't talking, and that wasn't, either.

Have to warm him up a little, the old Squiremaster thought. He went to guard, the poker a grotesque mockery. "Come on, lad, they're waiting dinner on us."

The gray eyes glinted. "Oh, you will not care that the roast is burned, I assure you."

"Like mine well done, anyway," the dwarf answered complacently. "I—"

The prince attacked so quickly, giving away no tiniest warning of it, that Korimson had barely time enough to get the poker between himself and the sweeping stroke that would have decapitated him. With a clanging shock that sent a dart of pain from the heel of his hand to the heel of his foot, the bright silver sword slithered down the black poker toward the dwarf's hand. Using his powerful shoulder, Kursh muscled the boy back off-balance, and they sprang apart.

Not a talker, the dwarf thought. Dangerous and quick as a snake. How many fights *has* he been in? His arm was already aching and his palm yearned for an ax haft. He clamped a lid on that thought quickly.

"You were saying?" Gerrit taunted.

For answer, Korimson pitched away the borrowed sword. He had started the bout with it, and that was all that was required. From now on the damned thing was a liability. The old weapons master watched the boy's eyes and noted approvingly that Gerrit had not let his attention be diverted to follow the sword's fall. The dwarf crouched lower, free hand out for balance. Very subtly, he dropped the head of the poker just a bit to entice Gerrit into an attack.

The boy snorted impatiently. "Don't toy with me, blackguard."

Kursh realized he knew that one, too. But a little color had risen in that pale young face. Ah, not quite the stone, our young—

This time there was the barest tightening around the gray eyes as Gerrit leaped again to the attack, feinting neatly to the dwarf's blind side and then ripping a cross-body slash that Kursh threw himself backward to avoid. He could feel the wind flutter his loose linen shirt, though, and it was not a pleasant sensation. He caught sight of Peewit standing half turned away with Imris's green hand resting on his shoulder, of Jak Nevelston's grim worry, and of the queen's hand raised to her mouth. But there were leers in the crowd, too, and the glittering blood-thirst that comes upon spectators at a bear-baiting. In that instant, when he realized he was mere entertainment for many, the duel nearly became as deadly to Kursh as it was to Gerrit, but then the old training took over, and the dwarf was in command of himself once more. "Not bad," he told Gerrit approvingly, "but you want to watch that left knee of yours. Ye're locking it." It was the tone of a master to a worthy apprentice.

The Greenbriar heir went wattle-red, and this time he made no pretense at art, he just threw himself into the fight, his sword an extension of the fist that wanted to knock the dwarf flat.

Kursh parried blow after blow, waiting out the first fury, and in the process discovering how to use the hook of the poker as an effective grappling tool. They dodged and circled in earnest now, Gerrit pressing the attack at every point, and Korimson gave ground, waiting. There came a slicing whir and he had his opportunity: while the shining sword was still in its descending arc, the dwarf spun aside and ducked under the boy's flailing free arm. For a split second, Gerrit had his unprotected back to the dwarf. Grasping the poker in both hands like an ax, Kursh brought it in a great flat swat against the prince's hind end. The Lordling was catapulted several feet by the force of the blow and fetched up in the arms of some of the bystanders.

There was a roar of laughter and some scattered applause. Though the mail coat must have protected the lad a bit, Kursh was pretty sure the royal rump was sausage. He laid the poker at rest on his shoulder. "About the roast being in the fire, Your Highness?" His free hand stroked his mustache. Men guffawed and women laid their fingers across their lips not to break into unladylike hoots. But even as he watched the boy with the Greenbriar woven into his coat turn stiffly, Korimson knew this would be doubly hard now.

Gerrit stared at him, the sword momentarily forgotten in his hand. On his face was an expression of shock, his eyes wide, mouth a little open. Then he smiled, genuine fun gleaming in his face. That was the most devastating thing he could have done to Kursh, for that grin was pure Ariadne, and the old dwarf's heart gave a painful thump.

Gerrit walked slowly back to the center of the practice field. "Not bad," he said approvingly. "You want to watch your weapon, though." He put a hand to his butt for comic emphasis. "You'll bend it."

Kursh credited him with a slight twitch of the gray beard, while people made giggling comments to one another. Under cover of that released tension, Gerrit struck.

Kursh was ready for him, because it was exactly what he himself would have done. This time, the swordwork was businesslike and polished. The poker grew dented, and time and time again Korimson had to disengage because the poker had no hand guard with which to catch the tip of Gerrit's sword and deflect it. All the dwarf could do was beat the blade aside and evade. The boy systematically worked to his blind side.

The queen tightened her hand on Rhys-Davies's arm. "Stop it."

"Your Majesty, I cannot," he replied, never taking his eyes from the combatants. "Even His Highness cannot stop it now. If I take either one of these men out of the duel, their seconds will have to continue it until Blood Honor is satisfied."

The dwarf stumbled as he jumped out of the way of a lunge. The crowd gasped and leaned forward expectantly.

Soon, Kursh was thinking to himself, I've got to end it soon. My bloody arm is killing me. Like arm-wrestling a whoreson octopus, this is. The canny old warrior knew what he was looking for, and when Gerrit came in with a low, straight thrust that would have disemboweled him, Korimson lifted the sword tip with his poker, let it slide down along the iron rod, and guided it home to slice into his shoulder two inches from the vein in his neck.

Though he was ready for it, the sudden flash of pain made him gasp, even as he grimly went on to hook the boy's blade. Using his own powerful legs as a fulcrum, he hurled the poker, the sword, and the boy halfway across the open circle.

Gerrit landed sprawling and stunned. He sucked desperately for air a moment, then rolled by instinct to pick up his sword.

Kursh got there before him, struck his fumbling hand away, and picked up the Greenbriar sword. The prince scrambled to his knees to find himself looking up along the length of his own blade into one unreadable dark eye.

At once the crowd went so silent they could all clearly hear the dozen or so creaks of crossbows from the battlements. The archers had him sighted in, ready to drop him at the queen's word. Kursh heard them, but did not waver. Blood soaked the front of his shirt, and his face was drawn. "Lad," he said for the boy's ears alone, "I'm sorry about your father. He was a decent man, for all he was a Shimarrat prince."

Gerrit's face contorted, and he spat in Kursh's face.

"Hold!" Lord Waterford commanded in the nearest thing to a shout anyone had ever heard from his dignified lips. "The Blood Honor Duel is satisfied! Master Korimson, put up that sword, please."

For a moment, one hideously long moment, Ariadne thought she had misjudged the dwarf.

But then the sword tip came up, Kursh stepped back, and he laid the weapon at formal rest across his forearm.

While the former First Watchman's friends rushed into the circle to attend him, the queen's frozen heart finally spoke.

"Fool!" Fidelis fumed, ripping the laces at the neck of the dwarf's shirt and pressing a folded pad of linen into the wound. Imris deflected another well-wisher's backslap.

Peewit tried to make some room for them. "Excuse me—step back—excuse me. Ho, Watchman! Give us some breathing room here, for pity's sake!" The fellow, a sergeant by his insignia, flicked a courteous half-salute, and signaling one of his mates, began to establish some order.

"Idiot!" The doctor was still shaken.

"Oh, ease off, Fidelis. It's not much more than a nick," the dwarf said stoically, but he did not object when Jak Cooper grabbed the back of his broad belt to hold him steady on his feet. "Drop of flotjin will put me right in a wink."

The queen's voice came near at hand. " 'Twill have to be Elixir, I fear." The crowd parted and fell back, and she came through with Rhys-Davies and Gerrit, the prince with his head held high and eyes looking straight ahead, above the dwarf's head.

Kursh almost saluted her, but remembered in time and bowed instead, straining against Fidelis's hand. "Thank you, my queen, but I'll require none. A scratch is no matter, if the good doctor here would leave off shoving his fingers into it."

Her face eased somewhat at his matter-of-fact tone, but she still looked to the physician. "Fidelis?"

"It's no scratch," he refuted briskly. "But if he wants sutures instead, it will be well enough, I suppose. The blade was clean, being new."

Ariadne nodded acceptance. Her gaze fell to Kursh. "That was a masterly exhibition, ambassador."

Korimson shook his head. "Clumsy. If I'd known I was to be the day's entertainment, I'd have practiced," he rumbled.

Here and there in the crowd, particularly from the military men, there were chuckles. The queen herself smiled. "Nevertheless, we marked that at the point in the match when you applied your poker to our son's posterior, you might very well have applied it to his skull. That would have been a legal stroke, well within your right." Heads turned in the crowd and people's lips moved to say, "That's true. He could have killed the Lordling." Ariadne swept a look around. "We thank you for your chivalry, sir."

Kursh tugged at his eyepatch. "Begging your pardon, my queen," he rasped, "but that wasn't chivalry: that was just want of a longer poker; he's a tall lad." For a moment, they believed him, then someone laughed. Korimson waited, and when they quieted, he added, "There was indeed chivalry in this match, Your Majesty, but it was not mine. When I threw away the borrowed sword at the beginning of the duel, I also threw away any right I had to be regarded as a legitimate opponent. All rules went out the window with the tosspot, if ye'll pardon my free speech." He had to salvage something for Gerrit: one day, this boy would be king, and the men watching would be in his army. The old dwarf drove the point home: "His Highness could have treated this like any tavern brawl, but he chose to hold himself to formal dueling rules. That is conduct worthy of a yeoman of the Watch, seems to me." Gerrit's head had not moved, but his narrowed eyes rested on the dwarf, and he wore a puzzled frown.

Though his point was not lost upon her, the queen did not see the matter that way. "Nevertheless, ambassador, the peace of our hall has been broken, the most solemn pledge of hospitality violated by our son and heir. He has made us an oathbreaker, and we do not relish the role." There was utter silence among the assembled nobles, Watchmen, and guests. "Now let it be known therefore that we do hereby unconditionally pardon both Ambassador Korimson and Master Brickleburr, and hold them both in honor for their long and sometimes painful service to the Crown. For though it may have been your hand that struck the blow all those years ago, Kursh, it was the Unnamed's will that directed it, and anyone may fall prey to the Wild One's powers." Her gray eyes were wryly aware. "We have not been wholly proof against them ourselves."

Many of those present remembered uncomfortably that she had once played the black crystal Pipes, and it had been widely rumored at the time she had refused the Elixir to heal the dwarf of the arrow Imris had brought him down with, a definite corruption of the healing power given to Beod's line by Ritnym of the Earth.

Peewit bowed wordlessly, and Kursh would have gone to one knee, but Jak's hold on his belt prevented it.

Ariadne's look softened, and she dropped out of formal diction. "Well, I fear the roast will indeed be burned, but much else has been prepared to please us, so I suggest we adjourn to the hall. I've no doubt Master Fidelis will take you in charge, ambassador, but will you join us afterward, if you feel up to it?"

"A man's Squiring Day should be a celebration, and it would take more than a scratch to keep me away from a hall full of victuals. I'll be there."

The queen nodded. "I rather thought you might. Meanwhile, you may require some assistance in securing fresh linen and clothing, and perhaps the flotjin you mentioned." She drew Gerrit forward. "So I give you my son to be your yeoman."

It took a moment for people to grasp the import of this: she had made the dwarf Gerrit's Senior Officer. People whipped startled looks from the queen to the dwarf to the boy. Even Kursh registered surprise. "But, my queen, I'm not even a member of the Watch anymore!" he blurted.

She raised an eyebrow. "Well, now, it wouldn't be much fun being queen if one couldn't bend the rules every once in a while, would it?" She gave the stunned dwarf a mischievous grin, laid her hand on Rhys-Davies's arm, and led the procession back to Rose Hall.

"Powers!" the Littleman breathed when the crowd had cleared.

Jak Cooper pursed his lips, Imris reached to brush some dirt off the prince's surcoat, and Fidelis smiled at some private thought as he checked under the soaked compress.

Kursh and the boy stared at each other.

Gerrit found his voice. "Orders, sir?" he asked quietly.

The words seemed to call the Squiremaster to himself. "Get to your quarters and clean up, yeoman. Ye look a sight, and both of us have got to dance attendance on a pack of curious fools at a party neither of us really wants to go to. But we'll put the best face on it for your lady mother's sake." He regarded the youth steadily. "Won't we?"

"Yes, sir." The gray eyes flickered. "But I still think you're a sodding bastard traitor. Sir."

"And I think ye're a little snot with a dirty mouth . . . and a sore ass," the dwarf replied genially. "That'll be all, yeoman."

Gerrit saluted. "Yes, sir." He executed an about-face and marched stiffly away.

They watched him until he went out of sight around the corner of the keep. Jak Cooper struggled to keep a straight face. "He has quite a lot of grit, you have to admit."

Kursh spat over Fidelis's arm. "So does sandpaper," he rasped, "but ye wouldn't want it close to you." He winced and glared up at the doctor. "Fidelis, will ye quit waggling the damned thing? I'd be halfway to healed by now if it weren't for you!"

Peewit began to laugh, and Jak dissolved. The Eldest smiled broadly, and Fidelis tried not to "waggle" as he chuckled.

Brickleburr grinned wickedly. "Congratulations, Squiremaster."

"Piss off or ye'll be a foot shorter, captain."

Somehow then they got him up to Fidelis's quarters, and he only broke one stool and a small pot while the doctor was putting in the thirteen sutures.

Chapter Eight

As arranged, they did not speak when they met so that it would look to a casual observer as though the assassin and his second-in-command were unremarkable strangers who chanced to be standing before a saddler's stall at the same time. Under cover of the noisy laughter at a mummer's farce going on two wagons over on the Sweep, the Shimarrat killer and his team leader examined bridles and harness and idly passed a few moments with the garrulous little leatherworker. The assassin gestured to some tack hung up in the back of the makeshift stall, the saddler turned to lift it down, and in the moment that it took, a key exchanged hands. "Ah, no," the killer laughed a few moments later in reply to the saddler's urging. "It's a beautiful bit of craft, good sir, but if I came home with it instead of the new cooking pot my wife sent me for, I'd be for the grave!"

Meanwhile, the team leader had drifted away toward the play, pocketing the key. He would go to the wagon after dark. He had marked it already: green, with a black roof. In it he would find the small keg of black powder, the disguises, and three lengths of split firewood already coated with the drug. It was a beautiful plan, very subtle, very ingenious. He had performed many unusual missions in the king's service, but this promised to be the crowning achievement of his career. And, of course, he intended to disappear somewhere far from Ka-Treer's long and deadly reach when it was done. It did not do to know too much of a king's business.

It had been a long day for all of them, Ariadne thought, and she probably shouldn't have asked to see the dwarf at this late hour, but there was something she must get straight with him before the morrow's presentation of the new yeoman to the common folk out on the Sweep. Though plainly in pain and tired, Kursh had looked across the hall when her page had delivered the message and given her a nod. Not long after, she had left the reception and come here to her library. Meara had readied tea and taken the heavy state crown to lock it up as usual, and now they were just waiting for the gentlemen. The queen was idly thumbing a dusty book of herb lore.

There was a muffled tap at the door, and Meara went to open it, stepping aside with a curtsey. Peewit and Kursh filed in, while beyond Ariadne caught just a glimpse of her son assuming guard position outside. "Good evening, gentlemen. Thank you for coming," she said, gesturing to the comfortable chairs before the fire.

Since neither of them knew what to expect, they merely bowed and waited for her to be seated first.

"I regret the inconvenience of the hour," the queen added, while Meara poured tea for them all. "But I needed to talk to you both, and this was the only available time. I promise I won't keep you long."

"Our time is yours, my queen," Peewit answered, and Kursh nodded, blowing on his tea to cool it. There was a slight frown on his face which might have been pain but might have been unease.

Ariadne smiled. "I'm sorry. It isn't so mysterious, really. I just have something to say to you, and I don't know how you'll take it, so I'm having a hard time finding the right way to begin."

"Simplest is best," the Littleman urged.

"Right. Well, then." She tapped her finger on the teacup nervously. "Peewit, I want you to accept a commission—or a promotion, I suppose it is, since technically you're still a member of the Watch—to Lord General of Ilyria."

The Littleman repeated slowly, "Lord General?"

"Of Ilyria," the queen finished helpfully. "Yes. It's a new post. In fact, I just made it up tonight." Her eyes began to twinkle. "It is a valid offer of commission, nevertheless. You would be charged with all military matters that pass in our domains, with power of command second only to my own."

But I wanted to go Home, Brickleburr thought numbly.

She misunderstood his silence. "It will be well with Will Quint, I assure you, and we need your wits. There is trouble coming with Shimarron; I feel it in my bones." Ariadne regarded his bent head and sighed. "But that isn't half the truth of it, Master Littleman. The truth of it is . . . I need a friend." His brown eyes lifted over the edge of the table, and she smiled. "Will you stay?"

The Pledged of the Hearthfolk straightened and answered her smile. "Of course. But I don't need a fancy commission to do that."

"Maybe I need to give it," the queen said honestly, and after a moment he nodded.

The dwarf tapped him on the arm, and when the Littleman turned in his seat, he stuck out his broad hand. "Congratulations, old sod!" He glanced in Ariadne's direction. "Beg your pardon, my queen. It slipped."

The cooper's foster daughter giggled. "No matter, Kursh. I have a surprise for you, too."

"Think I've been surprised enough for one day, my lady, if it's all the same to ye," he said wryly.

Her smile broadened. "I expect so, but I must ask your indulgence for one more tidbit." He was frowning, and she feared to lose him before she'd begun, so she paused and grew serious. "You remember at yesterday's reception I said I wanted some of your time during your visit, ambassador? Well, here is the matter: I hear that Jarlshof has had major trouble from pirates attacking your crystal shipments. True?"

It was scuttlebutt in every dockyard tavern from here to Skejfalen. The dwarf said warily, "It's true we've lost ships, but I don't think these are ordinary pirates." He and Peewit exchanged a glance. "In fact, in at least one case, I know they weren't."

The queen nodded. "We've lost shipping, too." Then she said directly, "King Ka-Treer seems to think he owns the high seas and our Willowsrill, too. I aim to put a stop to it. Does that sound like something our allies of Jarlshof would be interested in?"

"When do we start?" the Guildmaster rasped.

She held up a hand. "A moment. We of Ilyria have resources and men, but little knowledge of open-water sailing or of shipbuilding. Jarlshof has both. I have in mind a joint venture, a navy compounded of dwarves and men, to patrol both Willowsrill and the sea lanes between Waterford and Jarlshof. Our ships would fly dual flags and be answerable to the guild and to me."

His deep eye had narrowed. "That's a lot of people to be answerable to," he said frankly. "Ye're likely to wind up with nothing but confusion that way. Nobody will ever be able to give a decisive order."

She knew from the careful consideration he was giving it that Korimson was taken with the idea of the joint navy. Now to make him accept the rest of it. The queen put her teacup down. "Well, what would you suggest?" she asked, playing stupid.

He was still thinking of it as an exercise in strategy, not noticing Peewit's look to the queen and her wink. "What you need is one fellow at the head of the whole thing, somebody who stands between the guild and the Crown, somebody . . ." He got it then, and his eye flew open. "Oh, wait a bit! I never said—"

Ariadne turned to the Littleman with a merry cock of her head. "I could have sworn I just heard someone name himself to the post of Admiral of the Joint Fleet."

Peewit grinned. "Couldn't have been clearer."

"Pi—" The dwarf cut short the epithet, glared at the Littleman, and said gruffly, "It should be somebody else."

Ariadne put a hand on his arm. "There isn't anybody else with your particular set of talents, Kursh," she told him. "I need you to drive that Shimarrat bas—" My word, he's got me doing it, too, she thought, and hastily amended, "—Ka-Treer back to his own harbor and keep him there."

The old dwarf rubbed at his eyepatch. "I can only take the post on two conditions."

"Name them freely."

He regarded her. "The first is that I'll set this navy up for us and get it running smoothly, and I'll guide the opening engagement. But after that, I'll want to retire. It's a great honor ye've paid me, my queen, but I don't like to be from home too long. My daughter deserves a father."

"I would not stand between you," the queen answered quietly. "Your first condition is granted. And the second?"

His eye was steady. "Release me from being Gerrit's Senior Officer. I'll not take your son out on a ship with me: the danger would be too great."

Ariadne's face fell. After a moment she said, "I'm afraid you do not understand my son very well, Kursh. I assigned him to be your yeoman in front of the entire court. If I were to rescind that assignment tomorrow, he would feel himself shamed more than he already is." A smile briefly flickered. "You have seen how sharp is his sense of honor."

Peewit bowed his head while the dwarf muttered, "Felt it, ye mean. Still, he's the heir, my lady: think of the kingdom."

Her chin came up, and the Greenbriar gray eyes measured him. "I do assure you, admiral, that is exactly what I am thinking of. Teach him well, will you?"

Not too much later the two old comrades were marching past the guards on duty outside the royal apartment, the boy's limping tread the prescribed three paces behind them. The dwarf stroked his beard and said under cover of his hand, "Why the bloody hell can't she give him to the wizard?"

"Your luck," the Littleman commiserated, but he was giggling into his cloak.

"Maybe I'll put him on temporary assignment to the army."

"Don't you dare!"

Even now, more than two days after the attack, Firkin Flaxmaster could still see its eyes, flickering like distant heat lightning, as he had desperately rolled aside to avoid the glittering arc of the descending ice dart.

He had been asleep in a tallfolk barn, nested in the straw between the amiable milk cow and plowhorse, when he had been awakened by a moaning shriek and knew instantly that the Shadow had found him. He had not been quite quick enough; the point of the dart had broken off in his arm. Then there had been shouts approaching the barn and the sudden flare of a lantern, and he had grabbed his pack and run for the door, his useless limb flapping grotesquely at his side with pain burning in him like a fire along his veins. The Shadow had shrunk back into the dark vault of the barn rafters, and Firkin had escaped for that time. But it was following, of that he was sure, and he could not go still with a fragment of dart in him.

So now the Hearthman stood with the river water seeping into his worn boots and the willow withes swaying softly in the breeze, a curtain beyond which he could see the thickly crowded road and the occasional mounted officer who kept the queen's peace among the throng. He gathered from remarks he had overheard that the Greenbriar Queen's son was having his birthday, and the lady herself would on his behalf hold a special Healing. He drew a breath past the freezing pain that had crawled up his arm into his chest and allowed himself to hope. Just a little farther. He looked anxiously through the lacy willow toward the sky and was lightened a little. No clouds, bright sun. Good. As long as it was broad daylight, the Shadow couldn't attack, and he might be able to complete the mission given to him by the Matriarch.

Firkin hefted his pack. Now to find the Pledged and set the gift from the Matriarch into Brickleburr's hands. For a moment the weary Littleman leaned on his stick and tried to conjure in the midst of the tallfolk campfires the sweet smell of the peat of the Home hearths. Tansy Mossflower, Matriarch of the Folk, had pushed the gift into his hands. "Here," she said. "This must get to Peewit. And you will find out from him why he has not used the box, or whether indeed my message ever reached him." She had looked grave. "I misdoubt it. Heath has not returned Home." For a moment the fire had crackled on the hearth. "Still," she sighed, "we may hope that Heath is with Peewit at Greenbriar, safely delivered of the message and ready to use the box. Remember, tell the Pledged: 'Tansy says, I had it from him to send to you, with our hopes. It was told me, When Darkness falls, send this to the Greenbriar, for the key is with the house of Beod. Now is the dark fallen indeed—come Home!' "

Firkin shook free of the memory of the way her voice had been shaking. For a moment he stared up at all those tallfolk. Then, pulling his hood awkwardly around to conceal his face, he climbed up the riverbank through the willow screen. Carefully he threaded through the crowd, being extremely wary not to jostle anyone lest he should somehow draw attention to himself.

He got squeezed off the road by a mounted merchant and paused to wait by a vendor's cart, one of the many who sold piping-hot nutmeats, fried apple rings, and the maple-sugared griddlecakes that would be served in every home on the last morning of Kindlefest. The proprietor of the cart, a large woman with red chapped cheeks and dull blond hair scraggling from her spotted cap, pushed a wooden spoon at the bubbling apple spice rings and nodded significantly to her neighbor, who sat a few feet away selling the honey drops that were good for easing a child's croupy cough. "I tell you," the blonde said, "he's got a lot of gall, showing up here just as if nothing had happened at all. Makes a body simmer just to think on it."

The coughdrop seller finished a pancake and licked her fingers. "Well, the dwarf's back in her good graces, they say. I heard he give the prince quite a drubbing yestidday when the lad called him out."

The cook flashed a look around to see that no officers would hear, then turned to her companion with a grin. "Can't say as I begrudge the dwarf for that: there's many has wanted to give that little pipsqueak his deserts."

The other was not so bold. She shrugged, but hid a smile under her apron as she wiped maple sugar off her mouth.

Out of the corner of her eye, the blonde just saw the tin platter of pancakes on the tailgate of her wagon brushed to the ground by Firkin's limp hand. The Hearthman seized the dead limb with his good hand and shoved it back in his belt to keep it from swinging. "Hi, you!" she shouted in outrage at the stupefied Firkin. "Pay up, whoreson, or I'll have the law on you!"

"I'm s-sorry!" the Hearthman gasped.

"Sorry! Sorry, is it?" she shrilled. *"Pay up!"*

Firkin backed toward the road. "I—I have no—"

He backed into a horse's haunch. "What's the problem here?" the Watchman asked briskly.

"This dirty bugger won't pay for what he's ruined!"

The corporal looked down at the hooded figure. "Think about it, dwarf," he advised. "Wouldn't you rather pay the copper to the old hag?"

By now she had seized the Littleman's arm, right on the dart. Firkin's mind kicked like a rabbit in a snare, and he could make no answer.

The trooper took his silence for guilt. "Fair enough," he said. "Take hold of the stirrup." Mechanically, the Hearthman did as he was told. "Good. Now, understand—if you let go that stirrup for any reason, I'll have to cut you down where you stand. Hear me?"

Terrified of the sword and numb with pain, the Hearthman jerked a nod.

The soldier kneed the horse, and they walked up the road toward the castle. The corporal glanced down. "Nice cloak," he remarked. "Looks to be good wool."

"It is."

"Are you a shepherd, then?"

"No. Mostly I paint. I deliver toys to the children at Kindlefest, too."

"Didn't know the dwarves kept Kindlefest like we do," the bored soldier said.

"They—we do," Firkin murmured. After a moment, he asked, "Would you happen to know where I could find Master Brickleburr?"

To his surprise the trooper chuckled. "You must be the hundredth person who's asked! Everyone wants to get a glimpse of him and the dwarf to tell the folks at home they saw the famous traitors! Hoping the Teazle will disappear before their eyes, like as not, and take the dwarf with him again."

"But I have something for him—"

"Aye, there's a few that have said that, too, and meant it," the Watchman answered with grim humor. "But if you had any funny ideas, fellow, forget them at once: the pair have Her Majesty's leave to come and go as they please. It would be worth your head to try getting to either one."

"But I have to—"

"Look, just shut up, all right? And I'll forget you ever said anything. Where you're going, you won't be able to cause any problems anyway," the corporal muttered. There was at that instant a crash somewhere off to their right, followed by a man's angry yell and a woman's cry. The Watchman stood in his stirrups to look over the heads of the crowd. "Hey, you!" he bellowed. *"Stop, thief!"* He pulled his horse around, reaching down to push Firkin away. "Stay right here," he ordered. "Don't you dare move!" The Hearthman tottered back, and shouting "Make way!" the soldier rode into the crowd.

A voice said at Firkin's side, "This way. Take it slow, and don't look so damned guilty." A tall, thin man in grimy clothes had taken his good arm and now propelled him surely but unhurriedly through the press of people. Nobody gave them a second glance, being intent on craning for a view of what was happening over where the officer was collaring the thief. Muir stretched to check, and at that moment, Firkin wrenched away and was disappearing behind a wagon by the time the tinker whirled around. The tall man hissed a curse. Unless he missed his guess, that had been a Teazle and now he'd lost him.

From behind a stall draped with lengths of woolen yard goods, Firkin watched the tallfolk man until he moved off up the hillside. Tucking his numb hand, he made his way up toward the castle once more. Once he passed a hand over his eyes, but then realized it was not faintness: it really was getting darker. Thick clouds had rolled to blacken the sun. He shivered and knew the Shadows were coming.

From the peephole in the side of the green wagon, the three figures took turns watching. Suddenly the one at the peephole grasped the team leader's arm. "They've just thrown the first of our logs on the bonfire, Raven." Though they had worked together before, they knew each other only by code names.

The team leader smiled and uncorked the small bottle. "Excellent. It is time for us to take this, then."

The third member of the team, known by the name Claw, took the bottle and hesitated. "This antidote will really keep our minds clear of the fumes?"

"I tried it," Raven replied. "It works, and there's no poison in it."

The man nodded and with no further comment took a swallow, then handed it across the wagon to the first man, Scorpion. Carefully Claw rearranged his mouthpiece of molded, colored wax. "I don't know about you, but I feel like a bloody harlequin." He flicked a finger at the black robe. "Do you really think the damned Ilyrians are this stupid?"

Raven looked from the peephole to him, and the topaz eyes were a flat glint. "When the fumes hit them, they'll see what they are expecting to see." He surveyed the black robes, hoods with metallic "eyes" sewn into them, and the molded wax fangs. "Oh, yes," he said, turning back to the small window. "They are that stupid."

Behind him the other two exchanged a glance. And would the fumes reach the archers on the battlements? they wondered. And would the powder keg buried in the bonfire ignite when it was supposed to?

"This is damned ridiculous," the dwarf grumbled and gave an irritated pull at the broad red shoulder-to-waist sash. Since Ilyria had never had an admiral before, Rhys-Davies hadn't been sure what proper form would be, but he had suggested it might not be too farfetched to use a sash as a symbol of rank, at least until something more fitting could be devised.

Waiting with Kursh in the fresco hall for the presentation of the heir to the masses out on the Sweep, the lord general fingered his own Greenbriar teal band. "Oh, I don't know. I think it's rather dashing."

"Proper pair of mummers we look," Korimson fumed.

"Cheer up. It could have been a tattoo in the middle of our foreheads or something."

The dwarf grunted something Peewit was just as glad he couldn't hear. To change the subject, the Littleman remarked, "Chilly day for the queen to be doing a Healing." He pulled his cloak tighter and shuffled his feet on the marble floor.

Kursh glanced at him. "Hadn't noticed. I suppose it is." He folded his arms on his chest. "If you'd eat once in a while and get built up a little, you wouldn't feel the cold so much." This wasn't the first time Brickleburr had mentioned it, and his old friend supposed the long seasons of living out of doors had weakened his constitution somewhat.

Peewit grinned slyly. "You sound like Thyla."

He'd caught the dwarf fairly, and Kursh reddened. "Sorry," he muttered. "The woman's nattering clings."

"And a very good thing it is, too."

Korimson rubbed his large nose. "I suppose."

"You miss her."

The dwarf reacted quickly. "Miss the shop." A moment later, he allowed, "Yes. And the girl."

The Littleman smiled.

From the direction of the staircase leading up to the living apartments on the floors above came a rising murmur and then a footman's ringing cry: "Make way for Her Royal Majesty!"

The assemblage of nobles, ambassadors, and honored guests bowed as Ariadne was escorted down the stairs and through the hall by her son, who for this one day was granted relief from his yeoman's duty. Out on the Sweep he would receive such oddments as the folk chose to present in honor of his birthday, and on his behalf, his mother would use the Crystal of Healing, making the Elixir to ease whatever sufferers there might be. This was in token of the day that Gerrit himself as King of Ilyria would wield Ritnym's gift to Beod's line for the good of his people. As was customary, the heir had already tried to use the Crystal, dropping it to the floor of the royal apartment. He had failed, not surprisingly.

Peewit bent into his obeisance and heard Kursh's barely audible hiss of pain as the sutures in his shoulder pulled. Glancing at the dwarf, the Littleman caught out of the corner of his eye a movement behind them. But the only thing behind them was the mural itself; they were standing within inches of the painted wall. As the queen passed by, he circumspectly looked back and froze.

Korimson tapped him on the arm. "Ye can get up now, lord general; no need to make a show for the queen's sake. Brickleburr?"

The Littleman silently pointed.

"What?" the dwarf rasped, glancing anxiously after the queen. They were supposed to be with the royal party on the Sweep.

"The hare," Peewit said in a low voice.

Korimson glanced, then stared.

When they came out onto the Sweep the sun had gone in, and there was a penetrating wind blowing off Willowsrill. People were hunching into their cloak collars and tucking their hands inside their sleeves. Pennons flapped, and tents strained at their ropes. Though the occasion was a happy one, folk would be glad to get around a fire when it was done.

Ariadne's heralds were already reading her holiday proclamation to the crowd by the time Peewit and Kursh slipped through the press behind the royal pair. ". . . Wherefore we do hereby announce the granting of full pardons to them both, and take them back into our most perfect trust." There was no cheer from the crowd, but there were obviously no boos, either.

The proclamation continued. "In token whereof, we have created two new commands so that we may continue to have the benefit of their long years of military experience. We present to you with our favor the Lord General of Ilyria, Peewit Brickleburr, the Pledged of the Hearthfolk, and Admiral of the Joint Fleet, Ambassador Kursh Korimson, Guildmaster of Jarlshof." At the queen's gesture both stepped forward in precision and made the salute of the First Watch to the gaping crowd. For a moment there was thick silence, then from the place where Jak Cooper and his men were drawn up in a cohort there was the sound of a sword clashing upon a shield, quickly taken up by the entire troop, the traditional military sign of approval. It spread to others, Thom Quint and Rory Fisher, and then there was applause among the dignitaries led by Imris, Fidelis, Rhys-Davies, and Captain Quint. When the queen raised her own hands, the laggards got the message and obediently clapped.

The crowd of plain folk was swayed, and there was polite, if not warm, applause. Peewit and Kursh stood shoulder to shoulder, unmoving. The queen raised her hand for silence, and when it came, nodded to the chief herald. He proclaimed, "Be it also known that the admiral has our election for another important office." At this, Peewit went to parade rest, and Gerrit stepped forward beside Kursh. "He will be our son's Senior Officer during this year of his yeomanry."

There was an outright gasp from somewhere in the crowd of nobles, and Ariadne could have fried her sister June for it. Gerrit turned and saluted the dwarf, and Kursh gravely whipped an answering salute. Probably no one else saw anything beyond military decorum in either gesture, but Peewit was close enough to see the smoldering in the gray eyes and the steady dark glint that answered it.

The proclamation was done, and the trumpeters sounded the fanfare. Afterward, Ariadne walked before her people and in the familiar way she had, blew on her hands. "Nippy, isn't it?" she commented loudly enough for many to hear. There was a chuckle, and the atmosphere warmed in an instant. "Thank you all for coming to our little party. I hope the fair has been good?"

She had reminded them of the carnival mood, and there was a cheer. One old man raised his treble to yell boldly, "The vittles is right tasty, Your Majesty. Come have someat to eat with us." His shawled wife, red with mortification that the drink had got to him, slapped his arm and hid her face.

Ariadne grinned. "I shall, I promise. I've been smelling pancakes all day!" They laughed, and she nodded. "But first, I've some work to do for you. This is the Lordling's gift to our good people. If you'd assist the sick to line up along the road, it will help us reach everyone. And might I ask some of you to build up the bonfire? It's too cold out here for my taste!"

Willingly, they went about the tasks, and the smoke from the wood began to roll over the Sweep and rise up to the battlements. The queen herself went to Fidelis, who awaited her by the tall golden pole. This support for the Greenbriar had been set ready this morning, and the marble square was already embedded in the half-frozen turf. They had performed the Ritual of the Rose so many times now that it was nearly automatic. Ariadne glanced over the arrangements. "All right, doctor, let's go." She waved a hand before her eyes at the stinging smoke and reflected ruefully she might just as well have kept quiet about the bonfire.

Since this was a less formal version of the Crowning Day ceremony, they had decided to dispense with the symbolic crowning with flowers and the holding of the official diadem by the heir. Gerrit stood near at hand, though, to aid her to her throne once the trance hit, and Will Quint still stood behind Fidelis with his naked sword ready to strike off the physician's head if the queen cared to enforce the edict against spilling the ruler's blood.

Ariadne unclasped the Crystal of Healing from about her neck, poised the shining thing above the marble tile, and dropped it. The crystal broke as it would for no one but the rightful ruler of Ilyria, and the seeds of the Greenbriar rolled onto the stone. Fidelis reverently gathered them and transferred them to the patch of turf beneath the gilded pole, and the queen turned back her sleeve and presented her bared wrist to the doctor. With the deftness that comes of long practice, Fidelis nicked open a vein, and rich drops began to fall upon the seeds. A twining vine quested up the pole, branchlets already beginning to leaf out.

The bonfire crackled and flared in the wind, growing higher over the heads of the crowd. Three figures in black, hoods drawn close to conceal the rest of their disguises, emerged from a green wagon nearby. A lanky man in rough clothes appeared suddenly at the fringe nearest the road. There was a high-pitched, two-tone whistle, and Peewit swung his head to Muir, startled out of his military demeanor. "Captain, there's been—" the tinker urgently shouted.

Simultaneously, a small figure stepped out of the crowd. "Pledged, the Matriarch bids me ask why have you not used the box? The Door is—" But at that instant Firkin's voice was drowned out by a rising groan that came from the direction of the river, then was answered from the bog to the south of the castle. Another sounded from Gerrit's Wood, and the three together raised the hair on some people's necks, though to others the sound was of some deep-toned horn.

For some inexplicable reason, it had gone dark. The bonfire exploded into an inferno, its fiery lash reaching out into the crowd.

Peewit jumped to protect the queen, though his chin was on his shoulder to stare at the only other live Hearthman he had seen. Kursh dropped his dagger into his hand and leaped to cover Peewit's back while pulling Gerrit with him. "Get down!" he roared and pushed the prince into a crouch.

Ariadne heard their voices through her trance, but was powerless to move. In slowed motion, she watched Fidelis, stooping near the Briar, knocked over by the first of the things that came out of the unnatural night. Its hands, if hands they were, reached to pluck the Greenbriar out of the ground as a farmer pulls a weed.

She felt herself fainting. Kursh was shouting something, and she tried to focus on him, but there was too much blackness between them. Another of the things coiled about her throne and grinned up at her, fangs dripping blood. She tried to hit it, but it was Peewit's hand that came between them.

A sudden piercing radiance pained her tranced eyes that could do nothing but stare helplessly. She was looking right into the heart of that white brilliance, and Peewit was standing solidly dark in the middle of it. The thing melted away, fangs and all.

The third of the black things struck down the small stranger who had called to Peewit, bent to the turf, and held up before her streaming eyes her own Crystal, swinging on its golden chain. The Shadow laughed, closed its fist about the Crystal, and disappeared.

For some time then she thought people stood swaying, some staring sightlessly up at the sky, others clutching their hair and shrieking. At some time the ordinary gray light of a cloudy afternoon filtered back, and the noisome smoke lofted away on the fresh breeze. Near and far there were cries and wailing.

Before her, Kursh was staring at the dagger in his hand. Gerrit was getting slowly to his feet, white and trembling. Peewit, his skin flaming red, was running toward the small huddle of cloak near the fringe of the crowd. Ariadne lost her balance and fell heavily into her chair.

Dizzily the queen licked her lips and leaned her head back, sinking toward the faint.

Peewit was cold and hot at the same time, as with a severe sunburn, and he knew that it had happened to him again, but he had no thought to spare for himself just at the moment. An instant more he stared down at his kinsman and then, though his reason knew it was already too late, he yelled, "Hoi! Orderly! Elixir here!" It was a battlefield cry, desperate and overwhelmed, and it echoed in his own ears like something heard in a dream. His breath caught in his chest suddenly, and memory made its home in his hollow heart: there had been a battlefield once . . . another small figure like the one he held now, but sandy of hair and bearded . . . yes. Dazed, Brickleburr felt a sensation much as if some rusty lock inside him had turned, and for the first time in all the times he had dreamed, he was able to follow this one to its beginning.

Sandy hair and a face closed in death, yes. A light extinguished. And screaming, weapons clashing, the shock wave behind him as the wall exploded—no, he told himself. That was the other time.

Sandy hair . . . *when*? Who was it I held? his inner voice shrieked frantically. On a battlefield, cold, silent as a tomb, night. Eyes, hundreds of heat lightning . . .

Whistling down the years, the answer came, and struck him dumb: Comfrey. 'Twas Comfrey I held this way . . . Comfrey Lichen, forefather of the Hearthfolk, who died in Beod's war, nigh a millennium ago.

Impossible, his rational mind said staunchly. True, his intuition hissed. Torn between them, the Pledged of the Hearthfolk retreated into himself and went still.

BOOK TWO:

The Dead Man's Hand

Chapter Nine

❧

The dagger was still in the dwarf's hand, and Gerrit was just pulling himself to his feet. Will Quint stooped anxiously over the queen in her chair, and old Fidelis had gotten as far as his knees and was staring at the upturned earth where the Greenbriar had been rooted out. "Where did it go?" he was asking the air.

Slowly Kursh turned to look about. He seemed uncomprehending for a moment, then his eye found Gerrit. "Has anybody gone for Theodric? There must be Elixir aplenty from the Crowning Day Healing a few months ago. We always feed Elixir to the queen to bring her out of the trance." He was still wandering just a bit and made a visible effort to pull himself together. "Are ye hurt, yeoman?"

"Sir, I am not." The boy said it like a confession, his hand clenched on the hilt of the new sword he hadn't even drawn.

"Good. Make yourself useful, then, in tending to the wounded," the admiral ordered quietly. "The doctors will be needing litter bearers, and so forth."

"You are wounded."

Kursh looked down at his scorched arm. "I fancy I'll be all right. Bloody nuisance." The dwarf focused on Quint's broad back. "How's your mother?"

"I understood the captain to say she was not marked by the dark things, only tranced as usual by the Briar."

"The captain?" The one eye flew open. "Powers! Peewit!" He whirled, the burned arm held out stiffly. "Brickleburr?" he bellowed roughly, so that several people farther down the Sweep turned inquiringly. The admiral darted a look over all that smoking scene, but nowhere did he catch sight of a small figure in a dwarvish jacket and a teal sash.

By now, Gerrit had caught his urgency. "He was here, just with that stricken child down there, immediately after the attack. I remember watching him run down there while I turned to check on Mother."

Korimson ran toward the small bundle of cloak a little way down the Sweep at the verge of the road. Awkwardly because of his arm, he crouched and reached to flip back the cloak. It was small, gray-haired, black as if the body had been frozen in a bog, and for one terrible instant Kursh thought it was his friend.

Even while his mind was registering that this was not Peewit, he heard Gerrit's groan. The boy whispered harshly, "It's another one of them!"

Knowing nothing of the Hearthman the prince had buried by the brook, Kursh merely answered, "Yes, one of the Littlemen. But 'tisn't himself, thank the Powers. Now, where the deuce has Peewit got himself to, do you suppose? You say he came down here?" He glanced up at his yeoman.

Gerrit's face was pasty. "Yes, sir," he managed, staring at the corpse.

The one eye narrowed and Kursh looked from Gerrit to the corpse. "Brace up, yeoman," he advised quietly. "The people are watching, and there's some of them have lost family. It won't do for them to see their prince go to pieces. Now help me find—"

There was a piercing, two-toned whistle and a hail from their left. "Hallo! Ambassador! Over here!" The lanky tinker was summoning him urgently, looking at something near where the bonfire had raged.

Kursh heaved himself to his feet and scrambled between two market stalls, Gerrit following. When they came up, Muir Dach was standing on the lip of a deep gouge the sudden fire had cut in the hillside. At the bottom of the pit was Brickleburr, slowly scooping scorched earth aside with his hands. The old dwarf went over the edge without hesitation, waving a sign to Muir, who put out a hand to keep Gerrit from following. "Brickleburr?" Kursh called quietly. "What are ye doing?"

No answer, just the slow hollowing of the ground.

Korimson slid to the bottom of the gouge. "Peewit?" At closer range, the Littleman's skin was fiery red, but showed no blistering, and the dwarf allowed himself to hope that Peewit was not burned, that this was the same odd thing that had happened at Ledgelawn. Tentatively he reached with his good hand to touch Brickleburr's shoulder. "It's all over, old sod. They're gone. Come, now, let's get you some Elixir, eh?"

At that, the Littleman's head came up and he slowly swung his head to the dwarf's voice. For a moment he stared as if Korimson were someone he had known once, but could not quite place. Then he blinked. "Kursh?"

"Mm." He indicated the earth still clutched in Brickleburr's hands. "What were ye doing?"

Peewit's eyes dropped to the small digging he had made in the scarred slope. Then he looked around. "I was . . . trying to get him buried before they found him."

Alarm went through the dwarf like a dagger in the vitals. "Easy, lad. Let's get you to Fidelis. Come on, up you go."

"Your arm—it's all burned."

"Aye." Experimentally he reached with his good hand to touch Peewit's face. "Powers, ye're like a stove! Never mind my bloody arm, we've got to get some Elixir into you!" He grasped Brickleburr's arm and began to push him up the steep cut.

"I'm all right," the Littleman protested.

"That's what you say. I misdoubt Fidelis will think so."

Muir reached down to help them both over the edge. "The doctors are bringing the Queen's Healing around to those who need it," he said quietly, "but I think Doctor Fidelis should see him. And you, ambassador."

"Him, anyway," the dwarf rasped. "Yeoman, move some of these people aside, would you? I've had a bellyful of being stared at the past few days, and Brickleburr doesn't need it, either."

"Master Fidelis is over by the other Littleman," the prince said over his shoulder and began to forge a way for them toward the chief physician.

Jak Cooper was crouched beside the corpse, leaning to peer intently at something Fidelis was pointing to. "It looks like crystal," the queen's foster brother was saying.

"No, it's cold. I think it's ice," the doctor suggested doubtfully. There was a rent in the sleeve of Firkin's jacket, and from it protruded a needle-thin dart that glinted in the dull light.

Gerrit gasped as he saw it, and both men looked up at him. "A Null dart!" the Greenbriar prince exclaimed. "You know," he said urgently to Fidelis, "the ones Aengus talks about! Comfrey Lichen died of one!"

The elderly doctor's eyes widened. "So those black things that attacked us were—"

"Shadows!" the boy confirmed.

"And if the Shadows have risen, then the Skinwalker will not be far behind," the physician said hollowly. He pulled the stained cloak back over the small body.

Nevelston asked sharply, "What are these things you speak of?"

But Kursh elbowed past the boy. "Fidelis, take a look at this fellow, will you?" He urged Peewit forward, but the Littleman seemed rooted, staring down between the tallfolk at the small body.

"Powers!" The physician got heavily to his feet and limped the few feet around Gerrit to put a practiced hand against the Littleman's brow. "Flash burns," he diagnosed.

Jak frowned. "But none of his clothing is singed."

Peewit put Fidelis's hand away. "It's nothing," he murmured.

"It's happened before," the dwarf interjected. "He says it doesn't hurt."

Fidelis turned to look up the Sweep. "Theo!" he shouted, and when his assistant looked up from the man he was tending, beckoned.

The Door is breached, Peewit thought. He swallowed.

The portly doctor came thudding to them, holding out the blue Elixir bottle to Fidelis, but staring as they all were at the only other Teazle besides Peewit any one of them had ever seen. "Dead?" he questioned quietly.

Jak nodded while Fidelis measured a swallow of the precious healing fluid into a tin cup. "Use it sparingly, Master," Theo advised. "We can't seem to find the Crystal."

The old healer's eyes flew open. "What?"

Past them, the queen's voice said, "Nor will we. The last one of those horrible things got it." She was pale with the terrible import of that news, but she managed a half-smile for Peewit. "And the other would have got me, except for you. How did you make the light?"

The Littleman looked at the ground. "I don't know," he whispered.

Jak was too shocked by what she had said about the Crystal to pay much attention, but Fidelis paused in handing the cup to Brickleburr. "The light was you?"

Peewit reached to take the healing draught. "I think so."

He sipped the sweet Elixir and sighed. Tansy Mossflower bids you come Home. Peewit felt weariness coming upon him and passed his hand over his eyes.

Jak, still crouched beside Firkin's body, noticed the stranger's pack and drew it toward him. Reaching in, he brought out something that made him smile, as though at an unexpected jest. "This was for you, I think, captain."

Peewit stared at the cradle-bunny as though he had seen a ghost. Tansy . . . His legs went, and he slumped to the turf with their anxious cries fading in his ears.

It was cold, so very cold, it was an icy river in an underground cavern, a star chimed out of tune, a frosted tree. Dark, too, the kind that makes you lost, so that you could not find your way Home. . . . But if you pushed against the back of your eyelids, there was light, a bare glimmer, enough to make things out . . . the firefly lamps flickering, the garden gate and cottage door. Step across the scrubbed stone threshold. She always keeps the mat neatly swept. . . .

Hot applesauce and gingerbread. She had her back to him, leaning to the hearth and the stewpot. Before he could speak, the dark-haired tallfolk man sitting to his supper at the table looked up from his bowl, surprised to see him there, hastily wrapping the scarf loosely across his face, but his voice smiling a welcome. "Hullo, Master Brickleburr! Where are you back from?"

Where are you back from?

Where are you. . . ?

They had brought the Littleman to the chief physician's own chamber rather than to the hospital so Fidelis could personally supervise his care. Kursh was pacing up and down the corridor outside when the doctor came out and quietly closed the door behind him. "Is he all right?" the dwarf demanded.

"Better," Fidelis said. "I've given him something to let him sleep. That seems to be what he needs, though I don't know that it's doing him much good: he seems to be dreaming a lot."

"What's wrong with him?"

"He's exhausted, Kursh. Mentally and physically exhausted. I gather from what he says that these Shadows have been after him for weeks now."

"Aye. He said as much when he got to my house. One of them came after him there, and it wasn't the first time it had happened. They're from the Wild Feller, that's clear enough. Probably the other Teazle down there on the Sweep was sent to warn Brickleburr about them."

"I would guess so. But that isn't the first dead Teazle he's seen of late."

Where he stood at attention beside the door, Gerrit jerked suddenly, and his sword scabbard scraped along the wall. Fidelis and the dwarf glanced at the boy, then went back to their low-voiced conversation. Kursh questioned, "He told you that?"

The physician crossed his arms and studied the floor thoughtfully. "Peewit is very confused just now, but I believe he found a grave—at any rate, he mentioned a broo—"

Gerrit drew a breath and then leaned to massage the calf of his bad leg. "Sorry, sirs," he covered. "Cramp."

"Put your weight on it," Fidelis directed.

"Walk it off, yeoman," the admiral said. "To the hall and bespeak us some dinner. Yourself, too."

The prince saluted and limped off down the hall, how thankfully they could not guess.

"You were saying?" Kursh rasped.

"Ah, yes. A brook is what Peewit said. I imagine it would be some place where he and the tinker camped. It gave him quite a turn, and he says he's not felt well since."

"Ye can't wonder at that," Korimson said quietly. "Years and years he goes without ever seeing another of his own kind, and now . . ." He shook his head. "He's not as young as he used to be, Fidelis, and that kind of shock would be hard enough on anyone."

"Assuredly."

Both fell silent until Kursh stroked his mustache. "That light."

"Yes." The doctor nodded. "That is the question, isn't it? What was that light?"

Gerrit was on the stairs down to the hall when there came a hail from above: "Nephew!"

Ka-Treer came down the stairs behind him, attended by the Shimarrat noble who shadowed him everywhere. The king slipped a heavy maroon cloak over his shoulder. "Quite a birthday this has been for you," he remarked.

Gerrit smiled a little. "Hasn't it, though?"

"It still seems rather beside the point to have the heir to the kingdom go through this yeomanry, but I suppose each place has its customs."

"I suppose."

Ka-Treer studied his face. "So the dwarf is now your training officer." He thumbed his narrow waxed mustache and said in a low voice, "That is not an insult any man would have offered to another."

The prince was nearly as tall as his Shimarrat uncle. "The Admiral bested me in a contest I initiated. I don't like it, but that's the way it is. As for the queen's choice of him, I am in no position to quarrel with it."

Ka-Treer glanced at his man. "One might argue for you," he suggested.

"No."

"Ah, I see. Timing is everything. Yes. Very clever."

Gerrit said nothing.

The Shimarrat king smiled. "Do you sail with the admiral?"

"Would it matter?"

Ka-Treer's eyes widened at the directness of the question, then he chuckled. The sound was very much as if someone had drawn his nails down a rain gutter. "I like you, Gerrit. We are two of a kind."

Not on your sodding life, assassin. "And Ka-Bril is not."

The smile narrowed, and then the eyes. "No, Ka-Bril is not. But he is my son." There was a warning in the stirrup-iron eyes.

"And Ariadne is my mother." There was no less a warning in the dawn-gray ones.

The Shimarrat's onyx ear gem glinted dully in the torchlight of the landing as he smiled again. "Ah, yes. We are all one family. How nice to have kin we can rely upon."

"Yes. Thanks again for the stallion, by the way."

King Ka-Treer was not unaware of the gibe, but he nodded genially. "You're welcome, of course. Well, now I must take my leave of you—I've seen your mother and am on my way to my ship."

"You sail tonight?"

"At first light, before there's a danger of running anyone down in thick traffic. I wouldn't want to be accused for any accidents."

"Your helmsman will be obeying the channel markers, then." The Shimarrats had ignored them at their arrival.

Ka-Treer shrugged slightly. "Big ships are hard to handle sometimes."

"That must be why you plate the sides of all yours."

"Exactly." He moved a few steps down, then looked back up at Gerrit. "Incidentally, do you know the universal prayer of sailors, nephew? They pray to die on land." He stared. "It is a sentiment worth thinking about." Twitching his cloak around his shoulders, he turned down the steps once more.

"I have heard it," Gerrit replied. "Say, Uncle—can you swim?"

Ka-Treer walked steadily away from him and turned the corner in the steps. His voice echoed back up to the prince. "I have never needed to learn, Gerrit," he said with total assurance.

Treacherous bastard, Ariadne's son thought. He waited until he could no longer hear their footfalls, then made his way down to the Watch mess, thinking all the while that there must be some way to wipe that smile off the Shimarrat's face.

Ka-Treer was smiling in the privacy of the stairwell. His aide, Baron Te-Rosh, glanced at the king. "A most forward young man, even for a prince and a kinsman," the Shimarrat noble observed.

The holder of the Lion throne laughed gutturally and stroked his waxed mustache, halting on the steps. "Ah, yes. There is much of the family in the boy, Rosh." His smile flicked off as if someone had blown out a candle. "But not enough. In his place, I'd have had us all killed in our sleep last night and locked my lady mother someplace where she could make no trouble, then declared myself king. No, Gerrit is not quite Lion enough." He fingered his earring. "Interesting, though."

The baron cast a glance up the stairs and lowered his voice, though they had spoken in murmurs. "Shouldn't we be getting aboard, sire? I confess, I do not feel comfortable with all these Watchmen lurking."

Ka-Treer smiled again, a feral drawing back of the lips. "Don't let it bother you, baron. They're all still so stunned by our little charade, they haven't the will for more than a horn of ale and a maidservant."

Te-Rosh grunted. "I cannot blame them there, sire. Even protected by the antidote as I was, when our agents leaped out of the smoke and those horns sounded—" He shook his head ruefully, prompting another laugh from the king. "The 'other Hearthman' was a nice touch, too. Some insurgent's child, I presume?"

The King of Shimarron suddenly fixed him with a stare. "Do you think to fool with me, Rosh?"

The baron held up one hand, palm out. "Nay, sire! I—I was surprised when he appeared, that is all. I had not known that part of the plan."

"You didn't arrange it?"

The flat coldness of the voice made the nobleman flinch involuntarily. Rosh was plainly mystified. "No, sire. Most certainly not."

Ka-Treer's face was a mask. Then he turned in a swirl of maroon cloak and clattered down the steps. "Damn," the baron heard him mutter.

The council would be held in the library, the only place private enough for their deliberations, though it would be crowded. As Kursh came through the door with his yeoman, Imris quickly went to them. "How is he?" the Eldest asked anxiously.

"Better, Fidelis says," the dwarf answered. "I went in to check on him myself, and he was sleeping. The red, whatever it is from, has faded."

"Ah, that is good news. I feared the worst when we saw how the other had died."

"Gave me a turn myself," Korimson admitted. He looked up at the taller Yoriandir as they went to claim a couple of the chairs. "Didn't see you after it all happened out there, though I admit I had other things on my mind at the time."

Imris smiled. "The sparks from the bonfire were blowing right up the Sweep toward Gerrit's Wood. I was fearful, and went to be sure none of them caught. I should not have deserted you all that way, very likely, but at any threat to Nilarion's Children I cannot help myself."

Korimson shrugged. "If you didn't tend them, who would? Of course you get worried."

"Who would tend them, indeed?" the Yoriandir murmured.

The dwarf cocked an eye at him as they sank into two overstuffed chairs. "Now, I didn't mean anything by it, Imris. Besides, I thought your precious forest was aswarm with wizards from Covencroft, lending a hand with the trees?"

"Oh, they come." The bard smiled sadly. "But truly, I think it is more to study me than to tend Nilarion."

The fierce mustache bristled. "What do you mean, study?"

Imris' fir-green eyes were shadowed. "Well, if you have only one of a thing left, there is a great temptation to try to find what made it live. Or die." He tried a smile. "But as I remind myself, they only seek to know what is between Nilarion and me so they may make some provision for when I am no longer."

"Bloody cheeky of them, if you ask me."

The Yoriandir's smile widened into genuine amusement, and in the silent way of his people he sent a thought to the dwarf's mind: 'It is bloody cheeky. Perhaps one of these days I shall ask Nilarion to pick them all up with her branches and pitch them into the straits.'

"Be one hell of a surprise for the scrollmasters, wouldn't it?"

'Guard yourself well, Guildmaster! They'll be wanting to know how you blow crystal next!'

"Fat chance they'll find out anything." Kursh tugged at his eyepatch. "Except how to find the privy, maybe."

Imris laughed aloud, and several of the assembled men glanced their way, perhaps feeling that the occasion was too serious for such a display. The Eldest quickly changed the subject. Nodding to where Gerrit stood near the door, he said, "I was pleased her Majesty named you for his Senior Officer."

"I wasn't," the dwarf replied bluntly. "Oh, it's an honor and all, but I could do with a bit less honor and a bit more peace, to say the truth."

"I will not gainsay you, old friend, but it seems to me a wise choice."

"Well, we'll see what we can do," Korimson grunted, but the Yoriandir thought he looked pleased nonetheless. After a moment, the dwarf observed, "Not the stone wall he pretends to be, is he?"

"No. I have never thought so," Imris answered quietly. "Fidelis thinks highly of him, and that is something."

The eyebrows lowered. "Not much. Fidelis liked Alphonse as a lad, too, you remember."

The Eldest nodded, smiling. "The doctor has an open heart."

Kursh muttered something about a thick head and then fixed the bard with his one good eye. "Tell me just one thing: is he as good with a bow as he is with a sword?"

Imris cocked his head. "He showed promise as a boy, but has never pursued it further."

The admiral sighed. "Ah, good, I'm fairly safe on that score, then. If I can keep him in front of me, we'll have no problem."

Though his tone had been meant as a joke, the Yoriandir sobered. "You don't think—?"

"Yes. I do."

The Eldest was still pondering this when the door opened and men rose in respect for the queen.

"Sit, gentlemen, sit," Ariadne ordered, and when she was settled at the head of the long table in the middle of the room, they did so. The queen looked around. "Thank you for your prompt attendance, my lords. We have been much troubled at what happened this day, and desired to lay the matter before you." She paused, and some of the men looked at one another. The queen's chin came up and she faced them squarely. "The rumor you have no doubt heard by now is true: the Crystal of Healing is gone. We believe the servants of the Unnamed have taken it; at least, so it appeared to us who were near enough to see."

There was dead silence.

Jak stood. "I should like to know more about these things that attacked us this afternoon. Master Fidelis, you called them Shadows? Skinwalkers?"

The elderly doctor rose to his feet. "I must say first that I only believe the creatures to have been Shadows: I do not know it for certain. But they bore striking resemblance to beings Aengus the Painter calls in his manuscripts Shadows of the Unnamed. Wild, dark terrors, Aengus says, which prey on human blood in the night hours." He twisted his gnarled fingers together. "Particularly upon the blood of children." There was thick silence in the room.

Jak broke it. "Is there any way we can track them? Go after them?"

The queen looked to Fidelis to answer. He said, "You

cannot trail what does not leave tracks, my lord. The Shadows are not of this world, and they have returned where they came from. No, there is no way to follow them."

From his station behind the queen and to her right hand, Captain Will Quint asked in a hollow voice, "So we must presume the Crystal—"

"—is now, or soon will be, in the Unnamed's hands," the queen finished for him. "Yes. Exactly." There was a restrained murmur. She gave them time. "I am afraid there is more bad news." They went silent again, and Ariadne told them, "You have heard Lord Nevelston refer to something called the Skinwalker. Doctor Fidelis has told me of this creature. It appropriates the skin of its victim and goes about as that person, perfectly unknown until it kills again."

The military men stiffened, and the courtiers blanched.

Fidelis said quietly, "Aengus talks of the Shadows and the Skinwalker appearing together. I think it likely if the Shadows have visited us, the Unnamed will not fail to send the Skinwalker as well."

They took some moments to absorb this. Then a voice near the back was raised. "And what will happen now?"

Ariadne clasped her hands on the table. "Based on prior experience . . ." She smiled slightly. "I should say quite a lot." From different points in the room, a few tried to support her wry understatement with a chuckle, but it was not very successful against the sober fear. She swept a glance around. "The truth is we don't know, and doubtless that is part of the Unnamed's plan. But I was hoping to set out everything we know up to this point as rationally as we can, and see if something suggests itself that might be of help." She sighed and sat back in her chair. "First, then: it seems plain, since both of the Unnamed's prior attacks have been directed specifically against one of the other Powers at a time, this must be against Tychanor's Realm, the only one he has so far left untouched. This conclusion is borne out by the appearance of the Hearthman at the ritual down on the Sweep."

"Ah, so it *was* a Teazle, then?" a voice asked.

"It was," the queen confirmed. "Though I was entranced at the time, I know he yelled something to the lord general. Did anyone hear it clearly?"

Many shook their heads. Her brother Jak contributed,

"Something about a box. I couldn't hear because the tinker was yelling, too."

"Another tinker," Hilliard neBlackmore said in disgust. "Aren't they always around just at the worst times?"

Immediately they all thought of Tomasheen and the black pipes thirteen years before. Without giving away Muir's secret association with her army, there was nothing Ariadne could say to clear Muir now, but Will Quint spoke up. "Aye, fleas on a hound pup, they are." That drew a laugh, and the dangerous feeling against the wandering tinsmiths was defused for the moment.

Kursh had been thumbing his mustache. "I know the Hearthman called Brickleburr 'Pledged.' And whatever the rest of it was, Peewit heard it clearly. I saw his face."

The room went quiet again as each of them searched his memory of that shout.

Someone uncomfortably suggested, "Could it have been an incantation? I mean, the . . . Shadows came right on the heels of it."

Into the rising murmur, Imris's silver voice sprinkled cool water. "Nay, the Hearthfolk are Tychanor's own; they would not traffic with the Other Side. Clearly, the Shadows had been following this poor fellow and caught up with him here. They killed him so that he could not deliver his message to Peewit."

"I believe the Eldest is correct," Fidelis agreed.

"I heard," said neBlackmore, "that something strange was found among the Teazle's effects. Will someone say what it was? And does it give the message?"

The queen looked a little embarrassed. "Well, a cradle-bunny. Though of course that may not have been meant for Peewit at all," she added hastily against the grins that flickered around the room.

"No doubt this Teazle was on an errand to some child, and came here to consult the lord general first," the Eldest helped out gravely.

Ariadne thanked him with a glance. "No doubt," she agreed.

A Watchman asked, "Can't Master Brickleburr tell us what all this is about? Why is he not here?"

"He is under Doctor Fidelis's care," the queen answered. "To find and then lose a kinsman in such short order was a heavy blow to him, as you can imagine, and he felt ill.

When he awakes, we shall certainly give him the items. Quite likely he knows more than we about the business of the Hearthfolk."

"And what of the wizard?" another voice asked. "I'd like to know what Master Alphonse would say about all of this."

There were murmurs of assent. Ariadne's chin came up. "I expect he will be here shortly—as you know, Lieutenant Jamison is seeking him."

"Then what are we to do meantime?" Will Quint asked.

Ideas began to come. "Send a message to the Meld at once," Jak suggested. "With all due respect to Master Alphonse, we need all the wizardly help we can get. Perhaps if Covencroft knew the danger that has befallen, its denizens would use their powers in concert to protect what is most vulnerable: Her Majesty, the Eldest, and Nilarion."

"And Brickleburr," the dwarf rasped.

Fidelis pulled himself to his feet once more. "May I offer a suggestion, Your Majesty? We should send Riders out to all the Retreats and have them bring back all the Elixir we sent out after the Ritual of the Rose this past summer. If there is to be no more Elixir for a time, then it will be easier to protect our precious stock if it is all here, under lock and key."

Ariadne considered. "But if there is to be an attack, it will no doubt fall upon us here first and hardest. Perhaps the country folk may be spared for a time, and in that case the Elixir might be of better service where it is." The old man bowed and resumed his seat. The queen tapped a fingernail against the table. "But this brings up another important question I will ask you all to help me decide. Right now, I believe it is entirely possible no one outside this room except the lord general realizes the Crystal of Healing is gone." She turned one hand palm up and looked slowly around. "Shall we tell the people? Or shall we keep it silent as long as we can?"

The Eldest of the Yoriandirkin answered, "I should like the folk told, my queen. The times ahead are very dangerous, and there may well be things they would want to do, if they knew their time might be short."

Will Quint shook his head vigorously. "Begging your pardon, Majesty, but if word of this gets out, you can bet your last shilling trouble will break out everywhere, not the least from the Shimarrats and Barreners: it's only the knowledge that in a war we could heal our wounded quicker than they could bury their dead that's held all the scum back till now. Don't tell anybody, I ask."

There was a rumble of agreement from the fighting men in the room.

She looked around. Jak looked pensive, Kursh was nodding, Fidelis and Imris exchanged a glance, and her son, where he stood near the door, was pale and had his hand clamped on the hilt of his sword. Ariadne nodded to herself: she had known the decision would be hers. "Very well, gentlemen, then I will put you on your Oath not to reveal anything you have heard in this room concerning our Crystal."

Imris frowned. "How will you explain the fact you are not wearing it?"

Ariadne's hand went automatically to her breast, where she had worn the Crystal on its golden chain for nearly eighteen years. Her hand dropped. "There is a clever replica, an imitation done some years ago by the goldsmith, who gave it as a gift, saying he knew it was but poor flattery." She sighed. "At a glance, it will serve, I think." She rose, and the men clattered to their feet while Will Quint led the salute. The queen's chin came up. "Pray the Powers to help us all, gentlemen, and put the best face on it you can." She rustled out the door.

Gerrit held his position while men began drifting past him to the door. Korimson was across the room, talking to the doctor and the Eldest. The prince's hands were colder than they'd been yesterday when he'd challenged the dwarf to the duel. He had not realized until he'd heard it here what the Teazle out on the Sweep had yelled: 'Why have you not used the box?' The very box now wrapped in an old shirt in the bottom of the trunk that held his childhood toys, a place he'd felt certain Rory Fisher would not disturb. His stomach knotted, and he was positive his guilt showed. Why, the doctor was staring over at him right now!

Fidelis was only half listening to Kursh, and his brow was furrowed. What box? he was thinking. I don't recall Aengus wrote anything about a box, but I should reread . . .

The dwarf bumped him out of his reverie. "Supper, I say." The Guildmaster looked exasperated. "Why does everybody around here go all staring when the Wild Fellow pulls out his bag of tricks? Powers, ye'd think we hadn't ever tussled with him before."

Imris's fir eyes had gone the muddy green of a fall brook. "But always before there has been the Crystal."

The three old friends looked at each other. The dwarf straightened his eyepatch. "Right. Where the hell has the boy wonder gotten himself to, do you suppose?"

Chapter Ten

The black-and-white cat had had a rough journey. First there had been the daring leap from the rocks of the headland to the deck of the small fishing boat, and then she had been hard pressed to keep up with the booted one as he changed from boat to boat and finally to horse, spurring hard for the castle here. But she had smelled the mingled odors of this place of the human queen on him and so had followed. Her wizard needed help, and this was the only place to get it.

She had squeezed under the gate, unmarked by the soldiers, and run wearily up the marble steps into the stone house. Food first, her stomach had demanded loudly, but she had ignored it, going instead to the room where her wizard had sometimes slept in the bed. But the human queen had not been there, and the stout woman had tried to catch her, so Patience had left. Later, when she had satisfied her hunger, she would return, and perhaps she would be able to make the queen understand.

Now she was on her way down the corridor, padding swiftly toward the stairs to the food place, when a most intriguing odor stopped her in her tracks. It was faintly sweet and strongly spicy, and there was a good bit of pumpkin mixed in. Her whiskers twitched and she butted in softly against the wooden door she had been passing. The latch must not have quite caught, because the door opened a crack, enough for her to squeeze through.

This was the herb man's room; it smelled just the way she remembered. Cautiously she slipped to the deep shadow cast by the edge of the hearth and paused to listen. She could hear someone breathing evenly in sleep and then murmur and turn his head restlessly on the pillow. It was the Hearthman, the one she and the wizard sometimes visited out in the woods, who traveled with the human who reeked of horses and boiled sheep. She took a good look around out of her one eye to satisfy herself that the stinky one was not here. The spicy scent drew her toward the bed.

Light-footed, she hopped easily up on the stool drawn to the bedside and extended her neck to sniff at the Hearthman. No, the wonderful smell wasn't coming from him, though he had his own comfortable peat-and-honey scent, like every one of the Folk she'd ever chanced to meet. The spicy sachet was higher, on the table beside the bed. She craned to see what might be up there, then stood up on her hind paws to lean on the edge of the table. Ah! Right in front of her, set a little back so that it would not roll off the small table, was a round loaf in oiled paper, sitting next to a bit of fur that might have looked like a rabbit to a human. Behind both items was a knapsack. The multiple odors of the loaf fascinated her, and she stepped delicately up onto the table.

For a moment, she sat with a cocked head, regarding the bits of honeyed fruit which dotted the bread. Then she reached a paw to touch the thing. The fake rabbit wobbled, and she crowded back to the edge of the table, watching it suspiciously. It came to rest against the pack and steadied once more. She sat down to study it almost clinically. When the thing made no further move, she stretched her head to sniff at it.

And got the shock of her nine lives when a squeaky voice chittered, "Hey! Leave off, will you? Can't a fellow get a bit of a nap without the buffets of fortune cracking his noggin? I say, Master Firkin, this isn't like you at all, not at all, sir. A bit more consideration, if you please!" The flap of the pack bulged suddenly, and a large-eared, pointed nose with whiskers nearly as long as her own was suddenly staring up at Patience with indignation that became shock. "Oh, Powers!" the nose gasped and disappeared back into the canvas bag.

In one long leap, the cat reached the floor and streaked under the bed, whence her eye reflected the firelight as she stared up, every hair stiffly at the alert, nose quivering. 'What are you?' she hissed.

From within the pack there was silence. The bed creaked as Peewit turned in a dream.

Patience slitted her eye while she called to mind every feature she had seen. Ears, nose, whisk . . . oh. At once she relaxed and emerged from under the trailing wool blanket to sit primly with her tail curled around her forepaws. Her whiskers twitched. 'What are you?' she repeated quietly, though she knew.

The canvas muffled nervous murmurs. The cat pricked her ears to hear. ". . . cat, wouldn't you know? Lord of Summer, what's Master Firkin gotten me into this time? I don't need all this aggravation. Could have stayed home, should have stayed home, let the younger ones have a crack at it. But no, Matriarch Tansy's a hard one to say nay to. 'Sir Winston, you're just the one for the job,' says she, and here I am, cat out there, ruffian, aren't they all?"

Patience wiped a paw over her face to keep from sneezing her amusement. 'You can come out now,' she invited.

"I think not," the squeak answered firmly.

'I will not hurt you.'

A snort came from the pack.

Patience hopped up on the stool. 'Truly, I will not.'

"You're a cat."

'And you are . . . ?'

"Not a cat."

Patience's eye gleamed with good humor. 'Well, Not-a-Cat, it may surprise you to know that not all of my kin enjoy the hunt.'

The pack muttered, "Of course not. Why hunt when one can picnic?"

The pied cat sneezed a laugh and sat down upon the stool. She scratched her ear. 'You must be hungry.'

"And no doubt the same is true of you."

'I was on my way to the room where the humans keep the cheese.'

There was silence. My word, Patience thought, startled. He really is hungry. She thought at the pack, 'If I fetch you some, will you believe I intend you no harm?'

"It's just preposterous enough to be the truth. Very well, cat: you fetch me some cheese, and I'll credit you with not being the bloodthirsty murderer I took you for."

Stay awhile, then, Patience thought at him. She jumped

down from the stool, trotted to the door, and paused, turning her head to look back. 'Lipopo, or cheddar?'

The canvas wiggled, and beside the buckle two tiny eyes caught the firelight. "They have Lipopo here?"

'Of course,' the cat sighed. 'We queens feast only on the best, you know.' She nudged the door open and slipped through.

She made the trip downstairs quickly and had no difficulty following the pungent scent of the cheese she had come for. In the room where pots clanged and charcoal burners hissed, a wheel of Lipopo lay on a table. She crept under a crockery rack, waited until just the right moment, and leaped up to the table. Some slices were already cut, and she speared one with her claws, got a good bite on it, and jumped for the floor.

"Get out of it!" a voice roared, and she slithered under the rack and ran along the wall. She was nearly out the door when the human's heavy foot just caught the tip of her tail. Patience screeched around the cheese in her mouth, but with great resolution did not drop it. She whisked down the hall and ran up the stairs.

By the time she made it back to the room where the Hearthman slept, the pungent cheese was making her eyes water and her stomach rumble. She squeezed in through the door, trotted briskly to the stool, stood up on it, and dropped the slice of Lipopo beside the pack. There she panted, and took some for herself.

From within the pack there was no reply.

Patience sniffed, and the tip of her tail began to twitch. 'Oh, don't be such a nit!' she spat. 'If I'd wanted to hurt you, I could have knocked your precious hideaway right off that table.'

"No doubt. But that might make trouble for you, mightn't it?" The smug voice was beside her, in the bed.

The Queen of Cats jerked her head to look. From the pillow near the Hearthman's head two beady eyes and a set of large ears regarded her with amusement.

'Mouse,' she thought at it, 'you become tiresome. I got my tail stepped on for you. Now, come out here and eat this cheese, or I will.'

The mouse pulled at his whiskers. "Please don't take this ill, cat, but I'd feel better, I would, if you'd just remove yourself a bit. Say, over to the door?"

The black-and-white cat muttered something she had often heard her wizard say in like circumstances and stalked to the door. She sat down. 'Are you sure you wouldn't prefer me out in the hall?' she asked sarcastically.

"No, that will be sufficient as a test of good faith." Carefully the mouse crept along the pillow, up onto the headboard, then up to the table. He sat up for a moment, regarding the unmoving cat, then dropped to all fours and tore off a corner of the cheese. Holding it in his delicate hands he nibbled, noisily sucking his teeth between each bite. "It's a very fine strain of Lipopo," he remarked. "Strong but not overwhelming, nutty without being coarse, and the bouquet is really quite wonderful."

'There's an even better strain made by a cheesemaker in the little port town of Sparrow-on-the-Sea.' Patience licked quietly at her sore tail.

The mouse forgot his hunger in surprise. "By the bees! You've sampled Sparrow Lipopo, have you? Tell me, does it deserve the glowing plaudits one hears of it?"

The cat considered. 'It is a trifle too dry for my taste, but it is a very good cheese still.'

"Hmm. I like my cheese moist, too," the mouse admitted. "I have been anxious to try the Sparrow Lipopo, but perhaps now I shall spare myself the trip." He wiped his whiskers and cleared his throat. "I very much fear I have misjudged you, Mistress Cat. An understandable failing, I hope you'll allow, in view of the traditional troubles our kin have had. My apologies, dear lady." He clasped his hands and bowed.

Patience lifted her head regally. 'The human calls me Patience,' she informed him quietly.

"Yes, they do have a passion for naming things, don't they? The tallfolk, I mean." He helped himself to another bit and kept his hand over his mouth as he chewed. "Now, the Folk are very decent about things like that; they give one the courtesy of listening when one tells one's name."

'And yours is . . . ?'

He seemed struck. "Oh, my! It must be rattling around in that pack—my manners want polishing!" He drew himself up. "I, Mistress Patience, am Winston Thatch-rustle, of the Hedgerow Thatch-rustles, in the county of Gates."

'Gates? I have taken my wizard many places, but I have not heard of Gates.'

"Ah, well, you name things a bit differently down here, that is all. You would say, I believe, the Meadows of Morning."

Patience's ears pricked. 'Then you live with the Hearthmen.'

"Yes, yes. Charming Folk!" He seemed to recollect something, and slowly put the bit of cheese down. "At least they were." He glanced over at Patience. "There's trouble in the Meadows just now. That's why Master Firkin and I are here, you see."

Patience recalled a bit of conversation between the sentries. 'I am sorry to tell you, but I think your Hearthman is no more.'

The mouse sat back on his haunches and put a hand on his nose. "Oh, dear. Dear, dear." His voice was choked. "So they followed us down here, did they? I was afraid of it." His ears drooped.

'Who?'

Sir Winston closed his beady eyes for a moment as if to shut out some dreadful scene. "Terrible things, Mistress P. If you took a nightmare and turned it inside out so that it was most times invisible, you'd have something like these creatures. Horrible."

The cat was unmoving. 'I think I have seen one, mouse. It attacked my wizard and stripped off some of his skin. It is to get help from these silly humans that I have come here, though none of them will speak to such as you and me. And these things have attacked the Meadows of Morning where Lord Tychanor has his palace?'

The glistening black eyes fixed on her. "Oh, it's worse than that: they've attacked the Lord of Summer himself."

Patience rose. 'Let me hear it! The Dark One hates my wizard mightily!'

"He is in danger, then. Here." He indicated the bed with his long nose. "Do come out of the draft, and let us make ourselves comfortable. I feel in need of blankets to burrow in myself, for the memory is very unpleasant."

'Take care lest you wake this Hearthman,' Patience warned. 'He is very tired, and ill, too, I believe. I will stay here on the rug for that reason.'

When they were settled, he in a cave of blanket below

Peewit's updrawn feet, and she curled on the wool rug, Sir Winston began to tell her the tale.

Through his dreams wove a squeaky but somehow familiar voice and Peewit listened.

That day was, up to a point, like any other day in the Meadows of Morning, the mouse related.

The summer sun shone brightly, but not oppressively hot, and there was a sweet herb-smelling breeze wafting. The bees droned busily about their work, looping through an open window here and there to report news in the chatty way they had, so that every now and again somebody would pause in the painting, gluing, or sewing to rub his nose and smile under his hand not to give offense to the friendly insects. In cottages all over the Meadows—in the lush grass beside the river that was the Mother of Waters, in the patchwork fields surrounding the sunmill, on the heathery knees of the cupping mountains—the day's work went on amid snatches of whistled song. The Folk kept right at it, too, forsaking a break for muffins and tea, for it was late summer already and Kindlefest was barely four moons away. The cradle-bunnies had to be ready by then.

Near evening, when she was cross-eyed with looking over the lists and there was time to stretch and enjoy a bit of walk in the golden afternoon, Matriarch Tansy Mossflower decided to drop by Firkin Flaxmaster's shop and see what he was up to. As was his custom, Sir Winston had ridden along in the lace pocket of her apron.

The elderly Hearthwoman opened the gate in the fence around her cottage and struck off down Main Path through the village. "Hullo, Heath!" she called over her next-door neighbor's low wall. "There's a pie on the sill. Help yourself!"

His apple cheeks wrinkled in a smile. "And I've some buttermilk for you. I'll leave the pail on your kitchen table."

She waved her thanks, and the mouse could tell she was thinking as she often did what a shame it was that Heath should have lost his beloved Lily so many long years ago, when the Dark One had attacked the Lord of Summer.

"Evening, Matriarch. Ain't it fine, though? 'Course, there's rain coming."

Tansy had not heard Millet Bullrush, the village lamplighter, come up behind her, but she should have known he was there: an aromatic cloud of pipe smoke wreathed his head, as always, and he was whistling to the fireflies.

"My goodness, Mill, isn't it a little early for the lamps?"

He pushed his cap back on his head to squint up at the blue-and-golden clouds. "Well, seemed to me to be coming on for evening kind of quick tonight." He whistled a few notes, and part of the swarm of fireflies riding on his jacket flew into the streetlamp he held open for them. When darkness came, they would light, casting a soft radiance over the path. In the early dawn, Millet would be back through to collect them and bring them to breakfast.

Now that he mentioned it, the Matriarch noticed a slight grayness to the air, and the clouds were thickening. She pulled the shawl closer. "Looks as if I should have brought my umbrella," she remarked.

"Be a good excuse to duck in somewhere for a cup of tea." He winked and chirruped to the fireflies. With a nod to her, he strode briskly down the path to the next light.

She smiled and took the side turning that led in the direction of the millpond. From a chink in the stone wall bordering the fields a cricket chirped a greeting, and she answered, "Very fine, thank you. And yourself? Are the rocks warm?"

They were, and she passed on. There was a stile set into the wall, and she gathered her skirts to climb over. From the top step she could look out over the neat squares of the vegetable gardens, hay fields, and orchards. Her eye traveled past the sunmill, its huge gossamer sails whirring busily in the sun, and up the terraced slopes where the amber and deep burgundy grapes ripened in the fullness of the long summer hours. On the hillside opposite, the stepped levels of the Sun Palace reflected the sunset, but the ruby windows were not lighted, so the Power wasn't home yet. He would be soon, though: his Lamp was flaming down the western sky toward its lampstand under the Rim of Earth, and after refilling it in preparation for the morrow, Tychanor would step though the back door of the world and after supper join them on the broad lawn for a game of croquet, if the rain held off.

The Matriarch hopped nimbly down the other side of the stile and patted the inquisitive foal who came to whicker at her while the mare went about her cropping some distance off. Quietly, in case Firkin was still working, Tansy walked between the rows of turnip and cabbage and stooped to smell the sweet nicotiana. From the window of his work-room, Firkin saw her and came down the path. By the twinkle in his eye, she knew he'd been working on some-thing quite extraordinary. "Let's see!" she urged.

He smiled and brought it from behind his back. Captured in his lifelike carving was a young rabbit, flop-eared and wearing a flower chain. The expression Firkin had painted on its face was so comically sly that Tansy chuckled. Firkin wiped paint off on the rag sticking out of his back pocket. "Not too silly?"

Tansy giggled. "From your brush? Hardly!" Last year, he had given them a bunny wearing a blue coat with big but-tons and carpet slippers, for all the world like a tallfolk mayor. There had been some discussion about this depar-ture from realism around the hearths on Main Path, but most everyone eventually agreed that you had to let talent have its way. As long as it didn't offend Lord Tychanor, it was all right with them. The Power himself had taken one look and laughed. So now the Matriarch thought it politic to ask, "Has himself seen it yet?"

Firkin Flaxmaster stretched his back and rubbed a hand through his curly black hair, leaving a streak of white. "Not Home yet." He glanced at her and said cheerfully, "But if he's cheeky enough to send a family of chipmunks to live in the midst of my asters, he's got to expect something like this." They laughed and listened to the bees heading home to their hives. The sun sank toward the steep slope down to the world.

Watching that western sky, Tansy lowered her eyes from the purple clouds to the distant haze that told of the tallfolk hearthfires and wondered if her human friend, the village healing woman Biddy Chandler, was watching the sunset, too.

"Your eyes are looking far away tonight," Firkin said, stooping to pull a carrot. After cleaning it on his vest, he offered her half.

She shook her head and smoothed her apron. "Just the fidgets, I guess. I've been distracted all day. Mixed up the three-year-olds' list with the fours, if you can believe it." For the Matriarch, guardian of the list of all the children in the world, that was an unheard-of breach. Someone else might have smiled, but Firkin took the work too seriously for that. He levered himself off the wall to look at her. "How is Peewit?" Tansy suddenly asked.

He blinked. Though he held the honorary title Guardian of the Pledged and thus was tuned to Brickleburr's thoughts in a special way, still he had to consciously search his mind for trace of the Littleman who lived beyond the Gates. Bending his head and shutting his eyes, he was silent a moment. Then a slow smile broke across his face. "The Pledged is fine. I can see his pony and the wagon with a campfire already lit. They are arguing about a . . . hen, I think, and Peewit thinks Muir should return it to its rightful owner."

The Matriarch smiled briefly. "Good. I thought perhaps I was uneasy because of him." She sighed and drew the shawl around her shoulders. "Well, I should be getting home."

"Stay to dinner," he invited. "Fern will be home soon, and I know she'd love to have you."

"Thanks, no. I think I'll walk over to the palace and maybe chat awhile."

"I'll walk with you then. Fern will be coming up Main Path from the river. She was working at Daisy Hawthorne's today."

So they cut across the field toward the Sun Palace in the deepening dusk, startling some crickets, a few toads, and a rabbit or two. One of the crickets sang something hasty, and when they turned to look for it, the creature had gone. "What was that? Something about—?" Firkin questioned, puzzled.

They stood stock-still in the cricket-chirping field, Tansy stiffening as the thought struck her. "Oh, no," she breathed. "Oh, no! It cannot have happened again!"

The Hearthfolk had feared this forever. The Power himself had told them after the first war with the Unnamed, "My Brother hates you, because you are my own people. If ever he can destroy you, he will destroy me. Thus have I given you these meadows to be your home, and thus do I watch over you morning, noon, and night. Thus also do you share my aura for those months of the year when I must sleep to gain my strength for another cycle of seed, bloom, and fruit. Have a care when you pass the Gates to bring my blessing to earth's children! Untoward things may happen when the Gates are open, and the creatures of the Dark roam the world. Still, the great danger is not from tallfolk or dwarf, and certainly not from Yoriandir. The peril you face is from the other Gate. Keep that Door shut, locked, chained, and set watch upon it. For it is a Way Between, and the Skinwalker lurks beyond it, aura of my Twin. You stand between him and the children. They are yours to guard." So the Hearthfolk knew that there would come a time, for nothing lasts forever—not even Time.

Firkin and Tansy knew that it was now. The other word the cricket had stuttered was Door.

The Matriarch's hand grasped his arm. "Firkin, get Heath. He's the most experienced traveler we have. Tell him to meet me at my cottage immediately, prepared for travel." He nodded, kissed her hand, and raced off. Tansy glanced up to the palace, her heart thudding hollowly, then gathered her skirts and ran back toward her own cottage.

She went immediately to the loose stone in the chimney, which yielded to her wiggling. From within the hiding place, she took the small gold filigree box and the scroll. For a moment, the room was filled with the presence of a tallfolk man whose head brushed the ceiling rafters. He had cracked his head on them often, and she could still hear his inventive oaths. The Matriarch smiled, forgetting for a moment the desperation that lay in the pit of her stomach like stale bread. Then her smile faded as she remembered the last time they had met, here in this very room. He had said, 'When the Darkness comes, send this to the Greenbriar, for the key is with the house of Beod. And so they shall read the scroll and find their way, and then he will use the box. Courage, Mother.' Then he had stooped to kiss her cheek, and that was the last time. . . .

Tansy shook herself free of the memory. There was too much to do: she could not think upon it now.

Firkin and Heath came in, her neighbor still buckling on his pack over his leather apron. "It's getting dark," Firkin reported.

"Yes, I know," the Matriarch murmured. "It will get Darker." She turned with the box in her hands. "I charge you to take this and the scroll to the Pledged, Heath. They must fall into no other hands but Peewit's."

He fiddled with his cloak clasp. "Will he . . . remember?"

Tansy twisted her apron. "I expect he will." Their eyes met, and she added softly, "Poor fellow. You'll have to help him."

He nodded. "I will—all that I can. I'll bring him safely Home to you, Tansy."

They embraced quickly, two oldest friends, and then he was gone out the half-door. She put a hand on Firkin's arm. "Help me spread the word. The cradle-bunnies and all the lists must be taken to the caves. We can in no wise risk their falling into the hands of Shadows."

He looked shocked and drained of color. "Powers, no!"

"Also send a runner to the mill—they must be sure to hide all the extra barrels of sun oil we have. That's what the Evil Ones will be after when they come; the oil . . . and us." Firkin nodded jerkily and ran out. She could hear him calling the Folk together as he went down the Main Path.

Tansy took her shawl from the hook and followed more slowly. She passed through the gate and joined the hurrying stream of Folk trotting to and fro about their preparations in the night. Where the Road opened into the rolling country just at the edge of the village, she clambered atop the rock wall and looked off toward the palace, where the golden walls should have been glowing with a living light.

But tonight, this one night in the long Time of the Meadows of Morning, the palace was dark, the ruby windows reflecting the starlight. Tychanor the Warm had not come Home.

The Matriarch held the tail of the mouse that had climbed to her shoulder and stared with her at the fearfully quiet palace. "Oh, Winston," she had sighed. "I've waited for him so long."

He had patted her large hand with his much smaller one. "Well, at least he'll be here when you start baking Kindle-Logs. Mister Peewit always used to like to help with dicing the fruit peels and cracking the nutmeats."

She had tried to smile, and by her silence Winston had known she feared there would not be time for such homey tasks before the creatures of the Unnamed arrived in the Valley of the Sun.

By the time Sir Winston's tale grew toward an end, the fire in the grate had burned down to embers. Patience had settled on the rug, forepaws tucked under her breast. She looked now toward the hearth. 'Your tidings make my fur stand up.'

"I know," the mouse murmured. "I feel just the same way."

'And you know nothing further of what has happened to the Lord of Summer?'

Winston shook his head and nervously played with the end of this tail.

The cat slitted her eye in thought.

"But have you noticed, Mistress P, that it's got quite a little colder these past few days?"

She opened her eye. 'It does when white-ground time comes.'

One thin hand slicked back the hair on the top of his head. "Yes, quite right. And—oh, I know it seems absurd on the face of it, but the days . . . well, suppertime doesn't come at suppertime anymore, if you know what I mean. Why, I'm not even hungry by the time the sun tells me I should be anxious for my bit of supper." He pulled at an ear. "P'rhaps I've fetched up ill and don't know it." He touched his nose to take his temperature.

Patience slowly sat up.

Arrested by her intense look, the mouse straightened. "Ah, you've noticed it, too."

'Yes.' She swung her head to look toward the door. 'The peat-and-herb man is coming. Under the bed. Avoid humans, that is the safest course.' She sat primly in the shadows as Fidelis swung through the door. 'And all cats but me,' she added.

Quietly the doctor went to the fireplace and lit a splinter. The candle in its holder sat on the mantel, and when he had it going, he went to the bed to check his patient. For a moment he lay a gnarled hand on the Littleman's brow, then dropped it to take his pulse. Satisfied, he went softly out the door again. He met Kursh coming down the hall. "How is he?" the dwarf demanded.

"Sleeping more quietly than he was an hour ago when you last asked. You can go in and sit with him if you wish: I'm headed for the library."

The dwarf gestured. "Don't trip over the cat."

Fidelis looked down in surprise at the black-and-white shape twining about his bad ankle. "Where did it come from?"

"It was right behind you coming out of your room," Kursh informed him.

The cat turned her face up to them in the light of the

torchlit corridor, and at the same moment Fidelis exclaimed, "Patience!" and the dwarf struck his hands together. "Well, the boy wonder's decided to leave his bloody island, I see. Likely you'll find him with the queen. I'll watch Brickleburr, if you like, so you can go talk to the wizard."

"Well, this is a surprise! I wouldn't have put you down for the nursemaid type," the old physician teased.

"I've got a bit handy at it," Korimson confessed gruffly. "Never have been able to sleep when Gretchen's been sick."

Fidelis smiled. "As I recall, you occasionally sat up with Gerrit when he was small."

A shadow fell across the rough-cut features. "That was a long time ago," he said evenly, then abruptly added, "I'll see you later."

The doctor watched him enter the room a little down the hall. Stooping, Fidelis patted the cat. "Not so long ago that both of you can't remember it," he whispered. "If you want to."

It was dark and cold, inside and out, and fireflies froze to the lumps and the night flickered with heat lightning. A darkened palace, unnaturally dark, frighteningly dark, no light. He had not come Home, not come Home. The tall shadow of the dark-haired tallfolk man black against the storm sky, wind tossing his hair, eyes narrowed into the screaming wind as they looked together from the Rim of the World toward the Door . . . saw it shudder, saw the adamant locks explode and fragments fall away into the void. For an instant they had stood staring, the man's face drained gray and his eyes already seeing the horror to come. "By the Light," he had whispered. "He could not hold them. I thought— " and then the rising moan, the rushing fangs, and his hand had shot up, rainbow fire arching to shield. And "Now Peewit!" he had cried and begun a desperate Song. . . . The stones sharp against his feet, flying toward the Gate, the world tilting and the moan, the moan a banshee wail behind him screaming for his blood . . . and the wall exploding outward and the King-Light dying and he had to get him buried, had to because the Shadows would drink his—oh, by the Powers, they'd drink—!

Anxiously Kursh stooped over the bed. "Ssh, now, Peewit, it's all right," he said in a low voice, hoping his voice would reach through the nightmare. He did not touch the

Littleman, for as Thyla had convinced him, it was better not to wake the dreamer. "It's all right, old sod. Sleep easy now. Hush." Brickleburr sighed a breath and quieted. After a moment he was snoring gently.

The dwarf straightened, frowning. He regarded the small sleeping figure and then carefully drew the blanket farther up to guard against the draft and went heavily back to his chair. For some time he looked into the small blaze in the fireplace, sipping from his lukewarm cup of starflower tea. "Wish the wife was here," he whispered. "This stuff's bloody awful with no gingersnaps."

From under the bed two tiny eyes watched his heavy boots shuffle uncomfortably.

Meara had just eased the mail vest off the queen's bruised shoulders when there was a knock at the door. Ariadne sighed, and then thought who it might be. "If that's Alphonse, I'll—" she began angrily, and then told the waitingwoman, "If it's the wizard, I'm not receiving till morning."

"Very good, my lady," Meara agreed and bustled to the door to give the tardy guest a tart answer. But when she opened the door a crack, it was the young leader of the Riders who stood waiting. She signed to him and closed the door. "It's Lieutenant Jamison, my lady, new arrived, by the look of him." At the questioning glance Ariadne gave her, she shook her head. "No wizard."

An iron hand seemed to squeeze the queen's heart. Hurriedly she finished putting on a rabbit-trimmed houserobe and gestured Meara to admit the Watchman.

He came in and saluted. "Forgive the late hour, Majesty, but I knew you'd be waiting for my report, so I came straight up."

"You've had a long, hard journey, seemingly, lieutenant." There must have been a more circumspect way to ask, but she went directly to the point: "Did you find him?"

"Aye, Majesty. I tracked him to a little island east by south of Jarlshof. It's called Inishkerry." He stopped and pulled his riding gloves through his hands uncomfortably.

"Well, come to it, man! What's happened?"

Jamison straightened. "Your pardon, Majesty. I did not mean to fret you. The wizard was there, and as nearly as I could tell, he was well enough. I suppose."

Though Ariadne had not had many direct dealings with

Jamison she knew Will Quint spoke of him as a cool and competent officer. This indirect report was unlike him. "You have some hard news for me, I think."

"Aye, madam. It's not something I'd willingly tell."

If Alphonse was alive, it couldn't be as bad as all that. The queen seated herself and quietly ordered, "Let's have it. And no honey-coating, mind you."

He bowed slightly. "As you will, Majesty." Straightening, he began. "This Inishkerry sits by itself a day's sail northeast from Waterford. It is too small to support even a fishing village, a mere bit of rock and sea-gull droppings, and the waves crash all around it. There is one high spot, a rock cliff, where once the coastal wardens from either Jarlshof or Waterford—I don't know which—stationed a beacon-keeper. But that's a long time ago now, and the place hasn't been used for a generation at least." He was looking into the fire, picturing the remote spot for her.

There wouldn't be any porpoises leaping or crystal tinkling in the wind on Inishkerry, the queen thought. "A desolate place," she murmured aloud.

Jamison nodded. "Indeed, my lady. And . . ." He glanced at her. "It has since earlier this fall become a place of evil reputation among seafarers. I finally had to bribe one with a hefty bit of silver to take me out there."

"Evil?"

"There are storms, you see—thunder and lightning out of a cloudless day, high winds, seas that can swamp a boat, fog so thick you cannot see the end of your oar. The sailors have seen fires shooting up from the beacon hill, and they say if you happen to get near enough, you hear . . ." He hesitated. "Laughter. Only that, and the gulls."

The queen forced a smile. "If you were a wizard who liked your privacy, lieutenant, such stories would be useful, would they not?"

He was silent for a moment. "That is what I myself thought when we set sail from Waterford, Your Majesty. I figured Master Alphonse had just been working on a few spells and the locals were frightened out of their wits by them. And, knowing that he could Ward to see who was approaching in that small boat, I did not fear to be received as your messenger." He paused and swallowed. "I should have been afraid," he said flatly. "First there was hail big enough to tear the sail to shreds; then the sea kicked up and we nearly foundered. Finally, he threw a wall of Fire at us. I don't know how we managed to turn the boat in time. We could hear surf crashing, and I reckoned we must be nearly on the rocks, so I shouted to identify myself." Anger sharpened the soldier's features. "Then I heard the laughter, coming from somewhere above—the beacon hill, I guess. The wizard must have been standing up there watching the whole time."

Ariadne swallowed and looked into the fire, absently chafing her suddenly cold hands. "He may not have known it was you, lieutenant. He many not have heard you, and thought you merely another inquisitive fisherman."

"Even if that were so, it would be rotten taste in jokes. Besides, he did know it was I: he answered my hail."

The queen looked up quickly. "You gave him my message?"

She saw by his face that Jamison had come to the hard thing at last. He lifted his head. "Madam, I did."

"And?"

The Rider reported quietly, "I am to say, 'Tell the Greenbriar Queen she'll have to fight her own battles for a while. I cannot do it all.' "

For one frozen moment, Ariadne felt like a stunned child who has been slapped for no reason at all.

"I am sorry, madam," Jamison was saying softly.

Hot blood thundered in her ears, so that she barely heard the soldier. Cannot do it all? *Cannot do it all?* she shouted inwardly. Why, you lowborn son of a bitch, *you can't do any of it!*

She sprang up and walked quickly to the balcony door. With her face toward the cold night beyond the glass, she breathed deeply and fought the anger that made her hands shake. A draft stirred the drapery, and her eye was drawn beyond it to the dark. Out there, once, there had been fire rockets in the night when she was afraid. Ariadne wet her lips. "Jamison, did he . . . sound like himself?"

"It was surely his voice, madam; I marked it well. He sounded sharp, as though he was very tired or perhaps disgusted with me for seeking him out. Irritated, I suppose you would way, and sarcastic."

That sounded like . . . Rasullis. She clutched the edges of her robe.

The Rider added quietly, "Why, he has even driven the

cat off the island. I found her aboard when we made port at Waterford."

Ariadne whirled. "What? Patience has left him?" Oh, Powers, he has Fallen, indeed! No wonder the Unnamed attacks us again!

Jamison was nodding, a half-apologetic smile ready on his lips as he delivered the bit of trivial news.

The queen composed herself. "I see. All right, lieutenant. Thank you for this service."

He bowed. "My duty to you, Your Majesty." The waiting-woman let him out, and silently went to turn down the bed.

Ariadne held her hands out to the blaze on the hearth. "I should never have let him go, Meara. I should have kept him here by my side and let gossip be hanged." She straight-ened slowly.

The waitingwoman touched her cap and then advanced softly to reach for the soft rabbit robe. "He'll come home, my lady, and soon. He'll not leave you to face it alone."

"He'll eat his bloody words when he does, then!" Ariadne threw off the robe and turned away, but not before Meara caught the sheen of tears in her eyes.

The waitingwoman banked the fire and blew out the candles, but listening from her pallet in the tiring room, she knew her mistress was not asleep. Later, when there was a scratch at the door, Meara got up and let the black-and-white cat in, and then finally Ariadne slept.

Chapter Eleven

When Peewit awoke, sunlight was just beginning to slant in through the frosted windowpanes, casting a comfortable rose glow over the plastered walls. A moment's thought led him to the conclusion that he had been put to bed in Fidelis's room. He was snug under the wool covers and felt well, except he had the feeling something vaguely awful had happened he ought to remember.

He stretched and glanced toward the source of the snoring, expecting to find the physician, but Kursh was sprawled in the chair instead, beard toward the ceiling rafters, boots propped on a footstool, sound asleep. The Littleman smiled and turned his head on the pillow to look out at the sky. Two solemn little eyes and a set of whiskers were regarding him from the far edge of the bed, next to the wall.

"Good morning, Mister Peewit," Thatch-rustle offered politely. "I wonder if we might have a word with that great fellow in the chair over there about some breakf—"

The Littleman flipped the blanket. "Shoo! Get out of here!"

Sir Winston somersaulted backward into the crevasse between the bed and wall. He clung to the nubby blanket and hauled himself back up, panting, "Shoo? Shoo? Do I *look* like a cat, good sir?" Indignantly he straightened his whiskers.

"Get away, mouse!" Brickleburr lazily flapped one hand at him.

"My word! You can't hear me, can you? Mistress P. was right. For the life of me, I don't understand it: never met one of the Folk who was deaf." He stared at Peewit.

The Littleman stared back.

Defeated, Sir Winston dropped to all fours and crawled back over the edge of the bed. "I don't know how I'll ever explain this to Mistress Tansy," he was muttering.

'Tansy,' a voice whispered in Peewit's mind, and his heart began to thud hollowly. He shivered despite the warm cocoon of blankets. Why does the thought of that herb fill me with such sorrow. "Why?" he wondered aloud.

Kursh snorted and raised his head. "Hah?" he rasped. "What?" He blinked, tugged at his eyepatch, and sniffed. "Morning. Ye look a sight better than ye did last night." Rubbing a hand over his beard, he asked, "How d'ye feel?"

The Littleman firmly closed the lid on whatever it was in the back of his mind that wanted to get out. "Better than you do, probably. Did you sit up all night with me?"

The dwarf tried to flex the crick out of his neck. "No," he lied. "Just looked in on ye before I headed off to bed myself and sat down to wait for a word with Fidelis. Big mistake." He yawned.

Peewit hid a grin. "Yes, it was awful of Fidelis not to have come back at all. He probably just dropped onto a cot somewhere."

Korimson agreed smoothly, "No doubt." He slapped his hands on his knees. "Well, say the word: what will ye have for breakfast?"

("Lipopo," came a chitter from under the bed.)

"A piece of toast and a cup of tea would be nice."

The shaggy brows drew down. "That isn't enough to keep a mouse alive, Brickleburr."

("Yes, it is," came a hopeful squeak from under the bed.)

Peewit shrugged apologetically. "I just don't think I could eat anything else."

("Try," Sir Winston urged.)

"You'll try," Kursh ordered. "A soft-boiled egg, at least. You've got to get built up—you're nothing but skin and bone." He was gone out the door before the Littleman could protest further. Peewit sighed.

Outside, Kursh strode down the corridor, nodding to the Watchman on duty outside the queen's apartment. He went on a little way and stopped by another sentry. "Is this still the Lordling's room, lieut—?" he began to ask in a low voice, then suddenly stared. "By His Beard, young Master Fisher, is it?"

Pleased that his old Squiremaster remembered him, Rory Fisher grinned broadly and snapped a salute. "It is, admiral."

"And now you're an officer. His bodyguard?" He nodded toward the door.

"Aye, sir. At least, I was until yesterday. Since I've had no orders yet on the subject, I thought it best to continue my normal duty, at least for those hours when the prince is not in attendance upon you." Those hours when he was alone and unprotected, the Watchman meant.

Kursh nodded. "Very good, Fisher. I'll have a word with Captain Quint about it."

"Thank you, sir."

The dwarf reached for the doorknob, then hesitated and gestured Fisher a few feet up the hall. When they were far enough from the door, Kursh said, "You probably know him better than anyone, lieutenant: how do you size him up?"

The soldier had no hesitation. "Excellent material, admiral." He smiled a little. "But he sorely needed a Lesson, in my opinion." In his own training, the Squiremaster had taught him one.

Kursh stroked his mustache and rumbled, "Aye, well, the

Lesson takes better on some than on others." He tapped the young officer's chest and left him chuckling and headed for the mess hall. The dwarf knocked brusquely on the door and stuck his head inside. "Muster in the hall on the count of sixty, yeoman," he commanded. The heavy draperies were drawn over the window and the room was dark. Hearing no response, he slapped a hand on the door and whistled loudly. "Let's go, Greenbriar!"

From the direction of the table he could dimly see to his left there came a stifled gasp and snort, and a dark shadow raised its head. "Yes, all right, I'm coming," Gerrit managed, fumbling for his boots. He had apparently fallen asleep while reading, for Kursh saw him flip closed a book. Some bright object momentarily gleamed dully as he dropped a corner of the blanket that draped his shoulders over it.

Korimson closed the door and stood outside, leaning against the wall with his arms crossed on his chest.

He was on fifty-seven when the Lordling stepped out and stood uncomfortably waiting for his orders, still buckling on his sword. His eyes were bleary, and plainly he had slept in his clothes. Korimson eyed his rumpled Briar surcoat and his gaze traveled up to the uncombed hair.

Gerrit resisted an impulse to smooth it down and flushed.

Mildly, his Senior Officer said, "Don't let me have to look for you again, yeoman. Your job is to be there when I want you, in uniform and groomed."

The youth's mouth twisted. "Doesn't the same go for officers?"

They stared at each other. Kursh's palms itched. Very carefully, he clasped his hands behind his back. "As a matter of fact, yes. And if my baggage had been brought up from my ship before you retired last night, I could have had a shave and a decent change of clothes this morning while you were catching your beauty sleep. So now you will go down to the mess and fetch breakfast for the lord general and me—bacon, eggs, toast, tea—and then you will go three times to my ship and back on foot. Once to fetch my bag and twice more for the exercise, and you will do all this before you even *think* about your own breakfast. And if you *ever* use that tone of voice to me again, I'll break you in half," he grated.

"My mother wouldn't—!"

"Your lady mother would bless me for it!"

The Greenbriar gray eyes hardened to steel, and the breath whistled in the boy's nostrils. Then his chin came up and he took a step back and came to strict attention. "I'll fetch your breakfast now. Sir."

The dwarf gave him a curt nod and then watched him out of sight. He drew a heavy breath and went back to Fidelis's room.

Brickleburr sat up in bed regarding the Kindle-Log he had taken from the candle table. One of the bits of honeyed fruit had softened and slid from the top down to the side, and he picked it off and ate it, licking his fingers. The warm tang of mead liqueur lay on his tongue after he had swallowed. There was a sudden lump in his throat. In all his life, it was the first thing he had ever held from Home.

The latch rattled, and Kursh thrust the door open and slammed it behind him. The Littleman winced, and the dwarf saw it. "Sorry," he muttered.

"Who are you angry at?"

"I'm not—" Kursh grated and stopped. "Not at you. Nothing to trouble yourself about. Breakfast will be here shortly." He crossed to the window and stood looking out.

Gerrit, Peewit thought to himself. They've obviously had words. I wonder if the prince is conscious yet.

After a moment or two, Korimson turned from the frosted window, his face composed into its normal gruff demeanor. He gestured at the holiday loaf. "Smells good."

"Doesn't it, though?"

"Gretchen got a real cradle-bunny at Kindlefest the year before last." The dwarf tugged at his eyepatch. "Thought at the time you might have snuck in and left it on the hearth for her. I went about all day expecting you to appear suddenly." He smiled slightly. "Had it in mind to pretend not to see you to pay you out for staying away so long."

Peewit drew the oiled paper carefully back over the log to preserve its freshness for the holiday. "It wasn't I who left it for her, I'm sorry to say. The fact is, I've never actually seen a real cradle-bunny before, at least as far as I know."

Kursh's eyebrows went up. "Really? Didn't your mother and father make them for ye when ye were a little lad? I'd have thought a Teazle house would have been full of the things."

"Yes, of course," Peewit replied automatically. Then he

frowned. "No, I—" He stared at the sugared mint leaves through the paper.

The smell of maple-sugared pancakes . . . the house warm, himself snug under the covers, pretending to sleep while he spied on his father bending to the hearth and then straightening with a grin and a hasty sign at his mother through the kitchen door to stifle her giggle lest she wake the children . . . the image fading and the true one taking shape behind it . . . a broad green meadow spilling down from a high mountain gap, the rising sun standing full in the notch between the circling hills. Himself flinging the scarf on over his wool jacket and apron while he stood at the half-door and looked down toward the tallfolk earth, far away and glistening white beneath a blanket of what the Folk called icing . . . Tansy's voice behind him: 'Now, I've packed them all specially well this year. Try not to go skating on the icing again, hey?' And he had turned with a laugh on his lips to take the heavy pack and the mittens she held out to him. Her eyes were bright with fun. Tansy always loved the last morning of Kindlefest . . . there had been a dab of flour on her nose from her baking and he had reached to . . .

"Brickleburr? If ye can hear me, blink or something."

The Littleman focused on Korimson's anxious face. "Sorry. I guess I must have been thinking about something else. You were saying?"

Kursh dropped his friend's arm and slowly straightened. "Ye were out like a light, old sod. You were talking and then suddenly ye stopped. I couldn't get a word out of ye. Snapped my fingers, clapped my hands in your face—nothing worked. So I shouted to one of the sentries up the hall to get Fidelis up here on the double. He'll be here directly, I imagine. Maybe ye shouldn't be talking till he gets here," he warned uncomfortably.

Brickleburr laughed a little. "Very good, Kursh. You had me going for a moment there."

The dwarf shook his head and said seriously, " 'Tis no joke. Are ye feeling all right?"

There was no denying the look on his face. "Fine. How long was I out?"

Korimson smoothed his mustache. "Long enough to scare

me," he said flatly, then struggled for a reference. "About as long as it takes to boil an egg hard."

Brickleburr reached to put the Kindle-Log back on the table. He shook his head. "That's odd."

"Ye're telling me!" the dwarf muttered. "I didn't mean to give ye such a turn, asking ye about home."

. . . the half door and the distant blanket of white . . .
"Oh," Peewit remembered.

"What?" Kursh demanded. "What's the matter?"

The Littleman shook his head, confused. "I don't know. I just had the strangest . . . dream, I guess you'd call it. And do you know, it seemed like something that had actually happened to me once?"

"A dream?"

"Well, a daydream, anyway."

"Can't be something you ate—ye haven't eaten anything yet."

Brickleburr smiled and said lightly, "You're nagging again, Auntie," but the dwarf could tell he was shaken by the experience.

Starflower, the dwarf thought. *That's what he needs.* He nodded to himself, and for Peewit's benefit shrugged casually.

Fidelis burst through the door, and Imris was right behind him carrying his medical kit. The physician gasped, "What's the problem? The Watchman practically killed himself on the stairs!"

"Nothing—" Peewit began.

"He's had a fit or something," the dwarf said over his voice. "I couldn't wake him up."

Fidelis bent to take the embarrassed Littleman's pulse. "What happened, Peewit?"

"I'm sure I don't know. Kursh says I suddenly stopped talking, and he couldn't snap me out of it. I think I was only daydreaming," he finished lamely.

The doctor smiled a little and reached to thumb up an eyelid. "Maybe you were just ignoring him."

Korimson snorted and impatiently turned to make up the fire, for the room was chilly.

The Eldest set the kit down on the chair while Fidelis straightened. "Well, you certainly seem fine," the doctor announced. "No dizziness, tingling in the hands, anything like that?"

The Littleman shook his head.

Fidelis regarded him for a moment. "I think we may set it down to not having eaten in some time, then." At the fireplace, Kursh noisily shoveled ashes into the hod, his movements abrupt. The physician glanced at him for a moment, then returned his attention to Peewit. "You did pass a restless night, though."

"Did I?" The Littleman frowned. "I seem to have put everyone to a lot of trouble on my account."

Fidelis made a dismissing gesture, reached behind him to move his medical bag, and sank down gratefully upon the chair.

Imris asked, "Do you remember what you were dreaming about just now?"

Peewit drew the covers up as if suddenly cold. "Yes, but it's . . . silly."

"Dreams often are, on the face of it, but sometimes there is more meaning to them than it seems. Perhaps if you tell us about it, you will be troubled no more," the bard suggested.

"Look, it was just a dream, all right? Why is everyone making a mountain out of a molehill?" The Littleman flushed and looked away.

The outburst was so unlike him that for a moment none of the other three said anything. Then the doctor glanced at the Yoriandir, and the dwarf struck a spark from the flint into the tinder. The Eldest glanced that way and winced, then sat at the foot of the bed. "We don't mean to pry, Peewit, but we are all terribly worried about you after that attack yesterday." The Littleman lifted his head to meet the fir eyes, and the tree-tender told him, "The Crystal of Healing is gone: the Shadows got it."

Brickleburr's eyes flew open, and his fists clenched on the edge of the bedclothes. He went rigid, and then a sudden pain seemed to strike him and he groped for his chest.

Fidelis sprang out of his chair and thrust the Yoriandir aside. Quickly he put one hand on the small chest and another at Peewit's throat, where the pulse throbbed strongly under his fingers. "Relax," he counseled his patient. "Draw a breath, if you can."

For a moment, Brickleburr struggled to follow the instructions, and then he gasped. Almost immediately he went limp and fell back into the pillows. Sweat popped out on his brow, and he breathed heavily, closing his eyes.

"Easy," Fidelis murmured. "Slow down." Peewit nodded weakly and tried to comply.

Kursh watched tensely from the foot of the bed and then glared angrily up at the green-skinned bard. "Couldn't ye wait till the poor fellow had his breakfast? I told ye he was sick!"

Fidelis threw him a swift glance. "Hush, Kursh. You are not helping."

Korimson pulled at his beard, whirled, and strode to the door. He jerked it open and stamped out.

The doctor and Imris exchanged a look. The Eldest touched his own chest and mouthed, "Heart?"

Fidelis raised one eyebrow and shook his head no, quickly rearranging his expression when Brickleburr opened his eyes and raised a hand to wipe his forehead. The doctor sat down on the side of the bed and tucked the blanket around his patient. "Has this happened before, Peewit?"

"No." Something in Fidelis's face made him repeat, "No, truly; it hasn't."

"What did it feel like?" the doctor asked.

The Littleman licked his lips. "Like someone had driven an ice spear right through me," he answered in a low voice. He winced, and Fidelis quickly reached for his wrist once more. "No, it's all right—there's no pain," the Littleman hastened to assure him. "I was just remembering how it felt." He looked up to find their eyes on him and tried to smile, but there was a question in his eyes.

Fidelis patted his arm and answered it. "It wasn't a heart seizure: your pulse remained normal right through the episode."

Peewit considered. "What, then?"

"I don't know, but I think we've all had just about enough of it." The physician signed Imris to hand him his kit and withdrew the blue Elixir bottle. The Yoriandir handed him the cup from the bedside table and poured some water into it from the flask. Fidelis added some of the precious healing fluid to the mug and handed it to Peewit. "Blessings."

"Thank you." The Hearthman raised his cup to them and drank.

The smell of roses on the warm summer air and close at hand the Mother of Waters tumbling toward the tallfolk earth below . . . beside him a golden robe that shimmered in the sun, throwing off sparks of ruddy fire, and a hand that reached to lightly caress the flowers . . . a sad voice softly saying, "She told me, 'Mayhap at the end of our days, we shall—' "

Someone was calling his name. Brickleburr returned to find Fidelis leaning toward him, and the Eldest standing above the doctor, staring. "Peewit?" the doctor said again.

"I hear you," the Littleman said dejectedly. "It happened again, didn't it?"

"Yes. How do you—?" Fidelis started to ask, but Imris grasped his shoulder and cut in urgently, "Don't lose the memory! Tell us quickly—what were you seeing?"

Sighing, Brickleburr told him. "And the odd thing is, it doesn't feel like a dream at all. It feels more like an actual memory."

The Yoriandir's eyes were sharp. "You've been having odd dreams lately, haven't you? Perhaps for several weeks?"

Peewit looked startled. "Well, yes, but . . . they were just dreams. Not like this."

The Eldest prodded. "But they woke you from your sleep?"

"Well, yes. I'd—I'd wake up in the middle of the night with the rain drumming on the tin roof and Muir snoring on the other side of the wagon, and then I'd drift back off to sleep and in the morning I couldn't remember anything of what it was I'd dreamed about."

"Nightmares?" the Eldest asked.

"I think so. I was frightened," the Littleman reported uncomfortably.

"Can you say how long ago they began?"

For the first time, Peewit's eyes slid away. "Early fall," he replied almost inaudibly.

Fidelis held up a warning hand as Imris was about to ask another question. Quietly the doctor said, "Just after you found the dead Hearthman by the brook."

Peewit's head jerked and his eyes flew to the physician. "Did I tell you—?" He suddenly changed what he'd been about to blurt. "What did I tell you about that?"

Fidelis answered, "You mentioned only that there was another dead Hearthman before yesterday, and something about a grave by a brook. I guessed the two items were related."

The Eldest was certain he saw the Littleman relax fractionally. Brickleburr picked at a nub of wool in the blanket.

At last he nodded. "The rains must have washed out the grave. I found it near one of our camping places."

Fidelis asked, "Was there aught to tell you how he had died?"

Peewit kept control of his face. "No," he lied.

For a moment the doctor regarded him, then clasped his hands behind his back and walked slowly to the window. "Yesterday, when the Shadows attacked, you made a light or fire somehow that seemed to destroy one and drive another back, and Kursh said the same happened on Jarlshof." He turned to look at the Littleman. "Do you remember it?"

"Some of it."

The Yoriandir smiled. "Come, Peewit! Don't tell us you've been studying wizardry in your spare time from tinkering."

"I don't know what it was, Imris. I don't know how it happened."

"You did not intend to do it?"

Peewit's forehead was furrowed. "One of the . . . things . . . was getting ready to bite the queen, so I knew I had to save her and I reached for the black thing and . . ." He shrugged. "All I remember is feeling hot with anger and revulsion."

The doctor turned from the window and kept his voice calm. "What would have happened if the thing had bitten her?"

And before he knew it, Peewit had answered, "It would have poisoned her life's blood, just as it did Comfrey's."

For one tingling moment they were all silent, then the Littleman's hand flew to his mouth, the doctor cast a look at the Eldest, and Imris smiled briefly. Peewit gave something that sounded like a groan. "How did I know that?" he asked desperately, fear lighting in his eyes.

Fidelis cautioned. "Calm yourself."

"The Sight is a hard gift, but I'd say you have it, my friend," the bard said.

Somewhere far back in the Hearthman's mind, far back but clear, a voice said quietly, No, that isn't it at all. Reflexively he shied away from listening and demanded of the Eldest, "Why now? I've never had it before!"

"That is not so hard to answer, is it? We know that the Unnamed is attacking again, and we believe it is his Brother's Realm that is at risk. You are of Tychanor's own people. What could be more natural than that you should suddenly become more tuned to that heritage?"

Peewit wanted to believe this, for it was a reasonable explanation, and reason might banish the dreams, or at least banish the fear that went with them. "But if these dreams are Sight, why did I know that about Comfrey Lichen, who lived ages ago?"

The doctor came forward, shrugging. "Perhaps you will remember many things of your Kin's lore in order to understand the dreams you have of the future. If there is one." He suddenly looked piercingly at the Littleman. "Is there?" he asked.

Peewit raised both hands helplessly. "I don't know!"

The old physician smiled disarmingly. "It was just a thought. Now, that is altogether enough talk. Let us have some breakfast and perhaps a nap and then possibly everyone will be in a better mood." He caught the Eldest's eye and nodded significantly toward the door. The queen should be told that Peewit was awake.

"I'm glad you are well," Imris told the Littleman. "I have promised to breakfast with Her Majesty, so I shall see you later."

Peewit put his forearm over his eyes. "All right. My respects to the queen." When the bard had his hand on the latch, Brickleburr added, "And if you see Kursh out there, remind him to have a cup of starflower tea. Tell him, 'Thyla says.' "

Imris smiled and opened the door.

Gerrit was outside, juggling an enormous covered tray to get a hand free for the latch. "Oh, good," the prince puffed. "If you'll just swing it wide, sir, I'll bring this right in."

The Eldest stepped back out of his way and the yeoman carried the breakfast past him. Quietly Imris went out.

When Gerrit had set the tray on the table Fidelis hastily cleared to hold it, he hesitated. He longed for a private word with his kindly old friend, but the Hearthman in the bed was watching him, so he merely nodded. "Good morning, sir. I hope you're feeling better?"

"Yes, thank you." Brickleburr seemed lost in thought as he stared at the prince.

Gerrit bowed and hurriedly made his escape from that searching look.

Fidelis remarked, "The boy seems distracted."

Peewit glanced up at him. "Kursh has him hopping, I guess." He reached to remove the tea towels that covered the tray and groaned at the sheer sight of so many plates. "Fidelis, sit down. You've got to help me eat some of this. I can't vouch for my safety if the dwarf comes back and at least half these plates aren't polished off."

The doctor laughed. "Pass over some of that bacon, then, and we'll have a go at it."

Brickleburr handed him the plate and took a blueberry muffin for himself, splitting it and spreading it with butter. When it had melted in satisfactorily, he took a bite. And very nearly spat it out. "Ugh."

"I know," the doctor said sympathetically around a mouthful of savory bacon. "They're dried berries, of course, and that makes a difference."

The Littleman swallowed some tea. "Even so." He winced, pushed the muffin back onto the tray, and resignedly forked up some egg, though he did not feel like it in the least.

Gerrit hurried along the hall. He had taken the back stairs up from the kitchen, but he was headed for the front stairs now, since these gave directly onto the courtyard outside and were the most direct route to Queen's Gate. He still had to fetch the bastard dwarf's stuff from his rotten ship. His boots grated angrily on the stone flooring as he strode around the inside corner of the keep. Before him, not fifteen paces along the passage, the dwarf leaned on the sill at an open casement, motionless.

Gerrit had broken stride, but then reasoned his Senior Officer must already have heard him coming, so he marched forward and drew himself to attention when he came abreast of the admiral. "I've delivered breakfast. It's waiting for you in the doctor's quarters, sir. Plenty of everything, as you ordered."

The dwarf did not turn around. "Fine," he acknowledged quietly. His large hands were clasped before him on the wide sill.

The prince added flatly, "I'm on my way now to your ship to fetch your things, sir."

Again, softly, "Fine."

This was a new tactic, Gerrit thought, and he changed his to meet it. "I apologize for my behavior earlier, admiral." He hoped it sounded convincing.

The dwarf said tonelessly, "Begging your royal pardon, but you are the least of my worries right now, laddie." He continued to stare out the window. His hand began tracing the pathways of the mortar between the hewn stones.

Gerrit was nonplussed and debated whether to go.

Suddenly, still speaking to the window, Korimson said, "I'll wager you don't remember Brickleburr. From before, I mean. And that's a pity: you'd have liked him."

"I do remember him a little. He used to pipe to me, I think."

The dwarf's face twisted momentarily. "Right," he rasped the lie. His good eye turned to the boy. "He did." The fierce beard jutted. "Take my advice, Gerrit: get to know him." He resumed his stare out the window.

The Greenbriar prince put together the pieces. "Is he so ill, sir?"

Korimson's head dropped on his chest, and the silence was so long Ariadne's son didn't think he would answer. But finally Kursh pulled at his eyepatch. "He isn't well," he said flatly. Abruptly his shoulders squared and he slammed shut the window and jammed his hands into his pockets. "But he's still Peewit."

Mystified, Gerrit answered, "Yes, sir. I'll just be getting along now, by your leave."

The dwarf nodded, then put out a hand to catch the youth's arm as he went past. "And yeoman, just bring up my baggage and then get yourself some breakfast. Forget the extra laps: it's colder than the deeps of the sea out there this bloody morning."

"Aye, admiral. Thank you." He hurried toward the stairs before the clemency was taken back.

All the way down the marble stairs, past the fresco, across the courtyard, and even through the gates, he was turning the strange encounter over and over in his mind. It was a revelation to him that the dwarf could feel loyalty to anyone. He stopped halfway down the Sweep to look over the scattered litter of yesterday's fair. A few families were still making ready for the journey home, and he gave a mechanical smile to the daughter of one group struggling to yoke their oxen with numbed hands. The wife gave him a scathing look and roughly dragged the girl out of sight around the other side of the high cart. Gerrit did not notice, his restless mind consumed with trying to figure out the hated dwarf.

Loyalty, he thought to himself. And mercy, too. The old boy could have broken me in half this morning.

Irritably he clapped his gloved hands together for warmth. I wonder what else he's got up his sleeve besides that notorious dagger of his. And I wonder what's really wrong with the Teazle. His eyes briefly came to rest on the shining tin-plated roof of a tinker's wagon farther off across the Sweep, and then he stamped his feet and began to jog down the road to the wharves.

Imris stepped up on the iron step, rocking the wagon, and knocked at the studded door.

"Get away, you little bastards!" a voice roared from within. The door was suddenly swung back, cleaning the Eldest neatly off the step. Muir Dach glared, then, seeing who it was, spat through the gap in his teeth and jumped down to help the Yoriandir king up. "Sorry, my lord. Come in, if you're still of a mind to."

"Rather a rough welcome, Nan Dir Nog," said the tree-tender.

Silently Muir reached under the bunk and pulled out an earthenware jug. He snagged a tin cup off a peg overhead and poured some of the clear liquor. "You're looking a mite worse for the wear since the last time I seen you," he told the Eldest. "No offense, but you could stand a rest." He pushed the potcheen into the bard's hands.

"It is the cold. I have no love for winter." Imris sat on the opposite bunk and set the cup of potent liquor aside.

Dach saw the gesture. "Still can't get you to try it, eh?"

"I would not offend your hospitality," the harper smiled, "but once one has tasted Sileaught . . ." He shrugged.

"Have to drop by Yoriand some time and try it." The tinker seated himself and waited for the Yoriandir to say whatever it was he had on his mind.

Imris said quietly, "I need to know something, Muir—for Peewit's sake."

The dark eyes glittered. "Tell me what the problem is, my lord."

"His dreams."

Dach scratched his head. "Aye. His dreams have been bad of late. But that's his business, I'd say. What makes it so interesting to the ones up there?" He jerked his chin in the direction of the castle. "For nigh thirteen years, nobody has cared. Why now?" His eyes glittered with an anger Imris knew was not directed at him.

"I think those dark things yesterday were after him, not the queen."

The tinker grunted. "You're a little slow coming to that notion, then. Of course they were after him. Have been for a couple of months now. Ah, you didn't know that, did you?"

"No. Peewit did not say he'd been attacked before."

"The captain don't like his troubles spread about." His tone was a challenge.

Imris said slowly, "He is having seizures, spells the Elixir does not help." He threw the challenge back. "Now, what ails him? If you know, say!"

The tinker's feet had hit the floor of the wagon as he'd sat forward in concern. "What do you mean, seizures?"

Carefully the harper did not move. He didn't quite trust the man's mercurial temper. "He seems to be having walking dreams. There are times when he hears nothing said to him, and simply stares. I think they may be related to those Shadows yesterday. This morning . . ." He hesitated and then decided he might as well. "He had what we thought was a heart attack."

Dach leaped to his feet. "Where is he? Is he all right?" Though the Eldest was nodding, the tinker suddenly grabbed him by the front of his azure cloak and hauled him roughly to his feet. "*Is he all right*, I asked you!" the man roared in his face. Imris locked stares with the wild-eyed man, and suddenly there was a thick feeling in the wagon, as though a thunderstorm brooded over a forest. The tinker's jaw tightened, but he released his hold and reached instead for the potcheen jug. He tipped it up and took a long pull, then lowered it and wiped a dirty hand across his lips. Dropping his eyes he said gruffly, "You can never trust anybody, Eldest. If you lived my life, you'd know it."

"You can trust Peewit."

Dach eyed him and slowly sat down again. "Aye, harper. It's a great failing in the little man. I keep telling him that. He's all right now, you say?"

"It was not an actual attack, just something that mimicked one."

"Like what?"

"I know not," the Yoriandir answered truthfully. "But I

think the Elixir may have taken care of that part of his problem, at least. If we knew why he has these dreams, maybe we could better help him."

The tinker dug in his ear. "The dreams. Well, all right. They started way back—"

"Last fall, Peewit says. Just after you found that body by the brook."

Exasperated, Muir flipped the stringy hair out of his eyes. "If you knew that, then what the hell are you doing here?"

The Eldest smiled gently. "Tell me about that day."

Dach summed him, then reached into his pocket and drew out his pipe and tobacco pouch. He began filling the bowl with the fragrant, rough-cut shag. "It was raining. We got off the road early to get a decent fire going and dry out a bit before turning in. The captain takes the pail there and says he'll go fetch water. I gave him directions on finding the brook. I'd camped there before, of course. Well, he was gone a long time, so I set off to find him. Sometimes the rocks are slippery at a stream, and there's always the chance of some big animal deciding the little fellow would make a dandy meal." In the dimness there was a bright flare as he scratched a spark into his pipe. For some moments he drew to get it going, and the harper waited.

Muir Dach resumed, "I come over the brow of this slope down to the brook, and there's the captain, crouched on the ground. Had a queer look on his face when I hailed him, and he calls me down to him. When I got there, I saw he'd uncovered part of a skeleton." He puffed, and the ruddy light lit his sharp features. "We thought at first 'twas a child's, and we was wondering how the poor little mite got the brooch. The cap—"

The Yoriandir held up one green hand. "What brooch?"

For a moment as his train of thought was interrupted, the tinker looked surprised. Then he took the pipe from his mouth. "That's it, isn't it? That brooch."

"Nan Dir Nog!"

Dach looked across the wagon at him. "The brooch that your dwarf friend left in the bottom of his trunk all those years ago to be given to the Greenbriar prince."

Imris' stomach turned over. Slowly he picked up the half-filled cup of potcheen.

"The captain didn't tell you, did he?" Over the bowl of

his pipe the tinker's dark eyes gleamed. He jerked his head in the direction of the castle. "Yon bonny boy's a killer."

The Yoriandir king licked his lips. "No," he replied. "No, he did not tell us that."

Chapter Twelve

❧

Gerrit came swinging through the doorway chafing his hands and stopped dead on the threshold at the sight of the Yoriandir waiting for him before the fireplace, gazing at the portrait of his father. The harper gestured to the fireplace, where a small blaze of friava threw some heat. "I was cold, waiting. I hope you don't mind."

Gerrit limped over to the inner room, drawing off his surcoat. "Of course not, Eldest. Did you want something? I'm really in rather a hurry: I've got to change and get back on duty." The jingle of the mail coat as he wriggled out of it came clearly out to the other room.

Imris took the thick leather tome from the table. "As a matter of fact, yes. I was looking in the library for the third volume of the Books of the Painter, and it was gone. Master Fidelis wanted it."

"It's right on the table there. Help yourself." Gerrit stepped to the doorway, lacing a clean shirt. "Has Fidelis thought of something?"

The Eldest said quietly, "It must be lonely when one hides so much."

"I have friends aplenty," Gerrit said lightly.

"And secrets aplenty."

For a moment they stared at each other, the prince beginning to realize that there was something quite different in the fir eyes from the customary affection. "What are you driving at?"

"I haven't time for long explanations, Gerrit. I am not sure I want to hear them, anyway. You were at the council meeting: you heard what the other Littleman shouted to Peewit. I have come for the box you took from the Teazle at the brook."

The Greenbriar prince seemed stunned. His lips parted, and the flush of anger receded from his cheeks. Then his face hardened. "So. You can't trust anybody's word. Well, that's no great revelation, but I had thought better of Brickleburr. Does my mother know?"

It was the Yoriandir's turn to look surprised. "You have talked with Peewit about this?"

"Oh, come." He snorted with disgust and turned abruptly back into his bedroom to pick up the emerald-and-gold tunic.

Before he even thought about it, Imris was across the room and seizing the boy's arm to spin him around. "Would it interest you to know that the Hearthman has been having nightmares since he found the skeleton? That he has dropped at least twenty pounds since I saw him last winter and that he cannot eat? That he has had seizures of an unexplained nature? Would it interest you to know, in short, Master Greenbriar, that you killed one Teazle and now you're doing a fair job at killing another because he realized the day he held that brooch in his hand he could no longer serve the Blood?"

Their faces were inches apart. Suddenly Gerrit shook free and glared. "I didn't kill the other one, so save your breath for the real murderer."

"Name him."

"No."

"Why will you keep silent? This was no prank you can buy your way out of!"

"Look, if it comes out an innocent man will be hanged, and there will be pain for my mother. Leave it alone, Eldest, I'm warning you!"

Up to that point, Imris had been sure Gerrit himself had done the murder, but what he said had the force of truth. The harper regarded the prince silently, weighing him. "Why did you leave the brooch?"

After a moment, the boy said, "For honor. We—I could not bury him properly."

The Yoriandir nodded slowly. "Tell me about the box."

Gerrit hesitated, then walked to a corner where an old painted toy chest stood. Flinging up the lid so that it banged on the wall, he pitched aside toy horses, tops, a small tin dagger with its gilt paint all rubbed off, and a child's flute. He straightened, holding a smallish gold box and a tightly rolled scroll. Silently he handed them both to Imris.

The Yoriandir carefully unrolled the paper, some of it flaking away. When he saw the script, he grew still.

Gerrit, busily buttoning on his tunic, smiled thinly. "Yes. Aengus's hand. And now, as Fidelis doubtless will need no help from a Teazle murderer to decipher it, I'll get back to playing yeoman." He buckled on his sword belt and limped briskly for the door.

"Gerrit?" When the still-simmering youth looked back, he said without looking up from the vellum, "If you did not act so much the villain all the time, it would be harder to mistake you."

The prince paused with his hand on the latch. "But then, if I weren't such a snot, I would never know who my real friends were, would I?"

Imris raised his eyes. "Do you now?"

The gentleman-ruffian mask was well in place: Gerrit merely tipped him an ironic salute as he went out the door.

The Eldest silently rerolled the scroll, glanced once up at the consort's portrait, and went to find Fidelis.

The queen had delayed breakfast, waiting for Imris. But he had not appeared, and though she guessed he was probably with Peewit, she was still irritated and, though she would not have admitted it, disappointed.

Meara was clearing away the tray. Ariadne finished her tea. "Have Ka-Treer and that halfwit son of his left yet?"

"They have, my lady. Their ship sailed at dawn, I heard."

"Good riddance! Thank the Powers for small favors, at least. All I'd need would be for the Master of the Lion Throne to get wind of this." Thoughtfully she fingered the fake Crystal hanging from its golden chain on her breast.

Meara muttered an assent and carried the tray to the door.

There was a page outside, a rosy-cheeked boy of seven or so, with his hand upraised to knock. "Beg pardon, but I've a message from Master Fidelis for Her Majesty."

Meara stepped back for him, summoning another of the ladies-in-waiting in the antechamber to take the breakfast things. The boy whipped off his cap and Meara propelled him inside with a kindly hand in the hollow of his shoulder blades. He fell to one knee, almost literally. Must be new, Ariadne thought, and hid a smile. "And what would your name be?"

"Ethan, Your Majesty."

"Welcome to my service, Master Ethan. Now, what is your errand?"

In a singsong chant he'd obviously been reciting all the way to the queen's apartment, the page said, "Master Doctor begs to wish her Majesty good morning and to apologize for this intrusion. However, if it would please my lady to come to Master Fidelis's chamber, much may be made clear."

Peewit is awake and talking, she thought. She gestured the boy up and followed him.

When they opened the door at the boy's light tap, she was somewhat surprised to find them all there—Fidelis himself, Imris, Kursh, Peewit up and dressed, and her son Gerrit, who was by himself behind the door. The page bowed himself away, and the queen shut the door. They had all gone silent. "Quite a council, my lords," she teased gently. Fidelis got painfully to his feet and offered her the chair. No one had smiled at her sally. My word, what is it? she thought. It can't be Peewit; he looks tired, but well enough. She held out a hand to the Littleman. "You are feeling better, I hope, Master Teazle?"

He bowed over her hand. "I am, Your Majesty, thank you."

Patience came from under the bed, paused while tallying who was present, and then invited herself up on the queen's lap, where she began to clean bits of cheese from her whiskers.

Ariadne stroked the soft ears. "All right—what is it, gentlemen? And do sit down. You're making me nervous."

Fidelis and Peewit sat on the bed, but the others remained standing. Their looks went to the doctor, who drew a paper out of his robe. "We've found something that seems to bear on our problem, lady queen." He handed the vellum over.

It seemed to be cast in the form of a poem, but she could read none of it. "Old?" she asked, handing it back.

"Yes, very."

"Ah, Aengus again," she guessed. "And what does the Painter say?"

"It is a riddle, question and answer." His eyes flicked past her to where Gerrit stood in the corner, ostensibly guarding the door. "I will ask His Highness to recite it with me."

Why did they teach Gerrit this riddle before I got here? the queen wondered. And what does that look on Imris's face mean? She signed the doctor to continue.

He scanned the riddle once more, then folded it carefully. "It is named 'The Riddle of the Hearthstone,' " he told her. Then he looked to Gerrit. " 'What be the tyme?' "

" 'In the fall of the summer,' " came her son's voice, curiously quiet.

" 'How shall ye know it?' " the healer asked.

" 'By the meadow's mourning.' "

" 'Where is it hid?' " came the next question.

" 'In the dead man's hand,' " was the answer.

Ariadne let her hand sink in the cat's fur. Fidelis crossed his arms on his chest. " 'How lies he?' "

Gerrit was looking at the floor, concentrating. " 'Unquiet 'mongst the shadows under the scar.' "

Peewit's hands clenched on his knees, and the Eldest looked at him.

Fidelis continued, " 'What marks the path?' "

The boy hesitated, thinking a moment to get the sequence straight. " 'The finger's long shadow, thence by the Gate, and so Home.' "

" 'How shall he be called?' "

Gerrit lifted his head. " 'The Hearthstone of Tychanor.' "

There was silence in the room, except for a skitter that could have been a mouse scampering under the bed.

Ariadne murmured, "Chilling. It has the sense of doom about it." She collected herself. "But I fail to see why you think it may bear on our present situation, Fidelis. After all, the Book of the Painter has been around a long time, and much of what you've told me it contains has nothing to do with us at all."

The old man regarded his gnarled fingers. "This is not from the Book of the Painter, madam, though there can be no doubt whatsoever that Aengus penned it."

"Well, then, where did you get it? Are there more of his writings tucked away in our library?"

Fidelis scratched his eyebrow. Peewit sighed, and Kursh stood at parade rest, studying the floor. Imris's eyes were closed. After a moment, Gerrit said quietly, "I found it, Mother."

The air was brittle with tension Ariadne could imagine no reason for. She turned her head to her son in surprise. "Found it, Gerrit? Where? In a tavern?"

He flushed and limped past his Senior Officer to the fireplace. For a moment he stood quietly looking into the fire, then he turned to face her. "No, madam. In a dead Teazle's pocket."

So he arranged for the disposition of that poor little fellow yesterday and naturally went through his effects. What of it? the queen thought. "There is more, I think."

He raised a hand to brush the dark hair out of his eyes and briefly fingered the sapphire ear gem. Glancing at Peewit, he said, "First, I must ask your mercy."

If all her men knew, and all of them were silenced, it must be bad. The queen fought down a shiver. "If you think any judge would declare mercy without hearing the argument, Gerrit, you have still a great deal to learn about kingship."

He nodded once as though he had expected no more, then drew himself up. "It was not for myself that I asked, madam, but for others whose innocent involvement may not seem so innocent to this group. I gave my word to protect them, but without being forsworn, I can tell enough to fill in some pieces of the puzzle."

"Tell it, then."

Gerrit drew a breath. "Last summer we were on a hunt. One night for lack of something better to do, we . . . we decided to try to lure and catch a Teazle. To make him tell us where the golden Valley of the Sun is, you know."

Ariadne's face was a tight mask. "A juvenile prank."

"Yes. Yes, it was. Of course, we didn't expect it to work, not really, but it did." He dropped his eyes. "We had been drinking, as I will not need to tell you, and . . . in the course of the drunken game, the Teazle was killed."

She had known it, known it from their faces, from his face. Still she was stunned. "You killed one of the Folk?" the queen asked as though she could not possibly have heard him correctly.

The prince nodded, swallowing.

Her eyes leaped to Peewit's face. The Littleman could

have been turned to stone, so still he sat. She could not get any words of comfort out of her throat.

Fidelis stepped into the breach. "That Hearthman was carrying Aengus's riddle. I believe he had been sent as a messenger to Peewit, for with the riddle came this." He held out his hand, and there was a gold filigree box in his palm.

Her head was swimming with too much dire news, too fast. She could only see Peewit. Suddenly it welled up out of her: "Oh, Peewit, I am so sorry," she whispered. "I had no idea."

The Teazle slipped off the bed to pat her arm, as though she were the one who needed comforting, but he faced away from her son while he did so. "I think the prince takes more blame than is really his in this case," he murmured.

Gerrit said strongly, "A lord is responsible for his men, sir."

The lord general turned then to look up at the tall youth. "A man is responsible for himself. If the lord takes all the consequences, his men will excuse themselves."

Kursh said, "No. He's got the right of it, Peewit, y'know it. Let the boy heft this load by himself."

Ariadne raised a hand to forestall more discussion. "He will, gentlemen. I assure you." Her voice shook a little, but whether with pain or with anger would have been hard to say. The queen gripped the arms of the chair, stared at her son, then over at the doctor. "Now, what of this riddle? How do you read it?"

"I have never heard it before, and neither has Peewit, so we must start from scratch." He put his hands behind him and began to pace up and down the room.

Imris said, " 'In the fall of the summer' is a curious phrase. Why not simply say fall, if it refers to autumn?"

(From under the bed came a quiet chitter. "Because it refers to the fall of Tychanor, Lord of Summer," Sir Winston told him. Patience hopped off the queen's lap and came to keep him company. 'They can't hear you,' the cat reminded him gently. "I know, Mistress P, I know," he sighed.)

The prince cleared his throat. "If I may, sir? I've had quite a little time to ponder this riddle. In view of the fact that the Unnamed is mounting an attack on his Brother's Realm, might we not propose that the 'fall of the summer' means the fall of Tychanor?"

(Under the bed the cat sat up and pricked her ears, and Thatch-rustle caught the tip of his tail and nibbled it hopefully.)

Fidelis nodded. "Well thought."

"Well thought, indeed," the Eldest murmured, and some color came back into the prince's pale cheek. "What have you made of the rest of it?"

Their attention full on him was too much for Gerrit. He limped to the window. "Well, the meadow's mourning could be a pun on the Meadows of Morning. Especially if things were not well there, as they certainly would not be if Tychanor was somehow in trouble."

Ariadne had been listening with growing bafflement: this was more seriousness and more intelligence than she had seen since he was a little boy proudly pointing out words in his picture books. She had thought then that her son might be very bright, but in the intervening years she had come to believe his was but an early flare that had died to a smolder of mediocrity. She glanced at the doctor. Fidelis certainly was listening to him with close attention, she noticed. Something that wanted to be pride flickered in her heart, but she forced it down. He had killed a Teazle.

Fidelis nodded. "So far, so good. 'Where is it hid? In the dead man's hand.' So we look for a grave or tomb. There must be something else buried there we need for whatever task Peewit has been set. But whose grave is it? Who is the dead man?"

They thought about it. Imris suddenly said, "Beod. It must be: the king's tomb."

("Not his alone," Sir Winston said sadly.)

'. . . alone' the whisper came to Peewit's mind. He felt cold and rocked slightly on the bed. Fidelis glanced at him.

"He came to an evil end, then," Korimson contributed. " 'Unquiet 'mongst the shadows.' "

"Sounds it," the prince agreed, "but perhaps more important is that we have a clue in that line about the location of this tomb: it is 'under the scar.' "

"Surely that can't be it," the doctor objected. "It isn't a reference to a location, but rather to the death wound itself. Beod is dead under, or from, this wound. You know the preposition the Painter uses can have either meaning."

Gerrit tried it out under his breath. " 'Unquiet 'mongst the shadows from the scar.' No. If he'd meant wound, he would have written wound. Besides, a killing wound wouldn't have had time to make a scar." The physician nodded.

(Thatch-rustle wrung his hands. "It might," he said. "It might.")

The Littleman absently chafed his hands, and Imris reached behind him for a blanket to drape over his shoulders.

"Surely the end is a little clearer," the queen said, eyeing Peewit with a troubled look. "There is something about following a path to find the place?"

Gerrit recited, " 'What marks the path? The finger's long shadow, thence by the Gate, and so Home.' I'd venture a guess that one of the few landmarks still around which would have been here in Aengus's time is the Guardian, and it might be described as a finger of rock."

"And of course, it casts a shadow!" the queen exclaimed.

"Aye," Kursh agreed. "But the shadow's going to move all afternoon, every day, as the sun gets behind the thing. What good does that do us?"

"It would be a specific time," the queen mused.

The Littleman raised his head. "Kindlefest."

"Yes," Fidelis agreed. "Either the shortest day of the year, when the Lord of Summer wakes again, or on the longest day, when he is at the zenith of his power."

Powers, let us hope it isn't then, Ariadne thought. Could we withstand six months of the Dark's attack? Not without Alphonse, she answered herself. Her heart hardened against the involuntary yearning.

"Leaving that aside for the moment," the doctor said, "what gate is meant?"

"Nilarion? The Earthgate?" Imris suggested.

"Perhaps," the prince said. "But I suppose it could equally refer to any ordinary gate, or even some sort of door, perhaps into the tomb itself."

. . . the dark-haired tallfolk man black against the storm sky as they looked together from the Rim of the World . . . the Door, saw it shudder . . . 'By the Light!' . . . and then the rising moan, the rushing fangs, and his hand shot up, rainbow fire arching . . . 'Now, Peewit!' . . . the stones sharp against his feet, flying toward the Gate, the world tilting and the banshee wail behind . . . fumbling fingers so cold and no light . . . he opened the box, but then it was in front of him, eyes like heat lightning, spear poised, grinning as it threw and the spear shrieked as it came—

". . . sorry, lady queen," Fidelis was saying. "I'd not had a chance to tell you yet. It appears to be Sight of some kind."

Her warm hands on his cold ones. The anxious voice. "Peewit? Peewit?"

The Littleman opened his eyes. His chest ached dully, but it quickly faded. "I'm all right," he assured the queen.

Imris leaned over the bed. "What did you see?"

Brickleburr put a hand over his eyes to shut out their stricken concern. "The Gate. I'll recognize it again."

Quietly Fidelis asked, "Did something evil happen there?"

"No," he lied to spare them.

Kursh had started forward when the Littleman had suddenly gone rigid, but the Eldest and the doctor and the queen herself had come between him and Brickleburr, so he had stepped aside for them. Absently he had picked up the gold box and turned it in his broad hands, regarding the intricate filigree work.

Korimson glanced up to find Peewit's eye between the tallfolk. "A beautiful piece," the dwarf said and handed it to him.

("Yes! Yes!" Thatch-rustle urged excitedly. The tip of Patience's tail began to wave softly. Winston told her, "It's a puzzle, you see!" 'Ah,' the pied cat answered. 'And does Master Littleman know how to work it?' "I think so. Mistress Tansy seemed sure of him." They watched.)

Gerrit limped toward the bed. "It's a puzzle. I feel sure of it."

"Do tell," his Senior Officer muttered, and the prince shut his mouth. "Any idea how to open it, Brickleburr?"

The Hearthman frowned and stood up. "Several," he murmured. "That's the problem." Slowly he walked to the fireplace. He made himself comfortable, sitting cross-legged on the hearth with the fire warming his back. "Ah, that's better. Now, let's see."

The doctor and the queen exchanged a glance. If he took a sudden fit now, he might burn himself. The same thought had evidently occurred to the dwarf, too, because he joined the prince at the foot of the bed, within quick reach.

(Under the bed, Thatch-rustle scampered down to the end of the bed. Patience, belly low to the floor, followed.)

Peewit experimentally shook the box close to his ear. "There's something in it," he reported. He tried to twist or

slide various places, but nothing gave. "Hmm." He pressed
several points along the corners, but with no result. The
Littleman pursed his lips.

("That's it!" the mouse urged and in his excitement darted
out between the big boots. Patience quickly shot out a paw
and dragged him back to safety. 'I told you to stay hidden,'
she thought at him severely. "Yes, yes, sorry. Got a bit
carried away. Won't happen again." He licked his big teeth,
watching the Hearthman intently. Patience put her paw
down on his tail to hold him, just in case.)

Gerrit frowned and glanced down at his boot, then resumed watching the Lord General.

    . . . won't happen again . . .
    *. . . the soft sun, soft simmer of bees in the heather, smell
of open sky, scent of close earth . . . her lips had tasted of the
honeycakes they had been nibbling. He had reached to pick a
bit of magenta heather from her hair. "Must you go?" He
had nodded wordlessly . . . the clouds were reflected in her
eyes . . . then, "Let's call the bees to witness, then," she had
said and pulled him to his feet. "But, Tanse, I may not come
back." "You'd better, Brickleburr, you'd better," she had
whispered fiercely, tears wanting to start . . . he could hear it
in her voice . . . so he had whistled up the bees and the words
were said that bound them and now her lips were honey-and-
salt in the warm and blowing wind . . .*

He came to with the box open in his hand and the echo of
cheerful whistling in his ears. Kursh was crouched before
him. "How—? What—?" Brickleburr asked him, embarrassed.

The dwarf shrugged slightly. "Ye whistled something.
Sprightly tune. Mind the fire behind you," he cautioned.

The Littleman realized he was warm for the first time in
what seemed a long time.

Imris smiled. "I have not heard that air before."

"What did you see?" the doctor pressed.

    . . . heather and honey and her lips . . . The Hearthman's
ears went red. "Nothing to interest you," he said shortly.
He stared at the box.

"Aren't ye going to open it?" Korimson urged.

"I don't think I want to." But he thumbed up the lid.
Inside, cushioned in rich spruce-colored velvet, lay a smooth
oval of amber. The Littleman took it from its bed and held
it up. The fire behind him shone through it like sun through

stained glass and projected on the whitewashed wall of the
doctor's chamber the huge shadow of a bee in a corona of
gold.

For a moment there was stunned silence as they stared,
then the doctor gasped, "By Earthpillar!" and darted the
few steps, reaching to take the amber from the Littleman's
hand. He examined it. "A honeybee trapped in amber!"

"Yes. A queen," Brickleburr told him, but his attention
was on the box he still held. In the depression where the
amber had rested was a round gold locket with the rays of
the sun embossed around its edges.

Everyone else had crowded around Fidelis to see the bee
in the amber, but Kursh remained by the Hearthman. He
was alarmed to see a sudden fringe of tears on his friend's
eyelashes. He turned his head to Gerrit, who was also
regarding the Littleman. "What are ye staring at? Tea!" he
snapped.

Oddly enough, the boy took no offense, merely limping
quickly to fetch a cup from the breakfast tray.

Kursh put a hand on Brickleburr's knee.

Peewit opened his eyes and quite unexpectedly smiled.
"She's alive, Kursh, she's alive! I didn't know that!"

The gruff dwarf had no idea what he was talking about,
but he smiled back anyway. Peewit drew the golden chain
over his neck and slipped the locket inside his shirt. "Let's
have another look at that riddle," Brickleburr said, and the
dwarf helped him to his feet.

"What will you do to him?" Imris asked.

The queen rose restlessly and picked a pear from the bowl
on the table. She walked toward the window of her solar.
"I've a good mind to disown him."

That was plainly impossible, though, and the Eldest waited
for the real answer.

Instead, Ariadne asked, "How did he know what the
riddle said, even if he'd had the paper for a long time? Did
Fidelis translate it for him?"

"No, my queen. He never saw it till this morning."

She turned, twisting the stem off the pear. "Are you
telling me my son is a scholar in the ancient language?"
Imris nodded. "And deliberately fails at his lessons?"

"I do not think it is deliberate: my guess would be his

lessons do not interest him much, so he does not bother taking them in."

"Ah, an artful sluggard." She pressed a nail into the soft yellow skin of the pear. "Why did he hide it from me, Imris?"

The Yoriandir regarded her bent head. "Perhaps he has tried too hard to be Ka-Salin's son."

Sparks glinted off the gray anvil of her eyes. "What is that supposed to mean?"

"Consider, my lady: what does the boy know of his father? That he was a skilled hunter, a superb horseman, a boon companion, a graceful, elegant courtier."

Her gaze rested on the wine and the Eldest knew it, but neither mentioned the deceased consort's addiction. After a moment Ariadne nodded acceptance of his point, but added, "He was no Teazle killer, though."

"No, and neither is Gerrit. He has told us that in every possible way."

"You believe him?"

"I do." He rose and walked to her. "And so do you, my queen."

She looked away. "What of it? He knows who did do it, and will not say."

Imris gently took her hand. "When did loyalty become unwelcome at the court of the Greenbriar Queen?" Instantly, he winced, and she saw it.

They both smiled painfully. "If you thought to save him by bringing that to my attention, you misjudged it," the queen told him. She nodded as though he had made up her mind for her. "Right. Let's get the little snot in here and get this over with." She rustled quickly to the door and called for a page.

The Eldest sighed. "I shall leave you, then. I've no taste for bloodshed this morning."

She smiled tightly, but had it off her face by the time he left and the page appeared at the door. Ariadne said to the boy, "Please to fetch the Lordling. Let him make no demur: I want to see him at once."

Round-eyed, the page bowed and flew for the double doors at the end of the antechamber. As soon as the queen had closed the door behind herself, tongues began to wag among the ladies and courtiers. The prince was in trouble again.

*   *   *

"Well, sirrah, you have a positive talent for shaming me." Angrily the queen took a poker to the fire.

Gerrit kept silence, wisely stayed near the door, and watched the storm of sparks go up the chimney.

"You might at least offer a lame excuse!"

"That's the only kind—" No, he thought, bad joke. Not the time. He clasped his hands behind him. "I have no excuse, madam."

"You're damned right you don't!" she shouted.

In all his life, he could not remember hearing her curse, and the only time he had ever heard her shout was when a junior groom hadn't pulled a cinch tight and the horse had thrown him hard. He had been six. He could feel the heat in his face and looked down at the floor.

She flung the poker into the rack. "By the Powers, one moment you stand up to Ka-Treer in a right manly way, and the next you're smashing Weatherglass and spitting in my face by ignoring the peace of my hall. Now I find you've had part in killing one of the most innocent creatures on Ritnym's blessed earth and near killing Peewit with worry and sorrow! I wish to hell the dwarf had cracked your head open with that poker yesterday!" Her fists were on her hips, and her eyes were flashing dangerously. Suddenly he could believe the stories the folk told about her: that as a girl she had worked all day in the fields alongside her foster family. In fact, he began to suspect, when it came right down to it, his mother was no lady at all, and that she only reluctantly played the role. Retreating from the unpleasantness of the situation, he toyed with the new image of her.

"Stand up straight when I'm talking to you, yeoman!" she suddenly snapped, and he came to attention, which forced his head up. The queen took a step nearer. "I've excused you and excused you, and it's come to this. Why is that, do you suppose?"

"I never meant to hurt you, Mother."

"Powers, Gerrit, you don't understand it yet, do you? You have done the Unnamed's work for him! That box was obviously supposed to have reached Peewit six months ago!"

Their eyes met, gray to gray. For one brief instant his chin trembled. "I know it now," he whispered. Then he jerked his head up and stared over her shoulder.

I don't think he's cried since he was six, Ariadne thought.

So. Too much Ka-Salin's son. I wish you'd had a stronger man for a father, my dear. My beautiful blockheaded son whose neck I could wring just now if I could reach it. She signed. "Come here. Sit. Now, tell me how you learned to read Old Ilyrian."

At first, Gerrit could not believe he had heard her correctly through the thunder in his ears, but when she impatiently gestured to the other tapestried chair, he forced his stiff knees to carry him that far and dropped gratefully into the seat. "Well, um, it isn't particularly difficult, once one gets the hang of the declensions."

An eyebrow was creeping toward her hair. "I see. Fidelis helped you?"

"Yes, a little. That's all right, isn't it? I haven't gotten him in trouble, too, have I?" he asked anxiously.

The queen rubbed a spot between her eyes and signed him to go on.

Hesitantly he did so. "At first, I was just interested in reading firsthand about the Great War. Crummie—Master Crumbhollow doesn't know very much about it, you see. Not accurately."

"Is that a fact? He comes with quite good references," his mother said mildly.

"I'm sure he's a good master," Gerrit hastened to say.

"Yes. For somebody else." She had the feeling they both nearly smiled at the same time. "All right. Now aside from historical accuracy, what else were you after?"

Give her first marks, Gerrit thought admiringly. She had done that on very few clues, and not even old Fidelis had thought to ask it. "I was trying to figure out just what makes our family so important to the Powers," he told her truthfully.

The queen tucked up her hair. "And did you find any answers?"

"I think so, but I am not certain what it means." Gerrit sat forward. "The third manuscript of the Painter is much damaged—just a collection of miscellaneous loose pages, really. In it, he talks much of the Shadows and the Skinwalker and how they plagued the folk of earth when the Unnamed attacked the Lord of Peace and Plenty, as Aengus calls Tychanor the Warm. I imagine Fidelis has filled you in on most of it." At her nod, he continued. "Well, there's also a good deal concerning King Beod and the lady he loved, whom Aengus never names. But from the secretive way he speaks of her, it's fairly evident that this lady was the object of deep contention, and that she died tragically—how the Painter never says. I get the impression Beod wasn't the only one who loved her: Aengus berates himself at various points that he never spoke to her. And then it was too late: she was gone, and he lived on with the secret sorrow."

"Poor man," Ariadne murmured. And me with nary a public word for the one *I* love. She tapped a finger on the armrest. "But I don't see how this bears on the family's blessing by the Powers."

Her son smiled and examined his fingers. "I didn't, either, until I found one more tiny bit of information. At one point, the Painter calls her 'Ritnym's Daughter.' "

The queen's eyes flew to him. *"What?"*

Gerrit nodded. "An odd coincidence, isn't it, that the folk name the people gave you is the same?"

"Did she have the Crystal?" Ariadne asked quickly.

Her son shook his head. "No. That came later, long after she was gone, I take it. But she apparently made some enormous sacrifice that earned her the title." At her frown, he said proudly, "I think I've figured out who she must have been: Rose."

"Lord Tychanor's Rose?"

"Mm-hm. It makes sense, it really does. It explains why the legend of Beod and the earth spirit who mothered his son grew up, for instance—if you can't name the king's actual love, you cover it with a mystical story. And no wonder poor Aengus dared say nothing to her of his own feelings!"

"But . . . but if Tychanor loved her, and Rose loved him . . . ?"

Gerrit suggested, "Perhaps the Warm Fire allowed the union of the two mortals to, um . . . well, as a . . ." He was blushing.

Ariadne helped him. "Beod was a surrogate for himself, you think?"

"Yes. It would explain why our bloodline is so important to the Powers, wouldn't it?"

She was unconvinced. "Surely there are other possibilities."

"I suppose." A grimace of irritation crossed his face, and he asked earnestly, "Do you realize how rare it is for one bloodline even to survive through all these generations? I

mean, the odds are enormously against it! Ka-Treer's line
only goes back five generations, for instance."

"With all the assassins in that family, it's a wonder it's
lasted this long," his mother said disgustedly. "I own, I'd
not be sorry if there were no seventh generation of them."

"Oh, Ka-Bril isn't so bad," Gerrit said tolerantly. "He's
stupid, but not cut of Uncle's cloth, thank the Powers."

"So you will be content to have your vacant cousin on
your southern border?"

"I didn't say content." He glanced up quickly.

Excellent, Ariadne approved silently. He's at least given
some thought to this. She nodded. "I had not wanted to say
too much of this before, but we had information that there
would be an assassination attempt on one or both of us
during this celebration. The source believed the threat came
from Shimarron."

The prince nodded gravely. "I suspected as much. Do you
think the stallion was intended to kill me?"

"I own, I was frightened of it," his mother answered
frankly, "but I rather expected something more standard—an
arrow, poison, any one of the lovely things your uncle is so
renowned for. Then when he arrived and found us a great
deal more concerned about the change in the fresco and
what that portended than we were about him, I think he
gave it up as a bad job and decided to sit back and see what
the Unnamed would do to us, and save himself time and
effort."

Something niggled at a corner of Gerrit's mind, but he
could not pull it into the light.

Ariadne was saying, "Guard yourself well, nevertheless.
You have a grandson's claim on old Ka-Nishon's holdings."

He grew still. "That's what you've been working for, isn't
it?"

"I'd settle for a stable border, but if Ka-Treer dies and
leaves Ka-Bril his heir, I don't think we'll have one." There,
her expression said. That's the plan.

Gerrit laced his fingers and studied them. "I've not made
myself a very suitable heir, have I?"

"Oh, I don't know. I think we might salvage something,"
she said dryly. "It has been a great relief to me among so
many blows today to find I can talk to someone who will
understand what I am saying."

A warm glow started somewhere down around his stomach. "But in the eyes of the people, Gerrit the Wastrel has to take his lumps."

"Exactly. I am glad the suggestion comes from you."

"Was that why you assigned Korimson as my Senior Officer?"

"Partly, though I had no thought of it until he took you up on your challenge." Ariadne cocked her head. "And partly it was simply because despite the hurt he has done me, I love the old bear, as I love all of them. They are my friends, dear. They knew me when I was still me. If there is time left for any of us, you would do well to win their respect, for you will have no stauncher allies. I want you to use your secret studies to good use and find out everything you can from Aengus's account of the first attack on Tychanor." Her chin came up. "I have cause to believe we shall have to fight without the wizard. You must try to take his place, at least regarding the knowledge he has of the Wild Fire's methods. I charge you with it as your punishment: find me a way to fight the Dark!" For an instant he glimpsed the depth of her fear. "Peewit, in particular, deserves your every effort at help."

The prince nodded. "I like him. I remember him a little, you know, from before. He used to carry me on his shoulders, and we'd play horse."

Ariadne closed her eyes briefly, then shook her head. "No, my sweet. The captain is the bodyguard for the monarch; the First Watchman guards the heir." His eyes had narrowed, and she nodded at what she saw there. "It was Kursh you remember." Softly she drove the telling stroke home. "If you can imagine that unbending old taskmaster riding a giddy little boy around on his shoulders, you will know the depth of the hurt the Unnamed did us all that morning."

For a moment he stared wildly, then he leaped to his feet. "By-by your leave?" he begged, and when she nodded, he fled. There were tears in his eyes now. She was sure of it.

Afterward she could not recollect how long she had sat watching the fire die down in her morning room. She was roused from her reverie by the sound of agitated voices outside. She looked up just as there was an urgent knock at the door. Before she could call "Enter," Captain Quint was filling the doorframe. "You've got to see this," he blurted, forgetting any attempt at etiquette.

Ariadne jumped to her feet as he barged past her to the doors of the balcony and unlatched them. She was right behind him as he thrust them wide and led the way out onto the small terrace. "Look," he said, thrusting one gauntleted hand skyward.

The queen could not at first tell what he was so upset about: the clear blue winter sky was streaked with a hazy film of cirrus that told of changing weather to come; there was a flock of blackbirds winging toward the river; and the sun itself, too bright to look at directly, stood over the tip of her Greenbriar pennant. She frowned and opened her mouth to question Quint sharply, but he took her elbow and pulled her a pace farther onto the balcony. "There," the burly man said. "Now—can y'see it? Don't look at it too long."

She squinted along the line of his thick arm. Where his pointing finger stood out against the sun, there was a faint darkness. Her eyes burned and she looked away quickly. "What is it?"

Quint rasped, "It isn't moving and it's got no bigger since the sentries in the turret first spotted it a little while ago, so I don't think it's like that fireball Master Wizard burned up that time. But if it's an eclipse, it's one the Retreat Masters weren't expecting. I already checked. It's something unnatural, I'll be bound."

The queen was shivering, only partly from the cold. "Listen!" she said.

From that high balcony they should have been able to hear brisk hoofbeats clattering across the cobbles below as a Rider took his horse for shoeing, the laughing screams of the children sliding on the snow-covered Sweep, the creak of cranes and shouts of the dockworkers by the river wharves. Instead, there was silence far and near, except for the raucous cawing of the crows. When Ariadne peered over the icicled balustrade, she could see the cloaked and shawled children pointing with their mittened hands. They must have been pointing at the mysterious darkening of the sun, but the queen felt as though they were all pointing at her, and for a moment foreboding swept over her.

The captain's hand was under her elbow. "Come inside, my lady; you'll be froze to death out here with no wrap."

She allowed him to urge her back inside, and there they

found Imris just coming through the door. "Have you seen it?" she asked.

He nodded. "It has begun."

The queen blew on her fingers. "Actually," she whispered, "I think it's ending."

The Yoriandir asked quietly, "Did you happen to look toward the river, my queen?"

"No. Why? What else is wrong?"

His expression was gentle. "Alphonse is here."

Chapter Thirteen

⚜

"Your Majesty?" came the call again.

Ariadne sat up, thinking, Now what?

There had been the scene with Alphonse. All right, she had told herself when she watched him ride up the sweep, remember he's afraid, too. But it had been too much to hope that the bitter rankling in her heart over his reply to Jamison would not spill out. Her concern had quickened for a moment when she had seen the rag bound about his brow: a fall, he had told her abruptly. Then he had sprung the awful news that he could not remember how to Ward. Her heart had jumped into her throat, she had accused him of being happy about it because now he couldn't run the risk of wrecking the Song, he had smiled a peculiar smile, and she had exploded. Infuriatingly, he had not fought back. Finally she had dismissed him with no more ceremony than she would have given to a page. He had bowed silently and left. She had gulped down three glasses of wine, pressed a hand to the throb in her head that the wine had not killed, and let Meara help her into her soft wool nightgown. And Powers, the bed was so cold. Finally, she had drifted off to sleep.

Now, Meara was already at the door. When the waiting woman opened it, one of the Watchmen said without preamble, "Doctor Fidelis sent me running for the queen. Ask her to come to the hospice, please."

From within the curtains of the bed, the queen called, "Is it my son? Or Master Peewit?"

He kept his face averted. "Nay, Your Majesty. 'Tis nothing like that at all. But please come. I—I'd rather say no more, by your leave."

Ariadne nodded to Meara, and the woman gestured the man to wait, then closed the door. Hastily the queen threw on a velvet robe and a heavy mantle. She did a sketchy job of pinning her hair and walked to the door. "All right, sergeant, let's see what my chief physician is so all-fired hasty to show me."

Beneath the flickering light of the torches in the fresco corridor, Gerrit Greenbriar was leaning on a cane, looking up at the painting. He shifted to ease his foot and scanned the whole length of the mural once more. He had thought perhaps something new might have shown up, but that seemed to be a false hope.

His foot was aching abominably, and anyway he had his mother's directive to scour Aengus's ragged manuscript, so he had not even tried to sleep. He liked the quiet hours of the night usually; there were fewer people about to question his comings and goings. Tonight, however, there was a threat in every shadowed corner, a barely heard breath over your shoulder. Foolish fancy, no doubt, but still, he wished the bloody torches wouldn't flicker so. It made the gargoyles that crowned the lintel into the hall leer. Gerrit sighed and resumed his careful study of the Painter's cryptic warning device.

Blood still dripped slowly from the hare, running in a thin, muddy crimson trickle down to pool on the cinnamon marble floor. Gerrit regarded it thoughtfully. The hall was utterly silent, save for the flare of the torches and the muffled snores of the sleepers in Rose Hall.

In that echoing quiet he heard clearly the softest plunk, a drop falling. The prince's eyes narrowed, and he stepped nearer the fresco. Another plunk, and this time, because he was watching for it, he saw the crimson drop land on the hare and slide down to join the puddle. Gerrit looked up to the ceiling beams, heavily shadowed, and stuck out his hand.

A drop of blood spattered his fingers.

"Son of a whore," he breathed to the Painter's wall, and

traced the small hole in the ceiling. Turning quickly, he stumped toward the stairs to the floor above. Arriving in the main upstairs corridor, he imaged the hole in his mind and limped for the small room that served as an emergency armory, just down the hall from his mother's apartments. Gerrit took a torch from its bracket and went in, cautiously stepping past the neatly ordered pikes and buckets of sand kept there in case of spilled lamp oil. Now that he knew what he was looking for, he let his nose guide him: in the air hung the faint, sick smell that might have been dismissed as a dead rat.

Behind the weapons rack he found the pig's bladder full of blood. It was fresh, too. Someone must have replaced it that very night, hooking the bladder to the small tube through the wooden floor. Very clever, the prince silently saluted. Very clever indeed, whoever you are. Throw us into a panic with a trick every mummer knows. We've been played for royal fools this time.

But by whom? Uncle. It has to be. To what end, though? There must be easier ways to throw in your lot with the Unnamed. And how did Ka-Treer know the Dark would attack? The strips of paper in the manuscript . . . Powers! No, it can't be, that's too—

Clever by half. The Dark *has* attacked, though—the sun—

Thinking furiously, Gerrit disconnected the pig's bladder and stowed this piece of evidence carefully before going back down to the fresco.

The trickle of blood was already drying. The prince went quietly along to the kitchen and brought back a sponge, wet still from the evening's pots. With a few scrubbing swipes, Gerrit had cleaned the painting and dropped the sponge to the floor. Backing quickly to look at the entire fresco, he searched for some real change in it. Come on, old boy, he thought. What were you trying to tell us? You've got to do better than a mucking riddle!

A torch spit behind him, and the sharp pop drew his involuntary glance. When he looked back at the painting, some freak of the light picked up a gleam from his left, and he tilted his head to look up at the gargoyles.

One of them was looking back at him.

In a misshapen head of human form, one eye sagged and the crooked jaw hung open slightly to show a few large, square teeth. The carved wood had taken the patina of human flesh, and the good eye was a living one, sharp with intelligence and what might have been some humor. The lips moved and a quiet, somewhat slurred voice said, "Beware the Skinwalker, man-child!"

If Gerrit could have made his feet work, he would have run like a rabbit in that first instant, but then his fists clenched over the knob of the cane and his chin came up. "Who speaks to me?" he asked softly, not to wake any of the retainers who slept in Rose Hall. Wouldn't this make a fine piece of gossip, his ironic inner voice commented.

The gargoyle did not reply, merely fixing him in its steady regard. Then it said, "Let me out. It is Time."

The prince licked his lips. "Father? Is it you?"

A grimace of irritation contorted the hideous features. "It is Time, I tell you!" it said more loudly. "*Open the door* ere It takes Ritnym's Daughter!"

Gerrit straightened. "My mother is in danger from these Shadows? How shall it be prevented?"

"Fool!" The eyes in the gargoyle head rolled, and the jaw stretched in a cry of rage that shook the marble floor under the prince's feet and echoed off the fresco. Bits of plaster pattered to the floor. Gerrit expected everybody in the castle to come racing, but in that frozen instant there was nothing but silence, far and near, except for the hissing of the pitch in the torches and the dull thud of his own heart, and he understood that he alone had heard the roar. His eyes followed where the plaster dust rained to the marble, then quickly looked back up to the gargoyle. In the torch-light, the wooden head was dull with paint, and a cobweb's soft silk laced shut the crooked jaw.

Now Gerrit backed hard against the window wall, staring.

From the head of the stairs to the second floor, there was the sudden scuffle of hurrying feet. A Watchman came into view with the queen following him. Gerrit pulled his mouth shut and tried to hide the cane in the folds of his cloak. "Mother! Did you hear—?"

"I've had a message from Fidelis in the hospice. Follow me."

They took the stairs down to the front doors quickly, and the sergeant pulled a torch from its bracket to light them across the courtyard and around the left corner of the keep, where the hospital wing extended. As they cleared the corner, Gerrit pulled up. "What the deuce?"

There was a postern into the encircling wall that normally stood open during the daylight hours for people from the town to gain access to the hospital. This was unfailingly locked at sundown, and anyone bringing in a patient during the night hours had to present himself at Queen's Gate and argue with the sentries. Now, however, the postern stood open and the courtyard of the hospital was a bobbing sea of torches. Ariadne demanded of their escort, "Has there been a fire in the town?"

"Nay, my lady, but it's bad for all that."

"Lead on, fellow," Gerrit said, taking the queen's hand on his arm as they went down the couple of steps into the yard. The sergeant began making a way for them through the press of people, most of whom seemed to be carrying bundled children. For a scene of such huddled confusion it was strangely quiet.

"It's the queen!" a voice suddenly shouted as they were spotted. People turned to stare, and then Ariadne was cut off from Gerrit and found herself enveloped by a wave of reaching hands and imploring voices.

"My baby!"

"Little Tim!"

"Here, lady—here's our Alyce. Can't ye do somethin' for her, mum?"

Ariadne caught some of the hands and tried to press comfort into them. "Yes, yes, I'll help. Of course I'll help. Let me just get into the hospital now. Let me just get through. Doctor Fidelis and I will help." The wave closed behind her, and the Watchman tried to fend off as many as he could.

Gerrit was left with the stragglers. Someone in the press had trodden on his bad foot, and he was leaning on the cane, gasping for breath against the pain, when a small hand tugged at his cloak. "Please, sir? Please, sir?"

He looked up to find two huge eyes in a cold-pinched face fixed on him. "Yes?" he managed.

"If you please, sir, it's Sissy. Mum can't carry her no more, and Petey, too." The boy was gesturing off toward the postern.

Gerrit straightened. "Show me where they are, lad." The boy seized his hand in a ragged mitten and tugged him along. Near the farther edge of the courtyard just inside the gate they came up to a woman crouched with her back against the wall, one child hugged to her shoulder and a little girl sitting unsteadily across her knees. The prince quickly bent. "Madam?"

The woman opened her eyes.

"Here, let me take one of them for you."

"Powers bless ye, sir," she sighed wearily, as Gerrit lifted the girl.

"If you can make it to the hospital, they will help the little ones," he told her, folding the child in his cloak and leaning to offer the mother his hand as she dragged herself to her feet.

She smiled shamefacedly. "My knees give out. Must have been that last bit of hill."

Gerrit took the opportunity as they passed some torches to peer into the little girl's face. Only his training prevented him from dropping her. The small features, etched with misery, were swollen purple and nearly black, as though the poor little thing were frostbitten almost to the bone.

"She was bit by somethin'," the mother told him. "Spider, rat—who knows? But there's a mark on her neck, just like on Petey's."

Shadows, Gerrit thought with cold dread. He said nothing, but led them toward the hospital steps. When they got there, three Watchmen barred the way and tried to keep some sort of order. Gerrit bypassed the line. "Here, here, wait—" one of the men said, holding out his hand to stop them. Then he recognized the prince. "Oh, sorry, sir."

"Is my mother inside?"

"Aye, sir."

"I'm taking these two in next."

The man's eyes flicked to the poor woman and her three children. There were others waiting, but still: a prince was a prince, and would be king someday. The sentry nodded. "Of course, sir." He stepped aside. "I believe they've room for you."

Gerrit took the woman's elbow and brought her into the hospice's entry, where an orderly stood with a register. "Name?" the attendant asked without looking up.

"Greenbriar."

The fellow whipped a look up and flushed.

The prince indicated the woman with a nod. "This lady is with me. This little girl is Sissy and the littlest boy is Petey, and I expect you'll take care of them immediately."

"Aye, of course, sir. We can get the rest of the information later. Come this way, madam, and a doctor will see your children."

The poor woman really had an extraordinarily beautiful smile, Gerrit thought, and he smiled back.

The attendant coughed. "There is one small problem, sir. Doctor Fidelis has given orders that no child who isn't already sick should be allowed in. To keep the fever from spreading, you know. I'm afraid this little fellow will have to remain outside."

The boy, about eight years old, hung back against his mother.

"Fair enough," Gerrit said crisply. "Where are the well children staying? I'll take him there."

The orderly looked confused and folded his record book against his chest. "Um, well, I'm sure I don't know, sir. Out in the courtyard, I suppose, waiting for their parents."

The prince leveled the man with a stare. "It's cold enough out there tonight to freeze the t—" He caught himself in time, mindful of the round-eyed listening boy. "To freeze a cow's udder."

"We've just no place for them!" the attendant explained defensively.

The baby in the woman's arms stirred and cried softly. Gerrit hurriedly made up his mind. Turning to her, he said, "I'll make sure he has someplace warm to sleep tonight. Will you trust me with him?" At her nod, he said, "When you're ready to take your healed children home, send somebody for . . . the dwarf's yeoman. I live here. Somebody will know where to find me."

"Powers bless ye . . . Your Highness." So she had heard the 'Greenbriar.'

He blushed furiously, handed Sissy to the orderly, and held out his hand to the boy. "I'm Gerrit. What's your name?"

His mother pushed him gently toward his prince. "This be Nick, sir. Go with the gentleman," she told her son. "I'll come get ye in the mornin'." Silently the boy took Gerrit's hand. A doctor came to the archway, barked at the orderly for keeping sick people waiting, and led the woman and children away.

Nick tightened his hold on Gerrit's hand, watching his mother disappear. The prince told him quietly, "Don't worry—they'll be all right, you'll see. My mother is in there, too." But what the queen could do with no Crystal of Healing he didn't know. Judging by the crowd, they were going to run out of Elixir fast. "Come on," he told Nick. "Let's find you a warm bed." He began to limp toward the doorway, leading the boy.

"Sir? Gerrit?" When the prince looked down, the boy was holding up his cane. "You forgot this."

Gerrit stopped and took the polished rosewood with its heavy silver knob. "So I did. Say, do you know what, Sir Nick? I believe this might make a dandy practice lance for you." He pressed the stick back into the boy's mittened hand. "Now, a soldier carries his lance so." He put it over the lad's shoulder. "Good. You look a proper Watchman." The boy did not say anything, but his eyes shone. The prince put a hand on his head. "Come along to the barracks now."

Nick fell into step as they clattered down the steps outside. "Where the soldiers sleep?" the boy wanted to know.

"Where this soldier sleeps, anyway."

The prince received the Watchmen's salute and answered it, and Nick copied him. Despite himself one of the soldiers grinned. "Looks like ye've picked yourself up a yeoman there, sir."

"He'll probably outrank me by morning," Gerrit said dryly.

"Aye, sir, he will at that. My four-year-old already has two chevrons on me," the corporal said, then he suddenly sobered as though wondering whether his son might even now be coming down with the fever.

Wordlessly the prince clapped him on the shoulder and led Nick through the hospital courtyard and around into the keep. He did not look up at the gargoyle as they went down the mural hall. Not now, he thought. I haven't time now. Not long after, an amazingly dirty little boy was asleep between fleece sheets with a rosewood cane stuck tightly in one fist, and a prince was gathering all his old cloaks—and some of his new ones.

When Gerrit, his arms heaped high with wool garments, closed his door quietly behind him, he found Rory Fisher outside. The Watchman eyed the pile of cloaks. "I'm taking them down to the squire's barracks, lieutenant. There's need of them. I won't be back tonight," Gerrit told him,

backing down the hall. "So you can quit watchdogging me."
He stopped. "No, wait. Better yet, I've a small friend staying
with me tonight—Sir Nick of . . . Greenfields South. Distant cousin. Just stay right there in case he needs anything
during the night, all right? Thanks!" He walked quickly off.

Fisher peeked into the bedroom: through the inner door
he could see by the fire's light a small form mounded under
the blankets. He closed the door quietly and put his back to
it. "Bloody damn kid!" he swore in a whisper. "What the
hell is he up to now?"

Gerrit dropped the stack of cloaks inside the door and
blew on his hands. The long low room was filled with
snores, the creak of rope springs, and the rustle of straw
mattresses. The hearths down the middle of the room glowed
softly, banked for the night. His eyes gleaming wickedly, he
limped down to the nearest hearth and banged the shovel
against the ash hod. "Everybody up! Muster beside your cot
on the count of sixty!"

Heads popped up, bleary-eyed in the leaping light as he
threw wood on the fire. Duncan Tregallis squinted. "Gerrit?
Powers, man, are you mad? It's the middle of the blessed
night!"

A pillow sailed toward Gerrit from down at the far end.
"Throw him in bed! He's drunk again," Humfrey neBlackmore groaned disgustedly.

"On the count of sixty, gentlemen!" Gerrit bellowed.
"Unless you'd like to try the penalty for disobeying the
direct order of a superior officer. This is *Yeoman* Greenbriar
speaking, I remind you."

He had them there. One by one, they crawled from under
the blankets and pulled on their breeches. "It's freezing!"
Toby Naismith shivered, throwing his tunic on.

"Not nearly as cold as it is outside, squire," the prince
told him. By now he had built up the blaze on the lower
hearth, too.

Duncan sat on the edge of his cot, pulling on his boots.
"What's the drill, my lord?"

"You gentlemen have all graciously volunteered your time
and efforts for a very serious undertaking," Gerrit said.

neBlackmore came slouching up the wide aisle, buttoning
his tunic. "What? Are we going to steal the brewer's daughter again?"

"Grow up," Ariadne's son told him disgustedly. "It's far more serious than that. You all saw the darkening of the sun this noon?" There were nods and uncomfortable glances exchanged. "Well, tonight the Wild Fellow seems to be doing a flanking movement: some kind of fever has broken out in the town. All the victims appear to be children. At any rate, many of the parents are in the hospital wing, where Fidelis and my mother are trying to help the little fellows. But a lot of other kids who aren't sick are waiting around in the cold out there because they have no place else to go. I knew you'd want to change that, so I thought I'd give you the opportunity to let someone else use your bed for tonight."

"Hah!" Duncan snorted good-naturedly. "Opportunity!" But he was already taking his cloak from the hook by his bed.

"Somebody using your bed, yeoman?" neBlackmore asked insolently.

Gerrit locked eyes with him. "As a matter of fact, yes, squire." He grinned genially. "I'll bet there will be a lot of urinals to empty by morning, and you're just the person for the job of tossing out the piss, Humfrey. In fact, it's your exclusive province." There was a chorus of hoots and laughter as the squires filed past to either side. "Make nice, Humfrey," Gerrit grated when they were the last two left. "Be cordial to these poor children if it kills you."

"Get off my back!"

"If you don't like my discipline, Humfrey, there's an easy way out: tell your father what you did to that Teazle by the brook."

Fear flickered in the other's eyes, and he pushed past Gerrit to exit the barracks. The prince watched him go and jammed the poker savagely into the fire.

Toby puffed in the door, carrying one child and leading another. His cheeks were red with cold, but his eyes were sparkling. "This is fun!" Gerrit aimed a playful cuff at his ear and went whistling to gather in the waifs.

Fidelis straightened painfully, his stiff knees popping. "She'll sleep now," he told the child's anxious mother. "The boy is a little more serious because he's younger, but the Elixir caught it in time. You say you saw nothing near their cots—no rats—?"

"Nay. We've a couple of good tabby cats, my lord. There ben't rats in our house." She smoothed Sissy's hair. "When I see'd them marks on her neck and then the same ones on Petey, all's I could think was a snake must've been sleepin' the winter in the stack of peat my brother cut for us, and I brought the creature in when I went out to get us some turf tonight."

Fidelis was looking down the ward at all the beds. "That's a lot of snakes," he murmured.

The woman tugged at her shawl, embarrassed. "Aye, I knew that when I seen everybody on the road, master."

The old man smiled. "Well, thank the Powers we had Elixir. They may wake during the night: try to get them to take some water, if you can. There's a cup there."

"Aye, doctor. Thank ye for all ye've done." She kissed his hand.

Embarrassed, Fidelis patted the top of her head. "Now, now. It was none of my doing. Thank the queen if you get the chance." The old man looked around tiredly. "She's about someplace." Waving off her thanks, he surveyed the long ward. Most of the children were asleep, the candles in the niches above their beds burning brightly. If any had been blown out, it would have been a signal that the patient needed help. Parents dozed on stools drawn close to their children, and orderlies were quietly making the rounds. From the curtained apothecary at the other end of the room Theodric was holding up a teacup, one eyebrow raised. Fidelis nodded and limped down the ward.

When he pushed back the curtain, he found his able assistant and the queen taking tea at the long work table as familiarly as two gossips at an inn. "I don't think Gerrit ever went through that many diapers in his whole babyhood!" Ariadne was telling Theo, and they shared a low laugh.

"It'll keep the laundry busy for a while," the assistant doctor agreed, vacating his stool for the chief physician. He pushed a steaming cup of herb tea into Fidelis's hands and threw an old blanket around him.

The queen blew on her tea, holding back the question she wanted to ask until Fidelis had revived a little. She rubbed the back of her neck and stretched. "Gerrit was with me. Where did he vanish to, do you suppose?"

The doctor answered, "I heard one of the fathers telling a neighbor that the courtyard was full of 'squeeyers.' They've apparently taken very efficient care of the well children tonight, and even gone down the Sweep all the way to the town to be sure no one was lost along the way." Ariadne smiled into her cup and sipped her tea.

Theodric drummed his fingers quietly on the table, glancing at the older doctor. "Why do you think it struck only the children, master?"

Fidelis worked his gnarled fingers around the warmth of the cup. "Perhaps they were the easiest targets. We know very little of these creatures of the Unnamed, really, save that they apparently feed on blood."

"The odd thing is that they struck so quickly," Theodric said. "All the children fell sick between the third and the sixth hour today, and—"

"No," Fidelis interrupted quietly. "The odd thing is that some of the children were *not* harmed." He looked up at them. "I'd like very much to know how they escaped this attack."

Ariadne asked. "Why? Do you think there will be further occurrences?"

Fidelis sniffed the steam from his cup. "When has the Wild Fellow let us off so lightly before?" His quiet voice brought a chill to the room.

The queen stared at him. "How much Elixir is left?"

The old man lifted his head. "A week's worth, no more. And that is assuming the assault is no worse than tonight's. Remember that there may well be children from the country districts who will be brought in for Healing tomorrow. I should be very surprised if only the children of Castlenigh were affected tonight."

There was shocked silence.

"It's quiet now, Your Majesty," one of the Watchmen on duty at the hospice door observed as the queen paused on the steps to shrug her collar up farther on her neck. In the light of the torches in the portico a few snowflakes drifted lazily down.

"Let's hope it stays that way," Ariadne said wearily, and the man nodded and bade her good night.

She walked diagonally across the courtyard toward the keep, her guard in attendance. A snowflake landed on her eyelid, and she wiped its cold kiss away.

*   *   *

He would not make it to the inn. The Shimarrat team leader fingered the Crystal of Healing in the pocket of his dark robe and looked back over his shoulder. At the last mile marker he had heard following footsteps, and he had stepped off the road to wait till the other traveler passed. But no one had come along, and the footsteps had stopped. By that he knew someone was after him. Initially he had been angry: doubtless it was that damned assassin, sniffing around to take the prize back to King Ka-Treer and claim the bounty for himself. The team leader had drawn his long, thin dagger and waited.

Then he had glimpsed the flickering eyes. The real ones, not the fake metallic ones sewn into the hoods they had weighted and thrown into the river. Now the fear ran scalding on him. He had heard this tale in every inn along the way south—how the Eyes had attacked the Greenbriar Queen and stolen her Crystal, and he had laughed into his ale mug. But it was true, he knew it now. These damned Ilyrians—you couldn't trust even their legends to stay mere tavern talk.

He began to run, but he might as well have been trying to outrun the night. The footsteps clicked behind him, a Shadow appeared in the corner of his eye, and a piercing needle of ice sank into his neck.

The Crystal fell from his hand as the Shimarrat crumpled to the road, and the dark thing that had come out of the night picked it up with a hiss, its flickering eyes suddenly glowing iron-cold. With a rising cry of triumph, the Shadow vanished and took the Crystal of Healing with it to its master.

The latch rattled, and Rory Fisher turned to find a little boy peering up from under a rough shag of hair and holding his crotch uncomfortably. Any shyness the child may have felt was overridden by desperation. "I gotta take a whizz," he whispered loudly, "and there ain't no pot under the bed. Where's the backyard?"

The tall soldier choked down a snort of laughter. A very royal cousin, this! Gravely he said, "This way, Sir Nick."

When they reached the garde-de-robe, Rory took him in. "You . . ." He gestured. "Into the niche there and there's a chute that takes it down to, uh, the backyard."

The boy did his business, and Fisher waited outside the

door. When the urchin came out, he said with satisfaction, "I never seen the like: you don't even have to get your fanny cold. Maybe I'll ask Mum can we have one from our loft for me and Petey when he grows up." The Watchman thumbed his mustache and led him back to bed. At the prince's door Nick saluted. Fisher's eyebrows climbed, and he bit his tongue and answered it. The boy hung on the knob and confided, "I'm sorry Sissy and Petey is sick, but you know, this ain't half bad!" He went inside.

As soon as the door was closed, Fisher ran a little way up the hall where he could laugh without the ragamuffin hearing. Then he had a thought which gave him pause: Who were Petey and Sissy, and where were they being sick?

Kursh gave it until light before he set his hand to the latch of his door. Well, here goes nothing, he thought. And what will I do if he's not there? He pondered for a moment. I'll bet the floor of the Watch messhall could stand a hands-and-knees scrubbing. He nodded to himself. Right. He yanked open the door. No yeoman. "Damn," he swore under his breath. The old dwarf stiffened and marched out into the hall, intending to drag the bloody little whoreson from his bed and all the way down to the messhall by the scruff of his royal neck.

He very nearly tripped over Gerrit.

The prince was sitting on the floor next to the door, head pillowed on his updrawn knees, sound asleep. Korimson regarded him for a moment. Gerrit's hair was combed, his cloak was fresh, and a razor lay where it had fallen from his hand after he had shaved. The Guildmaster pulled at his eyepatch. Two steps in the right direction, anyway. He cleared his throat and nudged the yeoman none too gently with the toe of his boot. "Rise and shine, Greenbriar."

Gerrit's eyes flew open, and he came awake with a snort. Bracing himself on the wall behind him, he got to his feet and tried to snap to attention, but his snap didn't have much authority in it. "Morning, sir."

Kursh gave nothing away. "Don't morning me, yeoman: ye were asleep on duty. And look at those bloody boots! They haven't seen polish in a month, I'll be bound. Ye're a disgrace to the uniform, Greenbriar!"

Gerrit said, "Yes, sir!" A moment went by while Kursh digested this. The prince tilted his head slightly down to meet the old dwarf's eye. "Lovely morning, what? May I take your order for breakfast, sir?"

It sounded like cheek, but somehow Kursh got the impression it was just good spirits. He stuck his thumbs in his broad belt. "No need," he said. "We'll both take our meal with the rest of the Watch this morning. And ye'd better drink some strong tea, yeoman: ye look like ye've been up all night."

The boy's voice was innocent. "Do I, sir?"

Kursh pulled his beard. "Look, what ye do off-duty is really none of my affair, but about the girls . . . I hear ye've dipped your wick a few times." He narrowed his eye and frowned up at Ariadne's son. "If ye don't watch out, some father from the town will trim it for ye."

The prince burst out laughing, a free laugh with nothing of malice in it.

Oh, hell, Korimson thought. At least I tried to set the poor fatherless lad right. Shaking his head sternly, he motioned his yeoman to fall in and marched toward the stairs.

Gerrit gnawed the inside of his cheek and somehow managed to get back some semblance of military decorum, but it really was a bit too much that the one time he hadn't . . . !

Chapter Fourteen

. . . his feet were cold, but he couldn't let that matter . . . silence and the stars overhead, the thousand eyes around them flickering, and Comfrey was heavy. Even if he hadn't seen the wound, he would have known his lord was dead, but he had seen it, had, and there wasn't a tear left in him. There would be no dawn, just the eternal dark . . . sliding along the grass in the dark, hoping no stone rolled to betray him . . . he had to get him buried before—a figure, looming up out of the dark suddenly, the hand over his mouth, quick panic, fumbling for his knife, but then saw the ring and "Ssh!" the Painter whispered. "He's dead." "I know. So is Beod." Fate

*upon fate and wouldn't it ever let up! Then, cold right to the
bone: yes, it would. Now. "This way," the man beckoned.
Silently slipping through the night. Cold stone before them
suddenly, hewn stone blocks, a lintel carved with the Rose
that was hers . . . his eyes blurring again. The tallfolk man
must have raised it with his Fire, the invisible one, tonight,
after they knew. The Painter motioned him in where the other
waited already, a husk, no man, not that laughing, wild-
haired—"Hurry, not much time. It will have to do." In the
dark, fumbling, it was done, in haste, unseemly. They climbed
back out. "They'll find . . ." "No," the Painter said. "They
won't. Come away." Silent across the field, silent among the
bodies that caught at their heels like sacks of stone, so tired
they could have dropped with the dead. The man turned at
last, put a hand down to catch him as he tottered. "Far
enough, my friend. The Shadows will come after us, of
course, but their resting place will be safe." "Do it, then, and
may the Powers bless you for it." The Painter squeezed his
shoulder. "I am sorry." "I know. Do it. Time is too short for
talk." So the man had raised his hand for the peals of
rainbow light, shattering the dark, a beautiful strand of Fire.
From the battlefield to the overhanging heights it shot, burned
into the rock, and the mountain began to slide . . . "I told
you they would not find it," he shouted above the roar.
Fangs right over the Painter's shoulder suddenly, and his
own light kindling, flaring out to take them . . .*

The toast was burned and the eggs were runny. Things
have gone to hell around this place, Korimson thought
grumpily. Even Gret can cook better than that! Sourly, he
held his cup out for a refill, and his yeoman poured. "Get
yourself some breakfast, boy," Kursh told him.

"Thank you, sir." From the platter farther along the
table, the prince helped himself to some crisp bacon, which
he folded into a thick piece of bread. Sliding onto the bench
opposite his Senior Officer, he poured some tea for himself.
The dwarf wondered if that was what royalty normally ate.
"When you're done, I want you to carry my respects to the
lord general and bid him good morning. Then ask him, if he's
feeling more himself, to join me down to the armorer's shop."

"Yes, sir." Gerrit pushed his plate away, the image of the
gargoyle strongly in his mind, and the dripping pig bladder.
First the sun blotted, and now the children. No Shimarrat

work. "Sir, there's something you should know. Last night—"
Through the archway at the end of the crowded room,
Fisher was urgently beckoning. The prince said, "I think
Lieutenant Fisher wants to talk to one of us."

Kursh turned to look, then swung off the bench and went
out to the hall with Gerrit following. "What?" he barked.

The young Watchman looked worried. "Master Peewit
isn't with you, then?"

Korimson stiffened. "Obviously not. Why?"

"Well, sir—I thought to bring him breakfast as I was
going off duty. When I didn't find him in Doctor Fidelis's
room, I went along and checked his old room down the
corridor from yours. He wasn't there either, and he's not
been to see the queen."

"How about Alphonse? He must be with the wizard." At
the man's shake of the head, the dwarf bristled. "Well, he
can't just have disappeared!" A moment later it struck him
that, of course, that was exactly what the Hearthman had
done. But why? Unless he was having another of his spells.
"Yeoman, run a message to Captain Quint: he'll be in the
day room just now, giving his orders for the change of
watch. Explain what's happened; ask for a search, a careful
one. Peewit might be in his stillness spell, and I don't want
some oaf walking on him." The boy nodded and started off
at a run. "Gerrit! Alert the sentries on the battlements, too.
On the off chance he's visible, they may have seen him."

"Aye, sir." He broke into his limping jog.

Kursh whirled to Theodric. "Where's the wizard?"

"Breakfasting with Her Majesty."

Korimson's boots struck harshly on the corridor floor as
he strode for the stairs.

The sentry tried to slow him down, but the dwarf went
through the door like a scythe through a wheat sheaf. The
queen looked over her cup, and by the balcony the wizard
turned, a bannock in his hand. Kursh gave the queen the
salute of the First Watch without thinking, then demanded
of the wizard, "Where is he?"

The Skinwalker thought with satisfaction, In a place where
you will be too late to find him! Aloud he answered, "I
thought surely he was with you."

"Well, he isn't and hasn't been, so *ward for him!*"

Ariadne looked toward the sergeant still standing in the

doorway. "Thank you, Watchman, that will be all. Meara, the door." When the waitingwoman had shut the door, the queen looked to the wizard.

He feigned a sigh. "I can't."

The dwarf's good eye narrowed. "Oh, come—he's weak still from the fever. Surely the great enchanter that's yourself can look through his stillness spell, if he's in it."

The creature shook his head. "It isn't that. When I fell back on the island . . ." He indicated his wounded head, "I seem to have forgotten—"

"Oh, no." Kursh was shaking his head. "Don't you tell me that, Freckles!"

Ariadne intervened. "It is true, Kursh."

A fierce tug at the patch. "And the Elixir doesn't cure you?"

A glance passed between the queen and the wizard. "I had not taken it prior to last night, and now I will not use any of our precious supply." He set the bannock on the breakfast tray. "Surely we can find him without such drastic measures."

"Unless those damned black things have been back," Kursh ground out.

Shut your mouth, or I will let them have your blood.

"Surely someone in the hospice would have seen or heard something if that were the case," Ariadne said worriedly.

The Skinwalker beckoned the dwarf. "Come. We will find him."

Gerrit had delivered the call for help to Captain Quint, and now was on his way up the back stairs to the upper floors of the keep to alert the watchers on the battlements. This was a service stair and not so wide or smooth as the marble-paved ones that led up to Rose Hall. In his haste, the prince stumbled and scraped a hand on the wall catching himself. A blur of black-and-white came out of the torchlight of the landing above, and Gerrit drew back sharply until he realized it was the wizard's cat. Her tail lashed and her one eye seemed huge as she stopped on the step at a level with his eyes. 'You, boy—follow me,' Patience thought hard at the human.

"Look out, cat," he panted. "I'm going up. Shoo, now!"

'Don't shoo me! I have spent the night talking to stupid humans! Only one would listen, but he was just a kitten and new here, so he was of no use to us. Now, come along,' she hissed warningly. Sometimes you had to show humans you meant business.

Gerrit snatched back the hand he had carelessly extended to give her a friendly pat.

A high voice from above chittered, "Let me try, Mistress P," and Thatch-rustle came carefully walking down the stairs on the little curbing of stone. He sat up, put his hand over his nose for a moment, thinking, and then clasped his hands. "Now, young prince, I know we've not been properly introduced and such, but— "

'Tell him,' Patience hissed.

Gerrit straightened, catching sight of the mouse and thinking the poor creature would never even know what hit it when the cat pounced. But the cat showed absolutely no interest.

"Yes, I suppose that would be best," Winston conceded. "You are looking for Master Brickleburr, I assume and hope. If not, you should be. It's cold out, and he's been out there a long time."

'Tell him to go to the Sweep,' Patience urged. 'That is what the humans call the place.'

"Ah, yes. My companion says to try the Sweep."

The prince stiffened suddenly. "He can't be inside," he murmured. "Somebody would have seen him. He's got to be out there in the cold somewhere." The boy half turned down the stairs. "But where?"

Simultaneously, Patience and Winston both told him, *'The Sweep!'*

Gerrit's hand dropped to his sword. "Who's there?" he challenged, staring up the stair. "Gargoyle?" When no answer came, he shook his head as if suddenly dizzy and thumped his ear. "Could've sworn I heard someone speak," he murmured, then raised his head intently. "The Sweep. He must have gone down to Castlenigh to see the tinker: Fisher said they were friends. Ha! That's it!" Quickly he leaped away down the steps.

The cat and the mouse watched him go. Patience sat and scratched her ear, and Winston pulled his whiskers. "That might be a human we can work with," he speculated.

'I don't know,' the cat thought dubiously. 'He doesn't smell of cheese.'

* * *

Gerrit cast up his hood as he crossed the hospital courtyard. Though the sun shone, the air was cold, with an
intermittent breeze that slapped him with sudden swirls of
the night's powdery snow, which lay ankle-deep atop the old
layer. The hospital area was quiet compared to the frantic
scene of only a few hours ago, and he was thankful no one
stopped him on his way to the postern. No guard was
stationed there, but when he came up to the door, he saw
immediately it was not quite shut. Hope came alight in his
eyes, and he pushed his way out the postern against the drift
of snow that had held it. It was hard to be sure, because the
powdery snow had blown, but it looked very much as if a
line of footprints—small ones—stretched away across the
Sweep. Gerrit began to run beside them.

"Hoi, my lord prince!" one of the archers shouted from
the battlement. "Where are you going?"

The boy ignored him and went on. The tracks crested the
Sweep and led down across the children's sliding area, and
suddenly Gerrit knew where Peewit was. He paused an
instant at the top of the gouge where they had found the
Littleman on the day of the bonfire that had raged out of
control, at the bottom of the scar the wild fire had cut; the
tracks led over the edge, and as he scanned the bottom
quickly he saw a gentle mound of snow at the upper end.

Ariadne's son threw himself over the side, slid precari-
ously down the rough-cut embankment, and slogged through
the deeper drifts at the bottom until he reached the mound.
Dropping to his knees, he began furiously to dig, throwing
up snow as a terrier throws up earth. His hand hit something solid, and he brushed away the snow until he could see
the edge of a blanket. He discovered that his teeth were
clenched so tightly they hurt, and his eyes were stinging with
more than cold. Using his forearms as brooms, he cleared
more snow and uncovered the Littleman's head and outflung
arm. Brickleburr had fallen on his face, perhaps crawling or
reaching for some hold in the snow. Gerrit tried to feel for a
life-beat in the Littleman's neck, but his hands were so
numb he could not tell. Gently he wrested the small body
from the snowy bed, then sprang to his feet, clawed at the
clasp of his cloak till it gave way, and wrapped the warm
wool around Brickleburr. He lifted the Teazle. He tried scrambling up the embankment, but it was far too steep, so he

went down the hill until the scar rose to become the Sweep, and then turned uphill.

I've found him! he wanted to yell, but he had no breath for it, so he simply put his head down and concentrated on not falling.

His Senior Officer met him halfway back to the walls, demanding, "Is he alive?" Kursh immediately held out his arms, and Gerrit was glad enough to be relieved of his burden.

The boy bent, fists braced on his knees, breathing heavily. "Don't know, sir."

"He is," the dwarf reported. "But by Aashis's Beard, he's so cold!" They hurried toward the postern and burst through the portico into the hospice, scattering snow clumps off their boots. The nervous orderly waved them toward the apothecary, where Fidelis, Imris, and the queen waited with strained faces. "He was buried in the snow out there," Korimson reported. "Gerrit found him."

Without even bothering to unwrap the cloak or blanket, the physician poured Elixir and forced it gently through the blue lips. Each of the watchers counted several heartbeats of their own, and still nothing happened. Kursh swallowed.

The the terrible white mask of the Littleman's face was washed with a growing ruddy glow, and the snow began to melt on his hair. The prince sighed with relief, and his mother sat down suddenly upon the stool.

Brickleburr drew a breath and made to stretch, as one coming out of deep slumber, then discovered his arms were prisoned by the wrappings. His eyes flew open, and he beheld once again a circle of worried faces looking down at him. "What now?" he groaned and comically flipped the blanket over his eyes.

The tension shattered, and they all laughed the dregs of worry away. Almost.

Kursh told him, "You took a stroll in the snow sometime early this morning and gave us a scare when we couldn't find you."

"I did?" The voice under the blanket was very subdued.

"Aye," the dwarf confirmed. "What the bloody hell were ye thinking of?"

There was silence. Peewit pulled the blanket off his face and frowned. "I have no idea, but it sounds as though you'd better tether me."

"I'll do better than that," the dwarf promised. "I'll sleep across the doorway tonight!"

The Littleman nodded and flexed his shoulders against the wooden table. "May I ask a question? Is there some very good reason I'm not in a nice, soft bed?"

Fidelis chuckled. "It's good for your back."

"My back at present feels as though it's been bored through by these planks!"

Kursh helped him sit up, and Ariadne smiled. "There is no denying it, Peewit—you do make life interesting!"

"I do my best." He grinned.

She rose, gathering her skirts. "If I remember correctly, I had a breakfast to attend to. Does anyone know where Master Wizard has gotten to?"

"Said he'd check for the Midnight Wanderer here along Smithy Row down to Armorer's Gate," Kursh informed her.

"Ah. Well, I had better have a Watchman tell him the good news then. Good morning, gentlemen." They bowed, and the queen took her leave.

The dwarf looked at the Littleman. "Next time ye take a notion to build snowmen in the dark, ye might at least invite the rest of us to the party."

The Littleman laughed with his friends, but he was racking his brain, trying to remember why he had gone to the Sweep.

Gerrit rubbed the weariness from his eyes. "I am sorry to trouble you right now," he said to the Hearthman, "but the wizard has been closeted with Mother talking strategy, and I thought perhaps you would know something of this matter. Last night I . . ." Their eyes were on him curiously, and his Senior Officer was already frowning.

"I discovered someone had very cleverly tampered with our Greenbriar fresco. There is a hole bored through the ceiling above it, and I found a pig's bladder of blood hooked to it. Someone's been to great pains to frighten us. My uncle's agents, I believe. However, this does not account for the queer blot upon the sun, and certainly all the Shimarrat agents ever spawned couldn't have faked Shadow attacks on all these children. So we are dealing with two problems, and Uncle's tricks are no doubt the least of our worries. Also last night I think I had some kind of vision," he murmured almost inaudibly. "Um, does the name Skinwalker mean anything to you, sir?"

The laugh lines around the Littleman's eyes flattened, leaving his face all at once lifeless. "I cannot say why, Gerrit, but the name makes me cold, as though someone had opened a tomb." He looked up. "A vision, you say?"

"I think so. It warned me of this Skinwalker, and said there was danger to Ritnym's Daughter, to Mother. When I asked it what I should do to protect her, it just howled in anger. The floor shook, and it was gone."

Peewit ran a hand through his curly hair worriedly. "I'm glad Alphonse is finally here. Do be sure to tell him, though I don't know what he can do until he remembers his Wardings."

The Eldest said quietly, "His presence alone may deter it. Let us hope so, at least. I own, I feel better about leaving for home, now." He rose. "Nilarion needs me, else I would in no wise choose to be gone from here."

"Ye have your duty, Imris, but we'll miss your good bow," the dwarf told him. "I've a feeling ye could shoot the sun, if it came to that."

The Yoriandir laughed, clapped his broad shoulder, and lifted his harp case. "Only if you had a bet on it, my friend! Then I should not dare miss!"

At noon, there was a dark rim around the sun, thicker by half than it had been the day before, and quite visible to the naked eye. Kursh scowled at it and drew the drapery across the window. Peewit looked up. "Open or shut will make no difference, old friend," the Littleman said quietly. "Its infection will find me regardless."

"Maybe," Kursh rasped, "but I don't see any need to give it a better-than-even shot." He swung restlessly to the fire and stirred it up. "Have ye remembered what that thing is yet?"

Brickleburr blew a smoke ring and set the bit of amber back down on the small table. "No. Nothing comes to me."

Korimson chewed his mustache. "Drink the tea, now, while it's hot."

Peewit hid a smile and obligingly lifted his cup of starflower. He puffed for several moments. "Where is Gerrit?"

"I sent him to the armorer on an errand. Why?"

Knocking out his pipe, the Littleman got to his feet. "There's something I wanted him to check for me in the library, but I can do it myself." He walked to the door and opened it. "Coming?"

"You do take the suddenest notions, Brickleburr."

They were going up the hall arguing about his changeable notions when a small boy astride a stick horse galloped up behind them and pulled his "mount" to a stumbling halt. "Oh!" he said, pointing at Peewit. "You're the one the cat told me about, aren't you?"

Kursh frowned, but Peewit merely scratched his head and answered, "I suppose I am."

The dwarf snorted impatiently. "Cats can't—"

Brickleburr gave him a look. "This one can, remember?" He turned to Nick. "What did she tell you about me, lad?"

The boy caught his stick horse by its neck and put it over his shoulder like a lance. For a moment he thought hard, tongue in the corner of his mouth, then he reported earnestly, "It was in my sleep. Her and the mouse said you was out in the snow and you'd be awful cold if somebody didn't find you pretty soon. I said I was sorry and could I do anything? And the cat said, Go out to the Sweep, and I said, I'm sorry, cat, but I don't know where that is. Then she looked at me funny-like and said, Never mind, kitten. Go back to sleep." Finished with his narrative, Nick stood on one foot. "Isn't that funny? She called me a kitten!"

"It's funny, all right," the dwarf rumbled under his breath.

Brickleburr put a cautionary elbow in his ribs and Kursh subsided. "I don't recall seeing you before. What's your name?" the Littleman asked.

"Nick."

"Nick who?" the dwarf demanded.

At his tone, the boy took a step back. "N-Nick Carpenter, sir." He clutched the stick horse. "I don't live here. I c-come from the town."

The Littleman smiled. "Ah, you must be visiting, then."

Relief spread over the boy's features. "That's right. I'm staying with Gerrit."

Kursh stiffened at this familiar usage, but Peewit grabbed the dwarf's arm and asked, "And where did you meet Gerrit?"

"Down to the hospital, last night. He helped Mum carry Sissy and Petey in when they got sick."

The dwarf's eyebrows shot up as comprehension came to him. "So that's where . . ." he murmured. He looked uncomfortable and pulled his beard, rasping, "Bloody hell!"

"Ahem!" Peewit cleared his throat meaningfully.

"Sorry."

Brickleburr returned his attention to the boy. "You say there was a mouse with the cat?" A solemn nod. "If you should happen to see them again today, would you tell them I was asking after them, and I'd like to talk to them?"

"Right enough, Master Teazle." Nick thumped his horse to the floor beside him like ground-butting a lance and threw a salute.

Kursh thumbed his mustache. "Here, boy. If you're going to be copying the Watch, do it right. The arm comes up like so, and then a quick snap to the chest." He demonstrated.

"You do it good!" the awed child told him.

Korimson said gravely, "Thanks. It's practice. Run along, now, and mind you don't trip over your horse."

"All right," Nick said, and with an emphatic lash of the reins, he galloped away.

"Starting them a little young these days, aren't we, Squiremaster?" Brickleburr teased.

"I like to get a jump on things," Korimson replied and gave a tug to his eyepatch.

Peewit began a laugh that ended in a sharp hiss of pain, and his hand went to his chest. "No, I'm all right, really. Just a catch, or something," he said in answer to the dwarf's obvious concern.

Kursh glanced up and down the hall. "I've got it right here," he reminded the other, tapping the flask he had already told Peewit about as they were smoking their pipes. "Do ye want a drop?"

"No. Save it."

They went on up the hall, shortly passing the guards on duty at the doors to the antechamber of the royal suite. Admitted without question, the two went through into the library. The dwarf stood by the door as the Littleman headed down the rows of bookcases, running a finger along the bindings. "What are ye looking for?" Kursh asked.

"The Roll of Kings." This was the name applied to the collected chronicles of the kings of Ilyria. It would be in several volumes dating back to the time of Berren, Beod Greenbriar's son.

Korimson followed him down the aisle. "Top row back." He pointed, then brought down a chair and climbed up on it. Looking down at the Littleman, he asked, "Any particular volume?"

Peewit thought a moment. "Give me the one for Harald," he requested, naming Ariadne's great-grandfather. Kursh pulled the heavy tome from the shelf, blew the dust off, and handed it down to Brickleburr, who carried it to a long table.

Joining him, the mystified dwarf asked again, "What are ye looking for?"

"The roster for the First Watch." Peewit turned the crackling pages, running his index finger down the text while Kursh sat on a stool opposite and watched his friend's intent search. Suddenly the Littleman bent over the page, finger poised. He marked a page with a bit of paper from the box that stood on the table for wiping pens, then flipped the tome closed. "Kursh, would you mind? Let's try the one for . . . Blaise." Harald's grandfather. Obligingly, Kursh fetched the book he wanted. Again Peewit scanned it rapidly and must have found what he was looking for, because he straightened, looking very thoughtful. "Just once more, I promise. This time it doesn't matter which volume: pick one at random, one of the really old ones." Korimson gave him a sharp glance, but said nothing as he went to get another chronicle. The one he brought back was in a scroll case, rather than a bound book of manuscript pages. Peewit unlaced the ancient oiled leather case and tilted it to slide out the rolled parchment. He carefully unrolled the stained paper as he read. It took a little longer this time, but finally he murmured, "Hmm. Just as I thought." Holding a place in the scroll, he let the edges wind up around his hand and ran a hand through his hair, sighing.

"Ye look like ye've had cold water poured down your back."

Brickleburr smiled ruefully. "That's just about what it feels like. Now I'm not sure whether to be glad my hunch was right, or sorry that I looked."

"Why? What did ye find?"

For answer the Littleman pushed the books and the scroll toward him. "Read down the rosters."

Korimson rubbed his nose and bent over the chronicle from Harald's time. His eye stopped at one entry. " 'Brickleburr, the Teazle'? Relative of yours, maybe?"

Peewit pushed the Blaise tome forward and pointed. Kursh's face twisted. "Another Brickleburr. 'P. Brickleburr.' " He looked across the table. "Odd coincidence."

The Littleman smiled and unrolled the scroll for him. Kursh scanned it. "Oh, wait a bit!" He sat up hastily.

Brickleburr's smile turned into something like a grimace. "I just wanted to be sure."

"Peewit, this is ridiculous! We were cadets together, by His Beard! Why, I remember the first time I saw ye. 'Twas the day that big dumb oaf—"

"Handelson," the Hearthman smiled.

"Handelson shot off his foul mouth about that young Eastmeath fellow's sister and—what the deuce was his name?"

"Spinner."

"Right. And young Spinner smashed him one, Handelson went for his knife, and suddenly there you were between them, just as calm as if ye were calling two big hounds to heel. I figured ye were going to be killed sure, so that's when I jumped in."

"And things got very interesting."

They both grinned at the memory. The dwarf's smile faded. "So the other Brickleburrs in the chronicles can't be you."

"I have their memories, then. And Aengus called me by name in my dreams." They went silent.

"Ye were young, Peewit. We were lads together."

"I can't explain it, either, old friend, but I know what I know."

The dwarf knitted his blunt fingers and said a hard thing. "Maybe ye should go home. Likely your folk would know what ails ye and be able to fix it."

Peewit frowned. "I can't. I'm the Pledged." He slid off the stool. "In fact," he said, walking to the door, "unless I miss my guess, I've always been the Pledged." He left the door open behind him, but Kursh could not seem to force himself off the library stool.

Rot, the dwarf thought. Fever. Cold. Whatever the hell it is that ails the sun. But Brickleburr can't possibly be right about—no, he can't possibly be right. Forget it.

He jerked off the stool and gathered the books. With his hand on the scroll, he paused and unrolled it to stare at the crabbed script.

Rot, he thought again.

By the third hour after noon on this second day of Kindlefest the hospital was filling again. Curious to know whether the Elixir could be used as a preventive as well as curative, Fidelis administered a small dose to one little girl. Her fever promptly went down and she seemed recovered for the time, but by the time the lamps were lit against the early twilight, her anxious father beckoned the senior doctor once more, and the girl lay listless and burning. Fidelis applied cool compresses and ordered an attendant, "Take the word to Ambassador Korimson: tell him to wait as long as possible, else the fever will only return." The man nodded and hurried off.

There were fewer well children this time.

The fatigue of the previous night was catching up with him, and Gerrit hung on the mantel beneath his father's portrait, stifling a yawn. Nick swung his feet in one of the tall chairs drawn to the fire and noisily chomped a roast chicken leg. "Aren't you goin' to have supper?" the little boy asked through a mouthful.

"I suppose I should," the prince mumbled. He straightened and turned, deliberated a moment, and picked a heel of wheat loaf off the silver tray. Spearing a slice of Lipopo with his dagger, he resumed his restless pacing up and down before the fire.

"What's the matter?" Nick asked, drumstick poised for another bite.

Gerrit said over his shoulder, "A friend of mine is—" He had been going to say "ill," but not wanting to get the little fellow thinking again about his fever-stricken brother and sister, he substituted, "—has a problem, and to help him with it, I must solve a puzzle."

"I like puzzles," Nick informed him, sitting back in the chair, and crossing his legs.

"Do you? Well, try this one on for size." He recited the riddle. "What do you make of that?" He bit off some of the cheese.

Nick wiped his greasy chin on his shoulder. "That isn't a puzzle, Sir Gerrit—that's the Hearthstone game."

The Greenbriar prince froze. "The what?"

"The Hearthstone game," the urchin repeated patiently.

The bread and cheese were thrown back on the tray. "Do you know how to play it?"

Nick was incredulous. "Didn't you ever?"

Gerrit smiled tightly. "I grew up here, and there weren't so many other children to play with."

"Oh." The boy digested this. Then, as gravely as any chamberlain, he offered, "I'll teach you, then." He slid off the chair and put his hands on his hips. "We need a bigger place to play it: you can't hop so good in here."

"The hall?"

"Yes, that would be good. We need two hearthstones, too."

"What are they?"

The boy gave him a pitying look. "It must have been awful growing up by yourself."

"Not so bad," Gerrit told him. "A friend played horse with me. These stones: would these two potatoes do?" He lifted the two baked potatoes from the tray.

"Shit, no. You have to *throw* them," Nick educated him. "But them balls hanging from the light up there would be fine."

Gerrit looked where the greasy finger pointed, then wordlessly dragged the heavy worktable over under the chandelier, climbed upon it, and unhooked two of the bronze pendants. Hopping down from the table, he asked, "What next?"

"Got any chalk?"

"No chalk. Will charcoal do?"

"Sure. Come on." The boy strode for the door and had the latch covered with chicken by the time Gerrit had seized a stick from the fire and followed him. With some little difficulty, they got the door open and went out into the hall. "Gimme the stick and I'll draw it."

Gerrit watched as the boy quickly sketched a design on the stone floor with the charcoal. Three linked squares led off; then a large rectangle cut diagonally with a line; a series of three more squares leading off to the left; a small circle; finally a square in which Nick drew a small circle filled in with black charcoal.

The boy straightened, pitched the stick aside, and wiped his blackened hand on the good shirt the prince had given him. "All right," he said and came back to where his pupil stood. "Now: you start by running three times around the outside. You chase me." So they did. When they stood again at the starting place, Nick motioned for one pendant. "Now these are hearthstones, see, and that last box is home. Are you following me so far?"

"I think so," the heir replied solemnly.

"Good. The next part is kind of hard, so watch close." So saying, he drew up one foot, tossed his hearthstone into the first box, and hopped in, chanting, "*What* be the *time*?" Still holding his balance on one foot, he leaned, retrieved his stone, and straightened, answering, "In the *fall* of the *sum-mer*." He looked over his shoulder at Gerrit. "See, you have to know the words."

Now he let his foot down and crouched, flipping the stone into the next square. "*How* shall ye *know* it?" He hopped to follow his pendant. "By the *mead*ows *mour*ning." The stone went into the third square on the chant, "*Where* is it *hid*?" This time it was a hop on the other foot. "In the *dead man's* hand." He picked up his stone and stepped into the rectangle, then flopped at full length. Eyeing the prince, he said, "Some just sit, but you're *supposed* to lie down."

"All right," Ariadne's son nodded.

Resuming his instruction, Nick intoned, "How *lies* he?" He then sat up, put one hand on either side of the diagonal line, and swung into an expert handstand. Gerrit was impressed and complimented him. "Thanks," the boy replied proudly. "I'm good at this game. Oh, I should have told you before: you can't touch any of the lines or you're dead." With some difficulty, he moved one hand to grasp the bronze stone and gave it a little scuffle into the circle. His face was bright with the blood rushing to his head. "*Un*quiet 'mongst the *shad*ows under the *scar*. What *marks* the *path*?" Carefully he hand-walked into the circle and with enormous control and concentration, lowered himself to his feet. One toe almost touched the line. "Ha! I almost went out!" Standing up, he proclaimed, "The *fing*er's long *shad*ow." He picked up the stone. "*Thence* by the gate." He turned to face Gerrit. "And *so* home. This is the hardest part." Still facing away from the darkened circle, he told the prince, "You have to take your hearthstone and pitch it over your shoulder. See that little circle I made in the middle?"

"Yes."

"Well, if you're playing outside, you dig a little hole, but this works almost as good. If your stone doesn't land in the hole, you're dead."

"There's quite a lot of dying in this game," the prince observed.

"Aye," the boy said with relish. "Here goes!" Tongue stuck out, he dropped the bronze pendant over his shoulder.

It missed the circle. Nick took a look and stamped. "Oh, balls!" Disgustedly, he picked up his stone and walked to a very thoughtful Gerrit. "Your turn."

"Not right now, Nick. I have to go back on duty."

"Aw, come on."

"A soldier can't always come and go as he likes, you know. We have our orders." And mine right now are to get to Master Peewit with this, because if that's not a maze, then I never saw one! Clapping the crestfallen boy on the shoulder, the prince added, "I'll be back a little later. Then I'll teach you to play one of the games I know: it's called chess."

"All right," the waif mumbled. He looked up under the hand that tousled his hair. "While you're gone, can I play with your soldiers?" The toy chest was filled with them.

"Of course. Maybe Lietutenant Fisher will play with you," the prince suggested slyly.

The boy ran happily back into the suite, calling, "Bye, Gerrit!"

"Bye, Nick." As he hurried toward the room that had been assigned to the Littleman, he met Rory Fisher coming on duty. "He's waiting for you, lleutenant. He's had his supper, but you might try for a bath."

The Watchman kept his face impassive. "Very good, my prince."

"And if he wants to play a game called Hearthstone with you, I don't think I'd take him up on it."

"Not likely, my lord."

Gerrit laughed and walked briskly away, beating time against his thigh. "*What* be the *time*? . . ."

Kursh had his hands full. The previous night, Peewit had burned with fever, but he had not seemed to suffer with it. This second night the pattern did not hold true: the Littleman moaned in his sleep, turning restlessly every few minutes while the dwarf tried to keep a cold cloth on his head and not let him throw off all the covers. Whenever Brickleburr surfaced toward consciousness, Kursh tried to get him to drink.

In one of the relatively quiet moments there came a tap at the door. The dwarf, who had just put his feet up, cursed resignedly and went to open it. Gerrit stood outside. "A word with the lord general, sir?" Silently Kursh beckoned him in. The prince advanced a few paces toward the bed, then stopped.

"I'm afraid ye'll have to wait till morning," Korimson said and pitched the hot cloth he took from the Littleman's head into the basin to soak in cold water.

The cogs were already turning. The fever came back. Duncan the wardmaster, Toby to take his party down to the town again checking for any new patients trying to make it up the Sweep tonight, Humfrey on clean-up detail once more. "Sir, I wonder—if Lieutenant Fisher covers my duty to you, might I have leave?"

"Aye, yeoman. Go and run your orphanage."

"Thank you, sir. I—who told you?"

The gray whiskers might have twitched. "A cat."

Uh-huh, the prince thought. "Is there anything I can do here before I go?"

"No. I've a full bucket and an empty one, so we're fine. You're off duty. Go on. Make sure Fisher knows if I yell, he's to come running."

"I don't think he'd need to be told that, sir."

"Probably not. Young Fisher has a pretty fair memory." He put the cold compress on the Littleman's brow.

Gerrit was struck by the gentleness of the gesture. It was hard to believe that hand once held an ax which . . . He saluted quickly and left to take care of the well children.

When the boy was gone, Kursh regarded the figure in the bed for several moments, wondering how much worse he should let it get before he fed Peewit the Elixir. Brickleburr turned restlessly, disarranging the blanket. Korimson tucked him back in. "Let the mouse in," the Hearthman suddenly said clearly.

"Mouse? Are ye hearin' a mouse?"

Brickleburr murmured something, sighed, and quieted. The dwarf changed the compress.

There was a scratching at the door. Having nothing better to do for the moment, Kursh let Patience in. She trotted past him, tail in the air, ears pricked at the figure in the bed. Quickly she put her forepaws up on the bedside and peered.

"Don't get up there now. He's too warm as it is without a fur muff draped around his neck," the dwarf told her, closing the door. He hadn't noticed Winston scoot in and run behind the basket of kindling by the hearth.

The pied cat turned her head to regard the dwarf. 'I

shan't bother Master Hearthman. It is plain he fights the Dark One; I can see the shadows on him.' She dropped back down to the floor. 'Sir Winston, are you there?'

"Behind the basket," he answered. "Just waiting for Big Boots to take himself away. Is Mister Peewit awake?"

'No.'

"Bother! He left us the message with that boy. I had thought we might finally get to talk to him." Thatch-rustle heaved a sigh she could hear clear across the room.

There was nothing to do but wait. The dwarf had sat in the room's only chair. Patience rubbed against his outstretched foot and looked up, meowing quietly. She hopped delicately into Kursh's lap and sat down. 'Can you hear me?'

Korimson was somewhat surprised the cat would come to him since she'd never shown him any tolerance before. With one finger he scratched under her chin. "So you're the famous talking cat, are ye? I warn ye, I don't have much liking for cats as a general rule. My daughter's fond of them, though."

'She must have her mother's wit.' He was a fairly competent ear-scratcher, though, she had to admit. She twisted her head to present the other ear and began to purr.

Kursh grunted. "Like that, do ye?" She pawed at his hand softly. The dwarf held her paw lightly between his fingers and rubbed meditatively. "Ah, cat, I wish ye could tell me how this is all going to end. Much as I'd not be thought faithless once more, I own if it's down to the Dark for all of us, I'd like to see Jarlshof's shores again before I go. Don't know what I can do here by way of help, and it's hard being from home when the times are uncertain."

Patience felt the slightest of tremors in his broad hand and licked his finger with her raspy tongue, then curled on his lap.

"Don't get too comfortable, my girl. Yon lad's burning up, and I have to tend him."

It shouldn't have happened, but it did. Kursh hadn't slept at all the previous night, and not much for the nights before that. When exhaustion finally broke through his defenses, it rolled him under like a gently sifting snowfall.

"I say, Mistress P?"

'Yes, Sir Winston?' Patience opened her eye to a slit.

"Do you . . . hear anything?"

The cat gave it her attention. 'No,' she finally answered.

A long nose crept from behind the basket of kindling. "I do. I believe . . ."

In the bed Peewit suddenly rose to a sitting position. His face was heavily flushed, and his curly hair was pointed with sweat. His eyes were shut. "Mouse?"

Winston snapped upright. "Oh, very good, sir! Yes, right here!" He raced to the bed around Kursh's boot and leaped up the bedclothes. Pausing at the foot of the bed, he peered. "My condolences on your illness, Mister Peewit."

"It's nothing. I'm a little warm is all." His tongue came out to try to moisten his lips. "Tansy sent you?"

"Yes, indeed, sir, yes, indeed. The Matriarch felt you'd need some help remembering, you see."

Peewit wove a little. "Remember what?"

Thatch-rustle sat up. "Why, how to get Home, sir. She said you'd had your Homesickness held off with a dose of Meadowsweet every Kindlefest for so long that when its effects wore off, you'd likely feel quite wretched."

The Littleman seemed to be thinking this over, for he frowned. "Is that what is making me sick?"

"Oh, good grief, no! Not all of it, anyway," Winston amended. "No, your kin would never afflict you in such a fashion. Mostly what's making you feel awful is the dark of the sun. Bloody terrible it is that the Evil One is stealing the good life away from it. Just as he's stealing the life—oh, dear. Ahem. Blast my busy mouth!"

Brickleburr's hands knotted on the coverlet. "That's it!" he croaked in a parched throat. "That's it! The Light himself!"

The mouse nibbled the end of his tail. "I wasn't to have told you yet. It will bring too much memory down on you all at once, sir. Tansy particularly warned me to be careful—"

Peewit pushed a hand into the soft pillow and sat up a little straighter. "I want you to teach me how to get Home. I remember it has something to do with whistling and bees."

Sir Winston scratched his ear. "Well, yes, but whistling up the bees in the middle of winter is going to be difficult, to say the least, my dear fellow. Isn't it? So you'll need to use Aengus's Gate to get Home."

"Aengus the Painter?"

"Yes! Delightful chap, the old family stories say! Quite the gentleman to all and sundry. Why, my great-grandfather

Thatch-rustle had it from his great-grandfather, who had it from—"

Patience opened her eye and stretched. 'Winston, spare us the genealogy!'

The mouse put one hand atop his nose. "Ahem. Pardon. Yes, Aengus the Painter. He lived in the Meadows, you see."

"I know," Peewit murmured. "And I've seen Aengus's Gate. I've been through it before, haven't I?"

"Ah, you are beginning to remember. Yes, you have. A number of times, in fact."

The Littleman struggled with the memory. "At the end of each life," he whispered.

Thatch-rustle cocked his head. "At the beginning of each life, sir."

Peewit ran a dry tongue over his lips. "Where is it?"

"Just beyond—"

A tremendous downdraft blew the fire on the hearth into the room, and out of the embers leaped a black cat with eyes like heat lightning. In one bound it sprang from the ash-strewn hearth to the foot of the bed. Before Winston could evade it, before Patience could even coil herself to spring, the dark cat had the mouse under his paw.

With an earsplitting yowl, Patience launched herself through the air and met the black cat claw to ripping claw. Peewit by now had risen to his knees, swaying dangerously as he tried to focus on the flying ball of spitting fur. He had a glimpse of Patience, her fangs sunk in the Dark cat's throat, as his claws shredded her ear and raked over her good eye.

Kursh had jumped from the chair, fuddled with exhaustion. Grabbing the poker, he rapped sharply on the all-black back that was temporarily on top. Howling, the cats sprang apart. In the blink of an eye, the room was shot through with a growing brilliance, brighter than midday in summer and nearly as warm. The yowling ceased, and after a moment, the light went out.

When the dwarf could see again, he beheld Peewit sprawled back against the pillows, the bleeding black-and-white cat trying feebly to lick her wounds, and a small dab of soft gray fur in a ball at the end of the bed. There was no sign at all of a black cat.

Kursh dug in his breast pocket, found the Elixir bottle, and poured some for Peewit. Lifting his friend's head, he forced the Healing liquid down. Then while he waited for it to work, he ran a finger around the rim of the bottle and let Patience lick it off his finger. She purred, and the slashes around her eye began to close. "Give some to the mouse, too," Brickleburr told him weakly. He gestured to the foot of the bed.

Relieved that the Elixir had again worked its miracle, the dwarf felt inclined to humor him. He wet his finger with the fluid and gingerly flicked it at Winston. By chance, some got into Thatch-rustle's mouth. In a moment, he rubbed his whiskers and rolled over. Opening his eyes, he chittered at Patience, "I don't much care for some of your relatives, Mistress P, if you'll pardon my saying so."

"Damnedest thing," Kursh said to Peewit. "Look at this cat, would ye? If ye had a mouser like that to protect your barn for ye, the mice would eat ye out of house and home." He shook his head while Patience stared at him and sneezed when he came near.

Chapter Fifteen

🌟

All night as he scavenged blankets and straw pallets from all over the castle, Gerrit had been thinking about the Littleman he had found in the snow that morning, about *why* Brickleburr had been out there in the first place. By the time the last well child was tucked up and Duncan Tregallis' was deep in the midst of yet another story to lull their charges off to sleep, the prince had it.

He straightened from drawing the blanket over one little girl, surveyed the quiet barracks, and then went through to the weapons room. Taking a candle lantern equipped with tin shields to make an effective blackout, he struggled into his heavy woolen cloak, pulled up his hood, and headed for the door. "I'm just going to check the road once more," he told Toby Naismith.

The pudgy squire frowned. "All right, but there wasn't

anybody still left out there when we did our last patrol. I'll come with you, though, if you want to check."

"No need," Gerrit assured him quickly. "I won't be long, and anyway I really just want a sniff of fresh air to stay awake."

"It's cold out there!"

"I won't tarry," the yeoman promised. Above all, he did not want anyone to come with him. Toby gave him a shrug that said clearly if Gerrit was crazy enough to go out in such weather, Naismith wouldn't stop him, and then sat down on the edge of a cot to listen to Duncan's story of enchantments and magic winged horses.

Gerrit pulled on his gloves and picked a shovel from its post by the barracks door. He crossed over into the hospital courtyard and cut through it toward the postern. There would be less explaining to do here than at Queen's Gate. The Watchman on duty at the door in the outer wall eyed the shovel as the prince came up. "Aye, good thought, my lord. The gate's been sticking a bit. Here, I'll do it."

"Thanks, no," Gerrit forestalled him. "I need to get warmed up! Could I have a light from your lamp, though?" Obligingly, the man lit the bull's-eye lantern for him, and then Ariadne's son threw his weight against the postern, broke it open, and worked for some moments shoveling away the low ridge of drift. "There. All cleared," he called to the man inside. "Listen, I'm going to check the road. I'll be back in a bit."

"If my lord will wait, I'll summon an escort," the soldier called back worriedly.

"No, no. I'm just going halfway down—the sentries can watch my lantern." That should put the man in a quandary: he wouldn't want to gainsay the prince, but all the same the heir was under no circumstance to be left unguarded. Gerrit smiled a little to himself, calculating he had some minutes.

Briskly he shouldered the shovel, unshuttered his lantern, and walked down the road, able to go quickly on the footing of straw that had been scattered to make it safer for the horses of the Riders. When he came abreast of the children's sliding area, he looked back. The castle showed torchlight and embrasures on the battlements where the guards tried to warm themselves, and lamplight within some of the windows. It looked warm, and he shivered. Seeing no pursuers as yet, he left the road and cut across to the scar.

Entering the gouge from the downslope end, he slogged upward, using the shovel for a cumbersome walking stick and hoping he wouldn't slip and drop the lantern. He wouldn't have minded a fall, but the thought of being left with no light on this errand was not pleasant.

The snow was still trampled and churned where he had dug Peewit out, and the first thing Gerrit did was to unshutter the lantern fully and take a good look. Now, he reasoned, if I found him here and he was reaching off toward here, what was the Teazle trying to grasp? He scanned the now-covered embankment before him with the bright bull's-eye of the lantern, then fixed on a spot, set the lantern aside, and began to dig. Come on, let it be here! he thought with each thrust of the shovel.

Very soon he had cleared enough of the light snow to be down to the charred ground, but he had not found what he was looking for. He moved slightly right and cleared more snow. In the lantern's light he picked up the shadow thrown by a regular shape: a ridge straight as a ruler. Quickly he dug at the ridge with his shovel. The ground was frozen, and he chipped it away. The top couple of inches came away in clods hard as coal, but the recent frost had not driven any deeper than that yet and the turf beneath was still reasonably soft. Putting all his weight into it, he brought the shovel blade down in a chopping blow. The iron sank in perhaps four inches and gave back a sharp clang and a heavy shock that ran up to his shoulders. He had struck rock, linear rock. If this were a dice game, he'd have bet his birthright the formation wasn't a natural one.

The dirt flew as he dug and hacked. In another moment, he had exposed a solid edge of worked stone. Gerrit straightened, panting. "The damned tomb," he told the night. "I knew it."

The dark battlefield, the piled corpses . . . eyes flickering . . . above him the dark-haired tallfolk man—no . . . tallfolk boy with gray eyes bright with triumph. "I knew it!" Shovel clanking against stone, stone worked with the Bee-and-Rose . . the overtowering shadow rising up against the stars, the ice spear . . .

Peewit shot awake, a shout ringing in his ears which he dimly realized was his own voice. "By the Powers, no!" he whispered hoarsely, then jumped for his clothes.

Kursh had him by the shoulders. "Easy, easy," he was murmuring. "It's a dream."

But Brickleburr shook him off. "Gerrit's gone out to the Sweep alone and he's digging up the tomb! Oh, by the Light, if he gets it open! Get my boots!"

Kursh hesitated only a moment. "Right here." He threw a cloak at the Littleman, collected his own from the back of the chair, and led the way out. They hit the stairs running, Rory Fisher falling in behind them, not knowing what the trouble was, but realizing there must be some.

The Littleman pulled up his hood as they rounded the landing and raced past the fresco. "You can't come, Kursh. Get Alphonse and send him after me. It's the place where you found me when the Shadows attacked."

"Lieutenant Fisher, collect the wizard from his room, and then look for us on the Sweep," Korimson ordered over his shoulder.

"Aye, sir." The long-legged human spun and ran down the hall.

"I'm coming with you," the dwarf told Peewit, as if that settled things.

With his mind fixed on the boy, Brickleburr did not answer. Together they clattered down the stairway, jumped the steps out of the keep, then pounded around the corner into the hospice courtyard and toward the postern. The sentry held up his lantern and grabbed the hilt of his sword. "Who goes there?" he called sharply as they neared.

"We're going out, corporal. It's urgent," the Littleman answered in his clear voice, and the fellow made way for them.

"Get help, man—it's the Lordling!" Kursh roared, and the sentry sprang to life, calling for his squad.

The two running figures left the sudden clatter of hob-nailed boots behind and struck off across the Sweep. Wordlessly, the dwarf raised a finger to point off to their left, and the Littleman nodded; he, too, had seen the reflection of light on the snow. "Gerrit!" he cried loudly. "No!"

It was a door, slanted to the contour of the hill, like the bulkhead of a root cellar. Gerrit held up his lantern to study the motif etched in the stone. It was Beod's tomb, all right: there was the Briar, though it was clearly of a much older vintage than any other depiction he had ever seen of it.

Curiously there was a honeybee hovering above the Rose. Gerrit hardly had time to wonder at it when he noticed the golden ring set into the slab, as bright in the lanternlight as if it had never lain under the Sweep for an age of the world.

The prince was seized by an antiquarian's passion, and he was consumed with curiosity to know what marvelous artifacts the burial place of his kinsman might hold. By tomorrow's broad light, gawking onlookers would ring the scar and children would be all over the place, their attention diverted from sliding. Besides, wouldn't he like to see old Fidelis's face, and the wizard's, if he casually sauntered into the hospital with the announcement that he'd unearthed Beod's tomb!

He put a hand to the golden ring, pulled on it experimentally, and was surprised to find it yielded easily to his touch. Soundlessly the door to the tomb swung out. Gerrit propped it with the shovel, then shone the lantern inside. There seemed to be an antechamber of sorts, narrow, then a room beyond. The bull's-eye of light picked out the edge of a rough stone bier with what looked to be the fold of a heavy cloak of kingly scarlet draped over the side.

"Gerrit! No!" a voice cried from farther over on the Sweep, and the boy started, recognizing the Littleman's voice. Gerrit's lips tightened with exasperation, and an obscure obstinacy drew him across the threshold of the tomb. He ran quickly into the inner room, the lanternlight bobbing with his movement. On the hewn slab rested not one, but two figures. The first must surely be Beod, and the second was a Littleman. But in that first shocked moment it was not the rich robe worked with gems, or the Teazle's loose collar of beaten-gold sunflowers, or even the stern beauty of the mighty blade which lay under Beod's hand that stunned Ariadne's son. They should have been moldered to skeletons long ago; he had been prepared for that.

But they weren't.

His heart began to thud, and his mouth went dry. Holding the lantern higher, he went closer. The candle flickered sharply, and on the same draft that tossed the flame was borne a low groan.

Without conscious thought, his sword was in his hand and he lofted the candle lantern. It's the wind, he told himself firmly: the door is open behind me, and there's a tunnel leading off into the hill. It's the wind. He lifted his chin and crept around the bier to have a peek into the next chamber.

Another crypt, smaller, the bier lower and pillowing only one body, a tallfolk man. He had been wrapped in a sheepskin-lined cloak, as though to warm him against the cold of death, the hood drawn close around his head, and a soft linen scarf covering his face. He had no sword, but his crossed hands bore a ring, Gerrit noted, a gold band enclosing a single curious gem, pearl-lustrous, but many-colored, prismed like a milky dewdrop. Holding his breath, the boy reached for it.

The linen scarf puffed out with breath as the dead man said, "So it is Time." Even as he swung his feet to sit up, Gerrit leaped away back out through the other chamber. The door slammed shut behind him. A cry escaped the youth, and he turned at bay, sword shaking in his grasp. In the cold damp of the tomb, there was a hiss of draft, and then the moan came again. His candle went out.

At that moment, Gerrit came very near to going stark raving mad. "Go back!" he screamed hysterically at the dark, and the rock walls echoed his cry up into the hill. His heart seemed to be choking his throat, and he could neither swallow nor breathe. All his being was bent on listening for an approaching step.

Suddenly from the inner chamber there came a ray of light, low, comfortable, and a voice muttered, "What the deuce?" The scarfed dead man filled the low archway, squinting and holding up his hand slightly to cast the light of his ring on the half-fainting prince. "You're not the one I was expecting," the man said abruptly. "Where's Peewit?"

"Outs-s-side," Gerrit managed to stutter.

The man nodded, his free hand coming up to hold the scarf in place diagonally across his face. His visible eye searched Gerrit's face. "Ah. Beod's boy. I see now. Well, you will have to—" His head turned sharply.

Down the tunnel came a sound out of nightmare, a scuffling scamper like a multitude of rats on the move, and then a low, macabre laugh.

The dead man jerked straight. "By the Light! They've found that gate, too?" His ring flared to life, bitterly bright in the enclosed place till the tomb was a lamp with his hand the wick at its center. "Boy, take this to Peewit." He twisted the ring off his finger and thrust it at Gerrit, and the light hung still on his fingers.

Behind him now Gerrit could hear his rescuers outside pounding on the door slab. Get it open, dammit! he screeched at them in his mind.

The man looked down at the two who lay in death. "Ah, dear friends, I am so sorry about this. I had thought to spare you, but it was not to be. I should have known it had to happen this way." In his voice was a wellspring of regret. He put a hand for a moment on the hands of the king.

From the tunnel came the laugh, louder, harsher. The scuffling now might have been wings brushing against the rock walls.

From the door out to the Sweep came the grating of stone against stone, and the slab began to move.

The man swung to face the door, and the linen scarf fell away. For one instant Gerrit caught sight of what the covering had hidden: the sagging eye, the crooked mouth, the head within its hood oversized. The gargoyle.

"Save yourself, man-child," the dread figure advised gently and gave him a shove toward the widening inches of plain starlight. At the inner archway there were suddenly eyes, blue-cold, flickering, and a stench swept over Ariadne's son that was like the vapor of a carrion crow's breath. Gerrit gagged and threw himself against the door. As the light burst behind him, he rammed out into the clear cold of the Sweep.

A radiance, rainbow-hued, bathed the snow from the oblong of door into the tomb. Peewit and Kursh were knocked sprawling by the force of the opening door. The Littleman's lips moved, then he shouted, "Aengus!" and scrambled up, an expression of wakening joy on his face.

"Beware the Skinwalker!" came the bellow from within the tomb, and then there was a cacophony of sound, shrieking as though a thousand teakettles at once had all boiled dry on the fire and exploded! Gerrit stood and turned to look back.

All about, inside, outside, were a thousand flickering eyes, and towering over all, black against the distant stars, a Shadow loomed, grinning, with his spear poised over his shoulder. The prince shouted and pointed at it. The rainbow ring fell through his fingers.

"Close the door!" Aengus cried.

The Shadow hurled his spear. Peewit tackled Gerrit aside, and the ice point whizzed past and took the Painter right through the chest. As Aengus fell backward, the dwarf lurched to his feet and slammed the door shut against the foul wave of Shadows pouring out.

Somewhere near at hand there was a sudden flare of garnet light. "Get away!" the Skinwalker shouted with the wizard's voice.

Peewit was already running. Korimson shoved the prince into a scramble down the cut.

Sea-foam pearl twined about the garnet as the Unnamed's aura learned the wizard's second Warding, and the Fire roared like a foundry.

"Run, damn you!" the dwarf swore and hurled the boy up the embankment. They raced toward the solid bulk and many lights of the castle on the heights, the flickering eyes all about in the dark, fangs snapping at their heels, frost at their hearts.

In the cut, the Skinwalker brought his hands together, clasped them into a fist about the ring that burned the wizard's flesh, and let the last Ward tear through. Wine-color, pearl, and gold, the three-stranded Warding shot into the night. Gouts of earth leaped up, an explosion of rock rolling to cover the other ring and the tomb where, finally, the damned Painter would die.

The earth rumbled and shifted abruptly, some deep anchor point letting go. A star fell, then another, then a shower of them, falling straight down. A savage wind shrieked over the frozen snow, scything trees in Gerrit's Wood as a reaper cuts wheat. And in city and castle, every candle, every lamp, every hearthfire went out. The world was plunged into darkness.

In that cold Dark, there was an insidious laugh and a malicious hiss of satisfaction. "Well done!" the Unnamed whispered in the ear of his Skinwalker.

"Like taking candy from a baby, my lord," the creature laughed with the wizard's voice. He extinguished the Wardings and walked toward the silent walls of the silly woman's stronghold.

The guards at the postern slipped the door a few inches and the Skinwalker they thought was the wizard passed through it, the men drawing back silently. The queen, a dimly seen shadow mantled against the cold, waited on the

steps of the hospice as he walked across the snowy courtyard. He stopped a few paces away. Ariadne's hand reached
for him, but she dropped it. "I thought you couldn't Ward,"
she said in a chill, accusing voice.

Above his head another star streaked down the sky to its
death. In a truly cold voice, the Skinwalker told her, "I
remembered."

Ka-Treer was roused by the captain of his fast ship and
made his way to the flying deck, fighting the pitch of the
deck under his feet. Quite a storm had come up, he thought
to himself as he grasped the rails to haul himself up the
companionway. His attendant thrust back the hatch, and the
Shimarrat king stepped into a fiercely cold wind that brought
tears to his eyes.

When he got to the helm, the captain was waiting for him,
and the man had no need to tell the king why he had
summoned him in the middle of the night. Overhead the
dome of the night sky was streaked with falling stars. Ka-Treer
clung to the lifeline on the pilot deck and roared above the
wind, "Get the astrologer!" His bodyguard yelled the order
down to the second mate, and a sailor ran for the companionway. In short order the befuddled old man was being
helped roughly up the ladder to face the king. Ka-Treer
waved an arm at the sky. "Why didn't you warn me? Can't
you bloody stargazing vermin even predict a meteor shower?
The storm could damage my fleet!"

The astrologer's face sagged, but not at the king's anger,
and he scanned the sky anxiously. Finally he shook his
head. "No, sire, this is no natural occurrence."

The Lion King felt the cold bite into his exposed hands
and face. "What do you mean, it's no natural occurrence?
Next you'll tell me the Ilyrian gods are at war again!"

The old man's eyes were resigned. "You have said it, sire,
not I. But yes, that appears to be what is happening."

"I don't believe that rot! Find me an answer!"

The astrologer watched a star's fall. "Some things happen, my king, whether we give them credence or not. There
is nothing further I can tell you, except—" He glanced at
the captain and first mate, who did not know of the affair at
the Greenbriar Queen's castle. "Except that you may wish
to reconsider, and return the object to its owner."

"I don't *have*—!" Ka-Treer began to snarl, then broke

off. "And if I did, I wouldn't give it back, just when the plan is beginning to work."

The court wise man bowed gravely. "Then, sire, we must not be surprised at any events which may befall us from this time. The plan, as you say, is beginning to work, but it may not be *your* plan. By your leave," he murmured and went back down to the lower deck.

Ka-Treer stared after him, then glanced to Te-Rosh. The nobleman cast a look up at the sky, then back down to the king. Eloquently, he shrugged. "A meteor shower, sire."

The king tugged his cloak about him. "Of course it is. Captain, hold course."

"Aye, sire, though the prince would be more comfortable if we came about just a little, if I may suggest it."

"You may not," Ka-Treer answered abruptly. "And what if my son is seasick? Anybody might be on a night like this."

"Assuredly, sire," the mariner agreed and bowed.

Ka-Treer and Te-Rosh climbed down to the main deck and ducked into the companionway, passing the guards. The nobleman bowed outside the royal cabin and prepared to go on to his own, but Ka-Treer suddenly murmured, "Where by Molok's left one do you think those damned assassins of mine have gotten to with that bloody Crystal?"

Te-Rosh stroked his mustache. "Likely there has been some little trouble in Ilyria over the loss of it, sire. I fancy the roads must be clogged with pilgrims returning home from Castlenigh, carrying the story with them. No doubt our men have had to proceed most carefully."

"They were supposed to be at Waterford for our agent last night!"

"Truly, sire."

The king ground out, "Treachery, Rosh. I smell it. And if it's so, they'll wish they'd never been born when I catch up with them!"

"There is one comforting thought, my king: at least they have not tried to ransom it back to the Ilyrians. Our spies at court would surely have heard something by now and sent word."

Ka-Treer considered this, and finally nodded. "Probably they'll hold the Crystal and try to play a double-handed game, me against Ariadne." He smiled ruthlessly. "It's what I'd do in their position."

Rosh answered his smile. "Ah, but I'll wager they have never played against an opponent like you, sire."

They laughed over it, but later in the darkness of his cabin Ka-Treer clung to the latch of the porthole and watched the silver stars dive down into the heaving sea.

BOOK THREE:

❦

And So Home

Chapter Sixteen

❧

As a pale dawn lightened the sky, Ariadne pulled her mantle about her and left the hospital. The Watchman in attendance did not intrude upon her silence, and she walked down to her gates.

With the first light, the flickering eyes had paled away, though one could feel the malevolence of the Shadows all about. The queen grasped the wrought-iron grillwork and gazed through it. From the town at the foot of the Sweep there were a few tendrils of smoke rising above the chimneys as people discovered they could light fires again. Into her sight came two women, an older and a younger, leaving the castle by the postern. The older one, obviously the young wife's mother, had her arm around her daughter, and they clung together going down the road. Even from her vantage at the gate, the queen could hear the young woman's sobs. Ariadne knew why: during the night, three of her children had died because there was no Elixir left to save them. There had been accusing stares at the fake Crystal she wore, and finally the queen had been able to endure it no longer, but had gone with Fidelis up and down the narrow ward explaining why there would be no more Healing. Disbelief had turned to despair. This fifth morning of Kindlefest there would be many fewer children to wake.

Her stomach felt leaden, a fit match to the sullen sky, low with snow clouds. When the Watchman bowed her toward the keep, she meandered instead toward her private garden and signed the man to wait outside the gate and the thick boxwood hedge. Head bowed, Ariadne stepped into the one part of this courtly world where she felt truly at home, and her bitter reflections ran to the thought that if she couldn't do better than this by her folk, she might as well have stayed a peasant woman in Wolf's Glen. There had been the redeeming feature of innocence about that life at least, for all its hardship. She wished she had her mother—foster mother—Nelia here to talk to right now, but after the initial visit to court for Ariadne's coronation, the family that had raised her had stayed away, except for Jak and June. Jak had kept his head well enough, the queen thought, but June! What a silly woman the blithe maid had grown into!

Nearly as silly as me, Ariadne thought morosely. About the best you can say for either of us is that we married well and got the sons we deserved. Humfrey's a boasting, cruel little wretch, and Gerrit is . . .

It finally clicked. And Gerrit is protecting him, she finished the thought. All this time, and it was my sister's son's hand that killed the Teazle. She drew a deep breath. All this time, to protect me, so that I should not have to order my nephew's execution for murder.

Well, well, young master Greenbriar. You are the most damnable bundle of contraries that ever was: loyal and insubordinate, clever worthy of a king and stupid beyond any lout, light and dark, quicksilver and dross. You just could not restrain your pride in solving the puzzle, could you? And now Alphonse's Wardings have surged beyond his control, and all my friends hold you responsible for it. Oh, yes—you're my son, all right. And Powers help us all, we'll never get to see what kind of king you'd have made.

She paused to brush the snow off the sundial's bronze marker, a quite useless gesture: there wasn't enough sun to cast a shadow across the incised hours in the stone face. With one mittened finger, she routed the snow from the hours. What a way for it to end, the queen whispered in her own mind. We came so far, and to what avail? I saved Imris from fire and preserved him for the agony of being the last, the only, Yoriandir, and now he will go the way of his people when Nilarion falls, as it must inevitably do. Fidelis: faithful up hill and down dale; he has deserved his name. Alphonse, my last love . . . the only true one, maybe. My wizard who is too much man and not enough mage. He will not master the three Wardings that way; one has to be indifferent to wield such power.

And then Kursh, stalwart as they come, tormented by decency. I kicked him to something far better when Peewit took the dwarf home for protection. Thyla, and a little daughter, and Guildmaster. Who'd have thought? By all accounts, he's the best crystal-blower in the world. Peewit, too, has gifts I never knew. If I'd suspected how singular my old Teazle was, I'd have been far more careful of him. I have missed his whistling these years.

She picked a sprig of evergreen and held it absently under her nose. It smelled of snow, clean and sharp with life. Ariadne stepped carefully around the long glaze of ice down the center of the flagged walk where the shovels of the gardeners had left a skin of snow, now frozen solid, and walked toward the terrace at the end of her private sanctuary. Two flickering eyes watched her from behind the inverted rain barrel. The Shadow crept up behind the queen.

Well, what's to do? she was asking herself. There's got to be something. Two other times we have fought back doom. Of course, we had the Crystal then, or at least the hope of its being restored, and that does change—

Soundlessly it sprang, sharp fangs driving toward her neck. And then the Shadow faltered in midspring, covered its face with one dark hand, and coughed, backing off.

Ariadne whirled, saw the dripping teeth. With a cry of angry fear, the queen snatched for the Crystal that no longer hung on its chain and came up empty. The Shadow snarled and coughed again, warily backing away.

"It's different when it isn't a helpless child, isn't it?" she spat, and at the thought of all those poor babies, the queen's anger overcame her fear and she advanced on Tydranth's creature. Of its own volition, her hand came up as though it held her Crystal, and as it had twice before, her fist suddenly lit with a brilliant light, her living flesh translucent as an alabaster lamp.

The Shadow hissed, bared its fangs, and disintegrated in the light.

Slowly Ariadne came back to herself, her hand still at the level of her eyes, but no longer lit. "So?" she said softly, wonderingly. "The Powers have not left us, after all." There might not be a Crystal for her to use, but—

And then her heart finally heard itself clearly: the wizard, the crystal-blower, the Littleman. "Robin, you are such a ninny!" She struck her mittened hands together, spun around, and ran back toward the doorway into her castle, taking a daring slide the full length of the ice streak in the middle of the path. She giggled and pounded past the astonished guard. "Good morning, corporal!"

The man peered after her. " 'Morning, Majesty," he answered to the air.

She burst into the room rather more hastily than a monarch should move, she supposed, but so early in the morning there were not many folk about, and anyway she was too on fire with the idea to care. When she saw them grouped about the bed and the tense looks, she slowed and closed the door quietly.

Alphonse straightened and came to meet her. Ariadne peered past him. "I thought he was better."

The Skinwalker nodded. "And so he was, lady. This was a sudden turn a few minutes ago. He fainted, Fidelis doesn't know why, but he appears to be coming out of it. Come." He forced himself to smile with the wizard's lips. "Peewit will be glad to see you, I know."

She allowed him to lead her to the chair. Kursh glanced and sketched a salute, and Fidelis nodded over his shoulder. "He's waking," the doctor informed her.

The Littleman's eyelids fluttered. He suddenly shook his head on the pillow and woke looking straight at Ariadne. He blinked. "Good morning, my lady."

"Is it?" she murmured, concern for him in her eyes.

He waved it away and pushed himself up to sit against the pillows despite Fidelis's prompting to stay prone. "A momentary weakness, that's all. I feel much better now." Kursh snorted and poured some tea for him. The Littleman's intuition was still as good as ever, for a slow smile spread across his face as he surveyed the queen. "You've a sparkle in your eye, my lady."

"Do I indeed, Master Teazle? Well, it may be a tiny gleam of intelligence you see, and since it's been gone so long, it takes on the aspect of a beacon fire. Now, I have had a lovely walk in my garden, and I have done some thinking. I have also, incidentally, apparently, killed one of those rotten Shadows that had designs on my neck—later, I'll tell it later. For now, do you know what occurs to me? It occurs to me that what we need is a Crystal of Healing."

They looked from one to the other, sick dread in their eyes that was plain as tracks in snow. They thought the sun-fever coming upon her.

Ariadne's chin came up and she looked around at them. "So, gentlemen, we are going to make one."

Never, bitch! the Skinwalker told her silently and turned away, walking to the window until he could mask his eyes.

For a moment there was silence thick as cold grease, and then Kursh rasped, "We are?"

"We are," she answered. "We're going to try, anyway. What have we to lose?"

Only time, the Skinwalker thought with deep satisfaction, but he waited for the rest of them to take the bait.

They glanced to the queen and then studied their hands or the floor. Kursh smoothed his mustache. "I'm willing to give a try at blowing the crystal itself," he volunteered gruffly. "But by His Beard, I hope you know what you're doing, my queen. I don't like to think of misusing a Power's gift."

"Nor do I, Kursh," Ariadne answered. "Which is why I won't waste the people the Powers have sent to me. You, all of you, are the gift, if we had wits enough to use it."

"And Imris," Peewit pointed out.

She nodded. "I shall send for him immediately. I do not know what part was played by the Yoriandirkin in the fashioning of the original Crystal, but I am certain there must have been one. So yes, Imris, too." Fidelis was shaking his head. "What is it, doctor?" the queen asked.

"We have all forgotten one very important point, it seems to me," the old man said. "The heart of your Crystal, lady, was the Greenbriar seeds, and they were a gift from Ritnym herself. They are gone. Wherever shall we get more?"

Ariadne looked to Alphonse for help, but he was still staring out the window, seemingly lost in thought. "Well, Rasullis used Nilarion berries. I know his Crystal went awry, but still—it grew a briar of sorts. I suppose we could try the same."

The Skinwalker nodded and turned to face them with a smile. "We can."

. . . *the Power's golden robe beside him, the hand reaching to cup a flower from the vine* . . . "*Maybe you two shall have joy of each other at the end—*" . . . *the vine, the flower impossibly turquoise against the thousand greens and the hundred yellows that were the Meadows of Morning. And Rose she was called, Tychanor's beloved.*

Alphonse's eyes, peculiarly cloudy blue, and the jut of Kursh's beard behind him. The Littleman fastened on the wizard's eyes. By the Lord of Summer, Peewit thought, he's the Skinwalker!

He forced himself to say normally, "Sorry. Still tired, I guess. I'll be glad to help with the Crystal, though I haven't the foggiest notion what I can do." The blue eyes left him.

Ariadne rose, casting aside her long mantle. Though she did not quite smile, there was satisfaction in the look she gave her Pledged. "There now, you see? There is hope after all. I feel I could eat a bite. Will any of you join me?"

As though a knotty problem had been solved, the others stretched and straightened, the tension of the long night out of themselves, and assented to the queen's suggestion. Watching them, the Littleman did not dare say what he alone knew: that if there was any hope at all, it was very far from them. Much farther than the Skinwalker was from the Queen. Impulsively he drew off the protecting golden locket over his head and pressed it into the hand she held down to him. "Here, my lady, wear this for good luck if you will. You are very important in all of this." He was sure he saw a sudden flicker in the blue eyes, but he ignored it. "It will ease my heart to see you wear it."

"Why, Peewit, thank you! But if I have you by me, I shan't need much more luck than that." She brushed his forehead with a kiss. "If it makes you feel better, though, I'll do it." She put the golden locket about her neck, and then the talk turned to breakfast.

All that day an air of purposeful bustle pervaded the castle. The courtiers in the antechamber noted that the queen issued a steady stream of orders. The garlands looped along the outer walls were to be checked closely, and any which appeared to be coming loose were to be mended. Branches of the felled evergreens in Gerrit's Wood were to be collected for the purpose. Additionally, yards of new garland and boughs were to be woven to trim around all the the hospice's windows and doors. (There were sidelong glances at this bit of gossip, though, of course, courtiers were more politic than to voice the thought that decorating the windows of a death house for the poor children was really going a bit far.) When another directive was issued to the effect that everyone—everyone, from the lord chamberlain to the lowliest scullery maid—was to wear a sprig of evergreen, preferably something pungent, to ward off Shadows, there was much waggling of eyebrows and some wagging of tongues. But the Queen's Watch went about very efficiently making certain that the order was followed. Yes, they answered the incredulous, it did work. In fact, it had worked for Her Majesty herself just that very morning, and didn't it make sense that was the reason none of the flickering-eyed creatures had insinuated themselves into the castle during the darkness of the previous night? The waggling eyebrows stopped waggling, and everyone wore evergreen. The more pungent, the better.

Additionally, blazing fires were lit in every hearth, fed all day with chunks of seasoned wood to make heaps of glowing coals. If there would be no fire again that night, there would at least be some heat and a little light. Winter stones were set to warm for the children, both the afflicted and the well, and the castle folk got all of their warmest clothing out of the cedar clothes presses. Hot dinner would be served before sunset, and afterward earthenware crocks of mead would be set into the glowing turves of Rose Hall, the mulled drink rationed for all who wanted it. And Festil would play and sing, and there would be storytelling and spicy pepperbread. It was the queen's wish, expressed in rather more colorful terms to Captain Quint, that Greenbriar Castle would, by the Powers, keep Kindletest.

And the courtiers looked at one another, and the servingfolk scratched their heads, and the Watchmen wore evergreen in the cloak brooches. People decided maybe it wasn't as daft an idea as it seemed; after all, if this was going to be the last Festival of the Light, then why not try to make it a good one? So by midafternoon there was very nearly a festive air, except for the way people jumped when a potboy dropped a tray or a piece of knotty pine popped in the fire.

Kursh leaned on his fists over the drawing tacked to the table in his quarters. The fire roared in a satisfactory way up the flue, and a half-empty glass of black flotjin was within reach. He puffed on his pipe. "Hmm, yes, maybe," he murmured. There was a tap at the door. "Come," he called absently.

"Sir? Excuse me?"

Without turning, the dwarf growled, "Did you see the armorer, yeoman?"

"Yes, sir," Gerrit answered, half through the door and

not daring to enter further. "He tells me to report to you that he's made the modifications you ordered to your ship. I am to say that all is prepared, sir."

"Good."

"Sir?"

"What?"

Gerrit swallowed and made a sudden decision. He stepped in and closed the door behind him, drawing to rigid attention. "There's been talk, admiral, that you'll sail on a secret mission for the queen tonight."

"Can't be much of a secret, then, can it?" Korimson grated, still studying his drawing.

The Greenbriar chin came up. "I would like to go with you, sir."

"I only sail with people I like."

There was silence. The dwarf dropped his pipe onto the silver ashtray and took a swig of flotjin. The prince answered, "I know. I'm asking anyway."

Korimson turned, his face stone. "Why?" he barked.

Gerrit thought, Because you played horse with me when I was small, and I can't remember that my father ever did. He cleared his throat hoarsely, and his face regained its customary veneer. "My mother has important work to do, and I cannot help her. I'd rather not stick around to see more of the children go into a sleep they won't wake from. Drowning in an icy sea or being run through by a pirate's sword has got to be easier than that. So may I sail with you, sir?"

Dammit, why did he have to sound so much like her? the Guildmaster thought sourly. He sipped his drink, watching the boy narrowly. "All right," he rasped finally. "If you want a taste of what it is to be Greenbriar, you'll get one: I'm going to try to get home to collect a Weatherglass I left there. There's a very good chance we'll be attacked by the Unnamed. Not exactly punting on a millpond, or whatever it is gentlemen do of a summer afternoon. Still want to go?"

"Yes, sir."

Kursh nodded. "Go get whatever gear you think you'll need and move it to the ship. Tell Captain Jorgen I'll board soon after nightfall."

"After, sir?"

"Yeoman, if we can't make it down the Sweep through some scum-eating Shadows, we'll not bloody likely have the balls enough to sail across an unfriendly sea, now will we?"

"No sir."

"So get us some evergreen, and tell Captain Jorgen to grease the rails of the *Kite* with pine oil."

"Yes, sir."

"Then get back up here and have something to eat."

"Yes, sir."

"Then say goodbye to your lady mother."

Their eyes met, and though the room was warm with the fire on the hearth, both of them were suddenly cold. The prince saluted. "Yes, sir. I will." He about-faced and left quietly.

Kursh finished his flotjin, rolled the sketch and stowed it with his gear, then went along the hall to have a word with Peewit.

After so many years, the ones apart and the ones together, there really wasn't much to say, or too much, depending on how you looked at it. There was a job to be attempted, and that was that. So they sat with their feet to the fire and smoked. "I'm taking Gerrit with me," Kursh said.

"I'd hoped you might." The Littleman gathered the blanket closer about his shoulders and blew a smoke ring at the ceiling, fingering the raised bee on the meerschaum.

The dwarf pulled reflectively at his beard. "Aside from all our other problems, the Shimarrats are probably still out there on the high seas, you know. I doubt it's very safe for the pipsqueak."

"I don't think the pipsqueak cares. And who knows? He may be safer on a ship far north of here. If it's safe anywhere."

They smoked.

Korimson asked, "Is Muir around?" He was asking whether the Littleman would have someone with a dagger nearly as quick as the dwarf's own to guard him.

"No. He left Castlenigh two days ago, sending me a note. He said if he stayed much longer in town, he'd go mad. People are distrustful of him, it seems. The innkeeper suggested he remove himself."

"Why? Did the fellow find his pewter missing?"

Peewit looked at him over the bowl of his pipe, one eyebrow lifted. "No, but there was a disagreement about some candlesticks, apparently."

The dwarf grunted. They smoked some more.

Kursh studied the glowing shreds of tobacco in his pipe. He cleared his throat. "D'ye think we can do it?"

He meant make a new Crystal, Peewit knew. The Littleman bent his head to smell the sharp evergreen from the sprig of fir young Rory Fisher had brought to him earlier on the queen's instruction. "Aengus did it."

"Aye, but can Freckles do what the Painter did?"

Brickleburr laid aside his pipe and mopped his brow with a corner of the blanket. "I don't know." He's not Alphonse, old friend, he told Kursh silently.

The damned fever's coming back on him, Kursh thought. He took the blue bottle of Elixir from his pocket and put it between them on the candle table, then tugged at his eyepatch and got to his feet. "Right, then. I must be off." They stood before the fire awkwardly. The dwarf drew a breath. "Take care of yourself. If Fisher lets anything happen to ye, I'll throttle him."

He meant it, too. Peewit smiled briefly. "Take your star-flower. Thyla says." Kursh snorted, and the Littleman added, "My best to her and to Gretchen. Bring me back some muffins."

Just for an instant Kursh saw something in his friend's eyes that made him pause, but he put it down to the sickness. They clasped hands, and he left.

When he had gone, the room was somehow smaller and quieter. Peewit packed his pipe—his old one, now that Kursh was not there to see—and sat before the fire, thinking and trying to chase the fever from his brow and the chill from his feet. What do you do with a Skinwalker wizard?

First answer: you do not—repeat, do not—let it know that you suspect. If it has not attacked the queen directly, then it is waiting for something.

Counter question: what is it waiting for?

Possibility: for the last night of Kindlefest, when the Lord of the Sun sleeps his deepest. Surely it will be on the festival dedicated to his Twin that the Unnamed will make his final move to enslave the world to his death.

Now, then: what to do? Obviously I must go Home. The sun darkens and grows cold. That is not something about which I can do anything by staying here. It is in the Meadows of Morning that the answer lies, if anywhere. Haven't quite got a handle on that yet, but there's something for me to do—none of my dreams have shown me Greenbriar;

whatever I did before and am to do again lies in the Valley of the Sun. I'm sure of that much, at least. And if they're going to try to make a Crystal—without Alphonse—then I might have some time if the Skinwalker stays here. He'll have to play out the mummery, of course. I hope so, anyway, because I'd not like to meet the whoreson alone, in the dark, somewhere betwixt here and Home. That would really be too much. . . .

The Hearthman rubbed a hand through his curly gray hair and sighed. Have to do it: there's no other way. I'll have to leave the queen alone with the wretched thing and hope the Powers will protect her.

And where do you suppose Alphonse is? Poor fellow. I remember they did it to Aengus once. Must be unpleasant to be turned out of your skin . . . though, actually, the Painter rather welcomed it, I think . . . people couldn't stare at him that way. Of course, young Freckles isn't Aengus.

No, certainly not.

Awfully like him at times, though.

By the Living Light Himself!

Peewit's foot hit the floor with a thump as he sat forward suddenly. And she—oh, what a bloody fool I've been!—Ariadne is the living image of Rose!

He had unconsciously risen to his feet in stunned agitation, the pipe dangling forgotten from his hand, the blanket trailing. His mind clicked almost audibly. I'm not the only one who's passed from life to life! Some ash sifted to the hearth, and he discovered his hands were shaking. "Brickleburr, you untold idiot, you!" he berated himself aloud, but in the same instant there was in him a relief so great it buoyed him like a swan floating on a placid river. "So that's it!" He took a quick turn up and down the hearth rug, the memories flooding now. That's it! We were all there at the beginning, and now we are all together again at the . . .

The thought literally stopped him in his tracks. After a long moment he dropped back into the chair and realized he had been holding his breath, as at some news of terrible grief.

End.

He stared at the fire on the hearth without seeing it, his mind gray and still. Then there was a quick scamper across the floor of his mental attic, and a voice said, "But if it's truly without hope, why did the Powers wake your memories?"

Slow cycle of thought. "I don't know," he murmured. "For fun?"

The same squeaky voice chided, "Now, that's not Lord Tychanor's way, and you know it, Mister Peewit, though himself's all for fun in other ways, of course."

Peewit frowned. I never spoke in such a voice in all my life, he thought with irritation. Lives, I should say. He straightened in the chair, and for the first time in some minutes, his eyes focused.

There was a mouse beside the kindling basket, bright-eyed and solemn. "Ah, you're awake now. Good," Sir Winston said.

"You again," the Littleman said tiredly.

"Yes. Quite the pest, I suppose, but I do have my work, and you're it, so let's not be testy."

"I'm not testy, just tired."

"Of course you are weary! That's part of the Dark One's nastiness, don't you see? If you'd had enough appetite to try the Kindle-Log on the table there, you might have discovered it helps. Wouldn't you like just a bite, Master Pledged?"

As soon as the creature suggested it, Peewit felt hungry. He blinked in surprise and smiled. "How did you do that?"

Thatch-rustle pulled at his ear. "I didn't, in fact." He folded his hands on his belly, which had grown considerably plumper over the past few days on stolen Lipopo. "You did, Mister Peewit. It's your aura coming back, you see."

Brickleburr had half-risen from the chair. "Aura?"

"Think a moment, sir. You'll remember."

. . . darkness in the house, lightened with moonlight through the chimney hole . . . snores from the tallfolk man, the wife's quiet breath, a sniffly cough from one of the children in the loft . . . he crept soundlessly closer to the cradle, digging the small filigree gold box from the pocket of his red leather apron. The wee one, still too new to the world to be much more than a little lump of swaddling under the fleece, woke and fixed its half-open eyes on him as he smiled and smoothed the dark hair with the barest touch of one finger. The infant gurgled quietly, and his smile broadened. Aye, you know me, don't you, tyke? he thought. Opening the lid of his box, he took a pinch of the precious golden dust, set it on his palm, and carefully blew it over the baby. It sifted down, catching the pale moonlight in a golden shower, and coa-lesced to form for an instant a translucent wall about the

infant, which smiled a wide, toothless grin. The aura set and the golden limning disappeared, though it would be visible to those who could see for the rest of the child's life. There now, you're all set, he thought. Child of the Light. No Dark will harm you if the Folk can do anything about it! From the other large pocket of his apron, he drew a cradle-bunny, this one made of fleece with soft pink dyed in the ears and at the nose, and a ridiculous droll expression on its embroidered face. Firkin's work, he thought to himself and nearly laughed aloud, but recollected in time. He tucked the Folk gift into the cradle. Watch carefully now, bunny, he thought at it. The stuffed animal twitched one ear and raised a hind paw to scratch. 'We're fine, Master Hearthman,' it told him. 'See you at Kindlefest.' Right, he thought in answer. And you'd best have a good report for me! 'Oh, I don't fancy I'll have too much trouble with one this small, do you?' the cradle-bunny said, wriggling its nose. He gave it an affectionate pat, waggled his finger at the house mouse watching from the hearth to remind it to guard the household well, and then passed soundlessly out the door, releasing his stillness spell as soon as he was outside. Now for the next farm, over the rise and through the trees. . . .

Winston looped his tail over his arm. "You see? I rather thought you'd not forgotten something so important."

Peewit found himself still smiling at the memory. His smile faded, and he looked down at the mouse speculatively. "There's something wrong with my aura, isn't there? That's why I've been feeling so rotten."

"Quite! After all, your aura, Mister Peewit, is a rather distinctive one, if I may say so." Thatch-rustle had the air of one who keeps a delicious secret. "All the Folk auras are, of course, but yours particularly, you know, being the Pledged."

Another click. Auras. "The Hearthfolk bear a portion of the Warm Fire's own aura through the winter and give it back to him on Kindlefest."

"Just so," said the mouse with satisfaction.

"And I . . . ." Peewit struggled with the last fragment of memory.

"Yes?" Sir Winston prodded gently. "What about you, Pledged?"

The Hearthman sighed a breath and his eyes cleared. "I am Tychanor's secret self."

The mouse grinned his toothy grin. "So you are, indeed. Have some Kindle-Log, my lord?"

Dear Alphonse,

> *I am leaving this in the care of some friends who will be sure you get it, for I've a strong feeling you'll find a way back here to Greenbriar.*
> *The time is very dangerous, as you are aware. If you come to read this, you will already have discovered that the Skinwalker has been here: I only hope I have not erred badly in leaving Her Majesty without my protection. I did give her my locket, and it should work well enough until you can guard her yourself. I have been called Home, and such a summons cannot be denied. Besides, you won't need me to make the new Crystal. Melt down the locket for the gold filigree (copy the original pattern, mind you!), Kursh will blow the glass, and in the twist of paper with this note you will find more Greenbriar seeds. Never mind where I got them: they are real, and will work if the strength of your love for Ariadne overrides all other considerations. You can make this Crystal, Alphonse; Aengus was not stronger than you, nor cleverer, but he loved beyond reason, beyond time, beyond life itself. Someday, you may know who, and why, but it is unimportant to your task right now. Concentrate!*

> *Fondly,*
> *Peewit*

> *PS. There is something you will need buried out by the tomb—ask Gerrit, he'll remember.*

The mouse nibbled at a corner of the Kindle-Log slice Peewit had cut for him. "Nice handwriting," he complimented, leaning over the page.

"Thank you," Brickleburr answered past a mouthful of the fruited loaf. "I worked for a time as a scribe. I think it was in this present lifetime: they all rather run together now." He dipped the quill once more and hesitated as a sudden thought struck him. "You don't suppose your mouse friends will eat the Briar seeds before Alphonse gets here, do you?"

"Oh, gracious, no! I've told them quite rigorously who those seeds are from and left strict orders that they be handed over to the wizard in the same condition in which they were received." His long nose was wrinkled. "I assure you, my lord, there's not a mouse in the castle would dare touch them, though they smell deliciously of Kindle-Log."

Brickleburr laughed and pulled another sheet of paper toward him.

Dear Kursh,

Now don't look like that—I had to go Home, that's all, and no, I couldn't tell you beforehand. I wasn't sure myself till just now. There's a job I must do, you see, and we both know about duty.

So take care of Her Majesty and Gerrit and try not to be too hard on Alphonse—he really is a decent fellow, and none of what's happened is his fault. Good luck with the Crystal. Though I won't be cheeky enough to offer advice—you're the Guildmaster!—I remember the star you blew. I've never seen anything so lovely.

Chin up, First Watchman. I'll try to be back for Kindlefest.

A salute from
Brickleburr

Peewit sanded the ink, blew on it for good measure, and then rolled the thin scrolls, dripping a bit of candlewax on each with his thumbprint as a seal. He regarded them for a moment and smoothed an edge of the one he had written to Kursh where it had curled.

The mouse licked its fingers quietly, watching him.

The Hearthman looked up to find the mouse studying him. "This has been a good lifetime, Sir Winston—one of the best. It isn't every Time that one finds such friends." Thatch-rustle nodded solemnly, but said nothing. Brickleburr gave the letter a final pat, rose, and brushed crumbs of Kindle-Log off his clothes. "How did Tansy know I would find the Briar seeds she'd baked in the log?"

"Well, really, Mister Peewit, there was no other safe way to send them. We knew the Shadows wouldn't touch Kindle-Log, even if they got Master Firkin and me. When the Matriarch sent the box of aura dust to you last summer and you did not come Home to use it, Mistress Tansy knew you'd be needing the seeds, too."

The Littleman had been twisting the Briar seeds into a scrap of paper and now tied it to Alphonse's scroll with a bit of string. "There—that should do. Can you manage alone?"

The mouse hefted one end of the scroll experimentally. "I should say so. Just give me a few moments, my lord, and your secret will be safely stowed behind the wainscoting."

"Fine, Winston. I'll just finish packing, and then I think we may go."

"Very good, sir." He turned busily to the scroll for the wizard, spat on his palms, rubbed them briskly together, and picked up the paper roll.

The Hearthman hid a smile and began to gather up his pipes and tobacco.

In short order the pack was strapped and the mouse was sitting atop it on the bed. "Do you remember the way, sir? I'm sure I can lead the way, if you like, though of course it's deuced hard without the bees to guide us."

The Pledged of the Hearthfolk picked up the mouse by his tail and dangled him at eye level. "I think I remember how to get Home, summer or winter, to my own gates," he reminded the mouse mildly. "Even without Aengus's clue of following the 'finger's long shadow' in his fresco."

Upside down, arms and legs hanging loosely, the mouse looked abashed. "Quite, my lord. Just a reminder it was. No impertinence intended."

Brickleburr set him back down on the pack. "Make yourself comfortable. And stay out of the Kindle-Log—it's all the food we've got."

From within the pack as the mouse's tail disappeared came the somewhat hushed reply: "It's all the food we'll need, if we need any at all."

Peewit shouldered the bag, sniffed at his fingers to satisfy himself that the pine tar was still active, and in his stillness spell walked to the queen's apartment.

"Open up, Watchman," he ordered the man at the double doors brusquely.

In the pitch dark the fellow could not see him, but the Littleman could see him well enough from within the spell. The sergeant jerked to attention and asked, "Is that you, lord general?"

"Of course. I must see Her Majesty at once."

"My lady's down in the hall, sir."

"Oh. Well, I'll seek her there. Thank you. Good night."
Deft as a tinker, the Hearthman squeezed between the man
and the door, slipped through into the antechamber, and
shut the door behind him. The room was deserted, and he
crossed quickly to the queen's door. Quietly, he pushed it
open and peered around it. No Meara: she must have gone
to the hall with the queen. More important, no Skinwalker.
Peewit walked to the queen's writing desk and dropped a
third small scroll on it. Then he went through the tiring
room, opened the door to the secret stair, and went down—
but not all the way. About a third of the way on his left, he
pressed one of the stones and the other secret door opened.
In the stillness spell he could see the stairs, thick with dust,
that twisted down, back toward the mural wall. "Told you,
mouse."

From within the pack Winston's muffled voice answered,
"Yes, my lord."

It was nearly as bad as Gerrit had expected. The eyes
were all around, his pack was far too heavy, the
evergreen smell was enough to make his nose run, and the cat kept
herself right under his feet in the dark. He swore at her for
the umpteenth time and tried to scuff her away.

Beside him the admiral growled, "You're a hell of a one
to have along on a night patrol, yeoman."

"It's the bloody cat, sir. I'm going to kill the both of us,
falling over her."

The crunch of Korimson's boots on the icy road stopped.
"The wizard's cat is here?"

"Yes, sir. I know it's the same one—I saw her scoot out
the gate as they closed it behind us."

"That so?" There was a rustle of cloak as Korimson
stopped. "Patience? Come here." The cat's soft fur brushed
his outstretched hand, and he rubbed her ears. "What are
ye doing out in the cold, cat? Ye should be up to the hall,
getting under the wizard's feet while the boy wonder toasts
himself beside the hearth."

'It isn't my wizard, dumb dwarf!' Irritably she butted
against his boots. 'At least pick me up and carry me. I don't
care for it as a regular thing, but I'm willing to allow it
tonight, since the Evil Eyes are all around.'

"Shoo!" Kursh told her and gave her a gentle but firm push back up the hill.

She sank a claw in his boot and refused to let go.

"Oh, all right, then, ye damn black-and-white monster! Come along down to the river and see how ye like being left on the pier with yon Eyes all about!" Kursh scooped her up and was going to carry her in the crook of his arm, but the cat had another idea and scrambled up the front of his cloak to crouch atop the pack strapped to his back. Just to show him there were no hard feelings, she stretched her neck to purr loudly close to his hooded ear. "Make yeself to home, why don't ye?" the dwarf grumbled. But the purr was comforting somehow, and he surprised even himself by reaching a glove to touch her nose. Patience settled herself.

"Have you got her, sir?" Gerrit asked in the dark.

"She's got me, rather. Let's go, yeoman, and pinch up your evergreen: the cold might be taking some of the scent from it."

"I couldn't be that lucky," the suffering youth muttered, and his Senior Officer drove back a few of the nearer Eyes with his laugh.

In Rose Hall, the embers cast a warm red glow that was not at all to the Skinwalker's liking. And the smell! It sneezed through the wizard's nose.

Beside him the queen said worriedly, "I hope you're not coming down with it, too."

"Oh, no," the Skinwalker lied smoothly. "It's just pungent in here."

Ariadne sniffed deep of the spruce, holly, and cinnamon. "Yes, it smells like Kindlefest, doesn't it? I sometimes wish we could make a perfume of it to uncork the rest of the year, too."

He turned his head to regard her where they sat together on one of the long benches drawn near to the damnably hot mounds of wood coals, and managed to mask the flicker of his eyes. She was smiling and nodding to Festil to play the same ridiculous song again. As he watched the waning firelight etch her features with gold, the Skinwalker thought, *Since you like the stench so much, I'll drown you in it when the time comes, Greenbriar bitch. You'll sleep in a pitch-pine coffin and wake howling in the Dark. Oh, yes, it will be quite the Kindlefest.*

Ariadne poked him in the ribs. "Sing!"

Wouldn't I love to! the Skinwalker thought savagely, but restrained the Wild Song that rose to the wizard-body's lips. It was not Time yet.

Not quite.

He opened his mouth and let the wizard's voice pick up the refrain.

Chapter Seventeen

⚜

All that night they sailed without incident, a fast ship sliding without lights past the tidal rush at Willowsrill Mouth. At first they had scarcely believed the pine oil on the rails had repelled the flickering-eyed Shadows, but none were found aboard, and there had been no attack as they had rowed as quietly as possible away from the crowded quays and busy waterfront of Castlenigh. When they were well out in the broad river and the shore to either side was a pitch dark lost in the icy smoke that writhed off the water, the Guildmaster had ordered shortened watches, but doubled stations. More men would watch for shorter hours, though what they were watching for, none of them could say. Then he had gruffly ordered his yeoman to follow him below, and Gerrit had stumbled after him down the companionway.

"Cold?" the dwarf rasped.

"N-no, sir, not very."

"Liar. Sick yet?"

"No," the prince answered truthfully, though disheartened at the "yet." He had already wondered if he would be seasick.

"Good." There was the sound of the dwarf's heavy footfalls across the wooden floor of the cabin and then a clink and liquid gurgling. "Cat?" Korimson suddenly called. From the companionway came a meow. "Ah. Decided to sail with us, did you? You're not very bright, Patience: this is a grand

way to get your toes wet." Another meow, closer and with a
hint of growl. "She must like you, yeoman."

"Me, sir?"

"Well, it can't be me. I don't get on well with cats. So I
don't like to think what the wizard will say when he discov-
ers his familiar gone. Here—take this glass and drink it
down. All of it."

Somehow Gerrit found his outstretched hand. The stuff
smelled like licorice, and when he sipped it, he discovered
why flotjin was spoken of with wry respect. He coughed into
his gauntlet and was glad the old fellow couldn't see his eyes
tearing.

In the darkness, the dwarf's voice was gruff, but Gerrit
knew Korimson was smiling. "When you've finished it, there's
a built-in bench by your right hand. It will serve well enough
as a bunk. Try not to roll off. There's a port above it: do me
the courtesy of hanging your head out there if you must."

"Aye, sir."

"Good night, yeoman."

" 'Night, sir."

"Cat, get the hell off my damned pillow!" Korimson
suddenly roared, and then there was the sound of a mattress
rustling as the dwarf settled in.

Gerrit sat on the edge of his wide bench, nursing his
flotjin and wondering whether this was really the stupidest
thing he'd ever done, or only seemed that way.

From across the cabin, Patience watched the boy through
one slitted eye and then curled against the dwarf's broad
back and went to sleep with satisfaction. They were sailing
toward her wizard.

The Guildmaster stood at the rail with Captain Jorgen
late the next afternoon as they passed the headland and
entered the sheltered bay of Skejfalen, capital of the island
of Jarlshof. Korimson looked up at the dome of the guildhall shining in the wan light that should have turned its
crystal roof to a rose-and-gold magnificence. He thumped a
hand off the rail. "I don't like it," he rasped.

The captain of his flagship glanced at him. "The early
sunset, sir?"

"That, too. No, I meant the fact that we never even
caught a sniff of Shimarrat pirates, and the sea was as calm
as a duck pond. Ye'd have thought the human bastards, or

the inhuman one, would have made a try for us. I was expecting an interesting trip home."

Jorgen knew him well enough to risk a smile. "You sound disappointed, Guildmaster."

Korimson shot him a look that carried a deal of the venom reserved for the pirates. "I am. About the Shimarrats, at least. The Wild Fellow's missing us I'm not unhappy about. I've no fancy for being broken up by a whale or sucked down to the briny deeps by a whoreson giant octopus." He rubbed his nose. "Of course," he said as if to himself, "young Freckles could have been lying about that."

Jorgen had no idea what his master was talking about, so he wisely took the moment to signal the sails lowered and oars out. "We've covered the special weapons as you ordered, sir, and stacked empty crates around them. They're well hidden."

"Good. Strict hush, Jorgen—those things are our one hope."

"Aye, sir. Ingenious, if I may say so."

"They will be if the damned things work." Kursh knocked out his pipe, spat into the scuppers, and straightened. "We'll turn about for Greenbriar again at the turn of tide tomorrow night. Minimum crew—there's no reason to risk a full complement, just in case. Rig for dark running, of course, and be sure our flags are flying all the time. I don't want any loopholes."

"Very good, admiral." It was the first time any of the dwarven crew had used the new title to their Guildmaster, and there was pride in the officer's voice.

Kursh pulled at his eyepatch. "Oh, by the way, add another bar to your uniform, Jorgen. You're now the First Captain of the Joint Fleet."

The salt wrinkles around Jorgen's eyes deepened, and he flushed as he saluted. "As you will, sir."

Korimson looked around. "Where's my yeoman gotten himself to, do you suppose?"

"He's aft, sir, with the helmsman. He seems anxious to learn navigation. Actually, since this morning, I believe he's been over every inch of the ship."

"Has he made a nuisance of himself?"

"No, admiral. It is more than idle curiosity. He learns quickly." The officer's brows went up. "Actually, for a landsman, he's got the making of a deepwater sailor. I had thought he might have to stay below decks, next to a bucket."

Kursh smoothed his mustache. "Aye, he looks all silk, but there's grit in him, as a friend of mine has observed. I never even thought to ask him if he can swim."

"I did. He gave me a rather odd look and said he's never needed to learn."

The fierce brows drew down. "Is that so?" He thought a moment, glanced at the water rippling back from the hull as the rowers slowed, and said quietly, "Have him report to me immediately."

Captain Jorgen had a feeling he shouldn't have told the Guildmaster about that little conversation, but he inclined his head briefly and stepped aside to have a word with one of the sailors. The man touched his cap and ran aft. "If you'll excuse me, admiral?"

"Aye, Jorgen. Go watch from a safe distance. He's chancy to cross. Let the men know what's happening."

The captain of the *Crystal Kite* saluted and signaled his first mate as he moved away. They began to pass the word. Aloft in the rigging there were smiles, and the linehandlers on deck turned from their work to watch.

The Greenbriar prince came limping quickly up the deck, dodging coils of rope. He drew to a stop and threw a perfunctory salute. "You sent for me, sir?"

"I did. Attended me, yeoman." Korimson led him across the ship to the other rail. He halted and pointed to a loose end of line that snaked down from a sail someone had forgotten to knot off. The rope swung out about a yard from the rail. "Everyone has a job to do when we're coming into port. If you want to learn something of sailing, fetch the end of that line and I'll show you how to knot it properly."

Gerrit hesitated, smelling a rat, then swung himself up to the rail, slipping a little on the pine oil. With no pause, he reached out, grasped the swinging rope, and pulled it in, balancing easily on the rail. "There you are, sir," he said.

Kursh took the rope, casually tied it off on the spindle nearby, and shot out a hand to halt the yeoman as the boy bent a little to jump down to the deck. "Hold it, Greenbriar." The prince straightened a little, rocking now that he had no rope to hang on to. "The trip out has been easy: the trip back's likely to be a pisscutter. Every man aboard will have to know that he can depend upon the others. You agree, I hope, that officers are due respect at all time?"

Oh, shit, Gerrit thought. He nodded warily.

"Didn't hear that, yeoman."

"Aye, sir."

"Good. But this morning when Captain Jorgen asked you if you could swim, you made him a smart-ass answer, didn't you?"

I made him my uncle's answer. Smart-ass, nevertheless, I suppose. "I didn't mean it that way, sir."

"I'm sure. However, we need the truth now: can you swim, Greenbriar?"

"I can, sir."

"Wonderful. You will prove it, please." The dwarf crossed his arms on his chest. He had no doubt it looked relaxed and patronizing to the boy, but what Gerrit couldn't know was that both Kursh and Jorgen, to whom the admiral had given a hand signal, were prepared to dive in after him if he needed help.

The sodding bastard, Gerrit thought resignedly. I'll freeze my ass off. I hope it's just my ass—the Greenbriar family jewels could be in danger here. He stripped off his cloak and cast it down to the deck, then swept a glance over the grins of the crew. "I don't suppose there's any flotjin in this for me, is there, sir?" There was good-natured laughter, and on its sound, the prince sprang up and out, tucking his feet in a perfect backward somersault into the black water of the port. Quicker than a seal, he surfaced, swam the few strokes, grabbed for the rope ladder they flung over to him, and somehow got himself up the gently rocking side of the *Kite*. He was strongly tempted to make another smart-ass remark when the willing hands set him on his frozen feet on the deck, so it was probably just as well that he couldn't get his breath for the cold. He fumbled a salute.

In the one eye there was a gleam of satisfaction. "Ye don't swim too badly for a landlubber, Greenbriar." His hand flickered, and someone threw a blanket around the shivering, dripping yeoman and another sailor pressed his frozen hands around a tankard of flotjin.

Gerrit met his Senior Officer's amused squint. He raised the tankard. "Your h-health, gentlemen. Allow me to s-say I wish we'd met in s-summer." They roared, and he tipped the hot black liquor down his throat.

By the Powers, he's got the Greenbriar way, all right, the old dwarf thought. Already half these men would follow him in a fight, and the other half would wish they could. To cover the surge of pride, he tugged at his beard. "Get yourself some dry clothes, yeoman, and then move our packs up on deck. As soon as we clear the port authority, we'll head home."

"Aye, s-sir." Gerrit threw another stiff salute and limped away, leaving wet bootprints on the *Kite*'s scrubbed deck.

Damn, I wish I'd remembered that in time, Kursh thought. Of course the lad couldn't humiliate himself by kicking off the only pair of boots he's got before he dove in, and now they'll dry stiff as a board and probably cut him to ribbons on the bad foot. Korimson, Korimson, ye haven't got all your lamps lit sometimes. He shook his head.

Thyla shook her head over the boots on the wide tiled hearth of the living room. Too near the fire, and now they were stiff as a loaf that hadn't risen right. "By Aashis's stars, Father," she muttered under her breath, "ye'd think ye'd never dried a pair of boots before!" She stooped and carried them into the kitchen. "Do the best you can with them," her husband had requested over his eggs an hour before daylight. "It won't be very much," she had rejoined tartly. "My land, Kursh, the boots are the least of it! You'd better hope that young fellow doesn't catch a cold, because if he does, I'll make you take the same medicine I give him, measure for measure!" He had laughed and untied her apron strings while she had her hands in the dishwater.

The mistress of Ledgelawn smiled a little at the memory, though she had realized even while she spattered him with soapsuds that Kursh was covering over his fear of climbing the mountain. She didn't blame him: there was no guarantee that the Lord of the Winds would want anybody scaling his mountain twice in a lifetime. So she had kissed him long and hard when he got up from the table to light the candle in his lantern and watched after him from the doorway when he left with a wave and a growled word to their nephew Peter's dog, which had come running to gambol around his feet.

Thyla was fiercely rubbing oil into the leather of the boots when there was a soft scuffling in the hallway and the queen's son appeared in her kitchen. "Uh, beg pardon, madam, but I seem to have lost—oh, you've got them." He stood uncertainly in the sheepskin slippers she had set outside the door of his bedchamber.

"A bit of oil, and they'll be good as new. There—let them set by the stove a bit. The heat will soften them up. Now, what will ye have for breakfast?"

Gerrit smoothed his rumpled shirt that would not stay tucked in his breeches and pushed the hair out of his eyes. "Well . . ." He cleared his throat. "I usually serve the admiral first, madam."

Thyla put her hands on her hips and raised an eyebrow. "Do ye now? Well, there will be no more of that while ye're a guest under my roof, laddie. Himself's perfectly capable of getting his own breakfast if he has to. Sit down there and make yeself to home. Will pancakes do?"

Thoroughly nonplussed, Gerrit nodded and drew out a chair. He found his voice. "Pancakes would be marvelous, Mrs. Korimson, thank you." While she dropped a bit of lard on the griddle and gave a couple of stirs to the batter she'd already made, the prince clasped his hands on the table and glanced around. His eye traveled from the herbs growing in their wide sill box, to the spice jars handy above the marble counter, to the jug of milk souring on the top shelf of the stove for bread. He spied the two plates and cups drying by the sink. "I see I'm too late to serve him anyway."

Thyla glanced over her shoulder. "He's an early riser, Kursh is, and even earlier this morning. He'd a long way to go, and wanted to start before it was light out." She dropped a spoonful of batter on the griddle.

The prince frowned. "Where has he gone?"

"Up the mountain, dear, up the mountain. Had to take the Weatherglass back to Lord Aashis, you know. Said he didn't feel just right about melting down such a Power's gift without asking his leave first. So the old fool's out there in the cold climbing Barak-Gambrel. I own I'd feel better about it if Master Peewit were with him again," she added in a murmur.

While she turned the pancakes for his breakfast and poured him a cup of tea, Gerrit thought about the mountain, which rose almost right behind the house. He'd seen its crags and sheer faces on the ride up from the city yesterday. If the dwarf was on that mountain alone, he had more guts than brains.

Thyla put the plate before him and pushed the syrup pitcher within reach. "There. Don't be bashful now; eat up. You could stand a bit of meat on your ribs. I'm surprised your mother doesn't feed you better!"

The prince grinned, poured the amber syrup over the stack, and set to. When he tasted the first mouthful of light pancake, he knew why people still spoke reverently of Bakeress Njordson's cooking though she had left his mother's service thirteen years before. "Mmn! Is that apple I taste?"

Korimson's wife looked pleased. "It is. Keeps it moist on the griddle, I think." She bustled back to the stove and fetched the plate of thin-sliced, hickory-smelling ham from the warming drawer. "Here's a bite to go with it—I nearly forgot, and there's cream there for your tea, if you take it."

Gerrit had meanwhile discovered the starflower tea. "I don't believe I've had this kind before. What is it?"

"Oh, that's starflower. We prefer it—leastwise, I do, and Father puts up with it." She chuckled. "I make him drink at least a cup a day so's he won't go m—" She stopped short and looked startled, then plucked her apron.

"Go—?" Gerrit prompted with the beginnings of a grin. He was expecting to find the stuff was some kind of remedy for diarrhea or a weak bladder.

Thyla twisted her apron, then pushed at her hair where she had not worn the queen's cap for many years. Well, out with it, she told herself sternly. No sense tippy-toeing around it. "Go mad again," she said quietly.

The silence hung between them, thicker than the maple syrup that slid off the stack of pancakes.

Gerrit trailed his fork through the syrup, aimlessly tracking a pattern that filled in immediately. "It works, I presume."

Thyla grasped the back of the chair nearest her and looked at his bent head. "Starflower's sovereign for many things, Lordling." He looked up at this use of his childhood title, the only one she had ever known for him, and their eyes met. "Many things," Thyla repeated softly, "but not all. We do the best we can." She reached to pat his arm where it lay along the table. Straightening, she set her hands on her hips briskly, cocking her head at him. "I used to bake honeycakes for you when you were small. You don't by chance still like them, do you?"

Ariadne's son forced a smile. "They're not as good as they used to be, I don't think. Since I nearly broke a tooth on one a few years ago, I've shied away from them."

Her eyes flew open. "Land's sake! Poor lad! Well, we'll see about that! Finish your pancakes now, while they're hot, and I'll give a thought to tonight's supper and maybe a snack to take home with you."

The front door slammed and there was a skipping step down the hall. "Mama, Patience is out in our shed licking Mittens' kittens! Where's Master Freckles?"

Gerrit turned in his chair to find his Senior Officer's young daughter stopped on the threshold, her cheeks rosy with cold and black pigtails flying from under her bright woolen cap. The prince rose to his feet. "Good morning, Mistress Korimson." She had already been in bed last night when he and Kursh had arrived, though her father had gone immediately up to her room.

Gretchen stared until her mother cleared her throat loudly. "Oh." She dropped into the old-fashioned curtsy Thyla had taught her. "Sorry. Good morning, sir."

"Your Highness," her mother prompted in an undertone.

"Really, I'd rather just be called Gerrit, if you don't mind," the boy protested.

"My name's Gretchen," she informed him over the beginnings of whatever her mother was going to say.

He smiled. "I know. May I seat you, Lady Gretchen?" he teased gently.

"No, I can do it myself, thanks."

Thyla rolled her eyes and sighed as her daughter draped her cloak over the back of her chair and plumped down. Gerrit resumed his seat. "You look like a prince," Gretchen judged, head cocked.

Gerrit laughed. "And how is that, might I ask?"

"Tall." She grinned.

Her mother flicked the back of her head and scolded roundly for this impertinence, and both the girl and the yeoman ate silently for a few minutes while Thyla shoved things around in the dishpan.

"Mama, is Master Freckles here?"

"Not unless he's down to your father's boat."

Gerrit set down his tea. "No, actually he's at Greenbriar."

Thyla looked over her shoulder. "Ye don't say! I don't believe I've ever seen him without Patience around."

Gretchen's fork was poised in the air as she frowned. "How can they talk to each other if Patience is here and Master Alphonse is at your house?"

The prince had a feeling he was in deep water. "Talk to each other?"

Thyla dried her hands. "Apparently they do. Leastwise, that's what the wizard told Mistress Chatterbox here. And the cat does seem to understand what he says uncommon well." She shook her head. "There's no accounting for wizards, I guess. I suppose they can talk to 'most anything if they take a notion to do it. Still, it is strange that the cat would get herself caught on a boat without him."

Gretchen pushed back her plate. "Would you like to see Mittens' kittens?" she asked Gerrit.

"Wait, young miss," her mother said, holding up one finger. "Chores first, kittens later. Today is wash day, so I need wood brought in from the shed. I've got all your father's shirts to do. He can't go back to court with dirty shirts, can he?"

"No, Mama."

"I'd like to help," Gerrit volunteered. "Where is the woodshed?"

"Well, if you're sure," Thyla told him, "Gretchen will show you. And don't talk the young gentleman's ear off now!" she called after them as Gretchen led the way.

"Better put your cloak on," Kursh's daughter directed. "It's cold out."

Gerrit hid a smile. "Yes, ma'am."

Her hands were on her hips. "Are you going to wear slippers out in the snow?"

He shrugged. "I'll have to. My boots are still wet."

"I'll get you a pair of Papa's old ones."

"No, they, uh, won't fit."

"Why not?"

"They won't, that's all. Let's just go, all right?" He had spoken more sharply than he intended, and her face fell. Quietly she led him to the rack by the front door so he could sling his heavy cloak around his shoulders and then out and around the house to the woodshed built into the slope.

"I'm sorry I snarled at you," Gerrit apologized.

"That's all right. Everybody's snarly today. I think it's because Papa had to go up the mountain." They gazed up at the summit wreathed in clouds. "It's high, isn't it?" she said quietly.

"Yes. But I'm sure he'll be all right."

She nodded thoughtfully. "He promised me he'd be careful, and I think it will be all right, because Lord Aashis likes his crystal. Everybody says so." She looked up at the tall youth. "My Papa can do anything, you know."

Her clear blue eyes were confident. Gerrit glanced up at the mountain, then down at her once more. "Most papas can, I understand."

"It goes against the grain, that's the problem," Kursh confided to the air and the silver torches and the fountains, one hot, one cold, that spilled over in the corner of the cavern. He sat on the edge of the fire pit, cupping the Weatherglass in one large hand, the other braced on his knee. Whether Lord Aashis had an ear cocked to his workshop today, the dwarf didn't know, but some things had to be done decently or not at all, and since it had been Aashis himself who had changed this crystal from dark firmament, Kursh thought the Power of the Winds might want to have a say in unmaking the Weatherglass with the star captured in its center.

"The thing of it is, we've no other crystal that's come from you yourself, and if we're going to make a Crystal for my lady, we've got to use the best. Ye wouldn't happen to have just another wee piece lying around anywhere, would ye?" Korimson glanced around as if he might indeed find an unexpected shining nugget, but none was forthcoming. If there was to be a new Crystal of Healing, he'd have to destroy the Weatherglass Aashis had let him create.

After several moments of listening for some sign, the dwarf got to his feet resignedly and pulled the silver chain to open the crystal roof vent. Then he stepped well away from the firepit, put his fingers to his lips, whistled sharply, and shouted a word of command. The fire leaped toward the roof and then steadied to a low flame ideal for making glass. Since Kursh was not going to blow the actual crystal sphere right now, he would just melt down the Weatherglass into a rough blob of crystal.

He put on a pair of heavy leather mitts, took long-handled iron tongs, and began to warm the Weatherglass in the dancing edge of the flame till it was heated a little. Then he lowered it into the blue fire nearer the coals and turned it gently back and forth to heat it evenly. The cross-hatching of clouds around the middle of the sphere glowed orange and smeared, a shimmer of liquid just holding together. With his free hand, Korimson slid a long-handled iron bucket under the melting sphere and watched the slow dripping begin, jewels of fire dropping into the collecting cup.

The cut-glass facets of the flowing channels he had carved to represent the waters of Aashis's Realm shone red and gold and flame-blue, and they, too, began to melt. Soon the sphere was stripped of its surface decorations. Kursh stifled a sigh and watched stolidly as the heat melted his masterpiece.

Now there was just the pinpoint of light deep in the crystal to mark it for a Weatherglass. The miniature star, no bigger than a firefly's eye, shone silver in the midst of shimmering gold. Kursh watched the Weatherglass shrink to the size of a pigeon's egg, then a child's marble, then—when he wasn't sure he could hold it much longer with the tongs—a pea. He held it in the heat a moment longer.

Suddenly the chamber flared with a pure and silver light, so overpowering that the old dwarf had to close his eye against the radiance while he held the tongs and the bucket steady. The light went out. He squinted. As expected, the Weatherglass was no more than an iron bucket full of glass, and the chamber was lit only by the ruddy glow of the firepit. The Guildmaster withdrew his tongs, looped the bucket to the stone floor to cool, and slowly took off his mitts. "That Glass was the only magic I've ever done," he murmured to the Power, "and I thank ye for it. 'Twas a great consolation to me."

He paused for the thickly buttered bread, apple, and leather bottle of starflower Thyla had packed for him, and then put out the fire, closed the vent, and repacked his tools. Out on the landing beyond the cavern mouth he cast a glance up at the sky. Nearing sunset. The sky over the island was peach and rose-gold, banded by crosshatched clouds. The evening star stood brightly silver in the cooling violet sky to the east. He smiled.

Kneeling to the materials he had left ready, he quickly assembled the kite that he and Peewit had found waiting for them after the Weatherglass had quelled the storm. Kursh thumbed his mustache as he thought of the look on the Littleman's face when Brickleburr had realized he intended to fly down from the mountain. If it worked once, the Guildmaster reasoned, it would work again.

Strapping himself in, he tugged at his eyepatch, took a breath, and launched himself off the top of Barack-Gambrel.

*   *   *

Gerrit and Gretchen were building a snowdwarf when there was a whistle from overhead, a bellowed admonition to get the hell out of the way, and something green and rustling of silk cast a fleeting shadow over them as they looked up.

The kite coasted in well enough, but what Kursh had forgotten was that he would have to land in the snow. Before he knew what was happening, he was sliding on his big boots down the slope of the front yard toward the steep drop-off and the city below like a reluctant farmer being pulled by a runaway plowhorse. He sputtered a curse, threw out an arm, and hooked one of the garden benches as he went by. He stopped abruptly a scant garden's length from the edge. The Guildmaster shook his head, snorted with fright, and then had to pretend it was all very routine because his yeoman was suddenly there and making a mess of unbuckling him. "Stand aside, yeoman, ye've more thumbs than anybody needs!"

When he stepped out of the harness and sat himself on the bench, ostensibly to dig the snow out of his wide cuffs, Gerrit stood uncertainly holding the kite like some not quite saddle-broken horse and Gretchen put a mittened hand close to his ear and whispered, "You'd better hope Mama didn't hear you!"

Korimson grunted something indistinguishable, and his daughter straightened, pushing back her pigtails. "Did you have a nice day?" she asked brightly.

"Lovely," he growled.

"Mama and Gerrit and I made you some honeycakes! Well, actually, they're for Gerrit, but he says he'll share."

The old dwarf looked up. His yeoman's face was flaming. "Damned decent of you, Greenbriar."

"Thank you, sir. May I take your pack? And what's to be done with this . . . ?"

"It's a kite-flyer," Kursh informed him briskly as he stood up. "Don't tell me your training hasn't included learning how to manage one?" He knew absolutely that it had not: this was the only one in the world.

Ariadne's son swallowed nervously, the only betrayal of fright Korimson had yet seen from him. "Um, no, sir."

The dwarf hitched up his broad belt and clapped him on the shoulder genially. "Well, we'll have to remedy that as soon as there's time. It's an invaluable little piece of equipment. Just trot it over to the barn there, will you? My brother will take care of it later. Bring the pack up to the house." He turned to Gretchen and held out his hand. "Honeycakes, ye say?"

The girl slipped a wet mitten into his hand, and they walked up toward the blue door while she chattered about kittens and wash day, and dry boots, and snowdwarves.

All in all, Kursh thought, it had been a good day.

The parting had been hard. There were freshly ironed shirts, a sack of honeycakes, and a new pair of wool socks, knit for Kindlefest—which he would not be home to celebrate. Gretchen had obviously been coached by her mother to try not to make him feel bad, but her long face only got longer when she unwrapped the small enamelwork tiara he had bought for her in Castlenigh. To please him she had put it in her hair and smiled a grimace that wanted to be crying but couldn't.

Gerrit had said that she looked like a princess. Short.

That had drawn a genuine giggle from her. Kursh hadn't understood, but Thyla had smiled and then they had all sat around the fire, eating Kindle cookies and drinking hot cider, for as much time as there was. At the sound of stamping horses in the snow outside, he had risen to wave an acknowledgment at the carriage that waited for them, kissed his two women, waited while they both bussed Greenbriar, and then they had left as quickly as might be. He pretended not to hear the sniffling behind him, and pushed the cat over on the padded seat inside the dark coach.

The departure from Skejfalen had been quick and quiet, and they made for the open sea just a little after moonrise with a stiff wind filling their sails. The Guildmaster stood at the rail, shielding the glow of his pipe from any watchers, and thinking as his ears ached with cold that the nasty part was probably still coming. He could think no further ahead than the Shimarrat raiders. If they got through that, there was still the impossible to attempt. How by His Beard do you blow a bloody Crystal of Healing? he asked himself irritably. He snorted and shook his head.

Beside him Gerrit's black hair tangled in the breeze, but if the boy was uncomfortable, he gave no sign of it. He was peering into the darkness, trying to spot the headland. "Sir?

How does the pilot know where he's going on a night like this?'

"He doesn't," Korimson rasped and pushed off the rail to meet Captain Jorgen, who came striding toward them.

"Course, admiral? Straight for Greenbriar?"

"Aye, Jorgen. Steady as she goes. Crowd the sheets: they're waiting for us back at the castle."

"Very good, sir. The weapons have been readied."

"Fine. It will be at dawn, no doubt."

"No doubt, sir." Jorgen saluted and went back toward the helm.

Gerrit asked, "The attack, sir?"

"That's when they do it, yeoman. Out of the east at sunrise."

The prince rubbed his nose, a gesture he was unconsciously picking up from his Senior Officer. "Then if we tack to port when we're clear of the island and sail east in the night, we might have a tactical advantage come sunrise, might we not?"

"We might also find we've passed the bastard by and have him behind us and closing before we could come about. We have to catch him abeam of us when he attacks."

Gerrit nodded. "But suppose we sailed a bit south by east, came around the tip of Inishkerry, and closed with him so that we have the sun at our backs."

Kursh rubbed his nose. "Ye've been studying the charts."

His yeoman shifted uncomfortably. "Yes, sir."

The Guildmaster stroked his beard and nodded slowly. "Damned good thinking. It will take a bit more time, but these Shimarrats have got to learn their lesson now or they'll bottle us up in Willowsrill as soon as their spies get back with the word the Crystal of Healing is gone." He tugged at his eyepatch. "I like it. Jorgen!" he bellowed and strode aft.

By the Powers! Gerrit thought with pleased surprise. I've done something right for once!

The pied black-and-white cat sitting primly in the shelter of the nearby hatch cover pricked an ear at him and began to groom herself.

Miles to the northeast, King Ka-Treer listened to the wind and heard no flap of the pennant. "I told you to see to that, didn't I, La-Mere?"

The first mate of the fast ship winced in the darkness. "Yes, sire." He barked an order to a sailor, and the man swung up into the lines.

Ka-Treer finished scanning the horizon where the stars met the dark water and handed the spyglass off to the mate. "The fleet is keeping pace with us very well. Maintain the same course and speed. Call me an hour before dawn." He gathered his cloak and stooped to the companionway.

"And His Highness, sire?"

The Shimarrat king hesitated. "Order his slave to feed him some of that dwarvish liquor we took off the last ship. The stuff is supposed to work for seasickness."

"Very good, sire."

As the king turned away the officer heard him mutter, "By the Realms, something must!"

They had intended to stay well off the rocky island, but Jorgen—who was an impeccable navigator—must have erred, because the boom of surf was close in the darkness, too close. The Guildmaster whipped out his glass. "Dammit, what the hell is Jorgen thinking of?" He braced himself and peered through the eyepiece. To starboard he could see the white surge of foam. "Hard aport!" he boomed.

"She won't answer the rudder, sir!" came the helmsman's desperate cry, overridden by Jorgen's authoritative shout: "Reef the mains'l and topgallants!"

The huge mainsail came down the halyards, and the ship slowed under their feet. The breeze fell off suddenly. "Must have passed the headland," Kursh muttered, but for some reason he didn't think that was it at all. He pulled at his patch. The *Crystal Kite* rocked slowly forward, as though under oars and coming into her own slip in Skejfalen.

Gerrit came stumbling up the companionway. "What is it?"

"Nothing much," Korimson answered calmly. "We're about to pile up on the rocks, is all." The boy whirled to look landward and backed a step. From the top of the cabin came an anxious meowing, loud in the sudden quiet. "Stop that infernal yowling, cat," Kursh rasped, turning to glare up at her.

Patience yammered louder, stretching a forepaw toward the looming bulk of Inishkerry.

Kursh told her grimly, "If it's off the ship you want, that can be arranged easily enough, monster."

"Look!" Gerrit suddenly gasped, pointing. "At the foot of the tall crag there, sir, do you see?"

In the pitch night there was a faint glimmer of wine-colored light from the shore.

Korimson said slowly, "I do believe the boy wonder's left a night light on." He raised his voice. "D'ye see that, Jorgen?"

"Aye, sir. I thought the island uninhabited, except for Master Alphonse."

The ship nosed ahead. The dwarf and his yeoman both turned to look up at the wizard's cat. Patience was looking back at them, every hair electric with tension. "Hmm," Korimson rumbled in his beard. "Anchor, captain. Prepare to lower a boat. I'm going ashore." On his words the ship halted dead in the water and the cat leaped into his arms and began washing his face, purring like a kettle. "Bloody hell!" the dwarf roared and pulled away, pitching her lightly into the lifeboat that swung from its davits.

"May I go with you, sir?" Gerrit asked.

"Get in, yeoman, get in. Ye'd probably swim it if I said no." They were joined by the second mate and two sailors to row. "Stand by, Jorgen. If you hear me give a yell, got out of here if you can."

"Aye, sir."

The lifeboat was winched down until it rode the water, and they began to row toward the wizard's island with the pied cat standing in the bow like a figurehead. Whether the water actually smoothed as they approached the shore or whether it only seemed that way, Kursh could not tell, but the rowers had an easy time of it, and the garnet light grew steadily nearer. The Guildmaster checked the action of his spring-loaded dagger in its forearm sheath.

"Whatever it is, it's right down on the beach, sir. Maybe just at the edge of the water," the second mate observed.

"Draw up downwind of it, Thyrsson."

The man touched the rudder. They shot through the surf and landed on a sand bottom without hitting any rocks, and the sailors pulled the boat up on the strand. Patience streaked past. Korimson stepped out, and they fell in behind him as he led the way up the beach toward the garnet glow that now showed dully only about a hundred yards away. When Gerrit would have moved up with his drawn dagger to protect his Senior Officer's flank, Kursh waved him back.

"Hallo!" Korimson called. "Dwarves of Jarlshof here. We come in peace."

They listened, hearing nothing but the soughing of the surf. "Will you name yourself?" Kursh asked.

There was above the sound of the sea a moan.

"Shad—!" Gerrit began in a gasp, but Kursh cut across it.

"That's no Shadow, that was human or dwarf." He broke into a run, dagger ready.

If Patience had not been standing near his outflung hand, the dwarf would not have recognized the thing laved by the lapping salt water as Alphonse. In the dim garnet glow the naked man looked as though he'd been flogged. Flesh was missing from him in strips, sinew and even bone showing in places.

One of the sailors splashed a few feet away and was noisily sick. Gerrit swallowed hard and locked his knees. Kursh crouched beside the cat. "All right, lad," he told the still form. "We've come to take ye home."

The cracked and bleeding lips parted. "Kursh?"

"Aye. Who else? Ye still owe me money."

"The Skinwalker . . ." The wizard drifted off, his features slackening. The garnet light went out.

Kursh reached gingerly for a pulse and found one. "Let's get him back to the ship." He stripped off his cloak and dunked it in the water, making sure it was thoroughly soaked. They wrapped the wizard as gently as possible and carried him to the lifeboat, Patience running anxiously on ahead.

With the men bending their backs to the oars it did not take long. Gerrit helped to hold the wizard's feet. He looked up once to Korimson. "If Master Alphonse is here . . . my mother . . ."

"We'll crack the *Kite's* ribs if we have to to get there by sundown tomorrow, boy." They came within hailing range of the ship. "Ahoy, Jorgen! The wizard's sore hurt! I want all the white silk we've got aboard—there's likely a bolt left from the voyage out, and my best shirt is in my pack. Start Cook boiling salt water—a lot of it. Break out some brandy and brew starflower—strong. Line the bunk in my cabin with a waterproofed canvas. Stand by!"

They were winched aboard, and on the well-disciplined faces there were grimaces of pity when they saw. "Something called a Skinwalker's been at him," the admiral stated tersely. "That means that the bloody thing is at Greenbriar right now with Her Majesty and she doesn't know it." Some of the glances went to the prince. "Duty stations! Jorgen, get us the hell out of here! I want to raise Waterford light by morning!"

"Aye, aye, sir!" The captain spun, issuing a stream of orders, and within moments they were under way, racing under a full press of sails for Willowsrill Mouth.

Others carried the wizard carefully below, and mercifully he did not wake. "Poor bloody sod," Kursh murmured as he stood by and watched the ship's surgeon wind strips of silk that had been steeped in warm salt water around the wizard's body.

"As bad as it looks, some of the wounds are already trying to close, sir," the doctor reported in a low voice. "He has obviously been in this condition for quite some time. Thank the Powers he had the strength to drag himself to the water; if he'd stayed on the land, infection would undoubtedly have set in."

"Aye, but he's likely caught his death of cold."

"We will try to prevent that."

"We bloody will."

Later, when the doctor had done as much as he could for the time, the wizard slept cocooned in warm silk under a makeshift tent of wool blankets. Patience had put her paws up on the edge of the bunk and meowed softly, but ventured no further. Kursh and Gerrit sat across the cabin on the wide bench. "Come here, kitten," the dwarf said quietly, and she jumped up between them, and first the broad hand and then the lithe one rubbed her ears. None of the three of them slept at all that night.

The sky was just beginning to lighten outside the portholes when there was a light tap at the cabin door. When Kursh nodded and Gerrit answered it, Thyrsson touched his cap. "Tell the admiral we're three miles off Waterford and Captain Jorgen needs him on deck right now."

Korimson stepped past the boy and wordlessly ran up the companionway. When he appeared on deck, the captain pointed toward the west.

The line of the Shimarrat fleet—a score of warships and the single fast black racer—was strung out across the sea.

Jorgen looked definitely worried. "They're making no pretense at being pirates, are they, sir?"

"I wouldn't care if the Wild Fellow himself were sailing

with them, Jorgen. Nobody is going to keep me from reaching the river."

"Aye, sir. I've had the weapons readied. The crew is standing by."

"Good." Korimson glared in the direction of the Shimarrats, a feral grin beginning to curl his lips. "Ever hunted ducks from a blind, yeoman?"

"Yes, sir. Some days one gets lucky."

The dwarf grunted. "This has little of luck, boy, but it has a lot to do with accurate calculations." He held his hand out for the wax tablet Jorgen carried and the stylus. "I'll base this on closing to within two hundred yards, Jorgen. That will be your job: keep us steady and broadside. We should be out of range of their bloody crossbows."

"Aye, aye, sir. Steady as she goes."

"They've sighted us!" the lookout sang. "The lead ship is tacking! I think the first few of them are going to try to flank us, sir!"

"Of course they are," Korimson said complacently. "But that's all right. Better, in fact, except that I'll have to do the calculations a little quicker for the port side. No matter." He beckoned for another tablet and stylus. "Step up, yeoman. Are you clever at mathematics? The truth now, quickly."

"I could be better, sir, if I studied."

"All right, fairly answered. Work this problem out, using the Parameters of the Planes of Dorius." He thrust the tablet into the prince's hands, the figures already jotted down.

By the Powers, where's Crummie when you need him! the startled boy thought. Surprising himself, he had the answer ready rather quickly. "One hundred twenty-three degrees, sir."

Kursh ran a quick eye over the figures and nodded. He turned and shouted, "One twenty-three starboard! In sequence, on my signal!" A chorus of ayes came back. The crews at the weapons were busily cranking the equipment to the ordered angle. There was a smell of burning oakum. An expectant hush settled over the *Crystal Kite*.

They raced out of the sun, down on the line of Shimarrat warships strung out like pearls on a string. They closed to two hundred yards, straightened to broadside, and the admiral raised his hand. They were a little above the last ship in the line. "Number one, away!" He chopped his hand down. The fuse seared; the fire rocket ignited and shot out of its cradle toward the heavier vessel.

Across the water it streaked, straight for the Shimarrat's hull. There was a thunderous explosion, and as they sped past the enemy vessel they could see a gaping hole, already taking on water.

While the crew was still cheering, Korimson bellowed, "Stay with it, stay with it, damn you! Number two, away!"

This time the fire rocket tore through the stern of the other ship, raining splintered wood.

When they had made their first run, the *Crystal Kite* had destroyed or damaged eight of the eleven ships on that side. The Shimarrat flanking attack was in sad array: four of the ships had peeled off and were sailing as fast as might be for the open sea; another two were running for Willowsrill Mouth, and of the three remaining, their battle line was so ragged that Kursh had to make separate calculations for each. He shouted the individual orders and the fire rockets burned into the sunrise, taking two of the warships.

The black ship was heeling under her canvas, sneaking for open water. Jorgen had his glass trained on it. "Admiral, you'll want to see this."

When Korimson lifted the brassbound glass and took a look, he stiffened. He shot an unreadable look at his yeoman and held out the glass to him. "Amidships, on top of the flying deck."

The glass's round eye picked out his uncle, Ka-Treer, and beside him the Shimarrat prince, Ka-Bril. Gerrit lowered the glass. "I feel badly for my cousin," he said honestly.

"There's many a man younger than him that makes his own decisions, boy," the dwarf rasped, not unkindly. He added, "We'll pick him up if we can." While they sped toward the fleeing Shimarrat sloop, Korimson walked down to the fire-rocket station. "I'd like to send this one myself, men. A little remembrance for those bastards from Jan Reyason and the others aboard the *Jarlshof Star*." The fusilier wordlessly handed him the small lighted torch. "Close to fifty yards, Jorgen. I want to see him," Kursh called up to the captain.

Closer and closer they raced until they could see every line, every plank. The red eye glared balefully, and crossbolts rained ineffectually at them. As they began to flash past, Kursh touched off the shortened fuse and threw Ka-Treer a mocking salute. "Roste, you son of a bitch!" he bellowed.

There was just time to see the king's expression of open

terror, and the quick movement as Ka-Bril shoved him into the line of fire and twisted to dive off the far side of the ship. Then with a hot blast that rocked them across the water, the *Lion of Shimarron* blew up. They did look for Ka-Bril, but he was not found.

As they were navigating the river entrance, Kursh beckoned Gerrit and ordered the captain over his shoulder, "Break out the flotjin. Holiday rations." Then he led the way down the companionway and closed the door behind him. He poured from private stock for both of them and turned to hand one of the crystal tumblers to the boy. Quietly he said, "Let me be the first: all hail, King of Shimarron."

Gerrit looked down into the black liquor and swallowed. Then, for a reason he could not have explained, his face crumpled and he ducked to grasp the old dwarf in a one-armed hug.

Kursh thumped the strong young back. "Aye, you're right: the throne should have gone to your father instead of to that black-hearted bastard. But now at least the folk of Shimarron will get to see how a decent ruler does the job. Half-decent," he amended quickly as the boy straightened, brushing a sleeve across his eyes and gulped down some flotjin.

"If any of us lives that long," Gerrit added huskily.

Korimson rubbed his nose. "Are ye a betting man, king?"

"I've rolled some dice in my time." He finished the flotjin.

"Have ye now? We might have to discuss that later. For now, I've got a wager for you: your mother against the Wild Feller. My money says the queen takes him in three. What do you say?"

Gerrit straightened and tried to match his tone. "You'd ask me to bet against the family?"

Korimson grinned. "Can't do that, can we? Well, there's one sour wager: I won't bet against her, either."

The wizard stirred and asked weakly, "Are we having a thunderstorm? I thought I heard thunder."

"Go back to sleep, Freckles," the dwarf told him. "The storm's over. We'll be at Greenbriar by teatime."

"I hate tea."

"Go to sleep."

"All right." And he did.

Chapter Eighteen

❧

The archers on the battlements watched the slow horse plod its way up the straw-covered icy road. The sergeant of the watch was called, and he stood next to a crossbowman, leaning a little to peer. "It's the damned tinker, Muir Dach. Look at that: dead drunk. Doesn't even know where he is, belike. Disgrace on Kindlefest Eve's Day. Well, there's a warrant out for him by the innkeeper, so let's allow the whoreson to ride himself right into the dungeon." The men grinned, and he signaled to the gate-keepers to let the tinker through. The sergeant himself went down to make the arrest.

When the nondescript horse came closer, however, it was quickly apparent the tinker wasn't as drunk as they had supposed, for Muir Dach sat up and picked up the reins. The sergeant gave a hand code: at the ready. An arrow was notched, three daggers drawn. Then he stepped into the tinker's path. "Hold, Dach. What's your business?" he asked coldly, while two of his men slipped out the postern and circled behind the ruffian.

Dach pulled down the scarf wound about mouth and nose. "I need to see Captain Brickleburr right away. And put your daggers up: I'll make no trouble." He spoke wearily, and his face was pinched with cold. His left hand was out of sight in the folds of his patched cloak.

The sergeant could smell no liquor, and he was troubled by the hand. "Both hands on the pommel."

The tinker spat. "I've took a fall, man, and my ribs are cracked. I've come with a message for the captain. Now are you going to get him, or am I going to start shouting?"

The sergeant crossed his arms on his chest, glancing past the tinker to the men who closed behind him. "Brickleburr is the Lord General of Ilyria, fellow. I doubt he has business with such as you."

317

"You doubt it, hey?" He suddenly looked up at the keep windows and gave a piercing two-toned whistle. "Littleman!" he shouted raggedly.

The sergeant smiled. "He's gone."

Dach stared. "Gone?"

The soldiers rushed him. The horse shied sharply, and they dragged him from the saddle. Had they not manhandled him upright, the tinker would have fallen. The cloak fell open and revealed the broken shaft of an arrow embedded in his side, the shaft still painted with yellow and black.

The sergeant recognized it immediately as standard-issue Shimarrat. Muir grimaced with pain, gasped, and snarled, "Avalanche, you bastard! Get me to Quint!"

Avalanche was the current Watch code for extreme danger. The sergeant's eyes flew open. "Take him to the hospice. Corporal, summon the captain at once." The soldier left at a run, and they half carried, half walked the tinker through the courtyards to the healing station. Doctor Theodric came to the foyer, and despite Muir's snarls they got him down on an examining table. When Theo would have begun to treat him, however, a dagger suddenly bloomed in the tinker's fist and he ordered everyone out until he'd met the Captain of the Watch.

There were a tense few moments and then Quint ducked through the doorframe. "What the hell have you done to yourself, tinker?"

"You've got big trouble, soldier: I've just come from Swiftwater way, and there's a whole damned Shimarrat army on the move, burning villages as they come. By noon tomorrow, ye'll see the smoke." Quint looked stunned, and the tinker's ragged teeth showed in a grim smile. "Ye're at war, and you didn't even know it! Now get your healer to patch me up and tell me where the captain is. He and I will go out and see what us tinkers can do to slow them up—Brickleburr's got twice the smarts of any dozen whoresons in this castle put together."

Quint darkened, but he looked grave. "Master Peewit's gone home, tinker. Shut up and let the doctor work on you—we'll need every able-bodied man we can muster." He stepped to the archway and shouted for an equerry to fetch the chief of the Riders, and then light the signal beacons. Then he looked back at Muir. "You did well, Dach. There's a promotion in it for you, if we live that long."

The tinker suggested what he could do with his promotion and struggled up on an elbow. "Who went with Brickleburr? The dwarf?"

Quint sighed. "He went off alone. We don't even know when he left."

The ragged man threw his hat across the room and followed it with his dagger, narrowly missing the doctor who had come in. "By the bloody Powers, couldn't any of you pox-eyed bastards manage to keep an eye on one Teazle?"

"Not all of us can see in the dark like cats or tinkers. Give him all the whiskey he wants, Theo." Quint left. Muir lay back, weaker than he wanted to admit, and glared at the doctor. "Where's the bottle?"

"Let me just wash this off first, good sir."

"You touch my body with water, leech, and I'll kill you. Whiskey's good enough for the inside: it's good enough for the outside, too."

Theodric hesitated, then glanced at the orderly. "Have them bring up a large barrel of whiskey from the stores."

The queen rubbed a windowpane clear and watched the beacon flare. War. Eighteen years of peace, and now this. She wondered whether Wolf's Glen had been hit yet. Fast riders had already been dispatched there. Keep Gerrit on Jarlshof with you, Kursh, she thought. Don't come back here, to this doomed place. One way or another—Unnamed or Shimarrat—Ilyria will go this time.

Alphonse's voice said behind her, "It seems odd that Peewit would leave so suddenly, just when there's the new Crystal to be made."

She smiled slightly and turned. "Oh, Master Teazle takes his notions, and there's usually a good reason for what he does. If I've learned nothing else these past thirteen years, I've learned that. Probably he's out with the tinkers, cooking up some strategy that will rock those rotten Shimarrats to their toes."

The Skinwalker let the small scroll flutter back to the queen's writing desk. "Probably," he agreed aloud, but he was uneasy. He paced, staying well away from the fire so that it wouldn't flutter and possibly betray him. Well, my Lord of Darkness will deal with the miserable little Hearthrat, he thought. All is still according to plan. Just until midnight tonight. Without realizing it he smiled, and a momentary flicker escaped his eyes.

Ariadne, who had been glancing into the fire, blinked and looked quickly at him. She could have sworn she saw a flash of blue. The wizard had turned away, pacing toward her tiring room. He suddenly stopped and raised his head. "That way?" she heard him say. "So!"

"What is it? Have you figured out how to put the warding on the new Crystal?"

The Skinwalker turned. "Yes, I think so," he lied. *The ratkin has left a trail!*

Ariadne flew across the floor and flung her arms about him. Instinctively the Skinwalker drew sharply away, repulsed by the disgusting odor of the spruce she wore in her hair, but even more by the golden locket. *So!* he thought again. *An aura is on it! The Hearthman knows about me, then!* He refrained from gnashing the teeth of the wizard body. He forced himself to smooth the Greenbriar witch's hair. "Later," he told her. "We'll have our time later." Which was absolutely true. "For now, I must work. Wish me luck."

The queen regarded him narrowly. "Fine. Good luck." She turned to pick up the last of her breakfast tea.

In the instant the Skinwalker decided it would be just as easy and perhaps more effective to do it now. He reached into the pocket of the faded garnet robe, and his hand closed about the ice dagger.

There was a pounding on the door. "Your Majesty!" a man's voice shouted.

The door swung open, and Meara tried to hold the Watchman back. "I told him you were busy, my lady."

"Master Fidelis bids you come at once to the hospice, Majesty," the soldier panted. "The wizard's just come in with the Eldest!"

The Skinwalker stiffened, and his hand was coming out of his robe as the queen said, "Which wizard?"

"Master Nels, Majesty. It's the Eldest, though—come at once, please!"

Ariadne was already moving. "What's happened?" She passed within a foot of the Skinwalker. "Are you coming down?" she turned to ask as it made no move.

The servant of Tydranth knew immediately that it could not fool a wizard: this Nels would know. "I will see him

later, my queen. Likely Fidelis will have all he can do right
now. When I may, I will rejoin you."

Ariadne frowned but hurried out with the soldier.

The Skinwalker stood alone in the middle of the queen's
apartment, rubbing the garnet stone thoughtfully. It looked
up to find the waitingwoman still by the open door, hands
clasped on her neat gown, obviously waiting for him to
leave. Her expression said plainly that he should have ac-
companied the queen. The dark shadow walked slowly toward
Meara. Maybe I'll take this one, too, just for the amusement, he thought, staring down at her as he went past.

When he had gone, Meara shuddered. The wizard's eyes
don't sparkle like they used to, she thought. He's gotten
. . . dark, somehow. He should have stayed on his island
and left my lady alone. Her eyes don't sparkle much anymore, either.

Fidelis met her at the door with Nels behind him. "It's
Nilarion," the chief physician told her immediately. "Nels
here says the Tree and all of her Children have dropped
their leaves, as has every other tree in Yorland." He met
her terrified eyes. "I think autumn is finally over in the
enchanted forest, my queen."

Ariadne moistened her lips. "And what of Imris?"

It was the wizard who answered quietly, "He is failing as
well, Your Majesty. The Eldest will pass with the Earthpillar."

Until then, there had been a spark of hope in her heart.
Now the Greenbriar Queen despaired. The Dark had come
in truth.

The mouse had occasionally chittered from the pack, but
Peewit had admonished him in a whisper to be quiet. He
had found his way quickly and surely, having passed this
way so many times before. He even remembered the un-
even paving stone in the floor of the passageway where he
had fallen the first three lifetimes. Now he stepped over it
and smiled a little to himself in the pitch darkness.

They were somewhere in the network of caverns and
tunnels under Greenbriar Castle. Even he could not have
stood on the earth of the Sweep above and pointed down to
say, "This is the place." But he knew what he was listening
for, and when he heard it the journey Home would truly
begin. He walked a little more slowly and cocked his head.

Out of the echoing dark farther ahead came the barest brush of tinkling bells, as if a horse and sleigh had passed along a road just at the edge of earshot.

"There are the doorbells!" Sir Winston's muffled voice exclaimed delightedly. "Oh, well done, sir!"

The Hearthman chuckled a little and went on. When he arrived at the place, the doorbells jingled again, more loudly now that he was upon them. Peewit licked his lips and whistled the first few notes of the Painter's rainbow Warding.

Immediately a soft, multihued light illuminated the small cavern where he stood, showing the golden bells on their light strip of silk hanging from the ceiling and the golden filigree gate beneath them. Beyond the gate, it was as dark as the way he had just come. Brickleburr touched the intricate flowing lines of the metalwork. "You were always the craftsman, my friend," he murmured. Three linked squares led off, and these he turned until three diamonds touched point to point, the metalwork twisting on cunningly hidden hinges. Then the rectangle cut diagonally with a line of rigid gold chain: this Peewit gave a slight tug to, and the chain dropped into a loop that shimmered in the light like a dewdrop. Next were the three squares leading left toward the edge of the Gate. The Littleman traced the outline of each, but did not move them: this was the trap Aengus had built into his puzzle. "Don't for pity's sake move these," the Painter had told him. "Why? What will happen?" Peewit had asked. "Just don't do it, friend. You would not like finding yourself falling through the Foundations."

Brickleburr was smiling at the memory as he moved his hand to the circle of twisted Briar canes wrought in gold, complete with needle-sharp thorns. Peewit jabbed his finger on the right one, wincing only a little as a drop of blood welled. Last was the small square of the lock itself. The Littleman carefully let a drop of his blood drip into the tiny keyhole, and with a click, the covering plate swung open to reveal a small round cavity. He gave his finger a lick, and from his pocket took the amber with the honeybee that Tansy had sent him, the key to Aengus's Gate, the only entrance to the Meadows of Morning that the Unnamed's servants had never found. Brickleburr and the Painter himself were the only ones who had ever used it.

The amber lit with a warm golden glow, and out of its light flew the bee Cahokia, queen of Tychanor's hives an age of the world ago. Peewit whistled a greeting and pushed the golden metalwork back. Aengus's Gate opened noiselessly, and he stepped through onto the shimmering floor. Winston's long nose emerged from the pack. "Are we there yet?" The mouse took a quick look around. "Oh, I dislike this part, I do. It makes my stomach drop, sir, if you know what I mean." He burrowed back down into Peewit's tobacco pouch.

The Pledged laughed. "Hold your nose, then," he advised. "Here we go!" Swinging the gate shut behind him, he took a firm grasp on the pack straps, heard the bee buzz close to his ear, and whistled the Home and Hearth song. There was a rushing wind, a sudden drop, a rainbow arch overhead, and then—suddenly—wan daylight before him at the end of a dark place.

And there in the semidark of a shallow cave in the side of the mountain valley was Tansy to meet him with the stripes of a Skinwalker attack across her face. She raised trembling hands to embrace him. "Blest be the Light!" she sighed. "I knew you'd make it Home."

Gently he kissed her on an unburned cheek, and—Darkness coming on or no, the End or not—her hair, as gray now as his own, still smelled of chamomile flowers. He laid his head alongside hers, and they clung to each other for a long time while the weak sun passed the noonday and slid toward afternoon.

Finally he straightened. "Where are the others?"

Tansy looked up at him. "Oh, my dear, we are all that is left. The Shadows have been here, and it is Time, you know."

The queen bee lighted on her hair. "I know," Brickleburr said and blew the creature off. "But I'll see what I can do. I had hoped . . ."

She eased herself down to sit on a rock shelf spread with a dirty fleece and looked around at the cavern piled high with cradle-bunnies of every description. Their embroidered and glass eyes looked back at her. "We'd all hoped, Peewit, but it isn't your fault the message went awry, and what might have been doesn't help us now."

Winston scrambled out of the pack. "My goodness, Matriarch! This doesn't sound at all like you, if you'll pardon me for saying it." He rubbed his long nose and slicked his whiskers. "We've still a few hours of light left before

Kindlefest Eve. There must be something the three of us—er, you two—can do."

Tansy looked at Peewit, and the Hearthman looked down at the mouse. Brickleburr ran a hand through his curly hair. "Quite, Sir Winston. Where there's Light, there's Life." He raised his brown eyes to Tansy. "Are the house mice still about?"

"Many of them, I think, but most everyone else is gone. The Dark Fire, you know."

He nodded grimly. "All right, Thatch-rustle, let's snap to it." He waved an arm. "All of these bunnies must be packed and ready to take down to the world by tonight. Can your folk handle that end of things for us?"

Winston knew as well as either of them that the odds those bunnies would ever be needed were long, but he spat on his hands and rubbed them together. "Right, my lord. We might as well wrap up the Kindle-Logs while we're at it."

"Excellent. The Matriarch will direct things here." He stooped and unstrapped his pack to pull out the remains of the Kindle-Log and the small gold box.

"The locket?" Tansy questioned, watching him.

He shook his head. "I had to leave it with the queen."

The fear banked in her eyes leaped to sudden life. "But—!"

Brickleburr stood and put a light finger across her lips. "Hush, Tanse—it was the only way."

After a moment she nodded once.

Peewit tucked the gold box into his pocket and broke off a corner of the Kindle-Log. "Still as good as ever," he told her as he licked his fingers. That drew a faint smile. Then it was time to go. He kissed her again, waggled a finger at Winston, and walked toward the pale daylight.

Tansy struggled to her feet. "Peewit?"

He turned inquiringly.

"What do you want for supper?"

A slow grin spread across the Littleman's features. "Something hot. There will be a lot of snow down in the world tonight."

She waved as if he were just going off the sunmill for a day's work and turned to help the house mice, who were already gathering to Winston's shrill whistle.

Cahokia circled Peewit's head and flew out of the cave. "Yes, all right," he sighed. "I'm coming."

He went into his stillness spell, just in case any watchers

were in the Valley of the Sun. The sight that met his eyes shocked him more than anything had in all his long life.

Gone were the greens and golds of the Meadows. Where the terraced vineyards had dotted the slopes there was only a mass of blackened scrub, and the glasshouses where the Folk had kept the summer-flowering plants alive all winter were smashed in. The toy workshops were burned to the ground, and there was no village. The Mother of Waters steamed angrily through the charred valley, her waterway clogged with the refuse the Shadows had dumped into the river as they marauded the valley. The golden sunmill was no more than a mass of twisted gold wreckage, one piece of the huge sail flapping like a forlorn flag. And everywhere the Folk lay where they had fallen, frozen into the meadow by a thick rime of ice.

Peewit swallowed hard and glanced up at the Sun Palace crowning the opposite hillside. It appeared undamaged. Perhaps the Evil Ones had not been able to break through its defenses. He carefully began to pick his way across the Meadows. The pale sun drifted farther down toward the west.

By the time he was climbing toward the front gates, his knees were bruised from slipping so many times on the ice, and the bee had lighted on his shoulder, sheltering itself in a fold of his cloak. He looked quickly about, but saw no sign and felt no sign of the Shadows. The blasted things must all have gone down to the world to wreak their havoc there. He wondered briefly how the queen was getting on and then where Kursh was. His feet went out from under him once more, and he sprawled. Pulling himself painfully to a sitting position, he stayed that way for a moment, resting, and let his eyes run up the magnificence of the golden walls before him.

High into the clouds the stepped levels of the Sun Palace rose, the back of the structure backed against the very mountains themselves. Indeed, the Palace had been carved out of the mountain by Tychanor himself, who had stripped away the covering earth and made the Meadows out of it. Here the Power had dwelt among his folk in the beginning days, and then from anywhere in the valley one could see the windows gleaming red and orange and amber.

But now the windows were dark as eyes in a skull and the golden walls were dull with ice. No, Peewit thought, the

Power had not come Home. Well, he would have to go and fetch him.

But first there was Rose. The Hearthman got gingerly to his feet, raised a hand, and commanded, "Kindle!"

At once a brilliant radiance seemed to surround him, and he walked toward the opening gate in the midst of a cloud of golden fire. He passed through, and the gates shut behind him. He let the kindling wane. The bee buzzed near his collar. "Yes, it was nice and warm, wasn't it?" the Pledged murmured. "I suppose the Wild Fellow and all his foul creatures know I'm back. Let's see now: if I remember rightly, it's the second level left." The bee buzzed a confirmation, and he ran up the quartz stairway, limping a little.

The second level was still in the formal part of Tychanor's palace. Rich hangings of scarlet wool worked with golden thread adorned the walls, and elaborate chandeliers hung from the high ceilings. Peewit passed the wide room with silver and gold musical instruments still standing on their rests, waiting for the music of the Power to set them singing again. He passed the wide dining hall, and the savory smells of new bread, honey-baked squash, and sharp cheese still hung in the air, threaded with the nose-tickling scent of bubbling light wine. Brickleburr went on, counting the doors carefully. He came to the library with its clear golden reading light and ancient scrolls. One more.

The door opened into a room that seemed for a moment dim in comparison to the others. But the light there was deliberately low, a single gold candle burning steadily, and the window was positioned facing east to catch the sunrise across the bed, and across the figure of the woman who slept in it. The window showed dark blue sky deepening to violet now, framed by the ice-rimed branches of the Briar that grew outside.

Long had she slept here, Rose, fairest of women born of earth, and beloved of Tychanor. (And of Aengus, though the tallfolk man had not dared to say so for fear of her laughter.) She would not have laughed, had he but known, Peewit thought as he regarded her. He said softly, "Well, I've come Home, lady. I'm probably too late, though. Still . . ." He took the golden box from his pocket, placed a pinch of the dust in his palm, and blew it softly over her. The aura floated to limn her fair face. However, not even his aura had power to break the curse that was on her. He could only try to pave the way. "There," Peewit said. "Here's hoping."

There was a sudden noise from somewhere in the palace. He stiffened and listened a moment. The Briar outside began to send questing branches tapping against the window. Hurriedly he slipped the latch and threw it open. The branches grew quickly into the room. They would, he knew, form an impenetrable wall around her in moments. He ran for the door and paused with his hand on the knob. Throwing both arms in the air, he commanded, "Kindle!"

At once the golden walls of the room began to glow and curve to form a sphere of protection about Rose. He ducked out the door just as it was swallowed into the middle of the sphere. "Whew! Bee, are you still with me?" The insect buzzed and zipped into the air to lead the way. He could hear the rising moans converging throughout the Sun Palace.

One last thing. Sick fear shot through him, but mentally he took himself by the scruff of the neck. "Straighten up, Brickleburr. This is what you were Pledged to do." But at that moment, the thought was little consolation. He forced himself to run after the bee and tried not to think of his life in the world, or of Tansy, or of the way things might have been if he had not agreed to bear Tychanor's Aura. But he could not shake the image of Kursh's lowering eyebrows, and he could almost hear the dwarf growl, "Ye've put your foot in it sure, this time, Brickleburr."

I have, Kursh. I have at that.

Alphonse pushed away the dwarven doctor's hand. "Move, please. I'm getting up."

"But, sir, you can't!"

The cracked lips pressed together with the effort not to cry out, and then through clenched teeth, the wizard grated, "I must, idiot! Who the hell else is going to fight the Skinwalker? Find me a robe!"

Not long afterward, draped in a makeshift robe of silk covered with a concealing long brown cloak and hood, Alphonse tested his legs. The soles of his feet were nearly untouched by the Skinwalker's lacerating fire, and he found that if he shuffled slowly, he could maneuver well enough. The strip marks on the rest of his body hurt abominably, but by concentrating on a meditation, he was nearly able to ignore it. The pain-deadening unguent the doctor had salved him with helped a bit, also. He laid the hood back on his shoulders for the moment and took a careful sip of luke-warm starflower tea. There was a tap at the door of the cabin. "Yes?"

Gerrit stuck his head in. "If you can manage, sir, the admiral thought you might want to come up on deck for our arrival at Castlenigh."

"Very well," Alphonse answered in a husky whisper that seemed to be all the voice he had. He painfully raised the hood and draped the white silk scarf about his face. "Do I look very odd?"

The prince thought he looked very like a dead man in his winding sheets, but he shook his head. "Not very, sir, considering what you've been through."

"Bloody awful, then. Well, if I scare people, I scare people, that's all." But he was wondering what Ariadne would think. "Lead on, yeoman."

When they emerged on deck, the Guildmaster beckoned them to join him at the rail. "Would you like a chair brought?" he asked the wizard.

"No, it's actually easier standing up, thanks." Alphonse half turned to look about, because he could not easily turn his neck. "I don't see any Shimarrat ships."

When he looked back, there was a smile of deep satisfaction on the old dwarf's lips. "No, nor will you, I'll wager." He cleared his throat to change the subject. "Have any idea how you're going to drive the Skinwalker out of your . . . skin, or whatever?"

"Not really," the wizard admitted. "The damned thing's got my ring, so I can't Ward."

"I'll put a dagger into it for you," the dwarf volunteered.

"Powers, no! If you kill my skin, I won't be able to get back into it, and then I'll . . ." Kursh swung his head at the sudden pause. "I'll waste away, I suppose. You can't live this way indefinitely."

The dwarf smoked in silence. "Dicey bit of business."

They were clearing the first of the piers at Castlenigh. "And of course, we can't startle it into hurting Ariadne," the wizard continued. Suddenly he jerked upright, catching sight of the barque moored near the end of the pier. Immediately he caught his breath in a gasp of pain, and Korimson flung out a quick arm to hold him at the rail. "An Unmaker!" Alphonse cried. "And me without a Warding to my name!"

But then he took in the flag rippling from the topmast, and his expression cleared. "Nels!" His bandaged hand dropped to squeeze Kursh's shoulder. "Maybe now . . . yes, Nels ought to be able to put a hold on the Skinwalker for me. By Earthpillar, we may just bring this off after all!"

"Bet on it, Freckles?"

The wizard began a laugh, but it ended in a hiss, and so he settled for a slight smile and a grunt of amusement.

The *Crystal Kite* slipped into her berth, rails newly oiled with pine oil and secret weapons well hidden. It was the old First Watchman who spotted the smoke trailing up from the burned-out signal beacon on the heights behind the castle. Ice shot through him, and he looked quickly for the black banner and bunting that might have adorned the keep. But the Greenbriar standard flew proudly under the wan sun, and the evergreen garlands still gave the place a festive air.

"What is it, sir?" Gerrit asked, having seen the intent look on his Senior Officer's face.

Kursh pointed to the smoke. "It's war, son. Or would be, except for what we're carrying." The royal pennant from the *Lion of Shimarron* and a piece of black planking with the red eye were wrapped in canvas. Gerrit would take them to his mother.

The yeoman stepped to the rail, intensely serious. "Shimarrat army?"

"Probably coming up the Willowsrill right now."

The boy's hand rested on his sword hilt. "They'll get a chary welcome, admiral."

"They will, my lord."

Their eyes met in perfect understanding.

"What are you two hatching?" Alphonse asked, puzzled.

Kursh spat over the side and knocked out his pipe on the rail. "If ye didn't spend so damned much time sleeping, wizard, ye might know a thing or two."

The boy laughed, and the admiral ordered Jorgen to get them a coach immediately.

On this, the shortest day of the year, the sunlight was already waning by the third hour of the afternoon. Ariadne cast a glance up at the dimming sky and at the line of clouds approaching from over the Barrens. "Snow tonight," she predicted to Fidelis, who stood with her on the hospice steps.

"The children will be happy in the morning," the old doctor replied. There was a small silence in which each of them put up a brave face for the other. "Thank you for giving the locket to Imris. I think it made him feel better."

"Pray for us, Fidelis. We're going to try to make the new Crystal as soon as Kursh gets up here from his ship with the Weatherglass." A Rider had pelted up to the hospice court-yard to bring the news that the Jarlshof ambassador and the prince were arrived safely. The fellow had not been told about Alphonse, for obvious reasons.

The chief physician squeezed her hand. "I know all will be well."

"Is that an inside line, Retreat Master?" she asked dryly. "Or are you just hoping like the rest of us?"

His smile widened. He bowed stiffly and went back inside to tend his Yorlandir patient.

The queen waved away her Watchman attendant and walked slowly through the courtyard into the deep shadow of the keep to await the dwarf and her son. She wondered where Alphonse had been keeping himself all day. She thought he could have spared a moment to greet Imris, at least, if not for a reassuring word for her. Ariadne shrugged the heavy wool cloak up around her neck. Come on, old fellow—it's freezing, she mentally urged Kursh.

There was a step at her side. She glanced up to see Alphonse there. "Are you finished with your preparations?" she asked, returning her attention to the gate.

"Yes, indeed." The Skinwalker smiled with the wizard's lips and plunged his ice dart into her neck.

Ariadne stiffened, her hands flying up to find the cold place that burned like acid along the painways into her body. Her wide gray eyes fastened on the Skinwalker's face. "You're not—!" She tottered.

It bent over her as she fell, and its eyes were flickering heat lightning in the face she had loved. "No," it hissed. "I'm not."

There was a clatter of hooves through Queen's Gate and a bellowing hail. The Skinwalker looked up.

Across the broad courtyard the coach drew to a stop, and, heedless of his wounds, Alphonse sprang out of it. Instinct-ively, he threw up his ring hand.

The servant of Tydranth straightened with a laugh of triumph, both fists in the air.

The archers on the battlement saw only the queen on the ground and the wizard standing above her with what looked like a dagger clenched in his hand. A flight of arrows whizzed through the winter air, and the Skinwalker was driven backward into the wall of the keep by the force. As the wizard's skin sagged, a dark shape rose up out of it. There came a sardonic laugh from the darkening sky, and then a putrid blast of wind. When they could uncover their eyes again, the evil thing was gone and the swathed wizard was on his knees, cradling the queen and trying futilely to extract the ice dart, which writhed away in smoke. Desperately he tried to feel through his own bandages for a pulse in her throat and then put his ear close to her lips. And then Fidelis was there and the dwarf was trying to pull him away while Gerrit gathered his mother's hands and desperately called her.

The old physician lay a hand against the queen's neck and reached to turn up an eyelid. He stared, then gently let the eye fall closed and bowed his head, bracing himself with one hand on the cold stone of the keep wall. He had no need to say it.

"No!" Gerrit pleaded. Kursh dropped a hand to the boy's shoulder, not bothering to try to hide the tears that trickled from his one good eye down into his frozen beard. Alphonse began to rock her gently, and then the archer complement was crowded all around, doffing their helmets to stand bareheaded in the cold air.

The old dwarf straightened his back, dashed a hand across his face, and sniffed. He turned to face the Watchmen and the gathering household. Snapping his fist to his chest, the admiral intoned, "Hand, eye, and body hers."

The Oath of the First Watch was taken up by a score of hushed voices. "Heart, mind, and spirit hers. My blood for the Blood, now and forever."

Kursh finished the salute, and into the stunned silence raised his voice. "All hail, King Gerrit. Long live the king."

There were perhaps three heartbeats and then the solemn cry was raised: "Long live the king!" The creaking of the Greenbriar standard being lowered at the gate cut through the dusk like a knife.

Gerrit knotted his fists and managed to rise to his feet, his face drained of color. "Bear my mother in, some of you. I don't want her lying in the cold like this." They hesitated, and he added thickly, "Call her waitingwomen to make her ready f-for . . ." He could not finish.

Kursh gripped his elbow for support and flicked a hand signal. The disciplined men fell into ranks. Four of them stepped forward, but Alphonse was already raising her. "I'll do it," he said flatly, and no one gainsaid him. The ranks parted to let him through, and they bore Queen Ariadne to her rest.

Wailing began all over Greenbriar Castle as the news spread, and the sun went down.

It was Kindlefest Eve.

Chapter Nineteen

🛠

The silken bandages were stuck to him, and he had refused to allow Fidelis to treat him with more salve, more laving, more pain-deadening tea. This pain he wanted to feel, and he clutched it to him with an almost savage ferocity. The other pain Fidelis could do nothing about. After a time, the old doctor had left him and Kursh in his chamber and gone back down to the hospice to tend the comatose children and the Eldest of the Yorlandirkin.

The new king was closeted with Will Quint and the rest of his military commanders. A cohort of Riders, decked in evergreen, had volunteered to bear the Lion pennant and the Red Eye to parley with the Shimarrat generals. They would take the terrified ambassador, Fa-Salar, with them. Will Quint, a devastated bear of a man now, had loomed over the Shimarrat to promise that if he betrayed by any means whatsoever Queen Ariadne was dead, he'd be cut down before he could finish drawing his next breath. Fa-Salar had tried to put a good face on it, jangling about diplomatic immunity, but his pointed beard had quivered.

And then, of course, Kursh had realized it. He had hesitated uncharacteristically, standing over the tools he had laid ready on Fidelis's work table, turning a blow tube, picking up the crystal that had solidified in the shape of the iron bucket. The wizard stood staring out the frosted window at the moon. The dwarf glanced at his rigid back, cleared his throat, and said quietly, "I can't blow crystal without a fire, Alphonse. I'm sorry." He sat down upon the tall stool, leaning his head in his hands.

The wizard's voice was hoarse. "I know, old friend. It doesn't really matter now, anyway."

It matters for my wife and daughter, Korimson said in his mind. It matters as long as Brickleburr is out there somewhere: obviously he didn't go home for a lark. He searched for the right way to put it, but diplomacy had never been his strong suit. Kursh picked up the piece of crystal and turned it over and over in his hands. "It matters to me." When the wizard made no answer, the dwarf stared across at his back. "I think it would have mattered to her."

Alphonse raised one bandaged hand to scratch lightly at the ice on the window. "I'm sure," he murmured. The idle pattern took the shape of a rose. When he saw what he had done, he leaned to breathe on the sketch and rubbed it out with a balled fist. He turned quickly. "But what I want to know is why it didn't matter to the Powers." His eyes were dark in the low light of the fireplace embers, a muddy color like a churned lake. The wizard and the dwarf stared at each other, and then Alphonse whispered, "Why did they let the Greenbriar Queen die, Kursh?"

Don't pick at it, lad. It only makes the sore worse. "I'm no Retreat Master, boy. Don't ask me—I've lost too many. If it happens, it happens. Maybe the Powers have naught to do with it." His eye was steady. "Except to weep with the rest of us." He looked down, and then averted his face. Kursh drew a breath and squared his shoulders. "Let's try to do some work, Freckles—I'm not going to sit here twiddling my thumbs and waiting to see the Wild Feller come stepping over the Rim of the Earth in the morning." He got to his feet. "Are ye going to help me, or not?"

For a long moment he thought the wizard would not answer. Then Alphonse looked back at the rose he had blotted out. "We've no fire, no seeds, and no ring. Give me an idea, old friend. Just one."

The broad fingers drummed on the table. And stopped. Korimson's head came up. "Ye don't suppose there's any friava around, do you? The queen always makes sure—made sure to have it in the hearths when Imris was due to visit."

They stared at each other.

Then the dwarf whooped and hit the door at a run. "Yeoman!" he bellowed into the darkness. "Gerrit!"

"His Majesty is in council, sir," came Rory Fisher's hushed voice. "May I serve you?"

That brought Korimson down firmly to ground again. "Er, yes, lieutenant. I want to know if there's friava in the stores."

In the darkness they could hear his gasp. "By the Powers! Of course!"

"Good. Now, I want you to get some men and bring a deal of it, but not all there is, to—" He glanced at the fireplace. "Too small, and the hearths in Rose Hall won't do. Too many gaping fools about."

"How about the one in the shrine?" the wizard suggested quietly. "If the Powers still have any will to aid our task, surely it will go best in the place dedicated to them."

Kursh looked at him. "That's where they've taken her, you know."

"I know."

The dwarf turned again to the Watchman. "In absolute secrecy, Fisher, mind ye. I'll personally see to any man who breathes a word of it."

"Aye, sir."

"Look sharp, man. There isn't much time," Korimson snapped, and Fisher's footsteps went down the corridor toward the stairs. Kursh closed the door. "Well, that's my end of it," he said briskly. "Now, wizard, how about the seeds?"

Alphonse drew the silk scarf across his face. "Gerrit's Wood," he said. "Perhaps some of Nilarion's Children still keep their berries and will give them up to us for such a use."

He stooped with a grimace of pain to don the brown robe he had left lying across Fidelis's bed, the weight of the wool being more than he could bear against his wounds unless absolutely necessary. When he picked up the robe, two small scrolls dropped to the floor. "What's this?" he wondered.

Kindle Eve wore on. Most of the castle's inhabitants gathered in the darkened Rose Hall, but they made no pretense of holiday spirit tonight. The comfort was that of dumb creatures, instinctively huddling together. Festil's voice

was roughened with grief, but he did his best to play a soft
melody that screened out the rising moans from the Sweep.
In the hospice, closer to the outer wall, Fidelis and his staff
could hear the Shadows clearly, but it did not much trouble
the children: most of them had sunk deep into coma. It was
the chief physician's private conclusion that they would pass
with the night, as would the Eldest. Though the Yoriandir
was occasionally conscious, his heart rate and breathing
were slowing dangerously and no stimulant helped.

There came a tapping at the window above his bed, and
Fidelis opened it to admit the Binoyr. The white birds flew
to perch on the bedstead, their glossy emerald tailfeathers
sweeping the blankets. They cocked their heads and regarded the green-skinned bard. He smiled wearily. "They
ask why I sleep," he informed Fidelis.

The doctor who sat with him to wait smiled a little. "Tell
them you're tired."

"Ah, no, my friend. It will not do . . . to lie to . . . my
sister and brother." He drew a breath. "Ya ne-ventren," he
murmured in Yoriandir. "Go home now," he repeated. He
sighed. "There is no more . . . for you to do. She is gone."

Fidelis grasped his hand.

Imris made a faint gesture. "Let them out, please."

The doctor stood and opened the window once more. For
a moment, the Binoyr perched, still as if they had been
carved. Then one fluttered out, followed by its mate. The
Eldest and the doctor could hear their fluting song receding
toward what was left of Gerrit's Wood.

The Yoriandir subtly relaxed into the pillow, as though he
had been hoarding his strength for the moment and now
that it was done, he had no more need to hold on. His fir
eyes found the doctor. "Marian the Fair was the best song I
ever made," he said suddenly, and then he drew a ragged
sighing breath and was gone. Fidelis pulled the blanket
closer around him and blew out the glow of the small dish of
friava in the niche above the bed.

Alphonse had left some time ago, after Gerrit had remembered the Painter's ring. A team of diggers armed with
a friava brazier, plenty of pine oil, and shovels had been
assembled, and the new king had led them down to the
broken ground where the scar had been. It had been quite a
while ago, and Kursh was glad he wasn't one of them. He

called his mind sharply back from its wandering, glanced to check the heaped and gloriously hot friava glowing in the hearth, and took the long-handled iron bucket from the fire. The crystal in it had melted satisfactorily, so he selected a thin blowpipe from among his tools. He would not need all the crystal, just enough to make the small sphere, so he twirled the blowpipe in the bucket and got a small glob on the end. He dropped the Briar seeds down the tube, and quickly began to blow the crystal, turning the blowpipe smoothly as the molten red crystal ballooned. Deftly he dropped the small crystal ball into the bucket of steaming water to set.

There was a loud pop.

"Damn! Ye might as well go back to being an apprentice if that's the best ye can do, Korimson!" he told himself disgustedly. Shaking his head, he fished in the bucket, drew out the damaged crystal, and dropped it on the stone floor. From the shards he picked out the Briar seeds and set them on the makeshift worktable. The crystal fragments he put on the rim of the firepit. "Now let's see if we can't do it right this time, eh?"

Once again, he blew a crystal to balloon around the Briar seeds. This time when he transferred it to the bucket the small sphere sank to the bottom and then came up floating, just as it was supposed to do. He transferred it to the cold-water bucket, and the new crystal cooled to blue fire and then finally cleared. When he scooped it carefully out of the water and held it up to the friava's light, it was a smooth, flawless sphere. He permitted himself a smile and rattled the seeds inside.

The smile left his face. There had been four seeds. Only three were encased in the crystal.

His breath seemed to stop for a moment. Then he dropped the crystal back in the bucket, seized the small blowpipe, and upended it over the worktable. A Briar seed rolled out. "Bloody stinking whoreson *hell*!"

He slammed one fist down on the table and made the heavy iron implements jump. The Briar seed rolled over the edge, and he caught it. He rubbed his nose and glanced into the farther reaches of the shrine, where the glowing small braziers silhouetted the bier. "Beg pardon, my queen," he said guiltily. "I've just made another blasted mistake, is all." Quietly he set the seed into a shallow cup so that it could not roll again, and then he scratched his head. "Wouldn't ye know it?" he muttered. "And a perfect one it was." He shook his head and picked the crystal out of the cold water. Raising it to shoulder height, he prepared to smash it, then . . . stopped. His brows drew down. "It only ever took one seed to make the Ritual of the Rose work." After a moment more he lowered the crystal. "No," he said aloud. "I don't believe the Powers would mind at all."

Korimson wrapped the crystal in plush velvet, set it aside, and picked up a larger blowpipe. "Not at all."

Some time later the outer door opened and he heard them coming across the floor. Bent close over the work, the dwarf did not look up. "Got it?" he asked.

Alphonse leaned stiffly to the friava, hands outstretched. "Yes."

"Tried it yet?"

"No, not yet. What's that you're working on?"

Kursh glanced to follow Gerrit as he walked silently past down to the far end of the shrine. "Never mind," he said shortly. "A gift. The crystal's in the velvet there." He nodded at it.

The wizard stepped around him to take it, and the dwarf caught the iridescent sheen of the stone in the new ring. Old ring. Alphonse held the crystal up to the friava light. "Beautiful job," he murmured.

"Not bad. Not as difficult as some things I've done." He picked up a burring tool and bent again to the piece he was making. Tiny slivers of glass flew as he cut a flowing beveled pattern.

Alphonse's eyes widened as he peeked over the dwarf's shoulder. "I see what you mean," he said, awed.

Held in the vise clamped to the edge of the table was a Weatherglass, blown and cut by the Guildmaster's genius into a crystal rose. Kursh was engaged in the finishing touches, etching the veining into each folded petal, minutely polishing a sparkling dewdrop that winked with its own fire.

"How did you do that?" the wizard asked.

"The carving?"

"No, the drop. It's glowing!"

"Oh, that. It's . . . a star." He went on polishing. "I used one of the Briar seeds in this, Freckles. Gerrit will need only one of the three in his crystal to make a new Briar, and

I didn't think the Powers would begrudge one for her. I made the boy a Weatherglass once, though he didn't want it at the time, but I never made one for her." He swallowed, then went on steadily, "I wanted to do that."

The wizard nodded. "It was a fitting thought." He straightened and rubbed a finger over the new ring. Turning to the hearth, he gathered himself for a moment, then gingerly summoned the Wind Warding. A pearled blue glow shone from the stone, and a slight breeze blew the warmth of the firepit throughout the shrine. More confidently, he tried an Earth Warding, and spruce green lit in the ring, sending a smell of deep forest wafting through the room. Holding Aengus's two Wardings, he swallowed and opened his mind to the third, the Fire Warding. He was prepared for an eruption of Wild Fire and intended to break off at once, burning his own hand to snap the Ward if necessary. Instead, clear red-gold shimmered in the friava's light, a quiet breathing fire that seemed to pulse with his own relieved heart. Experimentally he braided the three Wardings together, circling the firepit with a gleaming rope of blue, green, and red light, finding the Painter's Warding crisper, clearer than his own. He waved his ring hand to dissolve the rope and sent up one small fire rocket to burst silently in the shape of a rose. There, he thought—if Kursh can make one for her, so can I.

But the dwarf was turned to his own task, and the boy was silent by the bier, and there was no one to see.

Slowly he let the Ward lapse. "It works," he told Kursh. "I guess we're ready." Raising his voice slightly, he called, "Your Majesty? It is nearly time."

The blue Elixir bottle was ready, the polished silver knife. If necessary the Briar would root itself in stone, as they had cause to know. Working quickly, Alphonse took the locket and Warded it into the golden filigree net that had held the original crystal. When that was done, he bent his mind to the making of a Crystal of Healing. The earth's rich harvest vitality he wove into the Ward, and then the sweet herb-smelling wind of spring, and finally the peace and warmth of a summer's day by a lazy brook. The rainbow fire encased the sphere, refracting into streaming rays that lit the shrine. The Warding set, the rainbow sank into the glass to bathe the seeds within, and the Crystal of Healing was made. Alphonse dropped his hand, and the lights went out, except for the friava's steady glow.

He looked to the boy. "Now it is for you, sire."

Gerrit licked his lips, put his chin up, and took the Crystal from the wizard's hand. He glanced toward the brazier-lit bier at the far end of the chamber, then closed his eyes and dropped the Crystal to initiate the Ritual of the Rose.

But the Crystal did not break for him.

They tried it several more times with the same result. The Crystal simply did not work. Kursh tugged at his eyepatch. Alphonse eased himself down on the edge of the firepit. Gerrit shifted his weight to his good foot and drew his sword to lean on it like a cane. "It's no good," the youth said quietly. "I'm good enough to be the King of Shimarrat, but I'm no King of Ilyria. I'm sorry."

He limped out.

When the door had shut behind him, the dwarf and the wizard looked at each other. "I think I blew the glass correctly," the Guildmaster said.

"You did," Alphonse affirmed. "And the Ward should have worked; it worked for the Painter. That was the way he did it. The ring showed me."

Neither said anything for several moments. Then Kursh murmured, "Be morning soon."

Alphonse buffed the rainbow ring on his brown robe. "It should be."

Each added in his own mind, But it won't be.

The wizard got painfully to his feet and shuffled toward the dark bier and the woman who slept there. The dwarf turned back to his rose and polished and polished.

Oh, lady queen, what playthings for the Powers we have been! Alphonse thought, lightly brushing back a straying brown-gold hair from the frozen forehead. They allow us to be stripped of any defense, and then think to draw the sting by offering one tiny hope. Then they dash that, too. I tried to make a Crystal for your son, lady queen, but if there is Greenbriar in him, it must be too deep to reach. The Painter's Ward came to me just that much too late: yesterday I might have given the new Crystal to you.

He traced the line of her cheek with a bandaged fingertip, and his chest heaved suddenly, though he would let the sound of no cry escape him. Even the old dwarf's stalwart presence was too much company for that. When the racking storm had calmed somewhat he pulled his head up. "Well, if this is all that is left to us, my love, I can promise the Unnamed will not harry you in death as he did in life," he told her still form in the barest of whispers. He patted the cold hands clasped around the dried flowers and evergreen sprigs, drew the silk scarf about his ruined face, and strode for the door.

Kursh looked up. "Where are ye going?"

"Just out to the Sweep for a few moments. I'll return shortly." The wizard's voice was muffled. The door closed behind him, and the dwarf was left alone in the shrine with the dead queen.

Korimson unscrewed the vise and held the Weatherglass Rose up to the friava's light. He nodded, satisfied, and carried it toward the bier. The dewdrop star showed a deep and distant silver in the dark, a tiny pinprick of light no bigger than a firefly's eye.

Hesitantly he approached the ermine-draped figure. " 'Tisn't much, my queen. I didn't have all the time in the world. But it's a fair thing, for all of that. Puts me in mind of . . ." A lump rose hard in his throat. "Better days," he rasped. "The star is for Peewit: he'd be here if he could, ye know." He reached and gently pulled the dried bouquet from her hands to tuck his gift in its place. There was just room enough within the frozen hollow of her hands.

Kursh stood back. "There, lady. Safe journey to Ritnym's Realm." He smoothed his beard. "It's not such a bad place for a gardener, such as yeself." He fancied he saw a smile. The old dwarf snapped the only other woman besides his wife he had ever loved a farewell salute, executed a smart about-face, and marched out of the shrine.

Rory Fisher stood outside, stamping in the cold. "Have ye waited all night, man?" Kursh asked in surprise.

"Aye, sir. It was no great hardship—the air's nearly as cold inside as out."

Kursh clapped him on the arm. "Ye were a stout lad, Fisher, and ye're a stout man now. There's one more service ye can render."

"Anything, Squiremaster."

The old dwarf stuck his hands in his belt to still their trembling. "I left an ax here thirteen years ago. Would ye happen to know where they've stowed it?"

*   *   *

The wizard halted near the place where they had exposed the door to Beod and Comfrey's tomb. It seemed the appropriate place, for inside the hollow hill also lay the Painter, who had been the first to sing his own Song. And I am the second and the last Wizard of the Three, Alphonse thought. He raised the rainbow ring. There was a flicker of black-and-white in the darkness nearby, and he very nearly hurled the gathering Ward.

'Are you going to sing?' Patience's soft voice asked.

Her wizard dropped his hand and exclaimed with delight, "Mistress Mousechaser! I haven't been able to hear you for so long!" He bent to pick her up and there amid the flickering-eyed Shadows he gave her a hug.

'There's no need to squeeze the breath out of me, wizard!' she said with some asperity. 'I asked if you were going to sing,' she reminded him.

He rubbed her ears. "Yes, I am. If we can no longer use the old Song of the Powers to protect us, then I must take it away from the Unnamed, too. It may rob him of some small measure of power and thus save something of earth."

Her eye seemed to flow soft amber. 'Master Chiswic said you would come to this.'

He buried his forehead in her soft fur. "Did he say what decision I should make?"

'No. He said only that you would know when it was Time.'

"I won't let him get Ariadne, Patience. I won't. And this is the only way to put her safely beyond his Power."

Her pink tongue rasped across his closed eye. 'Perhaps you love the human queen too much.'

"Maybe I do. And I'm not going to stop now." He gave her a final hug, set her down, and ordered sternly, "Now get yourself out of here, baggage. Go find a nice warm place to hide until this is all over."

She sat down and flipped her tail angrily. 'There isn't any place warm, fool, and they have run out of Lipopo.' She sneezed on his bandaged foot. 'So sing, will you?'

He smiled a little, raised the ring, and Unmade the Great Song.

Then, as the earth spasmed and split, and stars fell straight down out of the night sky, he made his way slowly up through the clanging gate of Greenbriar Castle. A voice that sounded like Kursh's yelled something, but he merely waved and went back into the shrine.

"Well, I've done it, love," he told her. And then, because there was not much time, he kissed her cold lips, raised the rainbow ring one last time, and with the last of the Great Power, cast himself down the black tide of death where she had gone, sealing the way behind them.

By the Light, they were close now! the Pledged thought as he pounded up the last stairway. The bee zoomed on ahead, and behind he could hear the clicking of long nails on the golden stair. His breath burned in his chest and his heart hammered in his throat as he raced down the narrow hall between two frescoed walls, more of the Painter's work. On one wall Tychanor the Warm himself in his golden robe with sparks of fire reached half across the arched ceiling. On the other wall Rose, chin on her shoulder, robes fluttering as she fled from the great dark shape that chased her forever in the painting, desperately flung out a hand that did not quite reach the Lord of Summer's. Never quite reaching, all down through the ages that the Meadows had stood.

Peewit sent them a breathless impulse of hope and leaped through the amber glass window at the east end of the hall. Something grasped at his heel with a touch of ice, but he ignored it, jumped for the back door of the world, hung on the knob until it turned, and swung out over the southern edge of the earth. He let go and dropped down to the doorstep, and the Door swung shut again and locked. There was a chorus of angry snarls, a howl, and hair-raising moans from the Shadows, but they could not come through, because The Dark One had bred them to be of earth and they could not leave it. Peewit leaned his head back against the earth and caught his breath a moment. "Bee, are you still with me?" Cahokia buzzed near his ear, and he pulled himself to his feet.

The edge of earth was ringed with a narrow rim of rock and dirt, the clay that had squeezed from the mold, covered with snow. To his back was the solid wall; in every other direction was Void. Even the firmament, the Sky Roof of dark crystal, ended at earth's edge. There were no stars out here to comfort him. For a moment, he quavered looking at two sets of footprints made of old, the tallfolk Painter's and his own small ones. Two went out, he said to himself, and only one returned. And it was not me.

A Skinwalker I am, Brickleburr thought, though a good

one, I hope. Tychanor's own Light against the Dark one his Brother sent to plague us when earth was new. It was the only way the Warm could walk among the people of the world to protect them. Well, he needs his aura back now, Brickleburr. And step lively: the Lamp is burned out.

He had taken a step off the threshold when the rumbling began. Bits of Earth Rim began to shake off into the void, and the cold Lamp suspended from its Lampstand under the earth swayed like a pendulum marking the passing of Time. Peewit's head jerked up. "Powers! Alphonse! It's worse than I thought!"

In answer there came a laugh out of the Void. "Go back, ratkin. You can do no good here. My fool of a Brother is going."

Brickleburr's face flushed, and he ran through the snow toward his right, toward the Lamp, following his own long-ago footsteps and the Painter's. He came to the remembered place, a promontory that jutted from the rim out into the Void, where the Warm Fire had stood one long ago day filling his Lamp with golden oil. And lying there in the snow, as he had lain there then, was Tychanor the Warm, his golden robe a tattered remnant, transfixed by a spear of ice as thick as a Littleman's leg. His warm brown eyes rested on Peewit. "Ah, my Pledged. I knew you'd come when it was Time."

"Aye, my lord. Rest you easy now. I'm here."

"It's the Lamp, Peewit, the Lamp."

"I know." Brickleburr scrambled out on the promontory to him, slipping a little on the ice. There came a whizzing blue light, and lightning blasted at the promontory where it was connected to the Rim. The Littleman dug out his golden box and fumbled a handful of the dust inside. Cold struck at him, but he went grimly about his task while the Warm Fire gasped and writhed in pain. Blowing gently on his palm, the Hearthman put the aura in place.

Through its fine golden shower, he and the Lord of Summer met each other's eyes. "Bless you, my friend," Tychanor said lowly. "I would not have had it happen this way." The promontory shuddered under them as something struck it hard from beneath. One link of the Lamp chain wrenched open. A huge black hand appeared over the edge of the promontory's point, and the snow sizzled from its touch.

"Get out of it, ratkin," the Wild Fire snarled, and the firmament shuddered, shaking a little loose from the Rim.

Peewit said hastily, "She's still waiting for you, my lord. Goodbye." He jumped to his feet, seized the ice spear with one hand, and raised the other. *"Kindle!"*

At once the dark ice stuck to his living flesh, burning its way inward toward his heart. But the golden aura surrounding Tychanor burst into brilliant Fire, and where it met the ice, the spear began to melt from the Lord of Summer's body.

Another black hand and then a knee and foot, and Tydranth the Wild Fire swung himself up over the promontory. His eyes sucked at Peewit's spirit, and his breath froze the marrow of his bones. "I told you to stay out of it."

Tychanor struggled to rise, the golden box falling from his nerveless fingers. The stub of spear had not quite melted yet, and Brickleburr knew bitterly that they had finally lost. Tydranth the Dark stepped toward them, smiling like an avalanche.

Then the bee that had moved under his fingers on the meerschaum came before his eyes, and a voice seemed to say quite close to his ear, "Come on, old sod—brace up. It's only the Whoreson himself, after all." The freezing at his heart eased for an instant. "Bee!" he gasped.

In the instant, the Wild Fire swatted at something on his smoking neck. Tychanor the Warm scrambled to his feet, flicking the harmless melted water from the front of his robe, which became incandescent.

"What—?" the Dark Fire croaked.

The Lord of Summer smiled grimly. "Mortality, Brother. It was your gift to earth's children. They give it back." He stepped quickly forward. "I can help you, if you will it."

With a snarl of rage the Wild Fire raised his fists to smite them both with his consuming fire, but the earth swayed, and the promontory sprang up and down like a plank. Peewit clutched his chest and tottered, the spear grown to an ice-web that encrusted him. Tydranth lost his balance and slipped, teetering on the edge over the cold Lamp suspended below.

"Take my hand, Brother!" Tychanor the Warm pleaded. "Let there be peace between us at last!"

The Wild Fire's hand whipped to grasp at the golden robe.

Oh, no, not all over again, the Pledged thought with the last thought left to him. Somehow he threw himself between them in a desperate dive that caught the Dark Lord at the knees, and together they fell off the Rim of Earth.

"Peewit!" Tychanor shouted, and grasped at the emptiness where he had been.

From far below came a faint cry: "Kindle!" And the Lamp's wick caught.

In the growing light bathing the Foundations from below, the Lord of Summer threw himself full-length on the soft grass beginning to spread like a wash of greenest paint around the Rim of Earth, and he wept.

But the time for sunrise was fast approaching, so at last Tychanor put aside sorrow and rose. The oil stood near to hand. He poured a steady stream into the Lamp below, and the golden light steadied and burned brightly. He took the chain and hooked it to the golden webwork that encased the firmament on the outside. Then, using the anger of his grief and his own growing awareness of truly being alive once more, Tychanor the Warm swung the Sun and hurled it up over the Rim of Earth.

And the sun rose on Kindlefest, bathing the Meadows of Morning in its strengthening light.

By the time the Power had climbed to his back door and unlocked it, the warmth was melting the ice from the sunmill, and the vines, and the fallen Folk. Standing on his rooftop terrace, the Lord of Peace and Plenty looked down and beheld with pity what had been done to his own in his absence, and love welled in his heart. He raised his hand, and a pure and radiant light restored the twisted wreckage of the mill until it started with a click and a whir to distill the elixir of honey and herbs which fueled his Lamp; he gestured, and the glasshouses sprang back into shining panels and the plants sheltered within began to bloom once more; he sang, and the Hearthfolk rose, the dreadful wounds of the Shadows healed, the memory fading. The Warm laughed, and the snow melted from the thousand greens and the hundred yellows that were the Meadows of Morning.

Then he went though the door into the palace, and now because of earth's shaking, his hand touched hers in the painting. His eyes sparkled and he ran down the stairs, calling, "Rose? Rose, I am come Home!"

Deep within the Sun Palace, on the second floor left, the woman stirred and woke to find the sun in her eyes.

The archers braced themselves on the shaking battlement as the stars fell. The dwarf rode the bucking platform as though it had been the deck of a tempest-tossed ship. One of the men pointed. "It is growing lighter, I think!"

Truly enough, the eastern sky over the rampart of the Barrens was graying. "Wait," the dwarf counseled, and he shifted the ax to his other shoulder. "It may not come up." But he wanted to believe that it would.

No, it was not such a bad place for a gardener. The queen sat on a carved stone bench, surrounded by beds of early iris and nodding daffodils. The sun shone through a mist, and a cherry tree dropped its petals on her shoulders. Beside her, Ritnym, Lady of the Earth, said, "Will you go back with him?" She smiled. "Your Alphonse is quite persistent. I can hear him calling at the gates even now."

"I intend to."

The Lady of Earth's eyes were warm brown. "Even knowing what I have told you? Remember: he will be here an age of the world, and you two shall not be together."

Ariadne smiled a little. "Oh, I'll bet you can make a gardener out of him for me."

Ritnym's laugh tinkled as dewdrops on leaves would. "Perhaps."

The Greenbriar Queen took one last look around, then rose. "I'm ready."

Ritnym stood with her. "So be it, my daughter." She raised her hand to touch Ariadne's forehead. "Your choice shall be the one Rose made, and when you die indeed, your aura shall pass into the Crystal as hers did, so your descendants shall have a token that we Powers have not forgotten the world or those who dwell in it."

Ariadne cast down her eyes. "Alphonse Unmade your Song. I am sorry for that."

"It was the only way to slow the Unnamed's advance sufficiently. He did correctly." She laughed again. "Besides, you should know there is no Song any wizard can sing which we cannot adapt to our own use!" She embraced the queen. "Go back, daughter, and take that impetuous man with you before he ruins my flower beds."

"But may I ask what will happen to Imris if I leave? May I not have a word with him?" Her eyes filled. "Truthfully, I don't like the thought of leaving him here alone."

Ritnym held up a finger. "Listen!"

Through the whisper of the rain on the leaves came the

distant humming of the harp, and then they heard many beautiful voices joining in the refrain. "The Yoriandirkin?" Ariadne guessed.

"Indeed. The Eldest has come home. Will you wish him to return to earth with you and be alone again?"

Ariadne listened to the laughter and the clapping. "But Earthpillar?"

"As you say, your wizard has changed the Song, and there is no longer need of an Earthgate. It is safe for Imris to be here at last. His burden has been laid down."

The queen swallowed her tears. "I understand," she whispered.

Ritnym smiled gently and pointed. "The path is there. Go swiftly! Time passes in Earth-Above!"

Immediately, without knowing whether she actually moved or not, Ariadne found herself walking up a flagged path bordered with azalea and rhododendron. From her right came a silver voice raised in song: "Liselle the She-Gull did love the land."

Thank you, Eldest, the queen thought. I did. I do.

Then there was an end to the path and Alphonse's anxious face pressed to the lichened wooden gate. "Ariadne!" he shouted.

"Hush! You'll stop the singing."

"What singing?" he asked as she walked through the gate.

"You are such a lummox, dear. Come, it's this way."

A single shaft of golden sun streamed through the Gap in the Barrens, streaked over the corrugated hills, turned the Willowsrill to buttermilk, crowned the Sweep with a spatter of diamonds, and arrowed through the east-facing window of the shrine to fall exactly on the Rose Weatherglass couched in the hollow of the queen's hand. The silver star deep within the crystal dewdrop kindled to a gold radiance that shone through her hands like an alabaster lamp, a light that jumped suddenly as she drew a breath and woke.

For a moment the radiance was in her eyes, and she hesitantly brought one hand up to shade and rub them. The golden radiance of her Rose steadied, and she held it up to look at it. A slow smile spread across her relaxed face. "Kursh," she murmured.

She sniffed, stretched, and sat up, holding the ermine

robe close around her. Powers, it was cold! Slipping off the polished marble table, she stooped to the wizard slumped against its base. His face was gray under the strips of bandages. She shook him slightly. "Alphonse? Wake up." He moved slightly, and she gently kissed his raw lips. "Wake up, please. There's a lot of work to do."

His eyes fluttered open, and he looked confused. "What singing?"

She laughed and left him to collect his wits. There was some sort of table blocking the entrance, and iron implements all over the floor. These she carefully stepped over to pull the door open.

The rose-gold of the rising sun glistened off the snow, and the sky above her battlements was an apricot glory. Unmoving figures stood staring eastward. The dwarf was clearly silhouetted. She called up to them, "Gentlemen? Excuse me—aren't we celebrating Kindlefest today?"

One man fainted and another crashed along the platform at a dead run for the nearest sheltering guardhouse. Two others stood frozen, gaping.

Kursh whirled, took one look, and pitched his ax to the platform. He flew down half the stairs, jumped the rest, and ran to catch her up, twirling in a circle till they were both dizzy and laughing like children.

Greenbriar Castle kept Kindlefest joyously. The bakers and cooks were busy, children were everywhere, getting into everything, the hearthfires leaped in the hall, and Kindle punch steamed in many a flagon. The musicians strummed their fingers raw, the singers sang themselves hoarse, and the mummers made the people laugh until their sides ached. Queen Ariadne danced with the wizard restored to his skin, and His Highness Prince Gerrit, ruler of the Principality of Shimarron, gave his crown to a grimy little boy named Nick to wear. The hospice was empty, the dancing floor was full, and no one forgot to pay his respects to the king who lay in state in the shrine until they could take him home to lie beneath Nilarion's canopy. Even the tinkers rode in a body up the Sweep on their wagon horses and were admitted, having played a great part in the Shimarrat army's decision to come to terms.

But most of the day, after the first blazing joy, Kursh stood on the battlement facing east, and though he was glad enough for the steaming punch they brought out to him from time to time, he would not come down. Toward evening, when it very properly began to snow in big soft flakes that spiraled out of the woolly sky, Ariadne paused at the doors of the keep and then walked slowly out to him.

She handed him a hot cup. He smacked his lips. "Ah, that's a decent punch. Could use a bit of flotjin, but it isn't bad at all."

She turned with a smile to lean on the battlement. "Cook will be glad to hear it." He sipped. The queen looked out over the soft gray-and-white landscape. "Kursh, he may not come back, you know."

"I know. But there ought to be somebody waiting for him if he does."

"And what if it takes all night? Or even a week or a month?" Or never?

"Time isn't important. When the Powers made it, they made a lot of it." He brushed the snow from his beard and looked steadily out over Willowsrill.

"How do you know where to look?" she questioned, rubbing her mittened hands together.

"The Meadows of Morning figures to be in the east, my queen."

"Oh. Right." She glanced sidelong. "Do you mind if I wait with you?"

"That depends. D'ye have any more of this punch?"

She laughed and called down to a Watchman for it. Alphonse came out of the keep with it, and more and more people drifted out to line the battlements looking east. After a time, the wizard began sending up a few fire rockets to amuse them.

From away over the other side of Willowsrill there came a sudden golden gleam in the winter's dusk. The dwarf's broad hand shot out to halt the wizard. "What was that?" he rasped.

It came again, but from farther down the valley this time. Then a third sudden wink of light from the northeast. "Whatever it is," the wizard said grimly, "there's more than one of them." He readied a Warding, but held his hand until he knew.

There came a faint shishing on the air, like sledge runners over snow, and now the golden winks steadied and grew stronger. The queen's hand dropped to the dwarf's arm and gripped it. Neither of them said anything. Gerrit peered beyond them, and Alphonse lit his ring. Something was moving on the other side of the river.

And then across the river. They could clearly hear the "Oooh!" that people make when unexpectedly taking a sliding fall and the sudden giggle of many voices as the streak of gold skimmed the ruff of willow trees. A shrill two-toned whistle carried on the snowy air.

"I *knew it*!" Kursh bellowed, launching his tankard in the air.

A toboggan crowded with Folk thumped to earth and whished up the Sweep, sluicing sideways and spilling all of the Folk into the snow as Peewit pulled it to a stop. Tansy pushed her hat back on her yellow curly hair and patted Peewit's back. "You're not too good a driver!"

"I'm learning," he replied serenely and stood up, digging snow out of his ear.

Those on the battlements saw the small, brown-haired figure bow. "Sorry we're a bit late," he called up to them, "but the cradle-bunnies kept hopping out of the packs!"

The tallfolk on the battlements laughed at what they thought was a jest and hung over the walls to watch the other toboggans come up the slope.

Kursh and the queen were the first two out the gates, with the wizard and Gerrit right behind them. They hugged Peewit until he was gasping for breath. "What did ye do to your hair?" the puzzled dwarf demanded.

Brickleburr grinned, but did not answer. He drew Tansy forward to present her to the queen. "Your Majesty, Tansy Mossflower, the Matriarch of the Hearthfolk. My wife."

Kursh's jaw dropped. "Your wi—!" He shut his mouth with a snap, blushed, and pulled at his eyepatch.

Alphonse laughed. "I can see there is more than one story to be told over the Kindle-Logs tonight!"

"Won't you all come in?" Ariadne invited. "You must be frozen!"

"Oh, not very," Tansy said, falling in step with her as they moved toward the gate. "It was a quick run, what with new oil for the toboggans."

A long nose and two big ears peered from the lace pocket of her apron. "Too quick by half," Winston chittered. "I say, Mistress P? Are you about? And have you saved a bit of the Lipopo for me?"

The black-and-white cat sneezed on the foot of a Watchman who had stepped too close to her tail. 'Just a crumb,' she told the mouse, 'and you had better hurry after it: these humans seem to have lost half of their few wits. I tell you, Winston, you have never seen such goings-on in your life. I strongly advise you to avoid the room with the pretty window, and leave the provisions to me.'

"Go ahead," Peewit directed the grinning Folk. "Get the packs out. There are a lot of children waiting!" They began to pull the toboggans up the last climb, Gerrit grabbing one tow rope and the wizard taking another, surrounded by people half their size who were doing most of the work.

The dwarf and the Littleman were left alone on the Sweep. " 'Twas a rough time here, old sod. How was your end?" the admiral asked.

Peewit pushed his wool cap back and rubbed his curly hair. "Not easy, but it's done."

"Aye, it's done. Er, is this the real you I'm talking to?"

Brickleburr laughed. "Do you feel up to some sport, First Watchman?"

"What did ye have in mind?"

"How'd you like to get home for Kindlefest?"

The dwarf looked down at the toboggan. "In this?" he asked warily, nudging it with his foot.

"I seem to recall an oversized kite once, and a huge mountain, and—"

"All right, all right, quit nattering on about it. Turnabout's fair play, I suppose." He smoothed his beard and turned to call up to the guards, "Tell Her Majesty we'll be back in a couple of days. We're going home for Kindlefest!" The men hallooed back, and the dwarf sat down gingerly in the contraption.

Peewit headed it downhill, jumped on in front of him, and took up the steering rope. "Hold on tight!" They began to slide down the Sweep.

Kursh, clutching hard to the red leather handles, leaned forward to ask above the shishing, "Will this thing jump over to the island?"

"It will if we get up enough speed on the hills!"

The sentries above the evergreen-decked gates heard from the dwarf the "Oooh!" that people make when unexpectedly taking a sliding fall, the Littleman's giggle hanging in the snowy air, and then a spark of gold whisked down the long hills toward the sea, and the night was quiet again except for the music and the laughter from the hall of the Greenbriar Queen.

About the Author

Sheila Gilluly was born in Rhode Island and attended high school and college in Arizona, graduating from the University of Arizona with a BA in English in 1973. Since then, she has earned an MA in Religious Studies from Maryknoll School of Theology, lived in Taiwan briefly, taught for a couple of years in Guam, and now teaches English and Creative Writing at a rural district high school in Maine. Ms. Gilluly is an avid gardener. Since midcoast Maine has only two seasons (winter and July Fourth), she has a lot of time left over from gardening to devote to her writing. Her previous novels, GREENBRIAR QUEEN and THE CRYSTAL KEEP, are also available from Signet.